MOON'S RISING

A Detective Lamont Novel

Book 1

ROB BROWN

A CIP catalogue record for this title is available from the
British Library.
The moral right of Rob Brown has been asserted.
ISBN-13: 978-1985048935
ISBN-10: 1985048930

ABOUT THE AUTHOR

A former health professional, the author recovered from life threatening injuries at the turn of the century.. A lover of music, he plays both guitar and saxophone. Rob has two grown up children and lives near Glasgow with his tolerant wife and two Spinone hounds.

CONTENTS

Chapter 1

August 2011

Whatever the season, it's a good day when rain doesn't fall on Scotland. Most months are cool and wet as precipitation piles in from the west on depressed Atlantic airstreams. As summers draw to a close, swollen, peat-brown rivers sweep down through narrow highland glens, forcing powerful salmon into nature's seasonal battle to reach the spawning grounds of their birth. This dramatic spectacle draws tourists and locals alike to gaze in awe as the struggle for survival unfolds.

In this romantic land of Rob Roy and Wallace, holidaymakers are drawn toward the beautiful Celtic myth. They huddle beneath waterproof clothing as moist, sweet mountain air fills their lungs and the fearsome female midges nip at exposed flesh. Others, less spirited, but perhaps wiser, gather in the cafés and bars to shelter from frequent heavy showers. For the stalwart local population, familiar with the climate's vagaries, it's just another Scottish summer.

This morning was different. Stormy winds that swept the mountains for a fortnight or more relented and, as cool air passed slowly over the rugged Perthshire landscape, a thick early morning mist formed over the waters of Loch Rannoch. Sprinting feverishly across MacCaig estate land, the powerful, sandy-haired Scotsman knew his only sanctuary lay in that swirling cloak of moisture. This was his battle for survival. Jock MacCaig was fighting for his life. He understood this and a torrent of fear raced through his mind, spurring him on. Charged with adrenalin, he urged himself forward recklessly, trying desperately not to lose momentum. Racing down through the forest toward the loch, he stumbled frequently over ruts and roots on the rough, steep terrain, but pressed on paying little heed to the risk. *What had he done that anyone should want him dead?* To his mind, there seemed no logical reason.

Setting the tripod and camera in position, he'd marked time in anticipation of catching the sunrise lighting Schiehallion's dramatic, conical outlines. As he waited for a break in the clouds, a sudden, violent shock drew the breath from him as something fiery tore across his shoulder. He was nearly spun off his feet as the crack of a rifle shot echoed through the forest. Stunned, Jock steadied himself and looked at the wound, but the bullet had only torn his skin. The gash was deep and painful, yet felt no worse than a heavy graze. As he gasped at the discomfort, it took no more than a second or two to realise what had happened. Then the second shell had sent small splinters of bark flying from the tree by his side. Some of them still lay in the thick tangle of hair as he sprinted for his life.

Now, less than fifteen minutes later and sweating heavily, he pulled hard on the oars, desperately seeking shelter in the loch's ghostly mist. Arms aching, his left leg burned with pain where it caught on the rowlock jumping into the boat. Glancing down at the torn jeans and blood-stained gash on his shin, Jock gritted his teeth. Again he found himself making feverish, unreasoned guesses as to why he was being hunted.

He'd been out catching dawn-lit photographs from Bothy Rock, high above the loch, when his world erupted. It had all been so normal, so peaceful, and then the gunfire. It had come from the far side of the clearing, but he didn't stop to find out exactly who'd fired, or from where.

Panicking, he'd knocked the camera over and dashed for cover in the dense woodland below. Whoever fired the shots had realised the impossibility of finding him in the forest and gone back to the kennels beside the ghillie's cottage for the hounds. Now *he* was being hunted like an animal. His pursuers must have known the dogs and known too they could track him and his familiar, friendly and very fresh scent. However, they couldn't follow him out on the misty water. Once there his whereabouts would be shrouded by thick moist air and the boat obscured from view.

Suddenly he stopped rowing, stunned. The pack, their chase thwarted at the water's edge, milled around, barking excitedly. Barely visible on the heavy shingle, and some way from the small jetty, a man stood, arms raised to his shoulders. To Jock it seemed he had appeared from nowhere. Then, through the drifting cloud he could just make out a rifle, pointing directly toward him. Positioned behind the telescopic sight, a man's face had become visible – a face he knew all too well.

He thought of throwing himself into the boat's hull, but before he could react a bullet tore through his diaphragm. Ripping the breath from his lungs, it cut through the tissues, and then shattered his fourth cervical vertebra. The spent, misshapen projectile disappeared into the depths of the Loch a few yards behind him. Dropping the oars, he grasped frantically at his chest. In those last, fleeting moments, an intense pain seared through his senses. Fighting to stay upright, Jock MacCaig lowered his head to see what had hit him. But, hardly had he registered the powerful sound of the first shot, when a second projectile entered his skull. He died in that moment.

As the body pitched violently backward into the boat's prow, blood-soaked bone and brain tissue joined the lead projectiles in the lonely depths of Loch Rannoch. For a few brief seconds before life left them, his legs twitched angrily where they hung over the for'ard bench. Satisfied, the shooter turned quickly and disappeared into thick forest followed by the noisy hound pack.

*

It was cold, even for Scotland in late summer and had rained for nearly a week. Constable Wilkinson was parked beside the loch at his usual breakfast station little more than a mile from Rannoch village. On a fine morning he could look out across the loch toward peaceful grazing land and the sharp peak of Beinn Mholach, but not today. Engine running, the small van's noisy demisters drowned out the radio as windscreen wipers tried in vain to clear his view.

Giving up, he turned off the ignition and began scanning the tabloid newspaper. Finding little of interest as he chewed vigorously on the crispy bacon sandwich, Wilkinson grunted, folded the paper and slid it into the door-well for later. Rubbing his hands together vigorously, the young constable's skin absorbed its daily fix of butter and bacon grease. Satisfied, he filled the plastic cup with hot tea from the flask and took a quick sip. Taking a deep, satisfied breath, he was resting it on the dashboard as the police radio burst into life. His shoulders sagged as the loud, flat tones of Sergeant Hugh Weir filled the police van.

"Since you're sat there by the loch," the voice echoed knowingly, "can you drive up to Brae inlet?"

Shaking his head impatiently, he asked, "Where?"

"Not far away from Mike Carie's croft. A tourist, out on the loch fishing, reported that a rowing boat's been left there. Says it's stuck by the shore under an overhanging tree's branches. He's not sure, but thinks there's a pair of knees sticking up from it."

Wilkinson could hear the sergeant's wife sniggering in the background. For a moment the young policeman wondered if the man was interrupting his breakfast for the hell of it.

"This isn't a wild goose chase, sergeant?"

"No," said Weir, chortling. "Not unless the geese've taken to wearing bloody jeans. Now get up there and see what the hell's goin' on!"

"Right, sergeant, straight away..."

With another shake of the head, he reached over for the cup and took a long draught of strong tea. He emptied it then screwed the flask top into place and dropped it into the carrier bag. Taking the local map from the glove box, Wilkinson made sure of the inlet's position, and then threw the map onto the passenger seat. Winding down the window, he reversed back to the roadside and poked his head out to check for traffic before setting off through the miserable drizzle.

After driving nearly two miles up toward the inlet he found a stretch of level hard shoulder, stopped and stepped out onto the sodden grass. Quickly zipping the waterproof and pulling on gloves, he began struggling through the thick undergrowth. Making his way toward the loch, the constable cursed as wild bramble thorns tore at his hands. Finally, after twenty or so yards of pushing through soaking wet brush, he came out onto the boulder-strewn shore. It took another five minutes of stumbling progress before he finally spotted a green-coloured rowboat. Caught under the branches of an overhanging ash, it bobbed around on rough water a yard or two from shore.

Drawing closer, he called out: "Are you awake in there?"

Stopping, he listened for a moment, but got no answer. Wilkinson gritted his teeth in irritation.

"Damned, drunken tourists!" he muttered, wiping the rain from his face.

Shaking his head, he clambered over one of the larger boulders, teeth gritted. The rain had now begun to thicken, driving at him on a strengthening westerly breeze, but he could see what the fisherman had thought were a pair of legs in the boat. Although thick tree branches were being blown across his line of sight, it did indeed look as though someone's denim clad knees were sticking up.

Wilkinson stopped for a moment, wiped the rainwater from his face and again called out. Getting no response, he cursed then continued picking his way gingerly along the slippery shoreline.

Breathing heavily from the effort, he finally drew level with the little boat. Muttering obscenities, he stopped to gather breath. Taking off the gloves, pierced by the razor-sharp briar, he rubbed at the minor abrasions and gritted his teeth. It was still impossible to make out what was in the vessel through the dense foliage. Balancing warily on a large boulder, the young constable stretched up and managed to catch hold of one of the tree's branches.

Convinced he would awaken a drunken reveller, sleeping off a hard night's drinking, he said loudly: "Right, you boozing bugger, let's see the colour of your eyes!"

Balanced precariously, he reached out as far as possible and caught hold of the boat's stern. At first it wouldn't move, but after several good tugs, it broke free and floated clear. He let go of the branch to get a better look, but recoiled with shock as two hooded crows, screeching loudly, rose and flapped away from the hull. The young officer lost his balance and cursed loudly as both feet slipped, forcing him to step back into the cold, shallow water. He looked down at his soaked boots and trouser bottoms in disgust. Taking a moment to regain some composure, he stretched forward and pulled the boat close enough to peer in.

Wilkinson stumbled back abruptly, horror etched

on his features. A man's body lay in the waterlogged hull, legs draped over the for'ard bench. The carrion had gotten to him first, for the grotesque, bloodied eye sockets were empty. Although the rain-washed, ashen face was still vaguely recognisable, the rear of the man's head was fully exposed. Mouth agape, he stared in disgust at the bloodied, dull grey tissue that propped the skull forward against the prow. Retching violently, the young constable turned away and spewed his undigested breakfast into the Loch's peaty waters.

Chapter 2

Perched rather uncomfortably on the folding wooden chair, Lamont tried hard to relax as he gingerly nursed a mug of hot coffee. The first drink of the day, he savoured it while soaking up the sounds and scents of the peaceful French countryside. He stared out from under the worn denim baseball cap admiring the broad canal as it curved off into the landscape through the endless ranks of plane trees lining its banks. Pushing the cap back, he scratched at the irritation a gnat was causing his hairline.

"Can't wait to get away from you little buggers," he muttered, checking his index finger for signs of life.

Pulling the cap down to shield his eyes, the detective continued to absorb the peaceful sights and sounds while ruminating about work.

Reflecting on why he disliked long breaks away from work always brought him to the same conclusion: boredom; and for him, holidays were boredom personified. The files on his desk kept the rip tide of boredom far from his shore. Somewhat ruefully, he thought juggling files carefully usually kept his boss, Deputy Chief Constable Moon from influencing the ebb and flow of casework priorities too dramatically. But Moon often had other ideas on the locus of work. Despite this, on most occasions over the years, their priorities had been in harmony. Occasionally, and only very occasionally, they were not.

He hadn't holidayed for many years: in fact, as he thought about it, not since his early days as a detective. It wasn't that he never dreamt of taking a break from work. No, in Lamont's case it was simply that he had never found a more productive way of passing time than chasing criminals. Yes, as a young man he had visited many of Europe's capital cities, absorbed their culture, and enjoyed the exquisite cuisine. And like many before him, had gazed in awe at some of the architectural creations of great minds; Mignot's in Milan, Gaudi's in Barcelona, or even Foster's historically recent work in Berlin. But those were only short respite breaks to appease his long-suffering wife and gather his thoughts: thoughts of unsolved problems nestling in the neatly stacked sets of files waiting by the desk for his return.

Like most others, he had sat on beaches under blue, foreign skies watching the beautiful people. The bucket list tour of the vineyards of Italy and France, learning the difference between wine and fine wine had been checked off too. Even the box marked, 'walked well-worn Alpine paths with friends and lovers' had been ticked, but now, as the middle years approached, he much preferred admiring a closed file. For him, that brought a quiet wave of deep satisfaction. Closed files, after all, meant closed cases – and convicted criminals.

The policeman had long since passed that time in life where a list of must visit places seemed important. No, he hadn't seen the African game reserves, the Taj Mahal, or Machu Picchu. Yes, they had all been priority destinations on his list, but were now no more than busy, souvenir filled aberrations on a multicultural, denim-dressed highway. And far too busy to be appreciated for the splendid isolation and grandeur his imagination had once afforded them. His schoolboy dreams, fuelled by romantic images from his father's encyclopedias, had been ruptured by the swarming crowds of people. Tourist traps, for him they held no more appeal than a high-season package holiday on the bustling Costas.

Sipping the hot coffee, he reflected briefly on the two neatly stacked piles of work he'd kept on the desk in front of him since first achieving the rank of detective: those cases his superiors wanted answers for, and those he saw as priorities. One-time Detective Inspector Lamont had always worked, as far as was possible, mainly to his own preferences. The rank he held had changed to merely 'detective' due to the head injury, but not the stubborn determination to focus on his own agenda. Although this had not presented too many problems over the years, it most certainly ended any hope of further promotion.

Having once been described in his annual police evaluation as being, 'not quite a corporate entity', he chose never to comply unquestioningly with the firm's aims, political or otherwise. From tailored, brightly coloured waistcoats and ties to designer spectacles, he was seen as one apart from the group. As in all organisations, this was perceived as a risk; but in the safe, orderly ranks of the Scottish Police Force, a risk no one was prepared to stake their judgment and careers on. It had certainly prevented a good problem-solver from fulfilling his apparent ambitions of promotion.

That widely held view of him was further amplified by a marked character change; the change brought about by a bullet in the head seven years ago. The SIG SG551 police assault rifle projectile had permanently removed the Chief Officers' desires to model him for any higher role.

Working for the Scottish Police Services Authority, his role was, in effect, pan-national. The Authority provided 'crime-scene-to-court' facilities, as well as running Tulliallan Police College and looking after national drug matters. Although the team offered a mainly specialised forensic service, Lamont's expertise was purely investigative and brought to bear only in special circumstances.

In the days before the head wound, his career aspirations were much the same as any other officer: go as far up the professional ladder as possible to ensure a full pension pot. After all, retirement should be full of comfort, joy and a second home in the Dordogne. But not now: now Lamont wanted his mind fully occupied catching criminals, especially if other policemen were struggling with the chase. Unlike many in the force, early retirement plans were the furthest thing from his mind.

So why was he so determined to pursue the wrongdoers? He had always loved chasing, catching and convicting the guilty, but now there was something more. Some saw him as having an obsessional attitude to work. There were indeed more brilliant police officers, but few with his cold logic and drive for success in every single case. Policemen could be deeply affected by particular crimes, especially the more violent ones, or those involving children. However, the type of casework being investigated meant little to Lamont; the man seemed deeply offended by all law-breakers and pursued them with determination and equanimity.

Growing up in a small mining village in the Forth Valley, near where he now worked, had certainly taught him right from wrong. He had seen the good, the bad, and the ugly at close quarters. However, any experiences he could cite were no different to those of many other 'children of the seventies'. But the slow recovery from the head wound had taught him about life; in particular, the stresses those who have to care for the victims must struggle through. He may have suffered pain, but his family had gone through even greater agonies.

While fighting to recover, it had been excruciating to endure watching them come and go from his bedside. Each visit seemed to be spent wondering if that might be the last time they'd see him alive. It was etched on their faces and echoed through strained words. Watching others suffer as he fought for life had driven an added determination to survive and flourish.

Relaxing, he took another thoughtful swallow from the cup. High overhead a peregrine falcon caught his attention as it swept purposefully across the bright morning sky. His eyes followed the hunter for a few seconds until it left his line of vision. Swiveling his head slowly from side to side, stretching stiff neck muscles, the Scot returned to his ruminations.

Despite the family turmoil created by those weeks spent receiving critical care, he was now convinced that the experiences had added to his drive for justice. From his perspective, sitting the five-foot eleven of his frame behind a desk while recounting successes had never been enough. He had always preferred being at the hub of the action. Yet somehow it seemed even more important now. On reflection, he thought this was possibly his way of paying back the debt: a debt the man believed he owed to all those who offered support through the bleak, dark days of recovery.

Strangely, this focus and determination helped resolve any guilt he felt for putting the family through that ordeal. For, whatever had happened in the seven years since, the understanding that he should never have been anywhere near the line of fire would always plague him. Time had passed quickly, too quickly, and yet looking back, 2004 seemed like only yesterday...

The unmarked police car swung off the motorway and into one of Europe's largest housing estates. He could clearly remember the uniform, compact homes sprawling over the southern edge of the city. Like many larger cities, clusters of high-rise blocks dominated Glasgow's skyline. A legacy of the sixties building boom, vast tracts of new homes had been constructed to remove the acres of impoverished inner-city tenements. The planners had changed the landscape, but not the people living there.

Parking the car, Lamont nodded toward the concrete mass that stretched out over the rolling landscape.

"We're here," he said, pulling on the handbrake.

"What's next?" Maitland asked.

Detective Sergeant Hugh Maitland could best be described

as reticent when it came to getting on with the job. But Lamont knew his team and they him.

"Over there and ask the uniforms where we're up to," he said, opening a pack of sweets.

"Why me?" Maitland asked, releasing the seatbelt. "Have you seen it out there? It's like the bloody Alamo!"

"I'm the Inspector," he said, popping a mint chew into his mouth, "and I do the jokes here..."

Watching the sergeant head off grudgingly toward the widening police cordon, he threw the sweets into the glove compartment and shoved it closed. Further up the street, a handful of blue uniforms were herding the onlookers away from the locus of the disturbance. He could see Maitland pushing his way through them, waving his warrant card. Dismissing the chaos, he carefully poked the new varifocals further up his nose.

"Bloody specs," the detective muttered, lowering the visor. He looked disapprovingly into the mirror. "As if things weren't bad enough..."

Pushing away the sun shield, the detective returned to looking out at the forlorn, concrete landscape and the milling gaggle of curious onlookers. He hadn't visited the estate for nearly fourteen years, since his early days as a constable on the beat...

He remembered those days clearly, and being left the unnerving task of standing sentry outside a murder scene, waiting for the forensics team to arrive. He'd only been alone by the door for five minutes when a tall, powerfully built man appeared on the landing with two sturdy looking associates. Walking casually toward him, the well-dressed character hadn't stopped until he was well within Lamont's personal space.

It was his first encounter with Pat McGlynn. The

underworld figure usually managed to keep a low profile running his 'business' activities from beneath the cover of one of the country's biggest travel agencies. He was, however, known to enjoy a bit of what some of the lads back at the station called 'active service'.

Leaning his right arm against the wall the imposing figure stood over the young officer. Lamont could recall his revulsion at the reek of stale smoke and expensive aftershave as the gangster spent a couple of minutes trying to cajole him into 'building a lasting contract' between them. Their 'contract' would depend on the young constable allowing him into the flat. But, despite his anxieties, he hadn't given ground. Ordered to stand guard at the murder scene, the young officer was determined that was just what he would do.

Sensing failure, McGlynn had resorted to veiled threats. However, even knowing some senior figures in the force at that time were suspected of being on the man's payroll, Lamont held his nerve. Believing the man could probably buy and sell police careers with impunity only strengthened his determination not to give ground. Then, frustrated by his stubbornness, the criminal revealed that the Chief Constable's teenage son had once unwittingly traded drugs for him. He went on to explain smugly, that after his hand opened a door of opportunity he, Pat McGlynn, would never allow it to close.

Watching Lamont's face for signs of weakness, the man once again stated the need for compliance. Either that, the gangster threatened, or his career could end abruptly. Things looked like turning nasty, yet he hadn't flinched. But luck had been with him back then. The lift doors slid open and the chattering six-man forensic team had spewed noisily into the hall.

McGlynn had stepped back, looked hard at him, and then smiled a slow, knowing smile.

"Lucky laddie," he said. "We'll see ye again, eh?"

With that, the gangster and his waiting henchmen had wandered off, muttering amongst themselves...

Shaking his head at the memories, he watched the large crowd of onlookers' jostle for a better view of events as they unfolded. He recalled the deep sense of relief when McGlynn had eventually left for a new life in Alicante.

At that time, it seemed the thug had been losing a gang war – and personnel – to the Peterson brothers, a notorious pair of killers from over Hamilton way. Apparently, McGlynn got wind of a high value contract they had taken out on him. Or so it seemed. Lamont hadn't been so sure about the truth of any McGlynn rumours back then. He remembered being uncertain as to whether the speculation about a contract hadn't been the work of the man himself.

However, enough had, apparently, been enough. The gangster had flown the coop to the Costas, living it up surrounded by a cohort of well-paid and trusted villains. According to informers, a healthy income had built up during his years in the travel business. By investing in Spanish nightclubs, he'd also been doing a fast and very lucrative trade in drugs for the young, moneyed tourists.

According to colleagues in the force, the business in Scotland had been kept ticking over by his glamorous lover and a couple of dangerous underlings who remained loyal. The gossip made sense. The travel agency had changed name from 'McGlynn Travel' to 'Lynn Global' in the early months of 1991. Since Lynn was his alleged lady-friend's name, this hadn't seemed an unreasonable deduction at the time.

He never fathomed why McGlynn had wanted access to the murder scene at the flat, for the forensics team found nothing incriminatory. Time had passed quickly, but it still irritated him. Now, nearly fourteen years later, the gangster had returned like a bad taste in the detective's mouth.

Rumour had it that when Jez Peterson, the elder and more violent of McGlynn's former gangland protagonists met his end, the territory had been left wide open. It transpired that the crook's young wife, sick of the man's bullying, infidelity and lies, had opened his throat with a kitchen knife as he slept. She was now awaiting trial for murder. He had been the planner and muscle in the family. His brother Rubin, a self-trained accountant, had already been banged-up for a fifteen-year stretch. A prolonged, covert police operation into his corruption and money laundering scams had seen to that. The powerful overlord brothers gone, McGlynn had seen his chance.

There were rumours too, that the drug and money game in Spain had been tied up by some very powerful gangs: ruthless eastern European cartels with even more muscle, firepower and venom than McGlynn. Whatever the reason, he'd now returned, seemingly free to reassert his authority thanks to Glasgow's brief underworld power vacuum. Word on the street had it that one or two of the more ambitious minor players had already been nullified, while the Peterson brothers' associates were either warned or bought off. Pat McGlynn was now trying to re-establish his empire.

Getting out as Maitland appeared through the crowd, he shoved the car door closed and scuffed a few stones at his feet. Breathing in deeply, he watched as the sergeant strode toward him. He already had a good idea what the man was about to say and knew he wouldn't like it.

"You were right," Maitland said as he strode up to the car. "That bastard McGlynn's back, but wait till you hear this..."

Sighing, Lamont felt the knot in his stomach tighten.

"There was a shoot-out with that waster Malcolm and some

of his lads. He's shot Malcolm's wife after she pulled a knife and somehow he's then got free and is holding him at gunpoint..."

"Well that's concise right enough," he said, eyebrows raised.

Delivered with a large dollop of sarcasm, the tone of his inspector's words had not been lost on the sergeant. Maitland shifted his weight and rephrased the explanation.

"There was a shootout between Malcolm's heavies and McGlynn's lot. Two dead in the house and one badly wounded. Apparently this happened after they took McGlynn by surprise. Seems a couple of Malcolm's lads were upstairs cutting drugs when McGlynn and his cronies appeared. Bit of a bloodbath by all accounts."

"Do we know why he's taken McGlynn hostage?"

"No, but it seems as soon as the fight started someone – a neighbour, they think – phoned in saying there had been shots fired. Luckily, the tactical team were running a training shift nearby, dogs and all. Nowhere for any of those in the house to go, so Malcolm's grabbed McGlynn."

"Ever the big man, eh?" Biting his lip, he tutted, then added: "Someone should have told him times have changed. Most of us would set the dogs loose on Malcolm's type, but not him."

Disturbed by a sudden burst of hysterical screaming, he looked over to see what was going on. A woman in the crowd was throwing abuse and blows into the faces of the uniforms holding her back as she continued trying to kick out at a neighbouring bystander who she obviously disliked. He watched as two of the uniformed back-up team helped bundle her away from the scene. A swarm of local press photographers were recording the minutiae of the action and obstructing the policemen in the process. He shook his head.

Maitland looked at his Inspector and said: "How come you know him?"

"Go back a long way," he replied, but didn't elaborate. "Do we know what Malcolm wants?"

"Safe passage, I think."

"To where, Castle-fucking-milk?"

Due to its historically bad reputation, Castlemilk was a large underwhelming estate of mainly poor quality, local authority housing. A mile or so north of their current position it offered even fewer life opportunities for the residents.

Maitland smiled. "Somewhere safe, he says."

Shaking his head, Lamont looked at the man and winked. "Phone NASA, tell them we need a Saturn rocket, ready in five," he quipped. "And don't forget to say please..."

"Space is the only safety from McGlynn's type, right enough."

Maitland laughed as his boss strode off toward the onlookers.

"Let's get up there before there's any more blood," he said over his shoulder.

With a view across the playing fields to four massive tower blocks, the lengthy row of two-storey maisonettes were among some of the estate's better properties.

"Which one is it?"

Maitland nodded toward a scruffy looking house, its windows hung with dirty, faded green curtains.

"Third along on the left."

"Where are the marksmen?"

"Two on the roof of the first block there," he responded,

pointing. "Another two you can see, over by those cars out front."

"Who's in charge of tactical firearms?"

"Wilson."

"And overall?"

"Wilson's senior apparently," Maitland offered. "Same rank as you..."

"And I'm ground crew." Lamont shrugged wearily, realising the overall responsibility lay on his shoulders. He muttered: "Just my bloody luck!"

Edging along behind the row of support vehicles, he found Wilson at the bottom of the steep banking on the other side of the road from the crime scene, chattering into his radio.

"Hi, I'm D.I. Lamont."

Wilson muttered, "Hold," and clicked off the radio.

Shaking his hand, the uniformed officer nodded toward the houses and said: "Pearson over there's been running the floorshow, but he's getting nowhere.

Malcolm's a dope, or doped; hasn't a clue what he's after."

"Your guys positioned?"

"Yep, all's fine," he said. "They spotted Malcolm through the window holding McGlynn by the collar. They think he has a gun against his head."

"He's been there before…"

"Doubt it," said Wilson. "Powerful man."

He smiled and corrected the officer.

"Was..."

Wilson nodded, but his eyes never left the scene.

He asked: "So, how do you want to play it?"

"I'll go chat to Pearson first, see where he's up to, if that's okay."

"All yours..." he said. A look of quiet relief seemed to flicker onto his features.

Lamont scurried over to where Pearson lay on the steep banking below the road. The officer gave him an update of the current manpower status under his command. As he listened, Maitland joined them.

"How does it look?" he asked.

The D.I. shook his head. "Not good,"

"What do we do now?" asked the sergeant.

"Well," he said, taking the megaphone from Pearson. "I hold the speaker out and point it toward those maisonettes. Then I scream at him through it for ten minutes in Gaelic, he gets baffled and surrenders."

"Only asked," he said, and turned to Pearson. "What's the bold Mr Malcolm's first name?"

"Stuart or Stu, apparently..."

With the sergeant trailing at his heels, Lamont made his way back to where the uniformed Inspector waited.

"I'll try getting him to the front door to talk. Maitland and I will go up for a chat if everything seems okay," he said, glancing over at his reluctant sergeant. "If you think we're in the merde, don't wait; give your men the go."

"Wire would be handy, no?"

"If he susses that, I'll be eating lead at a guess," he replied, wryly. "Besides, the wires spoil the line of my waistcoat."

"That colour, it might help!"

"*Blood red?*" *Lamont grinned and raised his eyebrows knowingly. "Hide the damage..."*

"*It's got to be better than chancing it, sir,*" *said Maitland. The sergeant threw his Inspector a questioning look. "No?"*

Lamont smiled at him and winked. It was merely another one of those critical choices.

After several minutes of intense negotiations, Malcolm finally agreed to talk face to face. However, he wouldn't release McGlynn, or let anyone into the house to tend the wounded – and he'd no intentions of giving up the gun.

The D.I. nodded at the firearms officer. "Get that?"

"*Understood. Good luck,*" *he said and returned to the open radio channel, checking the readiness of each of his firearms team in turn.*

"*Right lad, up and at 'em!*" *Lamont said, and scurried up the grassy banking into view of the maisonettes, followed by the reluctant figure of his sergeant.*

When they reached the garden gate, the front door opened a little and a voice called out, "Far enough!"

The portal opened wider and McGlynn's face appeared. His captor remained partly hidden in the shadows, but Lamont could see his nemesis' neck was tethered by a piece of blue nylon cord. Hands bound behind him, a pistol was jammed under his ribcage.

"*Well, well,*" *McGlynn said colourfully. "It's my old friend PC Lamont in a pretty suit and bright red waistcoat. Salaries must have gone up, or you're taking a decent cut of the action these days..."*

"*What do you want, Stuart?*" *he called, ignoring the sarcasm. He would chat with McGlynn later; they had unfinished business.*

"He's murdered ma wife!"

The man's voice sounded stressed and filled with highly charged emotions. Guessing he was most probably fuelled to the teeth with drugs, for a fleeting moment the detective wondered at the wisdom of presenting himself in front of the deranged and frightened, armed man. Putting the anxieties aside, he decided to press on.

"What would like us to do for you, Stuart?"

"Get me oot o' here. If this bastard lives he'll never leave me in peace..."

"Peace? I'll leave pieces of you everywhere," the captive laughed. "And 'PC' Lamont here will put a cross on your memorial. Won't you PC Lamont..."

"See! See!" Malcolm shouted. "See whit he's like!"

"Sea," McGlynn said humourlessly. "Fine spot for your body - swimming with the jellyfish."

"Ah'll use this," the man shouted, ramming the pistol barrel hard into his captive's ribs. "Am tellin' yeh ah will, ye'll join the other two. Ah know ye've mair pals, so ah walk, or it ends here!"

"Oh, I don't think you'll end anything, wee man, will he PC Lamont?" McGlynn chided breathlessly, clearly in pain from the blow to his ribcage.

Although winded, he suddenly kicked out viciously with his heel and ducked low despite the garrotte, struggling violently to break free. Caught hard on the shin, Malcolm howled and fell, allowing the tether to slip from his grasp. Seizing the opportunity, Lamont pushed through the gate and rushed toward the struggling men, but a shot rang out. Stopping abruptly, he watched as McGlynn spun, and then tottered backwards out of the narrow hall. For a moment the wounded man fought to retain his balance in the doorway.

Sprinting up the steeply sloping garden, the detective could see his right arm was drenched in blood from the earlier skirmish. Now desperate to get McGlynn to safety before the firearms team targeted Malcolm, he was about to pull him out of the way when a sudden blast of the handgun discharging filled his senses. Stopped in his tracks, he saw McGlynn collapse back over the entrance steps then tumble down the grass banking. Open-mouthed, Lamont watched as the man's body came to rest against the unkempt garden hedge.

Then Malcolm appeared in the doorway, gun in hand. His sergeant shouted a warning just as three shots rang out. Lamont swivelled round, but his last memory was a glimpse of Stu Malcolm's shock as two high velocity bullets carved through his chest. The third shell ricocheted from the wall and pierced Detective Inspector Crieff Lamont's skull. Despite fighting to stay upright, a sharp pain seared through his head and his legs began to give way. And then a sense of falling; forever falling into an icy cold, deep crevasse overcame him as he lost consciousness.

Maitland watched in horror as his Detective Inspector rolled down the banked garden, the inert body coming to rest beside that of Pat McGlynn...

As the painful memories of the head wound receded into the sunlit morning, Lamont the holidaymaker smiled. Taking a deep draft of coffee, he swallowed loudly and savoured the growing warmth in the morning air. He stretched, then yawned. No, he had never actively sought promotion back then, but it had seemed to come his way. Passing the qualifying exams and smiling the right smiles at the right people had worked. Now it was most probably the last thing in the world he would want. The shooting had given him time to find a clearer rationale for continuing his service within the police force. And demotion allowed him what he considered to be the highest privilege: that of being actively involved in casework. Conveniently, those cases kept another tide at bay: that sweeping tide of loneliness, guilt, and boredom.

Nearly six months had been passed on sick leave after the shooting. And sick he had been too; sick to the teeth of the hospital and every uniform-adorned, rehabilitation-focused species the doctors had thrown his way. Now, apart from the metal plate covering shattered bone where the bullet burrowed into his brain, and the occasional few hours of blinding headaches, little else had changed.

Elspeth often remarked that he seemed to have an even more acute ability than in the past to focus on and recall information. On the downside from her standpoint, he now seemed quite unemotional. Others, including Moon, had made similar observations and told him to his face. Although aware of the outward appearance of emotional change, Lamont wasn't quite so sure those evaluations were correct. Keeping counsel had always been his way, and he now felt protecting what remained of his inner self to be more important than open displays of passion.

As church bells pealed in the nearby Bastide village, he got up and wandered down to the waterside. The sound of a distant barge, chugging slowly toward the cute little rented gîte's moorings, caught his attention. He'd noticed the dull, heavy sound of the engines many times during the last week. It surprised him that he accepted such noisy, powerful machinery as being synonymous with the canal's tranquility. The boat was coming from the direction of Toulouse to the northwest and soon showed its heavy bow through the tree-lined shadows.

The Scot scuffed a piece of loose gravel with his shoe and watched as it splashed into the grey water. Then, popping a mint chew into his mouth, stood quietly and listened. The faint chatter from those on deck grew louder and more distinct as the dull green and red-painted hull drew near. The accents weren't French, but then, apart from the chartered craft afloat on the canal, few of the marine voices on the Canal Du Midi ever were. Most of those now sailing the canal were from multi-national backgrounds. Here purely for pleasure, many piloted their own craft along the beautiful, man-made waterway.

Constructed by Jean Paul Riquet in the late 1600s, the canal was built to haul wine, grain and wares across the Massif Centrale. Goods had originally passed through Bordeaux on the Garonne River, heading to northern Europe. Built with the support of King Louis XIV, the canal had helped Toulouse's traders avoid the Bordeaux merchant's levies on river trade as their wares headed out into the Bay of Biscay.

More importantly, the canal bypassed plundering Spanish brigands. Mediterranean goods and products had been 'brigand bait' as they ran the gauntlet through the dangerous, narrow waters in the Gibraltar Straits and sea-routes around the Iberian Peninsula. The Canal du Midi made this hazardous voyage unnecessary by cutting straight over the French mainland.

For the past century and more, its main use had been for pleasure boating. The cool, shady banks brought a welcome relief from the searing summer heat. The waterway also brought many tourists and much needed euros to southern France each summer.

As the vessel approached, its bow wave washed toward the shore leaving behind a dizzying reflection as eddies rippled over the still, dark waters. It was perhaps only fifty yards away when he began to discern two distinct and angry voices. Tipping the coffee dregs out onto the grass by his side, he guessed the first voice belonged to a man of central European, possibly Italian, origin. The second belonged to a young female English speaker. Despite her loud recriminations she was well spoken, the accent a hybrid of polite Scots and English Home Counties.

As their words became clearer the Scot was intrigued, for the couple seemed oblivious to his presence. Curious, he tried to distinguish the ill-tempered exchange above the heavy chugging of the boat's diesel engine. The woman blurted out something he couldn't quite hear, then over the bow he could see the protagonists facing each other across the deck.

"It could have been invested more wisely anyway!" the man exclaimed. "Risk should always be spread."

"What would you know?"

"Life!" The man gloated in fractured English: "I know life! It left him the moment the midwife slapped his bastard ass perhaps…"

"How dare you!" The woman sounded deeply hurt

as she howled defensively: "He did nothing wrong!"

"Then perhaps he should have left well alone," the man responded, though now in a softer, more placatory tone. "But we don't know the reason..."

At that moment Lamont, grinning broadly at the remark about midwifery, broke into the woman's line of vision. Her startled reaction stopped the dispute abruptly. Both turned to stare at the stranger on the canal bank.

"Morning," he called pleasantly.

Touching the faded blue baseball cap politely, he smiled, but both ignored him and hurriedly left the deck. He watched as they pushed into the cabin below and slammed closed the lacquered doors. From the angry gestures he could make out as the cube-shaped portholes passed his line of sight, the Scot guessed they hadn't quite finished arguing. He looked up at the wheelhouse as the tanned frame of the ship's pilot appeared.

Steering the vessel from its elevated controls, he called a loud, "Bonjour!"

The man politely tipped a casually worn officer's cap. Smiling broadly, he shrugged an expansive, Gallic shrug toward Lamont as he passed. He would have heard little of the argument, for the vessel's wheel was at least forty feet behind the prow deck and directly above the engine. Returning the smile, the Scot watched the handsome craft as it puttered slowly away. Ever the policeman, he locked in the image of two attractive young antagonists.

As he turned back toward the rustic stone cottage, Elspeth, his wife, appeared in the doorway.

"How's the head this morning?"

"It's fine lass," he answered. "I've the usual residual discomfort, but the pain's gone now, thank God."

"What was all the noise about?"

"Probably some romantic holiday tiff aboard that boat," he explained, casually sweeping an arm in the direction of the cruiser as it chugged off toward the nearby town of Carcassonne. "Though it sounded pretty intense from where I was standing."

Feigning interest, she said, "Really?"

Elspeth continued towel drying her auburn hair while stepping forward to look along the waterway. Pausing for a moment, she waved the towel toward the waterside. "And where were you standing; there, there, or there?"

Shaking his head at her mockery, he said, "It's a good job we're an item."

Elspeth wandered onto the terrace as the boat disappeared into the tree-lined shadows and kissed his cheek. At five-foot-nine she was almost as tall as her husband and in stiletto heels the willowy figure towered over him. Lamont liked that. He found her stature both intimidating and intensely sexual. Or at least he had before a bullet changed his world.

"You smell nice," she said. "Shaved early too. Going somewhere?"

"Same aftershave I've worn for twenty years," he said. "And yes, funnily enough, I was going to pick up another bottle this morning. The old one's nearly empty. Fancy a bike ride into the village?"

"Sounds great, but I don't think you'll get your usual from there."

He had worn the same aftershave since first buying it in Athens as a youth. She had tried many times to persuade him to use one of those she preferred, but without success.

"Supermarket's worth a try," he said determinedly. "The chemists are too expensive over here."

"When do you want to go in?"

"Anytime you're ready," he said, smiling.

Throwing the towel over the chair, she said: "Funny overhearing a passing lovers' tiff." Then, wrapping her arms around him added: "We haven't argued all week!"

"Yeah, but you're not blaming me for bad investments causing us financial losses."

The word, *loss*, sent an unexpected chill through her. Soon they would need to talk, but not now. '*It*' would wait.

He pecked her nose playfully.

She asked, "Is that it?"

"I don't want my glasses fogged again by your damp hair; can't see the guilty characters passing on the Canal through them when they're wet."

Shaking her head in mock despair, she let go of him and turned back toward the gîte.

"You're not at work now you know," she said. "Remember, we're on holiday – before your curiosity sends us riding off up the canal bank chasing imaginary criminals!"

Chapter 3

Brendan O'Leary closed the laptop and looked over the cramped little desk. Like the rest of the worn, out-dated office furnishings it needed either depositing in a skip, or setting alight with a can of petrol. The detective sighed as he looked around. Poorly painted walls highlighted random cracks in the aging plaster. Even the window frames seemed to be losing their struggle to hold onto the building's late nineteenth century mortar. A yellowed photograph of young Princess Anne meeting some of the local dignitaries during a visit in the 1980s hung wearily over an old, tiled fireplace. The hearth now played host to a rusting two-bar electric heater.

Trying hard to figure out how he'd ever managed to get himself transferred to this remote, God-forsaken hole, O'Leary scratched his head. After all, he was here, allegedly, for using one wrong phrase. A few weeks ago he'd been heading up a team of detectives investigating the looting rioters in Manchester, looking for connections to his own sphere of interest. Yet now, here he was, fighting crime in rural Scotland. He knew the job was important, but often felt he should never have agreed to the secondment proposal. Surely there were others who deserved this fate more?

Pitlochry, near the centre of Scotland's wild highlands, was certainly no desperate corner. But then, neither was it a metropolis of investigative police work. Making it the focus of investigations would be up to him, but there had been only one serious crime here in the last few years. In fact, so little happened, that in his opinion there was no need for a detective to be based here at all.

He had never seen himself as a country boy, or more importantly, a lover of Scotland, and yet here he was. The 'Jocks', as he called them, were in his opinion a rowdy lot whose best brains tended to evacuate the miserable, midge-infested, rain-soaked country immediately after puberty. These less than sanguine opinions of his temporary Scottish home hadn't been formed by chance, partisanship, or even prejudice: no, they were part of his family's history handed down through the generations.

His great-grandfather, Eugene, migrated to Scotland during the Irish potato famine. Many Irishmen left during what became known as 'The Great Hunger' to find work. A tenant farmer in County Donegal, he had little choice but to join nearly a quarter of the population seeking a new life – and food – when the potato blight struck.

Brendan could see a certain irony in his current situation. His ancestor had come to Scotland seeking wages; he had been sent to Scotland for more or less the same reason: work or starve. Unlike his seemingly brave and desperate ancestor who came in support of his family, he was relocated here for being an alleged racist.

Gritting his teeth and slapping a hand hard on the

little desk, he tried again to understand how he'd gotten himself into this situation. Yes, he held some disparaging views on the various ethnic groups, particularly those who hadn't bothered to integrate into his cultural world. He couldn't disagree that the phrase he'd been told to use would be interpreted as racist. However, he had never thought himself as influenced by skin colour and he'd certainly never disliked anyone for racial reasons – aside, of course, from the Scots. Even his disparaging views on the non-integration of immigrants had been hidden over the years: shadows in the folds of political correctness deep in his consciousness. It had only taken that one phrase blurted out in supposed anger in front of a black colleague.

Having held the rank of detective sergeant, he was now demoted to mere, 'constable', pending enquiries. Although his career would seem certain to remain in this fugue state until the hearing, he knew that those twenty-five years of policing weren't over. He simply had to tick the boxes in Pitlochry and then get back to catching the fallout down in Manchester.

It would take more than a good Police Federation representative to clear his name, and reputation, back in the city though. Racism allegations were a tenacious mud that didn't wash off easily. McLintock, his representative, said he had been lucky to get him this placement instead of a suspension. The man amused him. How could this be luck?

The rep had elaborated that his secondment was because the Manchester Police Authorities didn't want to be branded racists themselves. They were, rightly, very wary of any backlash in the face of a spate of inner-city riots. No, McClintock had repeated, that was the last thing they'd want, especially after he'd warned them of media leaks and rumours about the case. Those may even come from within the Force, he'd cautioned, and the damage would then become immeasurable.

He had listened attentively as the man indicated it may still take several months before they got round to dealing with his case. From his knowledge of disciplinary procedures, this time gap was not unusual in any disciplinary case put before the authorities, so he could relax and sit it out patiently. At least, to all appearances, that was the impression he would give while carving out his own niche.

McClintock, he knew, was a smart character. In his experience, the man could smell a rat – or an opportunity – at a thousand paces. He had hinted that racism was the national dirty word. However, he said, Manchester Police Force may eventually prefer to bury his little 'problem'. Senior officers, he'd argued, may even put pressure on the plaintiff to drop any charges in exchange for a juicy promotion, or posting of his choice. Besides, McLintock told him, the man they had been trying to arrest at the time of the allegations had disappeared into the wilds of the city's Levenshulme district. It was now one policeman's word against another.

"Brendan," the rep had smirked, patting his shoulder heartily. "I may be just the man to persuade them of the benefits of dropping this racism nonsense, and clearing your record too."

McClintock had thought for a moment before turning to leave.

"Federation relationships are critical in times like these..." Hesitating, he'd winked and offered a wry smile. "As I've told them on more than one occasion, they've got to think a great deal about the Federation's relationships with them." Nodding sagely, the man had left their meeting with the parting shot: "And those smooth relationships will be critical in these times of integration and budgetary constraint. They need our agreement to any proposed changes, Brendan, never forget that!"

And that was the last he'd heard from the Police Federation. Thankfully, a single disciplinary case was unlikely to be on anyone's list of priorities. He had been offered some good news too: due to the help the Scottish Police Forces had given Manchester during, and after the recent riots, it had been agreed that his own employers would be paying his salary and accommodation expenses.

Someone up there was taking care of things after all, he thought.

This arrangement would continue while he filled a gap in the Perth and Kinross Forces ranks. It meant he would remain part of the Manchester team for the time being.

Detective Chief Inspector MacDougall in Perth had told him formally that he thought him lucky, but wouldn't judge him – yet. The senior officer had said brusquely that he wouldn't tolerate any visits back to, or contact at any level with, the Manchester Force. Confirming to O'Leary that he considered him little better than suspended, he had warned him it would be wise not to forget that view. One foot out of line would be all it took as far as the Inspector was concerned, advising him with a smirk, that he'd been told by his Chief Constable: '*base the offender in Pitlochry. There, he'll have time to reflect on his alleged misdemeanours and look toward rebuilding a career*'.

So here he was: Thursday the thirty-first of August: three days and the office phone hadn't rung. Looking around the local area, chatting to anyone who appeared informed, had achieved little. Thankfully, email and the Internet kept him briefed on events.

Local professional contact had been limited to two uniformed policemen who occasionally used the building as an administration base. Always smiling, they would nod their hellos then go about any office business before leaving again. The station was usually left without a disorderly crumb on the floor. He presumed, judging from their relatively cool reactions toward him, that they had been informed he was persona non grata. No matter how perplexed he felt about the pace of things, there was no way of moving any quicker to build local relationships without raising suspicions as to his motives.

He didn't imagine the bureaucratic old Detective Chief Inspector from Perth, or anyone else for that matter, would pop in and check on his whereabouts. Guessing he could probably meet a starving, skeletal end in this first-floor office and never be found did, however, mean he was free to pursue his own covert agenda.

Life outside this self-inflicted isolation at work, he reflected, felt little better. His digs were a miserable bed and breakfast set in an old stone cottage on the edge of town. It was more normally frequented, he thought, by those desperate for a cheap spot to rest in the tourist high season. The room smelled of mothballs, the towels were damp and the bedding worn threadbare. It reminded him of the ransacked furniture store he'd visited after the looting back home where the thugs had used the premises as a very public toilet. Even the rented room's wardrobe emitted a deep, musty odour like the ones often found in homes where a body had lain. No, he would have to sort things out, starting with a move to new lodgings next week.

The desk phone rang loudly, startling him. O'Leary stared at it in surprise for a moment, then dropped his heels to the floor and picked up the receiver.

"Hello, Detective O'Leary," he said tentatively, uncomfortable with the strange sound of his own voice for a moment. Rarely caught off guard, he had remembered to drop *sergeant* from his title.

"Yes, sir." He raised his eyebrows and sat upright. "When would you like to see me? I can drive over straight away, sir," he offered. "Yes…Your office… yes… I'll be down there for…" He glanced at his watch. "Three-thirty…"

The phone cut off before he had a chance to ask any questions, but the Perth rendezvous sounded important. Buttoning his shirt collar, O'Leary straightened his tie in the old stained mirror by the door. Then, checking his jacket pockets for car keys and the ubiquitous notebook, he headed out to the Ford.

Perth had a feel to it O'Leary couldn't quite fathom. It was neither vibrant, nor thriving. From the twice he'd been here to check the place out and quaff a beer or two, the detective decided that it held more of a 'polite bustle' as its activity level trade mark. Most of the local people seemed to have lived here all their lives and knew one another well. He'd been told strangers taking up residence in the city were usually afforded a warm welcome, unlike the one he'd received on first meeting the Chief Inspector.

Locking the car and striding confidently into the modern police offices, he was immediately directed up to MacDougall's first floor office by the desk sergeant. This surprised him. He expected to be kept waiting the obligatory ten minutes while the Inspector let him cool his heels. Conforming reluctantly to protocol of rank, he knocked and waited. Finally, after a short delay, a harsh Scottish accent called him through. Looking crisp and formal, MacDougall gestured toward the chair as he approached.

"I have a problem, Detective Constable O'Leary," he said.

The DCI had taken the opportunity to ensure O'Leary understood his demoted status. He smiled to himself at this and undid the jacket button as he settled. He sensed the man study him intently, checking for any hint of adversity, but never flinched. Instead, he kept an impassive expression fixed to his features and casually crossed his legs.

"More realistically," MacDougall added, correcting himself. "*We* have a problem."

O'Leary raised his eyebrows as he said, "Really, sir?"

Hesitating a moment for effect, the DCI confirmed,

"Yes, really."

"In what way, sir?"

Taking stock of the file in front of him for a moment before continuing, the balding officer shook his head.

"It seems we have an unexplained death on our hands."

To the detective's ears, the line had been delivered with what sounded like a mixture of quandary and dread. "Unexplained," he said. Trying hard to maintain a serious expression, the detective added, "Always the worst sort, sir."

Placing both hands flat on the polished wood, the senior officer drummed his fingers for a moment. It almost seemed as though he was trying to decide how to respond to the detective's apparent lack of gravitas.

"We've discovered a corpse, detective," he said, then added warily, "body found in the early hours of this morning."

Raising his eyebrows again, MacDougall studied the officer on the opposite side of the desk for a moment with a curious, almost inquisitive, expression.

Despite the urge to laugh, O'Leary said nothing.

"It was in a small dinghy on Loch Rannoch,' the senior officer continued reluctantly. "Seems it had lain there for a few days. Three wounds visible on the body; one to the shoulder and others to the chest and forehead."

"Bullet or sharp instrument, sir."

"Not clear yet, though looks more like they were

inflicted by a projectile," MacDougall replied obtusely. "We'll await the coroner's efforts, I think and…"

O'Leary interrupted: "Isn't Loch Rannoch quite near my office?"

Despite trying not to sound offended at having trailed down to Perth for this briefing, he failed, and the vexation in his eyes stood out like a bold, neon sign.

"Yes, quite, indeed," MacDougall confirmed. He hadn't liked the interruption and was keen to reassert himself. "But nonetheless, I thought it better to bring you down for a chat about the best way forward. You see I'm not sure you're the best person for the job."

"I see, sir," O'Leary said, trying with difficulty to suppress his anger, yet still sound crestfallen for effect.

Knowing there were no other officers readily available, this case would be his, regardless. Again he allowed himself an inward smile.

"Anyway, detective, I hadn't quite finished what I was about to say…" Pausing for moment to confirm his authority, MacDougall reluctantly added: "As there's no one else available I'm afraid you'll have to fill in – although against my better judgement."

Uncertain what this man's better judgement might be, O'Leary said, with a hint of irony: "That's very kind of you, sir."

The Inspector caught the inflection, but chose to ignore it.

"Time of death is only a broad guess. We've had to

get a coroner down from Aberdeen. Our man's off sick and the one in Dundee recently left the mortal coil."

O'Leary could almost hear the stiff starch crack in the crisp, white shirt as the man spoke.

"Anyhow, he thinks the body's lain out on the loch for two or three days – preliminary timing, of course."

"And what does he think the probable cause of death is then, sir?"

"Gunshot wounds," MacDougall said with some distaste. "Though he can't be sure till he's got the body on the slab and prodded around a bit – his words, not mine."

A murder on his patch presented O'Leary with a golden opportunity. With no local detectives free to investigate, he could finally get closer to Rannoch village and Castle Druin.

"Is there a reason for the loss of investigative time, sir?"

Clearly upset by the challenging comment, the DCI asked, "What loss?"

"Scene of crime up at Loch Rannoch; me down here in Perth," O'Leary offered drily.

Staring at him in disbelief, MacDougall thought for a moment, then chose to ignore the remark. Regaining his composure, he said: "Because of staffing problems in pathology, we'll hear nothing definitive about the actual cause of death for a day or two more – at least."

O'Leary saw a ray of hope glint above the horizon

and sharpened his thinking.

"Did you say he *appears* to have been shot, sir?" Narrowing his eyes slightly and changing to a higher, more inquisitive tone, he said, "Probable murder, then?"

"That's what I want you to find out, Detective O'Leary!"

"Bullet and stab wounds are quite distinctive, and easily differentiated. What did the officers on the scene think?"

"A local officer…" The Inspector checked the file pedantically. "…Constable Wilkinson, reported the man's head had serious injuries commensurate with the skull exploding."

"Then it's gunshots – or the mysterious case of the erupting brain?"

"Well, quite," said the DCI, "but it's not a subject for humour; not in this office.

O'Leary checked himself and said, "No, sir."

After taking a few deep breaths, almost as though trying not to hyperventilate, the senior officer raised his eyebrows and said: "We believe – sorry – *we know* the body is that of one of the sons of Lord MacCaig."

"I see," said the detective, nodding slowly. His mind was awakening to the implications and potential benefits of any enquiries involving a MacCaig. If he got a result here and didn't make too many enemies, then he may be onto something of real benefit to solving his own investigative problems.

"Local Royalty then?"

"They're a very well respected family," MacDougall emphasised, "and friends of our Chief Constable…" He paused for a moment and held O'Leary's thoughtful gaze. "Sadly, one of whom now has the back of his head missing."

The detective could feel excitement rise as he thought through the benefits of having such an opportunity appear at this particular moment in time.

"The MacCaig family own most of the estate land around Pitlochry," the Inspector explained.

"I'd better get back up there then!" O'Leary chirped.

"Yes detective, but before you go, remember this," said MacDougall, his voice moving into warning mode. "That family require kid gloves. They've had a bereavement."

"Won't forget for a moment."

"Lord MacCaig gives generously to police benevolent funds," he said, in brittle tones. "Established 'Aid All Africa' and the charity works tirelessly to support our needy friends over there. He's also generous with both his time and money in the local community. In effect, detective, he's a pillar of the Perthshire community and part of our Scottish establishment."

"Important man, right enough then."

As he stared dully across the desk, the detective wondered when this buffoon would tell him something he didn't already know.

"I've spoken to him on the phone and offered my sincerest condolences," MacDougall said, the words heavily charged with empathy. "Tell him if he needs anything – anything at all – to give me a ring."

"I will," he replied warily, nodding. The detective finally understood why he'd been dragged down to MacDougall's office before being let loose on an unsuspecting Highland population. His tone was steeped in sarcasm as he added: "And you don't think I might prove offensive to their love of Africans?"

"No, Detective O'Leary," he replied firmly.

The DCI's expression had now changed to one of veiled anger. He narrowed his stare as though to underline his ire. For a fleeting moment, the detective thought he resembled a balding hawk and tried not to smile.

"They've no knowledge of your current disciplinary situation," said MacDougall. "But, I do want them treated delicately *and* with the utmost respect. More importantly, I expect a daily briefing on progress. I need something concrete to pass on to the Chief Constable."

The detective thought fleetingly of a heavy paving slab as he nodded in grudging agreement. About to rise from the chair, he was stopped abruptly when the rigid, formal figure waved him down; much as a teacher would a schoolchild trying to leave class before the bell.

"Don't forget," said the Inspector. "When I ask for a written report, I mean *written*; full and unequivocal. I want it delivered to this office by email the following morning. No excuses!"

O'Leary waited in his seat like a scolded toddler. Despite fighting the urge to reach across and plant a fist on the end of MacDougall's nose, he thought the better of it, subdued the temptation and played along. There was work to be done.

"That'll be all, detective," he said dismissively. Then, as O'Leary left his office, added loudly: "Remember the reports – I'll have senior officers, as well as Edinburgh, all over me with this one, have no doubt."

"And so you will," O'Leary muttered, pulling the door firmly closed.

"Damn the man!" he said aloud.

Chapter 4

Deputy Chief Constable Moon (emeritus) looked hard at his desk and the three bulging beige files and shook his head. The emeritus status had brought no less work his way. However, since his office lay within the boundaries of Central Scotland Police's jurisdiction, someone in Edinburgh had decided he could only carry an honorary title.

The Scottish Police Service Authority, (SPSA), had been established to bring cohesion to the disparate facilities and abilities of Scotland's eight, regionally based, police forces. Each one suffered manning, forensic, educational and financial limitations. After all, there were only five million souls in Scotland's relatively stable population base, which hardly seemed to warrant such an over-governed force. The organisation also had control over Scotland's Police College at Tulliallan. This brought Moon more than enough headaches, but it meant that Scotland only trained the manpower numbers the country's regions actually required.

The files stacked neatly on the desk reflected one single collection of priorities, mirroring his life to date. They were all in that orderly pile. He was currently reviewing the manpower and budgetary requirements of the Lothian and Borders force before they became part of the new, integrated Scottish Constabulary structure. Edinburgh's political types anticipated a report in three weeks.

He also managed Detective Crieff Lamont, the absence of whom was the subject of his current wave of intense dissatisfaction. He'd originally brought Lamont under his wing to allow the man to recover from an injury incurred in the line of duty. Back then, Moon had already decided that maybe a few of Scotland's higher profile crimes, or newly filed unsolved cases, could benefit from the SPSA's assistance. Some of the Chief Constables had resisted at first, but most had seen the writing on the wall. So here they were today: called on regularly from across the country to assist in a diverse range of cases. Such was his influence, that Moon's balanced views on the imminent amalgamation of Scotland's eight regional Forces were widely sought.

He had now been asked by the Justice Secretary's office in Edinburgh to assist in an urgent new case, the filed report on which rested on top of the others. For him, this was *the* priority. And he needed Lamont. Staring hard at the telephone for a moment, he tried to resolve how on earth he could ever reduce the size of the orderly pile of paper that filled the left side of his field of vision. But without his detective present – at the moment his only detective – reducing it was impossible.

The silver coloured phone sat directly in front of him, six inches from the far edge of the ageing oak monolith he used as a desk. It had always sat there. Positioning the phone on that precise spot allowed him to make the theatrical effort of leaning forward and stretching a full arms-length for the appliance when answering it. That effort, his old boss, Chief Superintendent Dalrymple had assured him, was significant. It told guests in his office that by answering, or making any particular call, he would be delivering a 'grand gesture'. That very act, he'd said, made the call look important and required the visitor's patience – and more importantly, their silence. Dalrymple would raise an arm and glance at his watch, then say: "Forgive me, I really do have to make this call, it's expected."

The line was usually delivered with a deeply apologetic, open-handed gesture. The officer was politely invited to wait in his secretary's office for a moment. The old man would then dial one or two digits too few for the particular call he was supposed to be making. When the telephone's 'engaged' tone cut in, he would begin an important conversation with some non-existent Chief Constable, or dignitary.

This fictitious dialogue always began in an aggrieved tone. His voice would then become louder as he pretended to complain about some impending, wretchedly diabolical liberty being taken against his department. This diatribe could involve resources, manpower, or any other subject and all the while, of course, he was quietly chuckling to himself. When invited to return to the Chief Superintendent's imposing office, the visitor would often have lost the thread of the argument, or the will to pursue it.

As he had found, particularly before heading-up the SPSA, taking time to reflect carefully on any matter could be of the utmost importance.

"Always allow time to change any decisions you've made, Moon," old Dalrymple would say in a scolding, wise owl tone. *"Never burn your bridges, or be seen to be judgmental – both bad for the career!"*

Having proffered these lines whenever he thought a junior had been presumptuous, Moon now used the script freely. He had become a 'Dalrymple' and carried the style with pride. Renowned for his thoughtfulness, he was a wise counsel sought frequently by many who trusted in him. It was these strengths that ensured he had been offered this role – extending his career well beyond his anticipated retirement. Now approaching his sixty-sixth birthday, Moon held an almost reverential status both within the Scottish Police system and the Edinburgh political hierarchy. Invitations to address seminars and conferences there, and in London, had become a regular part of his professional agenda.

Working assiduously to retain his Cumberland identity allowed him the privilege of being seen by many as carrying a neutral and non-parochial view of any local 'Scottish' situation. The man was free of regional bias, for which some prominent Scots had become notorious. These often bitter rivalries had tainted decision-making at important junctures throughout the country's colourful history. Moon's 'neutrality' therefore brought added gravitas to any analytical report on the Police Force's governance, structure, or efficiency he had been asked to compile by political masters.

He still owned a large, traditional, slate-built home, on the isolated western shores of Derwentwater in the Lake District. Overlooked by Catbells – a well-known walker's haunt – the substantial house and three acres of what was now National Trust land had been acquired by the family in the late 1800s.

After migrating from Ireland in the eighteenth century the Moon family had accrued great wealth from both lead and coal mining on and around Cumberland's west coast. Given the opportunity, he spoke with pride of his great, great, great-grandfather who had reinforced the family's kudos, power and wealth by importing rum from the Indies. The liquor had been brought in through the pretty, but now quiet town of Whitehaven, once one of England's largest ports. Moon conveniently ignored the historical rumours of their heavy involvement in the latter days of the slave trade. He rightly saw little to be gained by detracting from the more romantic episodes in his families past exploits.

The six-bedroomed home served him well. Whenever he and his gentile wife enjoyed a weekend free from social, or professional commitments they would leave the family home, which nestled near the foot of the strong walls of Stirling Castle, and head for their well-maintained Lakeland retreat. It allowed them to entertain an elite set of privileged guests, both political and professional, from either side of Hadrian's Wall. They were much-loved liberals.

Pursing his lips, the DCC drummed his fingers in frustration. He did not like being thwarted. Especially not on Fridays when it meant having to wait all weekend to resolve a difficulty. Moon scratched his head as he thought about ringing the detective's mobile again, but five other calls already made this morning had gotten the same 'busy' message. Instead, he picked up his Blackberry and sent another irate text. For the tenth time he failed to gain the intended recipient's 'delivery message' notice.

"Damn the man!" he muttered.

Chapter 5

"How did you find out about the restaurant?" Elspeth asked, as she finished tidying her hair.

"Saw it in the local information folder – over on the table by the door," he called back.

"Really? I tend to ignore those things."

"I know," he said, buttoning the grey, long-sleeved shirt and tucking it into his pants. "They're the ones the gîte's owners leave for guests, like us. Helps them find the local tourist attractions."

He was already on his way to collect the pair of boat shoes, left out on the terrace last night, as she muttered something about his sarcasm. Elspeth turned and studied him as he wandered back into the room.

"How do I look?"

"The dark brown shoes and the chinos don't work with that shirt," she offered. "Didn't you bring another one?"

"I've got that new black polo," he tried, "will that do?"

"Stick it on and let's see," she said, wrinkling her nose in anticipation of another sartorial mismatch.

Groaning, he left only to return a few moments later. "So?"

"You'll do," said Elspeth, shaking her head. Moving closer, she put her arms around him. "You know, I'd promised myself that we'd become lovers again this week and we have, metaphorically at least."

"Oh, I don't know," he quipped, "there was that effort on Tuesday, the lusty one Wednesday, then that one yesterday after you'd told me off…"

"You *are* a dreamer," she said, dismissing him scornfully. Elspeth knew the reason they hadn't made love, the time to share passion again with this man – her husband – had not yet arrived.

The restaurant was prettier than she'd expected and more formal too. Lamont tended to suck it and see, literally, where eateries were concerned. On several occasions over the years, after spending hours preparing to look her best, she would find herself seated in near transport-café conditions. Though in fairness, she was never left feeling out of place as he lavished her with attention wherever they went. However, this was the last evening of their first break together in many years and she wanted something special to help rekindle the fire.

The little cottage gîte they'd rented sat on the edge of the quiet commune of Sauzens, not far from a rural airport beside the nearby town of Carcassone. A medical colleague in Glasgow she'd recently consulted about her own health had recommended it. In gratitude, she had already sent a thank-you card and would take a bottle of the local vintage for him.

The well cared-for little collection of second homes and gîtes lay on the banks of the historic canal. It was close enough to town to use the old bicycles provided for daily shopping and café trips. August in France had been hot, but the nearest boulangerie for bread and cakes lay only a mile away along the shady canal towpath. Even then, earlier in the week it had been too hot to do anything involving movement, so they'd lazed in the shade. It was what they both needed for their all-too-short break in the sun.

The very idea of relaxation took a few days to seed in the detective's mind, but eventually it had, at least superficially. Elspeth hadn't yet been able to talk to him of the unease she carried about her health, or more importantly, of a developing relationship with a colleague, but they had learned to love again and be friends. Perhaps the professional relationship conversations wouldn't be necessary for a while longer, but that decision would have to wait till they returned home.

As they parked the bicycles he looked across and winked. She smiled warmly, even though her thoughts were more wishful than realistic. As he put out his arm theatrically, she looped her own round his and they wandered onto the restaurant's busy terrace.

After a few moments an immaculately presented waiter appeared. He offered a two-setting table that had, judging by the clutter of plates and napkins, just been vacated. However, Elspeth turned on her charm and asked him in French for a more romantic spot. The man pointed out that they were already very busy, but after consulting with a colleague, relented and ushered them carefully past several other tables to a seat directly outside the restaurant's window

After ordering, Lamont remarked ruefully: "That French dialect would have got an 'A plus' at my school."

"It was only a 'B' at mine," she retorted. "But then our standards were slightly higher."

"Your folks could afford to pay and look what that bought them," he smirked. As the drinks arrived he added: "You could even stroll to school chatting with friends – I needed a bus pass."

After thanking the waiter, she said, "Mind you, they thought you were old for your years back then – sixteen going on sixty-five!" Elspeth laughed freely and, feeling more relaxed than he had in years, Lamont joined her.

As the late August sun began to set the temperature was still more than twenty-five degrees. The meal had been excellent, topping a fine day together.

After the waiter cleared their empty tarte citron dessert dishes, Elspeth excused herself and went inside to find the Ladies Room. A number of others were waiting for a free cubicle. Two of those in front of her were English speakers. The elder of the pair, a woman in her fifties, complained loudly about exorbitant prices in the shops and restaurants. Her grating, high-pitched voice did little to garner support for her argument.

The younger of the two – a more confident looking woman – said politely, but firmly: "Quality always costs, don't you think?"

Failing to win any allies, the older woman bustled away into the first free cubicle. The young woman smiled at Elspeth and shook her head.

"It's always the same on holiday," Elspeth said quietly, nodding toward the cubicle.

The woman whispered: "Why do they come here?"

Elspeth shrugged, put out her hand and introduced herself.

"Amelia," the other responded warmly.

"Are you visiting Carcassonne?"

"No, we have a house here."

The attractive, dark-haired woman was dressed casually, yet looked exquisite. Tight fitting jeans and a loose, light blue, open-collared shirt seemed to accentuate her sophistication, and left Elspeth feeling a little self-conscious.

"How wonderful," she said. "Hope you don't mind my asking, but do you live here?"

"No, I don't mind at all," the woman smiled easily. "We don't live here all the time. Only came over for a couple of weeks to cruise the canal and rest a little."

"Does us all good," said Elspeth.

"I would guess from your accent, you're from Scotland?"

"Yes," she confirmed. "Stirling."

Before a cubicle became available, Elspeth asked her new acquaintance if she had finished her meal. When the woman confirmed that she and her partner were about to have coffee, Elspeth asked if they would like to join them.

Arriving back at their table with the young couple in tow, Elspeth began introducing them.

"This is…" She turned to the tall, athletic looking young man with a 'help, what's your name' look on her face.

"Gio…" said the young Italian. He looked at the seated figure for a moment as though he knew him, but couldn't figure where from. "Gio Genovese."

Nodding almost reluctantly, Lamont offered a weak smile.

"And this is Amelia," said Elspeth, puzzled by her husband's coolness. She threw him a sharp frown.

Taking the hint, he grinned broadly and got to his feet to offer the couple a welcoming hand. "Great to meet you guys!"

As they seated themselves, Gio, sensing his host's reticence, enquired politely: "We're not intruding, are we?"

"Of course not!" said the Scot, looking enthusiastically toward his wife. "We've been on our own all week, so the opportunity for a good old-fashioned blether is very welcome."

"You're here for the week then?" asked Gio, as the coffee arrived. He threw his partner a brisk glance. "This coffee…you have ordered?"

"We girls took the liberty," the young woman said.

Ignoring him, she put a hand on Lamont's forearm and said: "Your beautiful wife said you'd enjoy the company."

"It's a great idea," he responded warmly.

Having noticed the Italian's irritation at being interrupted, he guessed the couple probably still had unresolved differences following their earlier tiff on the cruiser. It seemed rather odd they had failed to recognise him, but he said nothing despite his curiosity. Perhaps their argument and it being so early in the day meant they hadn't taken much notice. Looking at it from their perspective, he'd probably been no more than another passing figure on the canal bank in the bright morning sun. And he had, after all, been unshaven, wearing sunglasses and sporting the old baseball cap.

"So, you have your own place here?" Elspeth enquired. "Must be great. We're back home tomorrow."

"We're going back next week as well, I think," replied Amelia. She looked toward her partner for confirmation, but he ignored the gesture and continued stirring his coffee.

"I was telling Elspeth our home is in Scotland, Mr Lamont. Well, my family do…"

"Really? The Scot asked, "Where?"

"I see by your face that our accents may have you confused," she said. "My father owns Castle Druin. It's not too far north of Perth."

"Yes, I think I may have heard of it," he proffered. "Isn't that by Loch Tummel?"

"Yes, you're close, but it's nearer Kinloch Rannoch," she enthused. "You know it?"

"Not exactly, but I know roughly where it is," he said. "Camped up there several times as a lad. Is that the baronial pile near-hidden by dense woodland?"

"Yes," she confirmed.

"On the South side of the Loch, isn't it?"

"Yes, very nice indeed," Gio enthused, "and with great views of Schiehallion!"

"It would have, right enough. Beautiful spot." Lamont nodded toward him. "Now that takes me back a few years."

Noticing their drained coffee cups, Elspeth asked, "Would you two like another drink?"

Amelia looked at her partner who nodded approval.

"Yeah, sounds great," the lithe, tanned figure confirmed, although his tone was not enthusiastic.

The two couples chatted comfortably for over an hour about France, Scotland and life in general. It turned out that Amelia's parents also owned a large maison père nearby. The MacCaig family had apparently owned the property for many years. To Lamont, their local home sounded very like a small Chateau – however they chose to label it. Extensive managed gardens and two hundred hectares of vineyards don't come with a mere 'house', at least not in southern France.

Amelia went on to explain that a local vintner managed the estate for the family. Harvested each autumn, their Cabernet Franc and Sauvignon grapes were blended with those of other local vineyards. These then went toward producing a locally well-known, though not expensive, wine label. This modest income, she said, helped with the running costs of the house and gardens. She avoided elaborating more about her family, preferring to deflect the conversation toward questions about

Elspeth's medical work.

From his viewpoint Lamont felt relief at not discussing his work, alluding only once to his career being in the public services. In his experience the words 'police' and 'detective' didn't always harmonise well in a social setting. He had also managed to avoid, in Elspeth's words, 'playing detective' by not asking 'interesting' questions. Her definition of his interrogative conversation style had often led to arguments. What he'd overheard by the canal intrigued him, but intrigue in this setting could offer little more than marital grief. They had found some peace and he wanted to keep it that way.

Besides, his wife, as he watched her chat freely, seemed happy and contented. This gave him great pleasure, for he was never a good conversationalist. Occasionally she would look at him and smile warmly and that was all he needed.

The couples said their farewells, but there were no promises to meet up again, or the usual exchange of phone numbers and email addresses. These were holiday social norms Lamont was happy not to pursue. As the evening wore on he had become convinced the Italian had indeed recognised him, but he guessed the young man preferred not to get into explanations about the argument and wouldn't blame him for that.

As the conversation evolved one thing had become clear; Gio Genovese had a controlling influence in the relationship. During the free flowing dialogue, he observed that Amelia rarely had the opportunity to expand on any topic without being interrupted. The Italian also had the habit of rephrasing her words. Despite the man's chauvinistic attitude, Lamont couldn't help liking them both.

When they finally arrived back at the gîte, Elspeth asked why he'd railed after being introduced to the young couple. Watching as the dark-haired Scot rubbed his chin before responding, she knew only half the truth would come out, but knowing the man well, preferred to let matters be and enjoy the time they had left on holiday.

They were free from the pressures of work, but not the painful truth she'd kept to herself these past few weeks. Their life together would soon need to face dramatic changes. Tomorrow's lunchtime flight would whisk them back to that reality. Later, as she lay awake listening to his shallow breathing, that mattered little. Neither did his personality change following the accident. They had once again found each other spiritually as soul mates and for now, she wanted little else.

Chapter 6

Moon leant over, pressed the speaker button and growled into the phone: "Call Tortolano in here, will you please?"

Jean McVeigh looked at the well-presented young officer. Sitting rigidly on the chair by the window, she looked no more than a teenager despite the age given on her C.V. Often working more as PA than secretary, she had glanced through the job application before handing it to her boss. The woman looked as impressive as her words had portrayed. Offering a sympathetic smile to the newcomer, she nodded toward the door.

"I think Deputy Chief Constable Moon wants you in there now," she said, with a soft highland lilt. Smiling as the girl rose to her feet, she whispered conspiratorially: "And don't let him intimidate you!"

Felisa Tortolano returned a weak smile, caught the door handle firmly, and then paused to take a deep breath before stepping into another world of policing.

Moon finished scanning the file as she entered. Looking at her, he carefully put his reading glasses back into the case clipped to the top pocket of the grey Oxford shirt.

Sliding the personnel file back into the desk drawer

and locking it, he gestured enthusiastically and said: "Come away in; sit down, sit down..."

Pointing toward the deep leather easy chair on the other side of the desk, a smile formed on his lips.

"You've now finished the Investigative Course at Tulliallan, Detective Tortolano," he offered. "Well done."

The slim youngster nodded. "Thank you, sir."

Although unaware of it, Tortolano was being shown more enthusiasm than was usually afforded to visitors. Now settled well beneath his eye level on a seat much too uncomfortable for informal discussions, she shifted her weight. Noticing her discomfort, surprisingly for him, Moon felt a moment of regret at using the 'Dalrymple' seat and felt his cheeks flush a little.

"And with flying colours too, apparently," he added after a moment. "One of the finest students they've had."

His pan-Scotland role meant the police college fell under his jurisdiction. Although that establishment rarely brought him pleasure – outside of the annual awards ceremony – the opportunity to find a partner for Lamont had been his most fruitful venture into its esteemed halls to date. Going to the Chief Constables, cap in hand for a recommendation, would almost certainly have resulted in the team being shackled with an officer unlikely to meet their needs. After all, which Chief would give away one of their prime personnel resources?

No, young Tortolano was the best he could have hoped for. Not that he thought her a compromise.

Her intelligence and academic commitment were beyond question. It was only a question of her experience and quality of personality where questions could be raised.

"Thank you again, sir. I always try my best."

Her response to praise – a wide-eyed look of anticipation – once again left Moon suppressing a smile. Without realising, he rested his elbows on the desk and sat there, chin on knuckles, transfixed.

"I saw in your file that you've stated a desire to work for the Scottish Crime Intelligence branch eventually."

"Yes, sir," she said, throwing a broad, even-toothed smile. "Eventually."

"Good, good…" Pausing for a moment, he sat up straight and worked to regain an air of formality. "This opportunity could help that ambition, I'm sure."

"I believe," she offered succinctly, "that pulling together the intelligence behind casework from a national perspective can offer Regional teams a far higher success rate, especially if those teams are to be amalgamated as proposed."

The young woman had high cheekbones, large green eyes and pale olive skin. As he looked at the silky sheen of her short black hair, Moon realised she bore a strong resemblance to a girl he had once adored from afar during his youth. Now understanding his attraction, he focussed fully on the matter in hand.

"I take it Tulliallan told you that I need someone a

bit special to work with our team?"

He raised the bushy eyebrows in anticipation of a positive response.

Unmoved and nodding carefully, Felisa Tortolano suddenly felt wary of the 'someone special' label.

Noting her reaction, he continued trying to describe the role on offer.

"The idea in principle, is that you'll be part of a team of two officers," he said carefully, eyes narrowing slightly. "Once settled in, you'll be expected to help investigate outstanding, mainly current, cases from across Scotland. This is where I think the role can benefit your National Intelligence ambitions. We need someone to help coordinate information. It comes through here by the cabinet load!"

"The role sounds very interesting, sir," she said. Then, eyes flashing, asked: "Would I be working in the field with Detective Lamont?"

Felisa, or 'Lucky' as her family and friends knew her, had heard rumours of the one-time Detective Inspector during her brief time in college, but only through the canteen gossip grapevine. After being told by the college Superintendent of the possible job offer, she'd put out a few feelers with tutors. Most of them, she'd quickly learned, were responsive to flashing eyes and warm smiles. Luckily, they were unaware of her impending meeting today.

The college 'Super' had been told by Moon not to broadcast the offer of a role to the young graduate. From his perspective, he didn't want the story of an expanding team spreading in these times of operational frugality. More importantly, he didn't want anyone trying to block an additional team member's appointment due to cost, or the imminent reorganisation.

One or two lecturers had talked openly with Tortolano about Lamont and a shooting incident several years ago. Seemingly, this had nearly killed the detective. In the eyes of some, it left him unfit for work. Apparently, only his friendship with Moon had secured a role, albeit one that some in the Force felt should not exist. A job working for the SPSA, it was rumoured, had been offered instead of the usual ill health retirement.

Stories of him being a dedicated, hard-working officer were many, but she'd picked up other snippets. Some, implying he was a cold fish and lacked emotion, others that he was very difficult to get along with even before the shooting. She heard other stories too, but many of them were a little more fanciful, describing a 'dapper detective' who always wore expensive clothes.

Most of the more professional views, she reflected, were of a difficult, often inspired, favourite of the seemingly unimpeachable Deputy Chief Constable Moon – the man now weighing her up from the other side of a wooden monolith. Putting little faith in any of the comments, Tortolano always formed her own opinions. Still, she thought it might be useful to check out the information picked up over at the college.

"Detective Tortolano…" the man's strong voice began.

The young officer sensed he was looking at her steadily, watching for a reaction.

"Yes, most of the time you'll be with Detective Lamont. Certainly, when it comes to assisting in case work, that's how it will be, though any free time you have…" The gruff character slapped a palm firmly on the desktop for emphasis. "…will be answerable to me and as I've said, pooling information."

Leaving things quite so loose and ill-defined, she thought, would be unusual for the police service. As far as she knew, every penny spent on manpower was counted diligently, while human resource specialists tied up job descriptions, ensuring they could meet the most stringent legal examination. Keeping role descriptions rigid within the police workforce helped prevent possible disciplinary breaches, but Tortolano needed to find out the root of the impending role's apparent accountability dichotomy. After all, the job could lead her into a career cul-de-sac from which there would be no way out.

"Can I ask," she enquired, expression a little puzzled, "how much free time will there be?"

"Not very much at all, I'm pleased to say," he chirped, his tone softening. "We're still working on a job description. Needs a bit of polish, shall we say."

'So, that was the intrigue in a nutshell,' she thought. *'They hadn't sorted the job description, simply because they hadn't yet agreed the best way for the new role to be delivered!'*

A small wave of disappointment flitted through her. Part of her mischievous inner-self had hoped for a hidden agenda to exploit. But no, it was merely two men who couldn't organise themselves sufficiently well to sort out a junior assistant's workload. She thought it best to confirm the point though.

"And Detective Lamont's role reports only to you, sir?"

"Yes, only me."

He sat up a little as he spoke and, from watching the man's reaction, Tortolano guessed he'd spotted the direction she was heading.

"Crieff Lamont," he began, and then stopped, almost as though deciding how freely he dared speak. "Let me correct myself, *Detective* Lamont is one of the best men in the force." Looking at her sternly, he added: "You'll learn from him and develop the role in collaboration with him…" Pausing for a moment, he scratched his chin thoughtfully. "And no, as I think you've probably guessed, we haven't talked enough about how your role should work. In fact, we haven't talked about you at all – yet."

Felisa Tortolano couldn't hide an expression of surprise.

"He's been asking for support for quite a while," he added. "And you're it."

"I see…"

The DCC glanced over at the wall clock.

"Aye, but worry not lass," he said quietly, almost reverentially, and leant toward her. "If I know the man, he'll soon have you dancing jig-time. You'll quickly find your feet just from being around someone with his experience – he'll make sure of that." Flicking an index finger toward her, he said: "Then we'll draw up some proper lines to keep the Personnel people happy, eh?"

This change of tone and style gave her only a brief

insight into the complex character that was DCC Moon. She had been offered a little cameo: enough to tease, she thought, and perhaps teach her never to try guessing exactly where he was coming from. Relaxing a little in response to the change of direction, she recognised it for what it was: his acceptance of the need for a new, untried role, working in support another detective.

"Has Detective Lamont said that he needed another Detective Constable in the team, sir?" she probed, but with an easier, more comfortable tone.

"No," he said, checking himself. "By the way, is it all right if I call you by your first name? Only it's a small team you're joining and we like to keep it informal – unless there are others within earshot, of course."

"Everyone calls me Lucky."

The young detective watched for a moment as Moon seemed to puzzle through the implications of having a team member with the name 'Lucky'.

"Hmm," he grunted.

"It's what my name means in Italian," she explained quickly. Yet she knew from his expression that the senior officer was thinking: 'Italian', 'Lucky', 'Mafia' and gangster movies.

"Clearing his throat, he said: "The name could cause some problems…"

"Yes, many people have said that," she agreed. "But my family manufacture ice cream in Ayrshire – have done for eighty years. And we don't market the stuff through Fedora wearing, dark-suited, sedan drivers in the dead of night."

Moon raised his eyebrows and almost managed a smile.

She explained further: "We're northern Italian, from near the French border."

He still looked a little puzzled, she thought, so she added for effect: "The Mafioso families have mostly kept themselves to the centre and south of the country, near their Sicilian roots."

Looking her over again, he appeared to relax, shaking his head and grinning broadly. Pondering on the role for a moment as he studied the plucky young detective, Moon found himself wondering what on earth had he let himself in for.

"I suppose you've got a point," he said finally, but somewhat reluctantly. "But remember, team Christian names are only for informal situations."

"Couldn't agree more, sir"

"I take it you accept the offer then?"

"Yes, sir," she confirmed and smiled broadly.

Beaming at her, he said: "Wait a minute and we'll get a cuppa in here, no?"

Tortolano smiled and nodded.

Stretching across the desk, he pressed the phone intercom.

"*Yes, sir?*"

"Jean, can we have a pot of tea in here, please?"

"*Two cups?*"

"Yes, two cups, Jean."

In the outer office Jean McVeigh smiled to herself, comfortable in the knowledge that she'd guessed correctly. Things would indeed be a little more interesting around the office from now on.

Moon scratched his chin again as he thought how to phrase what to say next.

"I perhaps need to explain things very clearly before tea arrives. Lamont wants an assistant, but he's never asked for a fellow detective. He likes working on his own. It'll be your job to broaden his horizons."

Swallowing hard, she knew her assumption had, in part, been correct: she'd not be joining the investigative team at Lamont's request.

"Yes, of course sir," she confirmed. "I think I understand."

"You'd better," he said, raising his eyebrows. "Can I share this with you in confidence?"

Tortolano nodded warily.

"Our colleague may not think he needs the support of another detective; at least not just at this moment," he explained, getting up from the chair to congratulate her. "But things are about to change as Scotland's forces merge. Your role will be to help him prepare the way for a positive contribution from the team in the country's future policing strategy. Welcome aboard."

"I'm honoured to have the opportunity, sir," she said, as he reached out his hand. "And a little anxious about the responsibility."

Appreciating the scale of the challenge, she accepted his congratulations, but her uncertainty hadn't gone unnoticed. Like the newly appointed detective, the old man too wondered if this choice really was a wise one.

Chapter 7

Clouds scudded high over the tall castle ramparts as Stirling awoke to a cool, blustery autumn morning. Dominating the Forth valley, the ancient fortress was spiritual home to the Argyll and Sutherland Highlanders. Acting as a defensive bastion, due to the rocky crag's strategic position it had stood, in one form or another, for nearly a thousand years. The statue of Robert the Bruce looks out from the esplanade toward the memorial tower, erected to commemorate Sir William Wallace, another Scots hero, in the 1860s.

Although he was neither hero nor legend, Monday, as usual, meant Lamont had been working since before seven. The detective always started early on Mondays. He preferred it that way; particularly on the rare occasions he hadn't been out covering a case over the weekend.

It meant being able to prepare personal strategies; his way of dealing efficiently with anything he'd mulled over during the weekend. And that same compulsive thought process overtook relaxation every weekend. Never looking at himself as being off-duty gave Lamont some raison d'être. It helped keep one step ahead of Moon, as it had with all his previous bosses. However, barely had he read through the lengthy collection of emails, than Jean's number came up on the desk phone.

Without bothering to answer the call, he closed the laptop, got up and stretched lazily. Strangely, he felt relaxed after the holiday and smiled to himself. Walking along the corridor toward the neighbouring office, he shook his head and wondered what had brought the old man's efficient PA in to work quite so early.

"Hi lady!"

"Good morning," she chirped, and put the receiver back in its cradle. "Had a good holiday?"

"It was relaxing, warm, French…"

"Jean!" Moon's voice boomed through the open door of his office. "Is that Lamont?"

"Old man sounds frazzled," he muttered.

Shrugging expansively, she went back to her computer screen.

The detective poked his head round the office door.

"Come in," the old man said, brusquely. "Sit yourself down."

Sinking into the chair, he asked, "All's well, sir?"

"If all was well, as you so casually put it, I wouldn't be here at this bloody hour, would I?" Continuing frostily, he spat: "Where the hell in France were you on Friday? I tried several times to get hold of you!"

"Sorry," he offered apologetically. "Let the phone battery die toward the end of the week. Didn't think you'd need me urgently."

Poking an index finger on the desk as though to reinforce the seriousness of matters, he spluttered: "Well, I damned well did!"

Knowing this usually meant the old man was too angry, frustrated – or both – to be reasoned with, he said nothing.

"Two things," Moon went on, testily. "First, I've got you the assistance you been asking for; and second, while you were off sunning yourself last week, somebody left a bullet-holed VIP drifting on Loch Rannoch."

The detective raised his eyebrows, but said nothing.

Clearing his throat indignantly while repeatedly prodding at the desk, the DCC went on: "I could have explained both if you'd not let the phone die – as you so succinctly put it!"

"Sorry," said Lamont, apologising again. "You know that's not my style. It was just…"

"Too much of your style, man, means too little substance – and never mind the 'just'," the old man said, though more softly.

A quieter tone, the detective knew, meant either the old man had been placated a little by the repeated apologies, or had run out of steam.

"Couldn't have got back any earlier with the flight schedules as they were," Lamont explained, "even if you had been able to contact me."

"It's about briefing and information sharing," he responded brusquely. "Keeping ahead of the game, as you would put it. You should have been on your way to Loch Rannoch by now."

The apology, Lamont knew, was normally unnecessary. The mere fact he was now available would usually be sufficient to pacify the old man's mood: but not today

Shuffling his weight uncomfortably, Moon added: "Lad, we get paid to be on-call, never off-line, and bloody well available for every situation. It's what keeps us at the locus of things in this mixed-up, tribal country of yours."

Pausing for a moment, he shook his head and let a weak smile form.

"Don't let me down again, eh?"

It almost sounded as though he was pleading. Lamont felt a fleeting moment of guilt.

"No, sir, I won't," he replied awkwardly.

The detective was now suffering twinges of remorse. Whatever the case up in Loch Rannoch involved, it sounded serious. Yes, the mobile had inadvertently died, but that was a good thing, for he'd needed to be with Elspeth. They had finally found some peace together, perhaps for the first time since the shooting.

"What's the situation then?"

"It's a long story, predictably enough," said Moon, picking the thin folder from its pride of place on the top of the pile. He was about to hand the file over the desk then stopped. The detective noted a weary shake of his boss's head.

"Right bloody mess, if you ask me. It's all there on paper, but in summary: a body has been found, belongs to the son of a local aristocrat who's 'connected' – both politically and socially. He's *Lord of the Manor* up there. To confuse matters, Perth have messed up their manpower allocation leaving an unwelcomed Mancunian..."

Already confused, the detective thought of raising his hand to interrupt the old man's flow, but recognised that he needed to get this off his chest. Instead, after discreetly shuffling a mint sweet from his trouser pocket into his mouth, he settled down to listen.

"Yes, a 'Mancunian'," Moon repeated, noticing his subordinate's puzzlement. "In this one's case – unloved, unwanted and unsupported – to lead the investigation!"

"Why is he here then? Assuming it's a 'he', that is..."

"It's a 'he' alright, but one that should've been suspended in Manchester for racism allegations!" Moon growled: "But, due to those blessed race related riots, they're desperately trying to keep matters like this one buried. So he's up here out of the way – supposedly – at least until the heat dies down. That's metaphorically speaking of course, considering the rioters tried to torch half of the infernal city!"

"Yes, grim business indeed."

"Needless to say, Tayside's Chief Constable rang me on Friday morning. He's now asking for support as he tries to dig himself out of a hole as deep as Loch Rannoch itself."

"Isn't that unusual now?"

His tone had held a hint of irony that didn't fail to

register.

"He's a cheeky beggar, if you ask me, for I was told a few years ago that he never wanted our roles established! When the Chief Constable's group originally discussed the formation of this team, his voice was one of three who apparently rejected the proposal out of hand. He cited cost as his primary objection. Then, possible interference with already fine liaison relationships…" Snorting critically, he continued, "…which supposedly exist between neighbouring Chief Constables. He suggested that there was already enough sharing of resources between the eight Forces. Said any unplanned manpower difficulties were already covered. And he then had the temerity to suggest that I should be ruminating in a field of long, green vegetation anyway!"

"Who put the original proposal on the table?" Curious, the detective asked: "Someone from the Edinburgh politico's?"

"Yes, the Scottish Office," Moon replied carefully, without revealing a name.

The old man began trying to poke his index finger through the wooden desktop again, but the detective knew that D.C.C. Moon himself was the most likely originator of the idea. He was certainly the main driving force behind the team's eventual formation.

"The sooner the Scottish Office has the bloody service across Scotland amalgamated," Moon growled, "the better for us all!"

Studying him, Lamont thought it better to try bringing the conversation back on track.

"Where are things up to with this Loch Rannoch

case then?"

"Not very far really," he shrugged, the tone moderating a little. "It's all in there, including a briefing note about the current investigating officer – so that you know what you're dealing with. His name's O'Leary." Handing the file over, he added, "Shred my handwritten notes when you've finished. Don't want the words dug up at a later date, do we?"

Taking a quick glance through the file, he asked: "What's the form on the MacCaig family then?"

"Their wealth came through jute, jam and jumpers…"

"Not journalism?" he enquired. Reflecting on the commonly held belief that Dundee's wealth had arisen from three core products, including newspapers, he wondered why they hadn't broached the written word. "So their money came from 'Oor Woollie', if you prefer, not 'Oor Wullie'."

The older man threw him a puzzled look.

"Jumpers and not journalism," he explained. "Woollies, not Wullie…"

"Oh, I see," said Moon, none the wiser.

Given the old man hadn't been born and raised in Scotland, he thought, perhaps the line about the cartoon character had been wasted.

The DCC went on: "Imported jute, which they turned into carpet; fruit grown on their land in the Carse of Gowrie, which they turned into jam in their own factory; and sheep's wool from several farms they owned and rented out. They turned that into winter warmth for the wealthy. Journalism's not their thing, though they've been prominent on the Dundee wealth scene since the invention of the printed word, apparently."

Lamont was unimpressed by the family's acumen. Monetary prowess had been valuable in securing employment, he knew, but very few of the movers and shakers were caring, or philanthropic like Muir, or Carnegie. The masses in servitude doffed their caps; or else, in many cases, starved.

"There were bigger players in each of their areas of business – like Mackellar with the jam," the old man explained. "But it seems none of the others had such diversity and vision. MacCaig's great grandfather wisely refused to put all his eggs in one basket. Clever thinking and ahead of his time."

"And what about the current Lord MacCaig, then?"

"He's from the same mould. His father sold up the jam and carpets businesses, though they still keep the farms and associated land."

"So where's the rest of the wealth coming from?" he asked, knowing the old man's contacts would have briefed him thoroughly.

It transpired that MacCaig had influence in Edinburgh and London, and seemingly strong relationships within the national press hierarchy. Noting that point, as Moon elaborated, he recognised that this would not be a man to upset during the investigation.

"So it's a pretty mixed portfolio, but very profitable," Moon explained. "The family have never stood still – in a money sense at least."

"Wise lot, then?"

"Aye, they are," he agreed. "No chinks in the armour, if that's what you're looking for. They're now into financial investments, property management in the South East of England, sporting rights around Castle Druin and a wide variety of overseas opportunities including charity work."

"I take it the latter's this Aid All Africa thing he's occasionally in the media for?"

"Ah, you've heard of it," Moon said, and nodded. "As far as is known, it's purely a charity."

"Giving something back type, then?"

"Apparently," he said carefully. "Philanthropic, or so it seems."

"You're not convinced?"

"With the very wealthy types, I never believe what I can't see," said Moon, finally. "Money corrupts."

He took a deep breath and watched as his detective flicked through the open folder, scanning the papers for anything that caught his eye.

"Look, finish running through it, tell me what you think and we'll agree a way forward."

"Ye've a point about money and corruption, right enough," said the detective absently, for he was already studiously reading one of the papers on his lap.

Eyebrows raised, index digit running the lines, Lamont scanned the murder file first. Preliminary investigations had been carried out, although it was too vast an area to put search teams on the ground and get a result at this time. Two local poachers, apparently the only ones known to the police, were in Perth gaol already. This effectively closed the local line of enquiry into known offenders, although Lamont knew that wildlife hunters were now a highly mobile lot. He had heard of them travelling from all over the country and, considering the monetary gains to be made as the price of venison soared, he thought that was hardly surprising.

While reading, he remembered the first little matter his boss had mentioned.

"Oh, I nearly forgot," he said, looking up, "you said something about assistance?"

"Aye," the old man replied brightly, putting down his pen and removing the gold-rimmed glasses. "Along the corridor in room seven. Come with me. We've a new detective for the team."

Lamont cringed momentarily, for the assistance he sought had never been that of another investigative officer. In his own opinion, he only needed a researcher and compiler to free his time for casework.

Getting up from the desk, ire long forgotten, the old man collected his jacket from the polished steel coat stand and bustled out of the office apace, the detective following along at his tail.

As they left, he waved toward his PA.

"Room seven, back in a minute, Jean," he said. "Man the phones, eh?"

Lamont shrugged and pulled a face, but the stalwart assistant never lifted her eyes from the screen. Jean shook her head and continued typing.

Room seven looked like every other office in

Stirling's sprawling, Randolphfield Police Headquarters. Built in the mid-seventies on what was rumoured to have been one of the key sites in the Battle of Bannockburn, archaeologists were now excavating the grounds in a search for evidence of the famous conflict. The detective had passed the dig site the University team were working on as he arrived for work.

Cream painted walls, long overdue a new coat of emulsion, lined the twelve by twelve foot box. A large, rectangular window, typical of seventies-styled office structures, offered some relief from the room's austerity. It was a bright morning and the desk was protected from the glaring sun by pale grey, vertical blinds. Around it sat four chairs, one of which contained the beautiful, olive-skinned figure of Felisa Tortolano.

Surprise filled the detective's face as Moon led him through the door.

"This is Detective Constable Tortolano," the DCC announced cheerfully. "Felisa, or 'Lucky', if you prefer…"

Quickly recovering, the detective put out a hand as the attractive young officer rose from her seat.

"Good to have you aboard," he said, almost hesitantly.

"I really hope so," she replied, and in a questioning tone added: "Much to learn, much to prove?"

He smiled broadly. The youngster knew her place. Lamont wondered if perhaps he would also have to re-evaluate his own role in the grand scheme of things.

Like her new partner, she was trying to gain a degree of understanding from his initial reactions. She had gauged, correctly, that he would be taken aback. Certainly, returning to his office and finding an inexperienced newcomer now working alongside him must be an unwelcome shock. However, she knew that, had their roles been reversed, her feelings would have been no different.

"Sit down, sit down man, you're making the place look untidy," Moon said, and waved. "And you too lass."

"Well, here we are," he breezed. "A tidy little team indeed. No time for introductions now though. I think you two had better start getting to know one another on the A9, as you head north for Loch Rannoch."

"Sir?" she enquired anxiously. "Me too?"

Rarely having ventured out in the field as a uniformed constable, to suddenly be thrust into an enquiry as a detective had thrown her. The role was always going to be a challenge, but now Tortolano's diaphragm tensed and her pulse quickened. In that very instant, the officer knew this was why she had joined the team.

"Aye, lass," he confirmed crisply, throwing her a questioning look. "Can you think of a reason why not?"

"Good thinking," Lamont responded, studying his new assistant. "In for a penny, in for a pound, eh?"

"I'm up for it," she said. Despite her voice reflecting excitement, at that moment the verbal enthusiasm portrayed a level of confidence the young officer didn't necessarily feel.

"I'll get up to speed with this file first," said Lamont, holding it up.

'Make it quick then," the old man agreed reluctantly, as he shuffled backward toward the door. "And remember: shred my personal notes before you set off."

Chapter 8

It was cloudy and cool for the time of year, but the odd shaft of sunlight flared over the city's castle ramparts from the southeast. Heading north toward Perth, the powerful Audi accelerated off the slip road into heavy motorway traffic. Nudging the turn indicator back to neutral, Lamont checked the wing mirror again and sighed.

"Not much of an introduction, eh?"

"No," she responded. "No time for the pleasantries really, I suppose."

Sensing her anxieties, Lamont waited a moment for the young detective to comment further, but she seemed to prefer watching the landscape through the passenger-side window.

"Did DCC Moon's notes bring any clarity to what you're being asked to investigate on Loch Rannoch, sir?"

"First," he began. "My name's Lamont." He glanced over and smiled. "I'm only *sir* if I happen to get promoted before you, and that's unlikely given my track record *or* my wishes."

"Sorry," she said, almost petulantly. "No offence meant."

The haughty tone caught him by surprise.

"My Christian name is Crieff," he said, "as in the town where my old man and my mother...well..."

"Interesting family history about the pre-Beckham trend setters, but it doesn't give me a clearer picture on DCC Moon's personal view of events Loch Rannoch."

Thinking he may have been a little too blunt, even if she did need to back off, he softened his tone a little.

"Besides some confidential information on the man we're going to meet," he explained, "there wasn't too much to go on."

"And?"

She was still looking toward him for an answer as he tried to compose his thoughts. It seemed the newcomer knew what she wanted, he thought, and intended to get it.

"Three bullet wounds on a body found floating on Loch Rannoch in a rowing boat. Tourist out fishing discovered it, early hours of last Thursday morning. Seemingly belongs to one Jock MacCaig; Lord MacCaig's adopted son by his first marriage. MacCaig owns much of the land around Loch Rannoch. He's a well-known figure in political and social circles – both locally and nationally. Big player..."

"Yes, I heard of him when I was at University. Set up 'Aid All Africa' and runs it with the help of his wife?"

"Yes," he confirmed, slowing a little as he waited for an opportunity to overtake. "Our involvement in the case probably has more to do with his charitable connections with Africa – and the business interests they bring to Scotland from developing countries – than anything else."

"Why's that?"

"Racism," he said bluntly.

"What's that got to do with anything?" she questioned. "I don't understand?"

"If I share this with you, I don't want it repeating, OK?"

"Whatever you say."

Catching the offhand tone in her response, the detective realised he'd been careless with his words.

"That wasn't meant as an insult," he offered, "more that it's all speculation and smears at the moment, pending an enquiry."

"What is?"

"The detective we're meeting this morning is being investigated for allegations of racism. There's concern that his apparent partisanship might influence the handling of a sensitive situation. Obviously, the concerns are built around the MacCaig family's African relationships and business interests i.e. 'Aid All Africa'."

"And why was he not suspended?"

"He's from Manchester."

"I don't understand," she said. "Why didn't this get explained to me before we left?"

"It's too complicated and sensitive at the

moment," he said carefully. "Besides, we're trying to find out why a rowing boat containing the body of a prominent figure's son was left floating on Loch Rannoch for three days. And catch whoever murdered him, of course. The officer on placement up in Perthshire is not really our concern. All we've got to do is ensure the politics and the investigation move along to a smooth conclusion."

"Too complicated?" She stared at Lamont as they overtook a wagonload of sheep being transported north from Stirling livestock sales. "I was supposed to be joining as part of a team. If it's too complicated, then perhaps thinking again about what I've let myself in for would be a good idea…"

"I didn't mean that," he said. "It's confidential."

"And I'm not trustworthy enough for confidential information?"

"No. Well, actually yes. But it's a matter concerning a colleague…"

"I can see he's a colleague!" she said angrily. "Even if he is from Manchester!"

He could understand now, why some wag at Tulliallan thought it a good idea to get rid of this fiery probationer and land her on Moon's doorstep. Smiling at the irony of it, the detective knew that if she left the team, the failure would fall on his shoulders.

"And you think it's funny or something, do you?" she asked pointedly.

Waiting till the opportunity arose, he slowed and swung the Audi over into a lay-by then stopped the engine.

"Look, detective," he began. "There's one thing you're going to have to learn while you're in the police. Professional life – and all that it contains – is on a need-to-know basis. We could be bloody stooges in some background game of politics involving the MacCaig family for all I know! Our only concern should be that we've a job to do, and do well – whatever the circumstances."

"And I don't need to know what those circumstances are?"

"Detective," he said firmly, "you must understand: you need to know no more than I do. And on many occasions you'll know even less. Comes with the rank; we're equals, but I'm older."

"But Deputy Chief Constable Moon told you what he already knows on a piece of paper which you've presumably shredded, as instructed."

Looking at her for a moment, he offered an apologetic gesture.

"I merely follow instructions and orders."

"Not what I've heard!"

"You're on the right line," he said and pointed out toward the rolling landscape. "But the River Teith, over there is where you'd do better on a 'fishing' expedition!"

"So, I'm not trusted enough to share that information?"

Breathing in deeply, he let out a long hard sigh.

"Listen," he said, using his most disarming voice. "Like me, you're a very small cog in a very big and dangerous wheel. It crushes and spits out those who think they're cute enough to defy it…"

For a second, the detective wondered if someone was playing a prank. Newly returned from holiday, an important investigation to undertake, and now saddled with an emotional newcomer. Worse, she failed to understand the discipline necessary to pursue an investigation, or even her own role.

"I'm sorry. This is your first day and it shouldn't be a baptism of fire…" He thought for a moment then continued, although with a little more empathy: "But you're not learning from other new recruits and tutors now. This world is full of secrets and shit. Someone must've thought you had enough character and bottle to handle it, yet still contribute effectively…"

Letting the words hang, he looked at her for a moment, but she continued to stare straight ahead, frowning.

"Don't prove them wrong!"

"The only person I have to justify anything to is myself," she responded defiantly.

"Perhaps lass," he replied.

"Whatever," she offered. "It doesn't mean I'm not trustworthy!"

After mulling things over, he decided to share what little confidential information there had been in the note. Not good form, he thought, but if he didn't show some trust in her now, he might never be able to.

"Okay," he began. "Moon said the man had been transferred pending an enquiry into alleged racial comments. He'd apparently made them during an investigation following the Manchester riots. A colleague – the type none of us need – overheard him utter an offensive remark toward a black suspect during an arrest. Moon has been told by Edinburgh that there are not to be any racial complications surrounding this investigation. O'Leary, the officer concerned, has to be kept on a leash."

"And what was it he's supposed to have said?"

"Damned if I know!" He was now feeling genuine anger in professional company for the first time in years. "There was nothing else in it!"

Moon had informed him of the Manchester detective's chequered past: previous allegations of sexism and untoward behaviour involving a female senior officer. He'd already decided that piece of information was too sensitive to divulge, even if he did want to build trust.

"Sorry to upset you," she said, "but that's hard to believe.

"Don't you understand," he said. "They are not going to tell Moon *exactly* what he's supposed to have done wrong. That's a matter purely for the Manchester force."

Omitting to tell her that Moon had also mentioned that he was going to find out a little more about O'Leary, he felt, was neither here nor there. What Tortolano did not seem to understand, as far as he could see, was that she was probably the first probationer of her kind to be offered such an exciting role. In the highly defensive and protective Scottish police system, everything seemed to happen by rote and within budget. It was possible that if she didn't succeed in this job, her career aspirations could be very limited.

Moon's note had explained that she'd been judged to be one of the most intelligent and perceptive new plain-clothes recruits in many years. However, Lamont knew that was no guarantee of career progression. And certainly not after joining the SPSA team. He recalled telling the old man any assistance they got would be better from someone unaffected by police politics. They certainly had that now.

Feeling a little crestfallen, Tortolano realised her stubbornness had gone too far, but she firmly believed herself an equal. In her view they had, for no good reason, cut her out of the information chain.

"You've given me the impression," he said, with genuine concern in his voice. "That if I don't meet your every demand we'll be no more of a team than Popeye and Bluto!"

"Who?"

"It's an age thing," he said.

Realising now that accepting her – fiery personality and all – as a partner, would mean more than merely persuading her to behave appropriately, he fired the car's engine. Checking the mirror, Lamont pulled out onto the dual carriageway.

"Now, can we get on?" he asked. Then in a placatory tone while revving the engine hard as he pulled away, tried: "And perhaps even 'get on'?"

"Sorry," she said. "I can't figure out why I've been chosen to join such a high profile team. When told I was the only one invited to meet the DCC it all seemed a bit strange. College tutors think it's possible I'll make Strategic Intelligence Analysis level one day."

"That's a possibility," he agreed.

"I think they just threw me into this job to see how I'd make out," she said with a sigh.

Accelerating past some slower vehicles, Lamont was feeling a degree of concern. Having asked for help, he now found himself managing an emotional, intelligent and highly opinionated young terrier.

"Possible too, knowing that lot..."

"And I do know this role is probationary," she said, surprising him, "but that doesn't mean I see it as an easy opt-out if I don't like it."

There was silence for a few moments as the rolling countryside near Auchterarder sped past.

"I'm not some rosy-spectacled fool." Her green eyes flashed as she studied his face for a reaction. "I know that if I can't make it here, with both you and Moon to help me develop, my career might be jeopardised."

"Oh," he confirmed. "Then you really do know as much as me."

"Yes, and it would be better for us both if, when you tell me your version of the truth, you don't forget the whole truth!"

Feigning a smile, he muttered: "Deal. The whole truth and nothing but."

Chapter 9

The bustling tourist town of Pitlochry lies where Wade's 18th century military road crossed the River Tummel. The old ferry service finally ended in 1913 when a suspension footbridge, which still stands beneath the rainy Perthshire skies today, brought the communities on either bank together.

Bridges were much on Brendan O'Leary's mind as he leant against his car waiting for the Stirling detectives to arrive. The bridge into Castle Druin already had its foundations set. Now, hopefully, his new partners would help him finish the job. That aside, could they build a relationship with an alleged racist? The thought vexed him. O'Leary kicked his heel against the car's tyre. Time would tell.

"That must be O'Leary," Lamont said, pulling up in the car park.

As they got out, he straightened his suit trousers and waistcoat. He had the uncomfortable habit of making people feel they were being weighed up, even before he spoke, and it appeared O'Leary was no exception.

"SPSA," the English detective said easily. "I'm honoured."

Casually stretching out his hand, he replied,

"Good. I'm Lamont – this is Detective Tortolano. 'Lucky' to her friends."

"Detective Brendan O'Leary, demoted," he said. "'Fraid I come with the patch."

"Nice to meet you."

"Lucky, eh?" The seconded detective looked Tortolano over as she rounded the Audi. "In case you've not been briefed guys, I'm an alleged racist from Manchester, temporarily demoted while awaiting professional lynching."

Lamont laughed coldly.

"Sort of concise version of what we've been told..."

Studying his new partners' reactions for a moment, O'Leary said: "My car?"

"Yes, why not?" the Scot agreed. "From what I remember of the road out to Rannoch, it'll be good to get a chance to take in the scenery."

Noticing the man scanning his partner's attractive figure while opening the Mondeo's rear door, Lamont resolved to keep both eyes wide open. Then, for an uncomfortable moment, he found himself wondering at his distaste for what had just transpired.

As the car headed toward Castle Druin, the Stirling detective had read the report prepared for the Superintendent in Perth before they'd left the outskirts of Pitlochry. Brief but concise, it told him a lot about the English detective, as well as the murdered man's relatives. Looking at the names, O'Leary saw he had already interviewed most of them during the preceding Friday. It was now important to confirm the accuracy and integrity of their original statements.

Supported by an outline coroner's report, it confirmed that Jock MacCaig, adopted son of Lord Alexander MacCaig, had been shot through shoulder, chest and head. No bullets had survived as evidence. Early forensic reports confirmed that he had been killed while in the boat. The amount of blood on the man's shirt suggested the shoulder wound could have occurred at an earlier point in time. There was nothing, other than small traces of alcohol, in the man's bloodstream. Some scarring, believed to originate from his childhood, and a fresh wound on his shin, understood to be from the boat rowlock, were the only other physical scars. Forensics confirmed that the deceased suffered the early signs of Type 2 diabetes, although he would most likely have been unaware of the onset at such an early stage in its development.

Speaking over his shoulder, he explained to Tortolano that from the report, the projectiles, having passed through the body, had most likely ended up somewhere in the depths of the loch. Glancing out at the scenery as he spoke, Lamont said he guessed they were unlikely to be recovered. The killer, he told her, probably wouldn't know this, and may have disposed of the gun to prevent a trace being made.

As he read on, O'Leary's report confirmed that the coroner thought it likely Jock MacCaig had been shot from a distance. The coroner had elaborated that he thought the chest shot had probably been for 'sighting' purposes and the head wound delivered in case the target survived the first bullet. It was, in his opinion, highly likely to have been a premeditated killing, going on to say that the perpetrator seemed to have considerable skill with a rifle.

Forensic examination of the boat had revealed little. It confirmed that, despite being distorted by their time in the rain, blood spatter patterns suggested the man had been shot from the front, and most likely from the shore.

The detective guessed it would have been nearly impossible to fire such accurate shots from a small vessel bobbing along on the Loch; not from any sort of range at least. Lamont therefore assumed MacCaig had probably been killed while trying to put distance between himself and shoreline. It seemed very likely that the man was either fleeing a pursuer, or had been assassinated by someone who knew exactly where he would be, and at what hour of the day he would be there. It seemed highly probable the killer was local, or locally informed, and may even have family connections. From the lack of equipment, it was obvious that MacCaig hadn't gone out planning to hunt or fish. From the position of the body it seemed there hadn't been time to defend himself either; but who was he fleeing from; where was he fleeing to, and why?

O'Leary's report mentioned that Jock MacCaig had been the progeny of a previous relationship. When Lord MacCaig had been asked for clarity it transpired that Jock had been adopted, which Lamont already knew from Moon's briefing. His mother had been Lord MacCaig's first wife, Catherine. She had died from liver cancer in the mid-eighties. O'Leary confirmed he had checked this out with the local records office.

Lord MacCaig's second wife, Angela, from whom he was now divorced, had borne two children. Ewan, twenty-six, was the elder and had left Castle Druin a few years earlier. He had become disenfranchised after his father introduced Helen, now his third wife, to the family home. The remaining sibling, Amelia, was twenty-three. A graduate in political science at Cambridge, she was involved in the family's charity work.

Driving with confidence, although too quickly for his passengers' liking, their host negotiated a small, narrow bridge over the River Tummel. Lamont, who had been taking in the scenery from the passenger seat, began to feel queasy, but said nothing. His thoughts were on why Lord MacCaig's daughter had concealed her emotions when they met in France. After all, from the timing of events it appeared she had already been aware of her stepbrother's murder.

Deciding not to discuss having met her with the other detectives, he would instead wait to see how they judged the family as a whole. Revealing his two chance encounters with the young couple in France might influence their thinking. He would prefer that didn't happen just yet.

His musings were interrupted abruptly as O'Leary, swerving to avoid an oncoming delivery truck on the narrow road, ran the car's offside front wheel along the pot-holed, stony verge.

"That was clever," he said calmly, although there was a sharp intake of breath from the rear seat. "Do you really need to rally this thing?"

"Sorry," said O'Leary without meaning it.

Not remembering the road as being quite so narrow and twisting, Lamont's knuckles paled and his left hand now rested near the door handle. Although O'Leary had taken the hint and slowed a little, in the Scotsman's view he was still pushing the car's capabilities, and his own, too hard.

They had covered nearly twenty-five miles when Castle Druin, on the southern side of the river, appeared fleetingly through the trees. Occupying a prominent position nearly a mile east of Loch Rannoch, it overlooked the picturesque, heavily forested glen. Taking in the geography of the area again, he was drawn to reflect on O'Leary's report. After the shooting the boat had presumably drifted, for it had been found nearly two and a half miles from its berth at the family's private jetty. As they turned off the main road through the large, wrought iron gates to the estate, he resolved to visit the jetty today.

Lamont took in the impressive setting as the castle swung into view. Forty-foot high walls, dressed with crenulations and arrow slits, gave the imposing granite structure character. Even more imposing were the two defence towers fronting the façade. Yet as they drove up the hill, the castle didn't appear to be a particularly large building.

"Clever architect," said O'Leary, referring to the illusion of scale. "And worth a few bob, right enough."

Over his shoulder, Tortolano was taking a good look over the building and its well-manicured surroundings.

"Yes," she agreed. "Wouldn't mind the building's annual maintenance budget as a salary."

As they turned into the parking area, a large, branded delivery van appeared from the rear of the grand house and made its way down the picturesque driveway toward the road.

"Take much in the way of supplies to keep this place running?" queried Lamont.

"Wouldn't have thought so," O'Leary guessed. "Not that many living here."

"What about staff then?"

"Very few, surprisingly."

"Why surprisingly?"

"Just am. It's big enough and runs regular functions."

"Got all the names of the residents and staff?"

"List's an appendix to that report," he replied. "Left it in the office."

"Helpful," said the Scot.

Tortolano interrupted the awkward moment.

"It's beautiful," she said quickly. "How old is it?"

"It was put up in the mid to late eighteen hundreds, girl," O'Leary said, guiding the Ford into one of the spaces marked 'Guest'. "Seems a castle in one form or another has stood here for nearly eight hundred years. This one was built for the visits to Scotland of Albert, Queen Victoria's hubby. Put up by Lord Alexander MacCaig's ancestor. Apparently he was a friend of the sovereign."

Switching off the engine, he looked over his shoulder.

"Seems it did them no good, for when Albert died in 1861, Victoria went into mourning. After that, she chose to ignore MacCaig's pleas for her to visit." He added, with an element of pleasure in his voice: "Old Queenie must've sniffed out they were a bad lot, even then."

"What's it like inside?"

"You'll see."

Having listened carefully, Lamont was about to offer a rebuke for pre-judging the MacCaig family – as well as calling Tortolano 'girl', but thought the better of it. Getting out, he followed the pair into the tall, ornate portico protecting a pair of wide oak doors.

One of them swung open as they arrived under shelter.

"Detective O'Leary," said Lord MacCaig, offering his hand. "Pleasure to see you again."

"Now not many say that..."

"At least not to your face, for certain," MacCaig said easily, smiling.

'No," O'Leary agreed. "Not to my face."

Sturdily built, though not very tall, MacCaig appeared both strong and fit, but Lamont could see the weariness in his eyes. The man looked as though he hadn't slept well for a few days.

"I see you've brought company," he said, reaching out a welcoming hand. "Reinforcements?"

Taking the outstretched hand, Lamont introduced himself and Tortolano as SPSA staff, assigned to assist the Tayside force at the Chief Constable's request.

"We're the cavalry, Lord MacCaig," he offered, taking in the elegant scene.

As the group wandered into a grand, galleried hall, MacCaig knew from the Stirling detective's tone that the reference to cavalry was not misplaced.

"So you're a detective too, Mr Lamont."

The man may be in his early sixties, he thought, but the sharply chiselled features and pepper-grey hair belied his age.

"Yes," he confirmed, without expanding any further on his role.

Looking around the beautifully dressed space in which they stood, he turned back to MacCaig.

"We're really sorry about your loss, sir," he began. "We know our being here is intrusive, especially at such a difficult moment for both you and your family."

"I fully understand detective, and your condolences are welcomed, thank you."

As he admired one of the well-polished suits of armour that stood on either side of the wide, central staircase, Lamont said: "And if there's any support you or your family need, don't hesitate to ask, Lord MacCaig. We're not here to add to your grief and dismay, but to allay it – if we can."

"Thank you," he said, watching as the detective looked around the paintings. "Very kind of you."

The galleries above were hung with a variety of landscapes and portraits, some, he presumed, of MacCaig's ancestors. It appeared to the Scots detective as though a great deal of renovation work had recently been completed. From the outside, he'd noticed the external stonework had been re-jointed and any damaged pieces replaced. It was the same here. There was an air of freshness one might not readily associate with an ageing structure. Both the walls and ornate plasterwork looked crisp, fresh and clean. A thick, grey-green woollen carpet dressed the broad expanse of the hallway and ran up the centre of the staircase to the first floor.

Missing – ubiquitous tartan rugs, he thought, taking in the lavish surrounds. He noted that the castle looked as though it had been spring-cleaned, yet O'Leary had indicated that there were few staff living in, or working for, the estate. Thorough domestic cleaning on the scale of Castle Druin, he thought, would probably take a contract team a week.

"Beautiful home you have, Lord MacCaig," he said. "You must enjoy showing it to your guests?"

"Aye, that I do."

Gesturing toward a large oil portrait at the head of the broad, sweeping stairwell, Lamont said, "The first Lord MacCaig, at a guess."

"Lord Gregor John Alexander MacCaig – Jock to his friends," he said, with some measure of restraint. "Built the castle. My son, Jock, was named after him. Didn't have the family features though."

"I'm sure he would still have been honoured, Lord MacCaig."

"No need for the 'Lord' title, here Detective Lamont," he said easily. "Alex will do fine."

"We prefer to keep things formal," he replied, at once laying out clear ground rules. "Experience has taught us that's the safest route to follow – if you don't mind."

"I appreciate the position you're in, detective."

Although already knowing the answer, he asked, "Was Jock your only son, Lord MacCaig?"

"No, Ewan lives with his mother – my ex – near Ascot." Then shaking his head, added, "We didn't get on."

"I see," said Lamont. "I'll need their address in Ascot please, if you don't mind."

"Yes, I'll get it for you when we've finished here."

"And I believe Jock was adopted?"

"Aye," MacCaig said, with an air of regret. "His mother and I…. well she couldn't…."

"That's okay, Lord MacCaig. Noble thing to do indeed, if you don't mind me saying." Easing the man's obvious discomfort, he added, "Sorry for having to ask. You've probably outlined a great deal to Detective O'Leary here already, but we need to clarify things. We're trying to put together a picture of your son's life before this tragic event."

"I understand," he replied stiffly. "Sorry for the emotion, but Catherine, his mother, died young as well. Cancer…"

"Yes, Lord MacCaig," he said. "It must have been very difficult for you."

Lamont thought for a moment that the emotion, and his empathy with it, might draw MacCaig to say more, but instead the man quickly regained his composure.

"How did Jock get on with people?"

"He was like the rest of us," he replied. "Many liked him, some loved him…"

"You know of anyone who disliked him enough to want to take his life?"

"No, no-one."

"You told my colleague here that Jock didn't have any enemies..." Lamont studied MacCaig's reactions as he spoke. "But did he have any *real* friends? I mean, was there a woman, or for that matter, a man in his life at the moment?"

O'Leary, who had been studying the many artefacts in the hall as he listened, looked across at Tortolano and raised his eyebrows.

"He wasn't gay," MacCaig replied indignantly, "if that's what you're asking."

"It's important for us to know all of those who were close to him, Lord MacCaig. Jealousy can often create tensions…"

"He hadn't had a girlfriend for over a year," MacCaig replied. An edge of contempt coloured his tone. "Last one was a glory hunter who smelled the wealth and I think that put him off."

"They parted amicably?"

"Yes, but she was a bit of a character," he responded, smiling again now. "Her name was

Honey. American girl he met over in Africa. We called her 'Honey the Money'. It was all she ever talked about. She said her father was big in real estate. Showed us a photograph of him once – he would have been big in every State..."

O'Leary quipped: "Bit of a 'waist'?" but MacCaig ignored him.

Lamont realised instantly that when Lord MacCaig joked, the moment was his, and his only.

"And has there been anyone else in his life since then?"

"No. Just as well really. He had a great brain, but was an appalling judge when it came to those he chose to let close to him."

"Thanks for sharing that with us," he said. "I didn't mean for you to have to repeat yourself, but there were one or two things we needed to clarify."

"Really, trust me, that's no problem at all, detective," he confirmed. After a moment, he said, "By the way, that's an appropriate name you have, considering you're a policeman."

The other two looked confused, not understanding what the man meant.

"Indeed it is," the detective replied. "Means 'law' right enough."

O'Leary glanced knowingly at the young detective, who blushed.

Lamont caught the exchange from the corner of his eye, but maintaining his focus, said: "We'd like to go over the statements Detective O'Leary took with those other members of the family. Would that be possible at the moment?"

Pushing fingers through his thick, dark hair, Lamont glanced at the young detective and pushed the glasses frame up the bridge of his nose.

"If you don't mind, D.C. Tortolano will accompany us."

"That's not a problem, detective."

"And then I'd like to go down to the jetty and gauge the lay of the land, so to speak," he explained. "That'd be no problem either, I hope?"

"No," said MacCaig. "Do whatever you need to do to find those responsible. I'll get the ghillie to show you the way."

Lamont noted the use of the word 'those' but thought he'd hold fire from challenging the comment.

"'*Those*', Lord MacCaig? Do you think more than one person was involved in your son's death?" the Englishman asked.

"Not necessarily," he replied firmly, although he had turned his attention toward Lamont as he answered. "But I know Jock was a strong, fit lad. It would have taken more than one person to get the better of him. Under normal circumstances anyhow…"

"Yes, I fully understand that, sir," O'Leary responded politely, "but we have to check."

"We believe your son was shot from a distance," Lamont explained. "Would only take one man and a gun."

"I see," said MacCaig, looking thoughtful. "I

hadn't been told."

"We've only just had confirmation ourselves."

"Oh, right..."

The man appeared perplexed, but Lamont said, "We'd like to take a look around Jock's room, if that's possible. Detective O'Leary didn't want to disturb your grief last week, but we really need to accelerate our investigations."

MacCaig nodded his agreement.

"We understand Jock worked for the charity?"

"Yes," the man replied brightly. "Completed some great projects for us. He loved Africa. Spent most of his time out there building relationships and working on the Charity's projects."

"Had Jock any financial wheeling and dealing to do out there?"

"Aye," MacCaig confirmed. "Without his negotiating skills it would have been impossible to move money to the areas of greatest need."

"And yet you say he had poor judgment when it came to some relationships?"

"Only close personal ones, detective."

"He dealt with local officialdom easily then?"

O'Leary watched the developing exchange with interest, for he'd felt MacCaig hadn't been fully co-operative on Friday. It may have been shock, but then it could have been something else. Having, himself, been warned-off upsetting anyone, it was interesting now seeing his colleague being overly sensitive to the family, despite the need for facts.

"Jock had a way with him," the man replied, smiling an uncomfortable smile. "He understood greed and yet seemed able to look past that predictable human frailty." The man paused for a moment, as though to underline his distaste for the blatant avarice he encountered through their work in Africa. "He made certain the money actually got to the poorest and neediest."

Accepting that his visitors were police investigators and not houseguests, MacCaig now seemed to understand that their enquiries had priority over his grief. The man may have had nothing to do with his son's death, however Lamont sensed the aristocrat's adept fingers weren't short of other pies to dip into.

*

According to the preliminary coroner's report, the bullets that killed Jock MacCaig had been delivered with a high degree of accuracy from whatever distance they were fired. Lamont knew that this information did little to help their investigations. There were many fine hunters littering the highland estates. That didn't include the regulars with high-powered rifles who visited each year for the shooting season.

He assumed, from the wound on MacCaig's shoulder and his leg injury from the boat's bloodied rowlocks, that the dead man had injured himself trying to flee at least one killer. After all, if anyone had damaged a shoulder, or limb to that extent, their first instinct would be to get it treated, not row out into the middle of a loch. Lamont's train of thought was broken by MacCaig's rich tones.

"Detectives, this is my daughter, Amelia," he announced, as the attractive, radiant figure breezed down the oak panelled stairwell.

Lamont said warmly: "Yes, we've already met."

Appearing shocked at first, Amelia MacCaig then began to smile as she approached the last few steps.

O'Leary and Tortolano looked at each other.

"So it's detective, is it?" she said, now laughing. "When you told us you were a public service worker then changed the subject quickly, we hadn't guessed you were a policeman."

"I'm afraid so," he confirmed. Throwing a glance toward his colleagues, he went on: "Don't like it to get in the way of social events, so I tend to keep it to myself when I can.

"Father, Gio and I met Mr Lamont over in Carcassonne…"

"Afraid it's Detective Lamont now, Miss MacCaig," he said through the smile. "I'll have to be a bit more formal given the tragic loss of your brother."

"I… I see," Amelia hesitated. "Oh, well, you have your work, after all."

"Is Gio up and about yet, Amelia?" MacCaig enquired. "Only I think the officers might want a chat with him too."

"Yes," said Lamont. "That would be very helpful, Lord MacCaig."

"I'll leave you to it then," he said. "Let me know when you're ready to go down to the jetty."

"I will."

After MacCaig left them, the housekeeper appeared and led the detectives over to the dining room. More than five minutes passed before Amelia returned with her boyfriend.

As the Italian responded to their questions, Lamont had the same unease with the young man that he'd experienced in the French restaurant while on holiday. His family, from what they could gather, had considerable wealth, although he did not recall gaining this impression when they'd first met. Not only were his family involved in investment banking, they also had interests in an aircraft charter company. The firm, Gio explained with pride, was renowned for its ability to shuttle the rich and famous to all corners of the globe. They transported clients, often at very short notice, but more importantly, with total discretion. The couple confirmed they had been on holiday in the MacCaig family home in Carcassonne – an alibi that was not difficult to corroborate.

O'Leary passed a hard stare toward their youthful colleague as a gesture of his disquiet with this state of affairs. After her earlier spat with Lamont, she too was more than a little put out at this dramatic turn of events. Tortolano assumed the ground rules for a professional partnership had ben set during their heated debate in the layby. However, she was now forming the impression that Lamont may have decided working alone was the only way forward.

However, her partner was well aware of his new colleague's disquiet. The Scot recognised his selfishness in deciding how the game would be played out. However, for the time being, Lamont would shoulder her ire. In his mind, the investigation took precedence over anyone's feelings.

After learning of Gio's family business' involvement in aircraft charter, he wondered if it might have been possible for someone to fly from France, commit a murder in rural Perthshire, and then return without arousing suspicions – and within the time available. He didn't think it seemed possible, but had heard of similar, well-planned, modus operandi.

Confirming her father had phoned on the Tuesday evening, Amelia explained that he told her Jock hadn't been seen by anyone for some time. She agreed this perhaps appeared unusual, but said that her brother had always gone his own way. With no hint of emotion, she confirmed receiving another call early on Friday morning telling her he'd been found dead.

Lamont never mentioned that she hadn't seemed too upset when they'd met. There were complicated family relationships at play, due mainly to Lord MacCaig's three marriages. It now seemed highly probable that she and Jock weren't friends, no matter how warmly she lauded him. After all, the deceased was several years her senior, and the fact that he was a stepbrother may have played its part too.

When he enquired in passing if Amelia liked hunting she'd responded with abhorrence, rejecting the cruelty aspect and re-affirmed her vegetarianism.

"Do you shoot at all, then?"

"Well, I do know which end of the gun is which; but no, I don't. It brings a great deal of money to the estate, which is good enough reason to shoot game, I suppose."

"Gio," he asked, gesturing toward the young man.

"I guess your family enjoy blood-sports?"

The question carried an air of distaste, missed by the respondent.

"We pride ourselves on it," the well-tanned figure replied cheerfully. "My family has had sporting rights in the hills above Genoa since the end of Mussolini's tyranny."

"I see," he said. "Sounds like a rural idyll." Holding the young man's attention, he casually enquired: "What sort of rifles do you own?"

"I have access to several of the finest pieces made for sport."

"Your own guns?"

"No, sadly, the best – a Finnish made Sako and a beautiful Mauser – are my father's. They originally belonged to my grandfather. But when I have need…"

O'Leary watched his new partner's interview style unfold with grudging admiration.

"Are you a good shot?" Lamont asked, glancing toward Tortolano.

"A very good shot!" he replied proudly. "I am…"

"He's one of the finest in Italy," Amelia interrupted. Having seemed uncomfortable with the tone of the interview, she flourished for a moment, adding coyly, "but he doesn't like boasting."

"I see," Lamont said easily.

"It's how we met," she went on, gazing into the Italian's eyes. "Mr Genovese came over for the deer season at Father's invitation. Brought his handsome son along for the trip."

"And your father has known the Genovese family for how long?"

"You should ask him," she replied, sounding slightly irritated.

Gio interrupted: "I don't think it's been too long – a few years maybe. We do some work for the charity."

"Alright then," the Scots detective said, sensing the interview had run its course. "I think we can leave it there meantime."

She asked, "Meantime?"

"Well, you never know, Miss MacCaig," he said. "It is possible we may have to chat again."

As the young couple left the room, he looked over to his colleagues and pocketed the notebook. He was about to discreetly ask their opinions when Lord MacCaig came in.

"Would you like a coffee, or a tea?"

"Yes," Lamont said. "But can we see Jock's room first, please?"

Leading the three of them to an oak-panelled door on the first floor, Lord McCaig swung it open and offered them free rein to search around.

The room turned out to be a private suite. The spacious lounge area on the first floor was well appointed. Its walls were covered with photographic prints of local and African wildlife, as well as some landscape scenes and one corner of the room had been turned into a mini-office. A lead-mullioned window overlooked the hills above Loch Rannoch and much of the glen stretching away to the west. A fax, laptop and printer were all set out tidily on the broad desk. An empty shredder sat on the floor to one side of a three-drawer filing cabinet.

Opening it, O'Leary pointed to the neatly organised files.

Lamont shook his head.

"Won't waste our time there," the Manchester officer said. "That's a week's work!"

"And the rest," he agreed. Shoving a mint into his mouth, the smartly attired Scot wandered around looking at the framed photographic prints adorning the walls. One or two of them were signed.

"Do we need to get someone to bring up a van?" asked O'Leary. He glanced over at the Scot questioningly: "Haul that cabinet over to Perth for a thorough search through it?"

"Not till we actually know what we're looking for," he replied. "Besides, if there had there been anything incriminating about the family, I'd guess it would have been cleared into that shredder after Jock met his demise."

O'Leary knew his colleague had a point. There were so many files pertaining to the charity's overseas operations, that it would have been impossible to access anything significant without luck, or many hours of painstaking effort. Realising it was probably a laborious waste of time, he closed the drawers, turned the key and placed it in his jacket pocket.

Noticing what he'd done, Lamont nodded. "Good idea that. Just don't lose it!"

The English detective smiled through his contempt for the remark.

"I'll put it on my work key ring," he said, testily. "Safe there."

"You two check the bedroom," said the Scot, asserting himself. After thinking a moment, he added: "I'll have a scan around down here if that's all right."

Shrugging, O'Leary glanced knowingly toward the young detective who then followed him to the second floor.

It was obvious from the moment they reached the large bedroom that it had been scrupulously cleaned. Both the dressing room and large ensuite bathroom were also immaculate. Tortolano went through the wardrobes and then checked the bathroom cupboards, while he carefully searched the bedroom itself. There was nothing of interest to be found.

"Nothing up there," said O'Leary, as they reappeared from the stairwell.

"Sure?" Lamont asked, as he leafed through a neat stack of papers.

"Well, I forgot to take my guide dog, right enough," he replied sarcastically. "But unless you want me to pull the room apart, then I'm sure. It's been cleaned; more liked sterilised, if you ask me."

O'Leary sounded weary and clearly hadn't liked being challenged. He recognised the Scot felt they hadn't spent enough time upstairs to conduct a thorough search, but cared little.

Despite noting the tension, Lamont ignored the remark and began reading through recent entries in

Jock's small desk diary. It held a number of references to the dead man's work in Africa. Deciding it contained too many notes to go through them there and then, he slid it into his jacket pocket.

"Here's a present," he said, passing O'Leary the laptop.

Putting the computer under his arm, he asked: "You want the hard drive on this checked through?"

"Good idea," he agreed. "You never know, there might just be something of assistance on it. It'll be done down in Stirling by one of the technical guys, though. Remind me to take it with us when we get back to the car."

He looked over to the young recruit, who was thumbing through a book she'd taken from one of the shelves.

"You okay?"

"Fascinated," she responded drily.

"Sorry," he offered, "but we need to work too quickly to spend time explaining every move. Can you do me a favour when we get back?"

Tortolano nodded grudgingly.

"Find out who Jock's natural mother was. Try the records office, then the adoption agency. Might get us nowhere, but you never know. Oh, and see what other links exist to any name you uncover. Then check those out too. Use your imagination."

"It's fine," she said. "I kinda got the need for that for myself – without the explanation. I'll check with the Perth registry first."

"You got the cat by the tail there," O'Leary smirked, although he hadn't really been paying attention to the exchange.

Ignoring the Englishman's remark, the fastidious Scot continued scanning the room for clues. Despite hating the feeling that he may have forgotten something, Lamont still concluded most searches looking over his shoulder reflectively.

"Alright," he said, finally. "Let's get on."

Taking the laptop and diary, they returned to the dining room where MacCaig was waiting with fresh coffee.

"Can we take these with us?" Lamont asked, holding up the diary while pointing toward the laptop.

"Feel free, officer. As long as they're returned when you've finished with them."

"We've taken the key for the filing cabinet up there too," added O'Leary. "We may need to take it to see what's in it. Just possible there's a name, or a clue to help us with the enquiry."

MacCaig seemed annoyed by the intrusion into his son's private world, but Lamont had already begun the old diversionary tactic of offering profuse thanks for his co-operation as they seated themselves at the table.

Reassured, MacCaig began pouring them drinks.

"How much time did Jock spend here?" Lamont asked.

"As I told your colleague last week, he often came home. Not too often, though." Replacing the pot on its silver plated stand, he added: "Perhaps four or five times a year."

"And how long did he tend to stay?"

"Not long. Two, maybe three weeks each trip."

"Long enough to maintain solid social relationships – if he sought them, that is?"

MacCaig nodded thoughtfully, then said: "Spent most of the time in his rooms working on projects."

"Preferred to get on with his charity work, then?"

"When he wasn't working the dogs, or taking photographs, yes."

"Would he have had the camera with him on the morning he died?"

"Usually took it with him whenever he went out," MacCaig explained. "Hated missing an opportunity."

"Any idea where is it now? There's no photographic equipment up there that we could see."

"Must have had the camera with him then," he surmised. "If he brought it from Africa, that is. Never saw his luggage when he arrived, so I can't really help."

"There was a camera bag in his dressing room, but it was empty," O'Leary said.

MacCaig shrugged. "Suppose it could have fallen into the loch from the boat," he offered. "I mean, if he was trying to photograph the hills through the mist or something..."

As his words tailed off, a sense of the man's loss hung over the ornate dining room.

After first offering it to the others, Lamont was pouring the last dregs of filtered coffee into his cup when MacCaig's elegant wife, Helen, appeared in the doorway. Dressed in a well-worn, dark blue Barbour and rust-red cardigan, she wiped her hands deliberately on the jacket and introduced herself.

"Hello, you must be Detective Lamont," she said, smiling warmly. "The housekeeper said you were in here. Forgive the outfit, but I've just been out with the horses." Throwing MacCaig a doe-eyed look, she added in a soft lilt: "Alex doesn't like me coming in with muddy Wellingtons on, do you darling..."

"Or that filthy jacket," he muttered.

With high cheekbones and smooth, pale skin, the woman hardly appeared much older than her stepdaughter. Complemented by neatly trimmed, light brown hair held back in a ponytail, her features carried an aura of sensuality. Two large pearl earrings, set in what he guessed to be diamond-encrusted white gold, dressed her face. In keeping with the report, she was at least twenty-five years younger than her husband. Obviously not the deceased man's parental mother, she could easily have been mistaken for his sister.

"Is it alright if we ask you a few questions, Lady MacCaig?" he asked. You've already met Detective O'Leary, and this is Detective Tortolano. We've been drafted in to assist."

As he rose to greet her, the detective found it hard not to sound too effusive. The unexpected, and very elegant entry to the proceedings, had thrown him. First Tortolano and now this, he thought. For a moment he felt glad to be married and safe from temptations, as her long, narrow fingers lightly touched his palm as they shook.

Making his apologies, MacCaig left the three officers with his wife. Slipping off the jacket and cardigan, she threw them over the now empty master's chair at the head of the table and sat down.

After clearing his throat, O'Leary said: "It's about Jock's death."

Noticing the effect she was having on him, Helen MacCaig smiled quietly. All men were the same.

"You weren't likely to be here about the local poachers, were you?" she said pleasantly, the words laced with a broad hint of sarcasm.

Enjoying men's reactions while tolerating overt responses often presented her with two entirely different worlds. Never faltering, when the need arose, to suppress uninvited male hormonal surges with a verbal slap, she was equally adept at offering just enough encouragement to tease the unwary when it suited.

With a fleeting confirmatory glance at his partner, O'Leary held her attention.

"We are sorry to trouble the family again at a time like this," he began. "But it's important we try to formulate a complete picture of events. I know we've already spoken, but it would be really helpful if you could assist us further."

Tortolano watched attentively as the English detective carefully chose his words. Something told the intuitive youngster that the man was not all he seemed, but found herself admiring his subtle, tactful style. Realising that he was 'playing for the points' within their own team, she also knew O'Leary was trying hard not to antagonise the MacCaig family. He should, she thought, have been very upset about Lamont meeting the young couple in France and not telling him, yet strangely, he wasn't. A brief glance toward her had summed his reaction up. He'd accepted, perhaps a little too easily, that her partner had his own reasons for not revealing having already met them.

Lamont had drawn similar conclusions about the seconded detective. He had also decided to ensure the man didn't get too close to the attractive youngster. Something didn't feel right, but he wasn't yet sure what the root of his disquiet was. Perhaps the Englishman's confidence was merely a front, but the bespectacled Scot was unconvinced. From his point of view, the seconded detective was not quite what he seemed.

Helen MacCaig's stressed retort interrupted his thoughts.

"Yes, that's all very well, Detective O'Leary," she remarked defensively. "But there's little more I can add to what I have already told you…"

"Can I ask," Lamont interrupted, "how long you and Lord MacCaig have been together?"

"Six years. Why?"

Ignoring the question, he asked: "And how did you meet?"

After pondering the question, she appeared to decide that perhaps this detective wasn't as malleable as his colleague.

"Through his wonderful charity work," she said, changing tack and managing to sound a little more at ease. "I was doing voluntary work in the Gambia when we first met."

"It can't have been easy?"

"No," she began, "it was very difficult at first, but we soon found time together."

"Sorry," he said, still smiling. "I was thinking of Africa, and more about your charitable work. As I was saying, it can't have been easy..."

"Oh, no," she replied, looking uncomfortable. "It was never easy. Especially with the banks out there; they never do things without lengthy debates."

Surprised by Lady MacCaig's reply, Lamont glanced at his young partner, but Tortolano gave no reaction. Popping a mint, he quickly reflected on his expectations of this woman's involvement in the charity. He had half expected her to be a young, attractive, healthcare worker: a nutritionist, or something similar.

"If you don't mind me asking," he said. "What line of work did you perform for the charity?"

"I was the accountant in Africa."

"Was?" O'Leary interrupted.

"Gave it up when Alex and I married."

"Must've been an onerous responsibility," Lamont remarked, regaining his thread. "I mean, trying to get the money into the right hands, so to speak."

"Very difficult," she agreed, now warming to the conversation. "Moving the money over from Italy to Africa could be complicated."

"Italy?"

Although her expression gave little away, the detective felt sure she hadn't meant to mention the monetary aspects of the charity's activities.

"Yes, money has to be traded in and out of the U.K.," she confirmed carefully. "It lets us avoid the onerous charges the British and foreign banks make when they move money abroad."

"Why Italy?"

"Costs," she said. "We use an Italian investment bank, owned by Gio's family: Banco dei Lourgho Basso. Their exchange deals and overheads for banking are the least costly."

Wheels began to turn in Lamont's mind as he wondered just what Gio Genovese's role in his family's business was. Although knowing the connections could be coincidental, his focus in this case was now being stretched beyond the MacCaig family boundaries.

"How do you get the money to the needy in Africa?" he queried. "Or even manage to make choices as to what 'needy' is? After all, with so much poverty staring you in the face, it must be very difficult."

"Ah," she said. "So many layers of Government and self-interest to be overcome. We do a great deal of work before the money even gets near the people in need!"

"Did Jock have an important role out there?" Tortolano asked.

Helen MacCaig paused momentarily, studying the young detective.

"Well, yes," she responded. "Of course! Actually,

he was Alex's right hand man on the ground, so to speak."

"And what was his role 'on the ground', so-to-speak," Tortolano continued. "What did he actually do on a day-to-day basis?"

Surprised by the interruption, Lamont let the detective have her head.

"Jock's role was to identify problems and locate key areas where money might benefit the local population. It was then necessary for him and Alex to agree the best way of getting the money on-site in any particular locale. He was a great help to many people there and loved them dearly. When a job completed, he'd then be responsible for reviewing the effect of resources used in resolving local problems..."

As Lady Helen relaxed and began responding easily to Tortolano about the resources' benefits, Lamont smiled to himself. Her fondness for Jock gradually became more evident and, as she defined the dead man's role more clearly, he began to form a clearer picture of MacCaig family relationships.

"Jock would talk to the local politicians about how well, or badly any project seemed to be faring – even put them straight, if required. Then he would begin all over again, discussing local needs on the ground with the tribal leaders," she enthused. "After ironing out the worst of the problems, he would come to me. We'd clarify the strategic issues together and quantify the sums of money involved. After that, we'd spend time with Alex sorting out how to get the resources to a particular area. Jock was at his best finding and nurturing those in the local communities we could trust – not to mention those that we'd have to 'pay off'."

"Who got the pay-offs?" O'Leary asked abruptly.

"Too many of them to list." Shaking her head, she added, "If you think for a minute that the local and regional politicians – and gangsters – would work with us for free, then you'd be very much mistaken!"

"So…" Speaking softly, Lamont tried hard to maintain the relaxed style to which she seemed to respond most easily. "Jock was a 'mister-fix-it' in every sense?"

"Yes," she said, tears welling. "Jock MacCaig was a wonderful man. Brave, resourceful and kind. He was very artistic too."

"Brilliant photographer," he enthused. "Are those pictures in his suite ones he took himself?"

"Well of course," she added. "He loved photography."

Lamont grasped from the response that she had at least visited Jock's suite of rooms, but suspected something more.

"He does have the best equipment though."

"Yes," she said wearily. "He would take it out most days. Loved scenery and wildlife."

Lamont recalled the argument he'd overheard on the Canal du Midi. Not all of those present in the family home shared her rosy-eyed picture of the murdered man.

"And everyone here shared your admiration of his work and personality?" Helen MacCaig seemed puzzled, so Lamont clarified the question. "What I mean is, would all the family and charity workers share your views on Jock?"

"Why wouldn't they?" she said, sitting back in the chair. "He was a great man."

"And you loved him?" he countered quickly.

"Loved him?"

The woman appeared confused for a moment.

"Yes," Lamont said softly. He studied her features carefully as he spoke, searching for anything revealing. "Loved him."

"I may have done, but not in the way you're suggesting!"

"I was only thinking in a mother-son way," he lied easily, and with enough conviction to ensure the words held credibility. "I wasn't for a moment suggesting anything else. I'm truly sorry if my tone implied otherwise, Lady Helen."

"Oh, I see," she said, looking a little flustered. "I thought…"

"Again, I'm truly sorry," he repeated, knowing he'd gained the upper hand. "But I see what you were thinking now."

"Do you?"

Studying her steady gaze for a moment, he said: "You were very fond of him as a colleague though?"

Grasping his line of thinking, her eyes displayed a sudden flash of anger and her thoughts raced momentarily. Then she breathed a quiet sigh of relief, believing they could never prove any wrongdoing on her part.

"Yes, I was *very, very* fond of him, detective," she responded silkily.

With one more puzzle to solve, Lamont studied her temper-reddened features. If her husband suspected the adopted son was involved with his wife then his reaction would not have been one of fatherly love. Despite the fact he was on dangerous ground, having opened the new line of questioning the detective decided not to lose the opportunity it offered.

"It must have been difficult for you though," he continued. "Answering to both Jock and Lord Alex?"

"It could be at times..." She appeared to think carefully before continuing through welling tears. "But I didn't really answer to Jock. He was more a partner."

Uncertain as to whether the tears were of genuine emotion for Jock, or frustration at having revealed too much about their relationship, Lamont knew he would get no further unless she became more indiscreet.

"They are both – sorry – were, both strong-willed," she added. "And driven to get whatever resources were needed out to the African people. Alex worked hard to raise the money, and Jock fought to spend it wisely."

"How much money are we talking about, Lady Helen?" Tortolano enquired thoughtfully. "I mean in terms of the annual budget."

Sitting back in the chair, Lamont crossed his arms.

"Last year alone, I helped manage eighteen and a

half million pounds on their way to good causes."

"You managed?"

"I still do the accounts for the collecting side of the charity."

"How does the money get to Africa again? I mean, eighteen million, or so, that's a lot of money," she said. "It doesn't go directly to Africa I know, but what actually happens to it?"

Lamont had leant forward to ask that very question. The Scot sat back again and nudged the dark-framed glasses further up his nose.

"Charity money is transferred to the Forex Company. It then trades for the best exchange rates when we need the money moved," she explained easily. "Funds are then transferred to local, respectable banks in Africa via our Italian bankers, Banco dei Lourgho Basso."

"How long can money stay with the traders before it moves to Africa?"

"Oh, that will usually be no more than a few weeks," she responded in a guarded tone. "More often than not, it goes straight to the point of need. The minute it's raised here, the best exchange value is sought for a sterling currency trade."

"Is money only raised here in the UK then?" Tortolano asked.

O'Leary glanced over at Lamont. He too was admiring the young detective's style of questioning.

"Well, yes, it all comes from Britain. The laws applied to charities are different elsewhere in Europe. It would be too complicated to manage charity funds abroad without a large number of staff and international accountants. Defeat the purpose really..."

Lamont interjected: "Defeat the purpose?"

"Well,' she said, "We raise the money to go to the poor in Africa, not wealthy financial and legal corporations around the globe. Raising money elsewhere would involve many more people. Not to mention the legal cover."

Tortolano asked: "What would they do?"

"Make sure we've complied with national and international tax and currency laws, of course," she said, confidently. "But we don't need to spend money on them. Every penny goes into our Forex broker's account and is then transferred to Africa via our Italian bank."

"I see," said Lamont. Apart from their enquiries, the detective was finding the information Helen MacCaig was offering about resource transfer abroad fascinating. "How much does eighteen million usually raise in the financial trading markets? I mean it must add value to the Charity's assets?"

"I don't know," she responded vaguely. "I've handled the money in Africa and now oversee its management here, but what happens in between is Alex's business."

"And how do you oversee it here?"

"Well," she said, thoughtfully. "I don't actually oversee the money in an accountancy sense. We pay people to do that. I go down to London for a couple of days most weeks and meet with the Forex traders to ensure everything's fine."

"So, it's more liaison than management you do," O'Leary clarified.

"Yes!" she agreed enthusiastically. "That's a very good way of describing things. It's easy enough to check the numbers on a computer. That's my role most days. I even chat on the telephone if necessary; but people feel you're more involved when they see you face to face."

"And you don't find gambling on the international money markets with a charity's assets an odd way handling the resources?" Lamont didn't get an immediate response, so he rephrased the question: "I mean, would 'Joe public' out there, still offer their hard-earned if they thought you were gambling with it?"

"It's hardly gambling insofar as I'm aware," she snorted indignantly. "Money is traded on the market and then moved to the needy in Africa via Italy. But it's only traded when it becomes profitable enough to do so. Better we manage the money for the charity's end-user benefit than some U.K. or foreign bank lining their pockets with the profits, don't you think?"

Lamont didn't like what he had heard about the charity's finances. As he understood it, the processes surrounding the movement of money had always seemed a little too open to abuse, but what she'd said was certainly true: assets deposited in any bank are used in multiple trading situations. It was one of banks' ways of raising their own profit margins. Because a pound is deposited in a bank doesn't mean that it is exactly the same pound you get back when it's withdrawn. The banks, he knew, would raise further capital for their own interests by lending the money, or trading it.

Now knowing a little more about the financial dealings of Aid All Africa, he decided to change tack. It was just possible Jock had involved himself in the money side of the charity before his death.

"Can you tell me, Lady Helen," he asked carefully. "How did Jock seem on the Sunday, the day before his death?"

"As normal," she replied, but beginning to sound impatient.

"Was there anything in his demeanour that you might describe as unusual?" he tried. "For example, did he have a daily routine, or habits you'd noticed, that might have changed around that time?"

"Well, it may be nothing," she replied hesitantly, "but he did say something about the dogs."

"Yes?"

"Well, he said they'd seemed unsettled after he'd returned from the kennels in the evening. Jock loved the dogs. He thought more of them than anyone in the house."

The kennels, Lamont knew, were nearly a mile from the castle, presumably positioned out by the ghillie's quarters to ensure the Castle's residents weren't disturbed.

"Was there a problem?"

"Sundays are the ghillie's night off."

"But Mackenzie Tosland, the ghillie, lives there?" he said, checking O'Leary's notes. "Am I right?"

"Yes, but he'd gone up to Kingussie to visit his

brother and wasn't due back till Monday."

"And he didn't return till Monday?"

"No," she said, looking dismayed. "Not as far as I know…"

Lamont took a deep breath and glanced at his partners.

"Thanks, Lady Helen," he said. "You've been a great help." The detective smiled as he closed his notes and slid the pen into his jacket pocket. "We're really grateful for your help. I think we've inconvenienced you enough, though. Many thanks again for your assistance at such a difficult time. We may need to chat again to have the benefit of your knowledge of Jock and his movements."

The woman threw him a glare as she stood up, confirming he had touched a raw nerve. Exploring her relationship with Jock had been difficult, but necessary. She had indeed looked less than comfortable with the direction of the enquiry at points throughout the interview. There would be plenty of time to expand on the discussion at a later date, if necessary.

"Yes, that would be not be a problem, I'd love to help find who did this to Jock. Anything I can do to help," she said. "Anything…"

"There is one more thing," he said. "At what time did you say you'd last seen Jock?"

Stopping, the woman thought for a moment, and then continued straightening the jacket over her shoulders as she spoke.

"I remember seeing him around eight o'clock, not long before dinner," she confirmed wearily. "As I've said, he seemed to think something was upsetting the dogs. Said he was going over to check on them again. There are foxes and all sorts wandering around out there…"

Pausing for a moment, she straightening her collar and looked out through the window into the castle grounds.

"I never saw him again after that."

"Many thanks again," he said gently.

So far, so good, he thought, watching her leave.

She seemed to have been very close to Jock, her stepson – possibly too close. Reflecting briefly on the finances of Aid All Africa, and how they moved between Europe and the African continent, something felt quite wrong. There was great deal of trading in the international financial markets, where currency values rose and fell on a minute-by-minute basis, twenty-four hours a day, six days each week. However, Forex trading was a risky business. It demanded a great deal of knowledge, time and skill on a trader's part to make a profit. Lamont wondered if the money in the Forex holding agency was being used to fund more than Aid All Africa's charitable needs.

Chapter 10

Despite thinking he would find little of interest at the Castle's jetty, the detective still needed to satisfy a vein of curiosity. Leaving the others interviewing the Castle's staff, he went with Mackenzie Tosland, the estate ghillie, down to the loch. Taller than Lamont, the man was in his early fifties and had the bearing and brisk manner of a proud Highlander. His smooth skin and pale complexion hardly appeared altered by a life of rugged, out-door work. Long, sandy-coloured hair was brushed behind his ears and tucked under a rough woollen beanie. A well-worn wax jacket hung loosely from the man's sturdy shoulders, its torn hand-warmer pockets and worn cuffs underlining years of daily use.

Looking out over the nearby mountain's reflections on the loch's flat calm waters, Tosland chatted easily. He confirmed that cool summer mornings often cloaked the Loch's waters in mist. Lamont wondered about Jock's apparent attempt to escape the shore. Was it possible he had headed toward mist-shrouded, deeper water in the middle of the broad loch to hide from an adversary? But why try to escape out onto the water? Why not hide in the acres of dense forest?

The ghillie confirmed that on the morning Jock

went missing, he had been at his brother's home in Kingussie and had not returned until the Monday afternoon. This was well after the time the murdered man disappeared. Noting the brother's address there, Lamont resolved to get confirmation of his story.

"And what time did you leave for Kingussie on Sunday?"

"Well," Tosland said, "I wis a wee bit late, right enough. But it would have been around five-ish."

"And had Jock been down to see to the dogs?"

"Naw," Tosland said, in his broad, vernacular Scots. "He didnae get doon tae the kennels until much later. At least not according tae whit he telt me he usually did, that is..."

"You saw nothing unusual then? I mean, before you left here."

"Not that I remember..."

"Lady Helen said Jock thought the dogs were upset on the Sunday evening."

The ghillie reflected for a moment, then offered, "That could be anythin' – a fox, or whitever."

"Anything odd happen that you can think of?"

"Naw, there wis nowt unusual," he said, and then took a sharp breath. "Well there was something odd, now that I think of it..."

Lamont waited, but the moments seemed to slip away as Tosland stared over out over the dark waters.

"Go on..."

"Ye'll think me a wee bit daft perhaps, but I could

have sworn I passed young Amelia in that four-by-four she gads aroond in," he said. "Strange really, but it was as I passed Frodyke Filling station on my way up tae ma brother's place."

"But I thought she was in France?"

"Aye," Tosland said, sounding puzzled. "So did I, that's why ah thought it a wee bit odd ma self. But, as I headed up the A9 toward Kingussie, I'm sure a saw her car leavin' the petrol station."

The ghillie couldn't confirm having seen the car's registration and neither was there any certainty in his mind that it was actually MacCaig's daughter. Apparently there had only been only one person in the car, but under the bright forecourt lights of the petrol station the man was convinced it had been Amelia.

Tosland also told him that as soon as he'd returned on the Monday, Lord MacCaig had sent him into the estate with the dogs to try to find Jock. MacCaig thought Jock might be out 'stalking' with the camera and had possibly been injured.

"Presumably the dogs helped?"

"No." The ghillie pointed up the loch in the direction of the Moor. "His body wis a couple of miles o'er that way. We were into a cauld northerly breeze by late afternoon; no easy scent clues for them."

Following the line pointed out by the ghillie, Lamont remembered the loneliness and isolation of this rugged landscape. He had sensed it here as a young man. In remote corners a tent could be a solitary refuge.

"And you got on alright with Jock?"

"The lad was just grand. Ah' had many fine days wi' him o'er the years," said Tosland, fondly. He looked at the detective and nodded. "No' a bad bone in his body."

Sticking both hands into his pockets he returned to staring out over the Loch.

"Many a day ah've spent oot there wi' him, fishin'," he added wistfully. "Ah'll keep ma fingers crossed ye catch the bastard that took his life away – if ah' dinnae get at him first – ye'll no be needed then."

From his demeanour, the detective believed the man meant what he said.

"Well," Lamont concluded. "That's been really helpful."

"Aye," he replied, yet believing he hadn't been of much help at all. "The dogs tracked straight down here tae the jetty."

As he rubbed his cheek, the detective tried to picture events leading up to Jock MacCaig's death. The man had presumably been shot at and wounded, then ran to the jetty. Standing aloof from an investigation was certainly important, but he often gained more from trying to build pictures: both from the victim's and perpetrator's perspectives. He understood how the man had died, he now needed to establish why, and find the killer. Love, lust or money, the usual motivators, were all at play here. Superficially, this case seemed no different to any other.

"Isn't that what you'd have expected?"

"Pretty much. Ah mean, ah knew Jock had used

the boat," said the ghillie, and laughed. "Though I usually rowed the bugger!"

"Where did the dogs lead you to?"

Pointing down toward the shoreline, he said, "Doon to the beach o'er there, by yon clearing in the trees."

The tree break was no more than fifty yards from where they stood.

"Can we have a look?"

Although the detective was now curious, what sometimes appeared to be a good lead was more often a mere distraction. And they consumed both time and precious resources needlessly.

"Aye, c'mon," Tosland said, leading the way.

After spending ten minutes combing the slippery shingle and boulders in the cool Highland air, he began scuffing stones large and small with his shoes.

"Are ye lookin' fur somethin' special?"

Tosland took a bag of loose boiled sweets from his pocket and offered the detective one.

Raising a hand in refusal, Lamont said vaguely, "No, just looking."

"Needle in an 'effin haystack, eh?"

The ghillie shoved a 'soor ploom' sweet between his teeth.

"It's to find a bit of evidence right enough," the detective muttered, as he pushed at his spectacles frame.

"Think how it must be for the local bobbies, eh?"

Tosland winked. "Awe sorts of pochlin an' thievin' they know nothin' aboot, ah'd guess."

"You know them?"

"Eh?"

From his expression, the detective could see the man thought he was enquiring as to who was doing the thieving. He smiled.

"The local bobbies…"

"Awe, them," he replied, scornfully. "Aye, jist in the passin' though,"

Lamont scuffed away more of the shingle while the ghillie watched.

"See either of them often?"

Shaking his head by way of a reply, the man added with a wicked grin: "Weary Weir – he's too tired tae answer a call, an' young Wilkinson Sword – good wae a cutting remark."

Trying hard not to laugh, the detective continued probing among the loose stones. Weir and Wilkinson were like rural policemen the country over: the butt of everyone's humour until they performed in an emergency and earned their stripes amongst the locals.

There appeared to be no obvious clues, apart from some scattered animal droppings – possibly those of the estate dogs. Lamont picked up a small firm piece with a plastic evidence bag and sealed it.

"Is this from your trip down here with the dogs?"

He showed Tosland the evidence bag.

"Naw," the ghillie replied, moving closer for a

look at the contents. "The dugs were well sorted before we got this far." He studied the bag for a moment. "It's one o' theirs right enough tho'. Ah kin tell by the carrots and vegetable bits. Cook saves the spoiled raw veggies – they come tae the kennels wi' the other food waste fae the kitchen."

Lamont nodded appreciatively. Now he needed a metal detector to search the beach more thoroughly. If the dogs had tracked to that spot, as now seemed highly likely, then it was possible that Jock MacCaig had been followed there by his adversaries – and where guns are fired, ammunition cases could fall. Even with a careful search however, it would be difficult to see a shell casing among the loose, wet stones.

"By the way, that'll no be fur yer tea, detective," the ghillie said dryly, nodding toward the specimen. "Ah mean, ye dinna look a poor man."

"You mean this isn't haggis?" Holding the bag up he studied it for a moment. "Hmm, thought haggis was round and brown with orange spots too. Never mind."

"Aye," Tosland grinned. "And they smelt like turd when ma dear, departed wife cooked them tae!"

Laughing, he asked: "How long have you been on your own?"

"Ach, a few years now," said the ghillie. "Car crash got her on the A9, on the way back from her mother's house up in Inverness."

"Sorry…"

Lamont offered the apology, for the ghillie seemed genuinely sad: almost as though the loneliness and grief had never really left his side.

"It's life," he said, a wistful expression settling on his features. "I get sad sometimes when I think o' her, tho' I never loved the woman."

Taken aback by the man's bluntness, he said: "No?"

"No. But I chose to be loyal. She wis ma best friend. Tho', in the greater scheme o' things, ah've nae regrets."

Lamont watched as an outboard-powered inflatable whined over the water in the direction of Kinloch Rannoch village.

"And how long have you worked here?" he enquired, changing the subject while sucking on a mint.

Tosland looked down at his fingers as though counting the time away.

"Near thirty years now," he said with pride.

As they wandered back to the jetty, Lamont felt a little deflated, despite the ghillie's pleasant company. He'd managed to uncover nothing major, but consoled himself in the knowledge that it could safely be assumed the dead man had been tracked to this lonely spot. The killer had probably used the family dogs, knowing that they'd find Jock, no matter where he hid. It explained why the dead man had gone out onto the loch.

"Would the dogs chase after Jock, no matter who let them out?" he asked, sharing his thoughts.

Tosland considered this for a moment.

"No," he said, shaking his head. "It would hiv' tae'

be somebody they knew, or whit knew them."

"What time would Jock usually have taken them out?'

"Ah'd guess aboot ten," he replied. "Then he'd clean oot the kennels afore they got back in."

"Who else knows the dogs well enough?"

The man thought for a minute.

"There are a fair number of people," he concluded. "Family and friends of the estate, mainly – and some o' the regular shots."

"Would the pack go with one of them after Jock?"

"Ah suppose so," he said, and after thinking for moment added, "Aye, it's possible right enough."

The detective's supposition that the killer knew the estate and the family had been confirmed. However, he'd hardly started to probe the family's relationships with the ghillie when Lord MacCaig arrived at the jetty in a pristine, estate liveried, Land Rover. A lemon-coloured outline of the Castle with 'Druin Estate' written in gold coloured letters inside the body of the Castle was emblazoned on the front door. It gave the dark blue, long wheelbase off-roader an almost regal appearance.

As the driver's door opened and the landowner swung himself down, the detective gritted his teeth. Tosland had lost interest in their conversation when the vehicle appeared. It didn't surprise him when MacCaig had a brief chat with the man and sent him back to the Castle on estate business. Watching the vehicle pull away, Lamont knew he would have to speak to him again, and soon – though not within earshot of any family members.

*

On their journey back to Pitlochry, he explained the decision not to discuss having met Amelia MacCaig and her boyfriend while on holiday. Although sounding a little peeved, O'Leary agreed this had been a good idea in principle. He hinted however, that it would have been more useful to be in the loop *before* the interview. Although his partner didn't comment, Lamont could guess her opinion.

Ignoring the angst, he explained that the couple had seemed very chatty when they'd in the restaurant, despite it being clear Lord MacCaig had let his daughter know of Jock's death that very morning. Lamont explained that he'd overheard them arguing earlier – and probably about Jock – as they had sailed past his holiday lodgings. And to him, the tone of the argument suggested neither of them had much respect for the dead man.

Similar opinions of the pair had been formed by O'Leary and Tortolano. The young couple hadn't seemed concerned by the man's death. They also thought the Italian very controlling of the relationship, but had heard nothing linking either party to Jock's murder.

Tortolano said the interview had troubled her. Yes, it was probable neither of them liked the dead man, but she guessed there was more to it than mere dislike. The pair, although involved with the Aid All Africa charity, appeared to have superficial and quite peripheral roles. She wasn't certain that this, apparently limited involvement, was as honest as it appeared. The Genovese name, she explained, originated in the north of the country, near Genoa on the Ligurian coast. Tortolano said this was near the Italian's home and where she also had family ties.

After listing to her with interest, Lamont suggested it might be useful for her to check out what was known about the Genovese clan. He thought, however, that the Italian had played no part in the murder; at least not from the impression of him given during the interview. However, he didn't believe the man to be as conscientious and honest as the picture he'd tried to paint.

"You up for that?" he asked.

After a moment, she replied: "Shouldn't be too difficult."

"Careful," he said, turning toward the young detective. "Explain the need for care and discretion. One wrong move in this case and we've a scandal on our hands. After all, we're not going to look good damaging a charity in the line of our enquiries."

"Got that."

"We only need information relating to what's known of Gio's family at this moment in time. I don't want them prying into their private affairs. If MacCaig gets wind of any probing, there will be serious repercussions from his connections."

"I'll explain that to them," she replied tersely. "Not that I wouldn't have anyway."

He caught the irritation in her voice, but could ill afford not to make the instructions crystal clear. If anything went wrong, he was uncertain of being able to rely on either officer to protect his back. Having not worked closely with anyone for a number of years, to be suddenly linked to two strangers from different backgrounds presented a challenge he didn't relish. Partnerships were based on trust, a commodity in short supply at the moment.

"We need to know more about the dead man's relationship with his stepmother," he said, almost to himself. "And the charity's financial dealings."

"How did you get on with Tosland at the jetty?" she asked.

"Oh, I picked up a sample there – not a lot of it about – probably canine," he said, taking the specimen bag from his jacket pocket. "One for the Lab."

She leant forward to see what Lamont was holding and almost had the sample bag in her face.

"For God's sake!"

"Don't worry," O'Leary jibed. "He's trying to get up your nose."

Ignoring the exchange, Lamont took out the notebook and made a one-line entry.

"That worth sharing?" asked O'Leary, gesturing toward his lap.

"One for the memoires..."

As he closed it, the Scot glanced over at their driver. Something wasn't right, but he couldn't put a finger on it. Then the thought struck him again: for someone suspended from his own force and awaiting serious disciplinary procedures, he seemed remarkably composed and confident – almost too confident.

As they neared his temporary base, O'Leary confirmed he would purloin a small team of officers from Perth to help search the loch's shoreline. Thanking him, the Scot said he'd emphasise, when briefing the old man, the need to keep DCI MacDougall in the background. Throwing the sample bag onto the rear seat, he asked Tortolano to get it to the laboratory for confirmation that it was canine with carrot residue.

"Carrot residue?"

"I found it on the shore, near the jetty. I think the dogs chased Jock MacCaig down there," he explained. "If it is canine, then the contents suggest that the pack were there. The cook over at the castle throws the veg cuttings out – along with the food left overs – for the hounds at the ghillie's kennels. Nothing's wasted."

Braking, O'Leary swung sharp left into the police station car park.

Pulling on the handbrake, he queried: "What does that tell us?"

"That whoever killed Jock knew the dogs well enough to use them to track him."

Tortolano looked at him.

"But we can't be certain, surely?"

"No, not really," he replied, shaking his head. "According to the ghillie a lot of people are familiar with the pack. The lead dog is apparently quite trusting too. Seems it would have trotted out with someone who knew roughly what they were doing, even though they weren't trained to lead them."

149

O'Leary had parked up beside the Audi. Getting out, he said his farewells and hurried off to further his own line of the enquiry. Watching him use the code to open the Station door, Lamont decided he would keep an eye on him.

"Something wrong?" asked Tortolano.

"No," he said. "Nothing."

"You don't like him, do you?"

"I wouldn't buy him a pint, if that's what you're asking."

"Is it the race thing?"

"Might be, right enough," he said thoughtfully. "But I suspect it's not the type of race you're thinking of. He's in a race of his own making."

Not quite certain what her partner was alluding to, Tortolano shrugged and got into the Audi. As they travelled back down the A9, he asked her to take the laptop into the technical forensics team and get Phil Mason to take it apart. He wanted to scan the contents of Jock MacCaig's diary himself.

*

"So you don't think it's a simple murder then?" asked Moon, his wizened expression displaying curiosity.

Leant against the doorjamb, Tortolano watched the men converse with interest. Having returned from the technical department where she'd dropped off the laptop for content analysis, the young officer was curious about the direction the enquiries would now take them. From her perspective, they had travelled a great deal and resolved little.

"No," Lamont said wearily. "There's something else but I'm buggered if I can put a handle on it. O'Leary's a further complication thrown into the mix..." Glancing toward his new partner, he went on: "It may just be that I've not had other officers working with me for a while though. I'm probably being impatient."

The woman nodded knowingly, but said nothing.

While he recounted the day's events, Moon listened diligently to his analysis of the situation at Castle Druin. However, he seemed unconvinced of anything being badly amiss with Lord MacCaig, or his family. Eventually, and seemingly with some reluctance, he agreed to their seeking further information. After eventually accepting that Tortolano should begin subtly probing Genovese's family background in Italy, he told her to begin immediately, but warned her against causing waves. After she left the office, he set out his own concerns surrounding the investigation.

"Strangely enough, like you, I'm beginning to think this is a not a simple murder investigation," he offered. "I had hoped we could avoid any political fallout from a case like this though..." The old man rubbed his chin as he reflected on the enquiry. "MacCaig is, after all, extremely well connected. The last thing we need is someone with his clout stirring the mire for us over in Edinburgh. But, if you're right, then it may be unavoidable, despite my reticence."

"What stage of the national change process are we at over there?" asked Lamont, referring to the restructuring of the Scottish Force.

"The politicians are close to the merger announcement," said Moon wistfully. "That means seven fewer chiefs and deputies. Could see me taken out of the frame."

"Why?"

"Well, I'm an over-aged expense heading – as the accountants might say – that could be replaced by one of political classes."

"Police experience is essential for your role!"

"No," he argued. "Only for yours. I'm more admin than anything else."

After pondering the gravitas of that statement for a moment, Lamont said: "Do you really think MacCaig will stir things?"

"Funny one that, for despite the political clout he wields, I haven't had one call from any quarter asking in which direction our enquiries are proceeding. Seems a wee bit strange, don't you think?"

"Possibly..."

"Now, if I were MacCaig and had his contacts, I'd have been pressing for information about the investigation into the death of my son. Especially now that we're involved." Moon chewed on the end of his pen for a moment. "No, there hasn't been one word from Edinburgh, or even from the Chief Constable in Dundee for that matter. And he's a close friend of the man."

"So you don't think he wants the investigation team pressing too hard?"

"I would want answers," Moon reasoned. "Wouldn't you?"

"With his contacts I'd have us dancing on hot coals, right enough," he agreed. "But it'd not be just MacCaig himself. As I said during the briefing, none of the family seem too grief stricken. At a guess, his lordship is in some sort of denial process. Perhaps that's why he's not been pressing for information."

"After what you've told me," the older man said. "I've a feeling there's more to it than his reactions to bereavement. And Lady Helen, well..."

Moon rolled his pen on the desk for a few moments while Lamont took stock of his boss's observations.

"Young Tortolano may get us some background information about the Italian's family," he offered.

"I don't think that'll help, do you?" growled Moon. It was more statement than question and impatience was now showing on the rounded features.

"No, perhaps not. But there's something not sitting comfortably for me both in what he says, and in his general behaviour. And O'Leary's a complication in the equation as well. He's not behaving like someone on suspension for a serious misdemeanour. More like he's on a busman's holiday, if you ask me."

"Never mind O'Leary, he's not our problem," Moon directed.

"No, right enough."

"Anything about the MacCaig family you can whiff in the wind?"

His subordinate gave a brisk shake of the head.

"This little affair could lead us up an embarrassing cul-de-sac," said Moon. "We need answers, or we'll need to back off before MacCaig gets the opportunity to stretch his political muscle. The one positive point is, that if he has done something wrong, we'll know soon enough."

"How?"

"He'll use his social and political contacts to block our lines of enquiry."

Moon was rightly wary of the investigation's ramifications for his Unit. One reasonably well-founded complaint from a well-connected figure like MacCaig at this stage was all it would take. They already had enough enemies, especially at a time of major change in the Scottish Police Force's structure. In survival terms it was 'dog eat dog' and he knew it.

Agreeing grudgingly, the detective accepted his boss was probably right. MacCaig no doubt had his reasons for holding fire. At any moment of his choosing, the man could call on an array of allies to divert or even scupper their enquiries. And possibly destroy the team.

"I'll work as quickly possible on all aspects of the enquiry," he agreed. "In particular the dead man's relationship with Lady Helen. I think there's some mileage there for us. There may even be a useful file hidden in the dead man's laptop our boys can find. O'Leary can dig around in the charities funds and money movement..."

"I'm not too comfortable with him getting into the financial aspects of this case – if there are any," Moon interrupted. "Better with him working closely on the family relationships aspect of things. That way you can keep a wee eye on his comings and goings – and ensure no-one gets offended."

"And the money?"

"I'll make one or two preliminary probes," he confirmed stiffly, while realising his anxieties about the case had been too transparent. In a more relaxed tone, he said: "I've good contacts down in London. We'll see if one or two 'Canaries' can't sing from the money hub at the Wharf, eh?"

"O'Leary's getting a small team up from Perth to search the shoreline of the Loch," the detective confirmed. "They'll scour around the point to where we think the dog pack tracked the dead man's scent. It's near a clearing in the trees – I went down there with the ghillie."

"What's he like?"

"Good type," he said. "More helpful than he appreciated too. It appears Jock MacCaig was definitely trying to get away from someone."

"Let me know if you get anything. I'll brief Perth for you and keep things quiet up there."

"Thanks." The detective was grinning as he turned to leave. "Old MacDougall will be apoplectic when he receives the request for a police search team. Should send his manpower budget well into the red."

Heading for Room 7, his anxieties about the case remained high. Something was vexing him, but he had no idea what, or who. He tapped the young detective's door and went in. She was on the phone.

"Yes... Of course... Great... Yes, I will, thanks... Yes. I'll tell Dad... Bye."

"That sounded cheerful," he said. "Get us

anywhere?"

"Not sure," she said. "We'll see."

"All your family bilingual in English and Italian?"

"Of course," she confirmed. "Most of them live here and only go home to Italy three or four times a year with the van for supplies. Imports cost a fortune. Better to haul the stuff over. My father's relatives are still in Saint Eusabio, in the hills behind Genoa."

"So you think they might be able to help?"

"It's got to be worth a try," she replied, speculatively. "But, as I said, who knows."

"If you get anything, anything at all..."

"Of course," she said. "Have you set up on-going briefings for O'Leary?"

"O'Leary and I will use the old Blackberry and email mostly – that is, if we're not together and still need to communicate."

Tortolano seemed pensive and after a moment asked: "Do you think he's getting a fair crack of the whip?"

"I see you having the occasional look at him," he confirmed. "Forgive me saying, but I think I can gauge your feelings too."

Tilted his head, he smiled and paused for a moment. Tortolano gave him neither eye contact nor a response.

"Detective, there's a job to do here," he said, as the young woman blushed. "We find Jock MacCaig's murderer – end of."

"I'm well aware of that, but when you were at the jetty he was telling me what had really happened in Manchester."

When she began elaborating, Lamont studied the floor for a few seconds then interrupted her.

"Emotions, and whatever he says to you, don't really have a role here – at least not in my view. If you like him, then fine. But don't pre-judge the investigations into his conduct by swallowing his line of reasoning, or explanations. Never completely believe what a colleague says – not even me."

"Well…" she began, but let the words hang.

He looked at her long and hard.

"Christ," he said, animatedly. "On first impressions he seems fine – might be Snow White in drag, for all I know. Like you, I've seen nothing during our short acquaintance to suggest he's racist. But that doesn't mean he isn't bad to the core either. Wait until the dust settles and see how it goes, eh?"

Tortolano decided her partner was in one part infuriating, on the other, a possible font of professional wisdom. Desperate not to dislike this man, for she understood it critical they form a working relationship, Tortolano drew a deep breath. There and then she decided that tomorrow was a new day and a new start. She would try again.

Chapter 11

By the time Lamont got home from Randolphfield, Elspeth was already asleep on the sofa. When she didn't respond to a soft touch on her shoulder, he flopped into the old armchair and watched as she lay, softly breathing. Sitting quietly for a few minutes listening, he pondered the day's events with MacCaig, O'Leary and Tortolano, the other new complication in his working life. Moon knew he wanted secretarial or admin assistance, yet had recruited another detective. Not only that, he wanted her to study and learn from his every action, right or wrong. Each move, at least until he knew the detective well enough to trust her, would now have to be strictly within the rules.

He had grown used to being alone, thinking and acting autonomously, solving problems in his own time and style. Not any more: his new partner had already been critical when she thought it necessary. She was strong-willed too. From his standpoint, the only positive aspect of having the woman as a team member was her obvious intellect.

Sighing wearily, he watched Elspeth's chest rise slowly, then fall as she exhaled. He loved her, always had, but time, work and the burden of guilt carried from the injury, had taken a heavy toll. Loving her wasn't easy. Argumentative and highly gregarious, the attractive auburn-haired woman always knew her own mind. But, he believed the blame lay mainly with him for the problems nurtured during the past few years.

The head wound had taken away more than his career prospects. Life had been fragmented while he grew into accepting the injury brought with it fundamental personality changes. And that transformational period, as he adjusted to a new reality, probably caused more arguments and stresses than could be counted.

Guilt still coursed through him too. It was at its most intense during the quieter moments, leaving him feeling both empty and very much alone. Getting to his feet, he wandered through to the guest bedroom and collected the duvet. Draping it over the settee, he carefully covered her shoulders and arms then, gently touching her forehead, left her sleeping and went into the kitchen. Taking a piece of cheddar from the fridge, he made a sandwich and ate it quickly.

Washing the food down with water, he soon became frustrated by the self-analysis. Striding up to the bedroom, he took off his jacket, waistcoat and tie, and then hung them up. Lying down, he removed his glasses and soon fell into a deep, disturbed sleep, where a never-ending chasm relentlessly sucked him down into its black depths.

Elspeth had returned, tired and weary. Managing the complex care of two difficult medical cases over in Glasgow had taken its toll. Yet, despite having personal health problems to manage, she hadn't forgotten the importance of restoring their marital harmony. The holiday had re-awakened a mutual tenderness. She didn't intend to let those feelings drift again, especially not now.

After writing a short note explaining her sorrow at failing to chat more while on holiday, Elspeth had placed it under a flower vase on the kitchen windowsill. He always had a sandwich washed down with water after a late return from work. He'd see it, read it and waken her.

By the time Lamont got up she had already left for work. Surprised to find her gone, he showered, dressed and headed out to the office without so much as a cup of coffee. This wasn't unusual, for he rarely ate breakfast. The note remained folded under the vase on the kitchen windowsill.

Feeling unwell, Elspeth returned home at lunchtime and found it unopened. After thinking briefly about whether or not to save it, she took a deep breath and dropped it into the waste bin. Sitting at the table, even the familiar surrounds of her home suddenly felt very lonely. Holding back tears of disheartenment, she decided to return to the hospital. At least there she had a role and wouldn't focus on her own health. The holiday was indeed over, she thought, and not only from a timescale perspective. France – and her husband's reawakened emotions – seemed to be moving quickly into the past.

*

Standing in front of the whiteboard, hands in pockets, Lamont was trying not to feel frustrated. He didn't usually need diagrams to map out an investigation, but with a new recruit on board and O'Leary very much in the foreground, he knew it could be helpful in keeping things up to date. He would use the board's facts and musings on Friday morning for the team meeting. Resolving to activate the headquarters' conference calling facility would also keep the Manchester detective in the loop - and his partner happy.

Studying the different coloured lines of enquiry carefully, he made certain the work already done was correctly set out. As he turned to put down the markers, Moon came into the office, shirtsleeves rolled up.

"Ready for action?"

"In action!" Moon replied positively. "Money…"

"Interesting?"

"Well, I think it's a 'yes'," he said. There was a broad grin on his face as he passed the mobile across. "But tell me what you think."

After scanning the text, the detective looked up and raised his eyebrows.

"Is this useable?"

"The answer to that one is, simply, no." Moon pointed at the phone. "That information is highly confidential and cannot be revealed. Apart from anything else, it would expose our source to legal action and possible disqualification from the bar."

"How did he find this out?"

"Let's just say that some members of the finance community down at Canary Wharf owe him favours for keeping them out of prison."

Lamont picked up a marker and turned to the whiteboard.

"So we've a suspicion of money laundering," he said, while writing. "Eighteen million plus goes into a Forex registered company in the 2009-2010 fiscal year. And yet, even after highly successful trading on the Yen and Euro, a slightly smaller sum – although again, still around eighteen million – goes forward to the African continent. So someone's probably making a personal profit out of the money trading." Looking at over at Moon, he offered: "The dealers?"

"Possibly…"

Turning back, he scribbled on the board where he thought it most appropriate, then drew a short line to an image of MacCaig he'd printed from the Internet.

"This, 'money movement', from the charity to Africa, takes place via a bank in Genoa," he said. "Then the money trading company…called 'AidenallafricA' – *nice name too* – get their sums wrong?"

Moon stroked his chin and agreed, saying, "Seems so."

"In the last financial year, even though a similar amount is raised – and put through the books of the company in London," Lamont continued, as he scribbled, "the amount leaving AidenallafricA and going to Africa via Italy is slashed to somewhere short of seventeen million pounds."

"Yes, in a nutshell," said Moon, tapping his forehead with his fingertips. "What we really need to know is: how much of the original profit stayed within the hands of the charity and how much went on 'expenses'?"

"And who received it?"

"Quite!"

"What about last year?"

"Bad trading, possibly…" Moon appeared pensive as he reached out for his phone then shoved it in his pocket. "But here's the juicy bit you'll like. I rang Companies House and the Directors' names for the company changed before Jock MacCaig's death."

"Well?"

"He was replaced on the Board by Giovanni Genovese."

"Gets better."

"Doesn't it just."

"So what's the strategy? I mean, we now have an interesting situation: Gio Genovese on the investment arm of the charity; family banking links with Italy, and possible money laundering?"

"And despite my playing matters down," Moon said optimistically, "it's quite possible Tortolano's family will know something useful."

"Will I get her through?"

"Good idea."

He returned a few moments later with the detective in tow, a resigned look on his face.

"Sir," she began, before Lamont had settled. "My sister-in-law got back to me. I'm afraid the family know very little about the Genoveses. They're similar to nobility over there. Not much about their activities ever gets into the public domain. They live inside a walled estate in an eighteenth century Castello – and very grand it is, apparently. It's masked by cypress trees and can only be seen in the distance from one of the neighbouring hills."

Moon cut short the romantic imagery.

"And what did you manage to find out?"

"Well, there are two brothers. They inherited the firm directly from the grandfather after their father died young. They're major political players through their ownership of the bank."

"Nice to hear," said Moon, ironically.

"It apparently began as a post-war investment collaboration with two Dutch financiers," she went on. "Hence the name, which translated means, 'Bank of the Low Places'. The Genovese family bought them out in the 60s."

"Is the bank only an investment operator, then?" Moon asked.

"They don't know for sure, but think it handles offshore investments. Money from wealthy private investors the length and breadth of the country, apparently."

"Can't we find out anything else?" Lamont asked.

"Doubt it," she said. "They keep very much to themselves. Our source is my sister-in-law, a journalist on *Gazzetta del Cordana*. She tells me not much is known about them in the public domain."

"At least she's heard enough to give us something else to think about though."

"Yes," she confirmed. "Big players in the financial world, certainly. Apparently known to donate large sums of money anonymously to children's charities."

Looking at her quizzically, Lamont said: "Anonymously?"

"Seems they have ways of making certain that people know how much they've given – and where it's gone – using friendly contacts in the media," she elaborated. "They've strong relationships with leading financial editors and newspaper owners – hers included!"

"Just what we need," said Moon. "If we have to poke around formally, and my information's not one hundred percent correct, we'll be eaten for breakfast by politicians and the media."

"I need some thinking time," said Lamont.

"Good idea," he agreed. "I'll leave you two for a moment and check out which way we need to play the politics. If I can, I'll also get the published accounts for 'AidenallafricA' and the Aid All Africa charity itself. A good root around in the finances may tease out something to confirm our suspicions."

"Hopefully," said the detective, trying to sound optimistic.

As Moon went through the door he added over his shoulder: "I'll talk to Inland Revenue. Let's see if they have anything that could be of assistance without us probing publicly."

When the door closed, Lamont said with gratitude: "That was useful information. It opens up a number of avenues. Might be worth a trip over to Genoa if things develop."

"I'll get the high factor sun-tan lotion ordered," she smiled.

"In the meantime," he said, nodding at the new phone console on the desk, "sit there and we'll have a chat with O'Leary. Let's see how he's getting on. I asked him to establish that gamekeeper's drinking habits. If he can bump into him in the local, then great."

"I thought you wanted thinking time?"

"Gives me a headache," he said, winking.

The screen broke into life.

"There you are, large as…"

"Video conferencing in darkest Scotland," O'Leary retorted, his face too close to the screen. "Next we'll have pigeons for the big messages, eh?

"It's a recorded line, Brendan," he said in a matter of fact tone. He leant back from a close-up of O'Leary's face, staring at him from across the ether. "If you don't sit back from that camera, I'll be having nightmares."

"Oh, sorry," the Englishman said, grinning broadly. "Didn't mean to alarm you."

Lamont pushed at the glasses frame as he spoke. "Did you manage to get the ghillie's local tagged?"

"Yes," O'Leary replied. "And ended up chatting to him as he left."

"How'd that happen?"

"Well, he seemed to want to talk." O'Leary shrugged and then scratched his nose, for a moment seeming distracted by something to the side of him.

"Really?" Tortolano said.

"Waited till I came out of the Laird's Lair – that's the local over in the village – late last night," he explained. "I'd popped in to see if I could find him, or catch a chat with the locals. Anyhow, after half an hour he came in to the bar, had a quick drink, nodded toward me, then left without speaking. After waiting a minute or two, I followed. He was waiting in the car park."

"Promising," Tortolano said. "Did you get to chat with the locals first?"

"Yeah, but the minute you mention the castle, the draw bridge goes up, so to speak."

"Suspicious?"

"No, they know where their bread's buttered though," he replied. "Just my luck, only a handful of punters in there and the two I was nattering with were estate gardeners. Great ale though!"

Sounding impatient, Lamont pressed the detective for answers.

"What did Tosland want?"

"Said that young Jock was a fine lad, loved the estate and his work in Africa," O'Leary reported. "But wanted to tell me how familiar the lad had been with Helen MacCaig."

"Did he say how close they'd become?"

"Close enough for the housemaid – a pal of his – to notice that Jock's bed wasn't often slept in. That tended to be when Lord MacCaig was away on business too. More often than not the bedding had been disturbed to make it look as though he'd slept there. The housemaid could tell that he hadn't though…" O'Leary added with a smirk: "Apparently they can always tell with things like that."

"Hmm..." Lamont thought for a moment. "Anything else?"

"Seems our Lady Helen has the habit of changing her own bed sheets on those particular occasions."

"Nothing too conclusive then," Lamont said, "but more confirmation of our suspicions, nonetheless."

"Yes, unless you want DNA," O'Leary said brightly, "or pictures. Besides, at least we now have someone on the inside, so to speak."

"Is he loyal to Lord MacCaig?" asked Tortolano.

"Yeah, I think so. Says the old guy got duped into marrying this one, but wouldn't expand on it. Didn't want to be caught chatting to me, so it wasn't long before he cleared off."

"Okay," said Lamont. "That kind of explains some of the entries in the diary. He had her phone number at the front and then odd little entries with only the time and 'HER' on them. Wouldn't be possible to link them, but they seem to coincide with his visits to the castle and she is 'HER'."

"Bit spurious," O'Leary fired. "Any woman could be a 'her'."

"Not many called Helen Elizabeth Radcliffe though, her maiden name before the marriage."

The face on the screen concurred, adding: "Looks like a strong enough tie."

"Possibly," said Lamont. His tone sounded circumspect. "Keep digging if you can. Oh, and suss out those two local bobbies. Perhaps they can throw some light on things. Try not to make them too suspicious. That's a small community and they'll no doubt be networked to the estate through wives, kids and God knows what else."

"Church as well, eh?"

"Yes, indeed," the Scot said, his expression unchanged. "Very possible too. This is the rural Highlands after all, not Manchester's Moss Side. You know the score anyhow. Play it tight."

"Yes, no problem." O'Leary asked, "Anything else?"

"Nothing for the moment, just keep an eye on things – and an ear open. If you hear of any unusual visitors to the Castle, let us know. I'll let you know ASAP if there's a sniff of anything down here. Our boss is looking into one or two financial matters in the background. Hopefully, he'll gain further information.

"Such as?"

"We've word of money irregularities, as well as some overseas relationships that might be interesting. That Genovese lad is well connected too. His family definitely own the bank used by Lord MacCaig's charity to move money across to Africa."

"That's pretty useful to know," the detective said, then added wryly: "Getting a bit tasty up here in the Highland hinterlands, eh?"

"Yes," he agreed, smiling. "Very tasty."

"Okay, I'll get onto the local bobbies, then try to get another chat with my 'ghillie friend', after I've briefed MacDougall in Perth, naturally. Anything on that laptop we collected from the dead man's room?"

"The technical buff here, Mason, gave me a brief verbal report, but said little. I'd asked them to scour the drive for any links they could find to the investment company or the charity. Also asked him to look for emails, or online diary links to Helen MacCaig."

"No help then?"

"Nothing so far," he confirmed. "No sniff of a mobile phone for Jock either. I rang Lord MacCaig and asked him to check it out with the family, but he says none of them know anything about it."

"Not a helpful lot anyhow." O'Leary, who was looking away from the screen while shuffling papers on his desk, asked: "Anything else I can do up here?"

"No, not at the moment," he said, before adding: "Oh, and don't worry about briefing MacDougall. Moon has already had a word with the Tayside Chief about our progress. We're putting together a report for him. And forget about that filing cabinet in Jock's suite. On reflection, we think it'll have been well cleaned out. Besides, unless we need to, Moon doesn't want MacCaig upset too much and hauling those files away ain't gonna win many smiles."

"Tell 'sir' a big 'ta' from me for the reports," said O'Leary. "Keeping that desk-bound misery in Perth at bay is very welcome."

"By the way, if that 'ghillie-friend' is your best shot at humour…"

He cut the connection before O'Leary could

respond.

"That was cruel," Tortolano said, grinning.

"No gain without pain!"

"Anything I can do?"

"Yes, see if Moon's free, then pop through and update him on O'Leary's tale of 'incest' between the dead man and his stepmother. Then ask him if he'd like you to prepare the draft briefing note for the Tayside Chief, where of course you'll be careful not to mention anything…"

"Anything?"

Lamont nodded and threw her a wide-eyed look.

"Anything!" he confirmed. "Enemy territory, Tayside."

"Need to know basis, then?" she said, tapping her nose while grinning wickedly.

Lamont raised his finger.

"To know how to use knowledge is wisdom," he said as she left the room.

After a moment, Tortolano put her head back round the door. "Grasshopper…"

Chapter 12

Mrs Robb walked stiffly into the dining room balancing a tray carrying Lord MacCaig's breakfast. Waving a hand in gratitude, he continued chatting on the phone. The housekeeper placed it carefully on the table then left, trying hard not to listen to the loud dialogue as she retreated.

"Well Brian, that's been really helpful of you and the whole family will be grateful, I'm sure," he said. "No, I don't want any pressure on them, thanks... No, no, it's a sad job and they've got to do it... yes; I'll tell you if I need anything... You too... yes... have a fine day. Thanks again for your kind thoughts. Bye."

Putting the receiver on the table, he was about to cut into a thick rasher of bacon when Amelia appeared in her dressing gown.

"Early for you," he said. "Gio on the go yet?"

"No," she said lazily, lifting a piece of dry toast from the rack. "I couldn't sleep. What, with all this police fuss and things."

"Difficult, isn't it, lass."

After scowling at the toast, she dropped it back onto the rack and slid her hands into the cream coloured dressing gown pockets.

"Will we ever get back to normal?"

Swallowing a mouthful of bacon, MacCaig pursed his lips.

"Eventually, lass," he sighed. "Didn't take one of your sleeping tablets last night?" Spreading soft butter onto a piece of crispy toast as he spoke, MacCaig worked hard to sound interested in his daughter's usual morning moans. He could never understand how the children hadn't inherited his driven lifestyle. "Help things get a little more normal if you got yourself some sleep…"

"No," she said. "I'm trying to stop using those bloody toxic capsules. I can hardly get up in the mornings as it is."

'True."

Amelia thought about pouring herself a tea, then hesitated. "Who was that were you talking to?"

"That was my friend over in Dundee, Brian Macalister, the Chief Constable," MacCaig said, crunching into the crisp bread. "Jock's body will be released in a few days. We can then finalise the funeral arrangements and tidy things up a little, eh?"

"Did he tell you what the police were up to?"

MacCaig swallowed, and then wiped a few crumbs from his mouth with the cotton napkin. "Says there's not a lot happening. Not that he knows of anyhow."

Studying his daughter's tired features for a moment, he bit off another mouthful of toasted wholemeal.

"Though I'm not so sure Detective Lamont won't keep his nose clear of our charity work," he added, almost as an aside while chewing. "Apparently quite keen to explore Helen's financial role."

"Why would he be interested in that?"

"Oh, I'm not sure," said MacCaig, as his daughter sat down opposite and poured a tea. "But I think he sees things that don't exist. Typical policeman I suppose…"

"Dad," she asked carefully. "We haven't done anything wrong, have we?"

Putting the napkin down on the large yew-wood dining table, he went over to comfort her.

"There's nothing wrong, lass," he said.

Standing behind his daughter stroking her hair, he said: "The police have a job to do, but I dislike anyone getting too close to our private lives."

"But Dad, what have our private lives got to do with anything?"

Pushing away his hands, she got to her feet and turned to face him.

"Gio seems anxious," she said, uneasily. "You're both keeping everything to yourselves. Then you two have your little chats – after which, he spends hours on the phone to his father in Genoa!"

Nodding, MacCaig put his arms around her reassuringly.

"Jock's death upsets you, I know," he said. "But you mustn't worry about things. Gio and I have our business arrangements. His father ensures the funds flow smoothly for the charity work, so we have to talk frequently. He then has to discuss our proposed agreements with his father. Apparently old Genovese has to approve all the bank's exchanges of capital to satisfy Italian currency laws – and himself!"

Amelia MacCaig had always seemed much happier leaving financial matters to the men in her life. So long as a source of income existed, her preference was to leave well alone – providing it allowed an almost unchecked spending power. Currently, she was remunerated to the tune of £30,000 each year. Her title; Aid All Africa's Continental Press Liaison Officer, was a role established by her father to reduce tax obligations, and ensure her an income.

"As long as there aren't any problems, then that's fine," she said. "I just wish Gio was as communicative about things as you are."

"Don't worry," he said. "The financial crisis is still causing uncertainty in banks the world over. Even in countries like Switzerland. Why, I only heard this morning…"

"Yes," she interrupted. "I read on the Internet that some guy has traded away millions – and after all that's already happened with the Lehman Brothers. Terrible isn't it?"

"Yes," MacCaig agreed, surprised that she could name the Lehmans. "It's about as bad as it can get, so don't go harassing Gio, eh? He's only trying to make sure all moves smoothly in relation to our money. Any losses we, or his father take, are kept to a minimum, thanks to him."

"Yes, I see what's going on a little more clearly now," she said, relaxing a little.

Preferring to appear ignorant of the financial

dealings between the two men in her life, Amelia rarely challenged either of them for an in-depth response. After all, she felt certain that if you maintained an apparent ignorance about anything important, it was highly unlikely anyone could challenge you if things went wrong.

"Do you know what Jock's wishes were for a funeral and things? I mean, had he asked for burial, or a cremation, or what?"

She hadn't been fond of Jock MacCaig. In her view, he had been jealous of the children his father sired after the death of his own mother. Amelia believed this loss had led him to dislike both herself and Ewan, her elder brother. He frequently described them as spoiled or greedy – a view he had made known openly at times – and not only within family circles.

"We don't know what type of funeral Jock wanted and there's no will. We never discussed it…" After thinking for a moment, MacCaig said: "He didn't like cremations, I know that much."

Looking round the dining room, MacCaig caught his tired features in the mirror above what Mrs Robb called, the flower shelf. Close enough to absorb the scent of fresh yellow roses from the gardens she put there earlier, he smiled. Depending on the season, the green and gold Ruskin vase on the mantle always held flowers. Neatly trimmed, they fitted perfectly into the space between the ornate grey marble fireplace and a large gilt mirror he'd purchased at an auction in Sotheby's many years ago.

"We'll give him a good send off!" he said suddenly. For a moment the man seemed inspired by the simple beauty of his surroundings. "Though he'll not be interred in the family crypt."

"Because he wasn't one of us?"

"He *was* one of us," MacCaig said quietly. "But I think that's what he'd expect. I do know he disliked the very idea of the crypt; considered it elitist and old fashioned – even creepy."

"I don't blame him on that front."

Alex MacCaig had avoided condemning her assertion that Jock hadn't been 'one of us'. However, that he hadn't been one of the MacCaigs by birth was a fact; one with which Jock himself had never been entirely comfortable.

"He really was one of us, but not blood," he said, finally.

"Can I say, Dad..."

"Yes?"

"You don't seem terribly upset that he's gone, yet you were always so close to him."

"Yes," he confirmed. "We *were* close. He was a good lad."

MacCaig and his adopted son had been close, although when Catherine, his first wife died, the thorny subject of his only son's adoption had become increasingly uncomfortable. The discomfort had been amplified when he eventually remarried. The birth of his two, what he called, 'natural children', sealed matters.

At the age of nine, Jock had been unceremoniously packed off to private school in England. This choice had been made despite having the once famous Rannoch School right on their doorstep. Alex had done this in order to distance himself from what he'd thought, at that time, to be a serious error of judgment. He had gone ahead with adopting Jock to appease Catherine, who was distraught over her sterility. Subsequently, he had spent more than thirty years living with the outcome of an agreement he had never really wanted to make.

"So why aren't you very upset?"

"Well," he said uneasily. "Things weren't always comfortable between us, at least, not recently. We were arguing about silly little things. It reached a head in the past few months…"

He paused for a moment, as though unwilling to explain things further.

"Yes?"

Taking a deep breath, he continued reluctantly: "I told him he could go his own way, and that I would no longer support him financially through the charity. Then I took him off the AidenallafricA board and replaced him with Gio."

MacCaig seemed pensive, and almost appeared to be sad. After having exposed the rift with Jock, which had ended with his son's removal from the payroll *and* the board, he realised this was something he had not intended to reveal to his daughter. He had already asked Gio to say nothing till after the funeral.

Immediately seeing the opportunities in Gio's promotion, she looked pleasantly surprised, but said nothing.

"Gio didn't tell me."

"He wouldn't, at least not until it was disclosed publicly."

"I see…"

Reflecting on what she'd been told, Amelia felt angry. Secrets were one thing, but having important family and personal details kept from her was another matter.

"Still, no one would have wished such an end to a fine young life." MacCaig went on, although with deep compassion: "For that's what he had: a fine life."

"What else were you two so at loggerheads about?" she asked, ignoring his sentiment. "I mean; the way things are you sound like he's still here; like you're still rankled. Especially after you two being so close."

"I never fully understood what happened myself lass, that's why I sound like nothing's changed," he lied easily. "We had quarrelled a lot, though."

"I'm sorry," she said, now determined to unsettle him. "It must make his death really difficult to come to terms with, no matter how it looks to the rest of us."

The comment jarred, as she knew it would.

"What do you mean, 'the rest of us'?"

His anxieties centred on how others might view his having argued with the lad, then displacing him on the company board – especially since this occurred immediately prior to his murder. As far as he knew, till now, only Mackenzie Tosland had an inkling of the growing, unresolved enmity between them.

MacCaig knew nothing of the household staff gossip about a possible affair between Lady Helen and Jock, but he had his own suspicions; suspicions dealt with in the only way he knew how.

"I only meant Gio," she replied. "He said it was worrying that you didn't seem to miss Jock."

"And what the hell does he know?"

"Well," she said, apologetically. "I suppose, well... nothing..."

The sudden outburst of anger subsided as he looked at her strained features.

"Sorry for my irritation, but it's a sad thought that people didn't know how much I cared for my boy!"

"It's not that he, or anyone else for that matter, didn't know," she offered, thinking her father now appeared to be perplexed. "Perhaps it's all been a little too much for you to absorb, or something. Perhaps Gio misunderstood things."

"Amelia, no matter whether Jock was adopted or not – he was my son!"

Gently touching his arm for a moment, she then kissed his cheek and left, having opened an emotional Pandora's Box without knowing how to replace the seal.

MacCaig sat down at the table and finished the pot of tea. With the search team due to arrive by ten o'clock, he phoned the ghillie, telling him to get over to the jetty. It was now eight-thirty. The casually dressed peer thought it better to make his way down to the loch before the police arrived to see what he could find.

O'Leary was leaning casually against the bonnet of his car as the liveried Land Rover pulled-up beside the small, wooden pier. An odd spit of rain blew through the cool, damp air. It was indeed, autumn in the Highlands. He raised his jacket collar as MacCaig approached.

"You're sharp on the go, Lord MacCaig."

The well-groomed older man came over and extended a hand.

O'Leary asked: "Didn't expect company?"

"Just passing," the peer lied. Putting his hands into his jacket pockets, he said, "Saw you and wondered why you're here this early. Life too hectic in Pitlochry for sleep, is it?"

"It's the nightclubs," O'Leary joked. Gritting his teeth, he waved ineffectually at the cloud of midges that had gathered. "Strobe lights, pole dancers and loud music until five in the morning, then there's the breakfast bars…"

"It's the Highlands right enough, officer. You'll get used to the peace."

"Constable Beattie was here all night," said the detective. "So I thought it might be kind to let him go home to Perth."

"All night?"

"Aye, well, Lamont thought it better to make sure," he said, studying MacCaig's expression. "You never know, eh?"

"So what's his thinking here?" he asked, gesturing toward the Loch. "He must have a hunch to go on if someone's been stationed out all night in the cold."

"I'm not quite sure," O'Leary lied professionally, then tilted his head and gestured flippanty with a wave of his hand. "And even if I did…"

"I see…"

MacCaig was clearly disappointed that he couldn't gain the policeman's confidence. Then Tosland's noisy pick-up swung into view, pulling up by the jetty before he could try further to elicit any answers.

"Aye, aye!" Tosland gave his familiar greeting as he got out of the old Ford. Sticking the four-by-four's keys in the upper pocket of his green fisherman's waistcoat, which seemed to hang permanently from his shoulders under the scruffy, wax cotton jacket, he said, "Fine mornin' for it, eh?"

O'Leary nodded, left the men to their conversation and wandered over to where his colleague had suggested they might search for clues. According to him, there may be some evidence of Jock having been there, though the Englishman felt more sceptical. Lamont had asked them to search for an ejected shell casing from the gun used to shoot the deceased. He had sent an email with a map attachment. Opening it, the detective skirted the marked out zone and tried to picture what might have happened.

Hearing the two estate vehicles pull away, he breathed a sigh of relief. The loch was near flat calm, and a thin mist hung low over the cold, dark water. It was possible, he supposed, that Jock MacCaig could have sought shelter from his killers on the loch. Contemplating the gloomy, yet picturesque scene, he wondered what Lord MacCaig and Lady Helen were doing in the early hours of the Monday Jock died, since all household staff had taken the Sunday off.

Taking the mobile phone from his pocket, he checked for a signal, but was interrupted by the arrival of a police van. Then a large minibus turned into view and parked on the hard standing beside it. O'Leary was pleased to see the team arrive so early, for he felt somehow unnerved by this damp, lonely spot.

While the officers were unloading their equipment and getting the police dogs out of the van, he introduced himself to the sergeant. They laid the search map on the vehicle's warm bonnet. According to the burly uniformed figure, the suggested search area wasn't too large, but would still take a few hours to scan. Acknowledging his understanding of what was expected, he slid the map into a cellophane holder.

"We'll get down to business then," he said cheerfully.

While watching their meticulous search pattern develop, he grudgingly sent a confirmatory text to Lamont, but put nothing about MacCaig's arrival in the message. The detective understood that everything counted as evidence and any sloppy, or revealing text messages, might possibly end up in the wrong hands and used in court. He knew, as did every officer, that mobile phones had the unfortunate habit of losing themselves.

Chapter 13

Having enjoyed a little too much of his host's hospitality, Gio didn't waken till gone nine-thirty. The coffee left earlier by Amelia was cold by the time he emerged from beneath the duvet. As he finished showering, the leggy, elegant figure wandered into the en-suite and watched him towel-dry.

"Do you think my father suspects anything, or anyone?"

"No, my darling," the Italian replied. "I may be wrong, but he seems quite relaxed about everything. If I did not know him so well, I would be concerned that he seemed too, perhaps – how do you say, 'chilled'?"

"Yes, it's almost as though Jock's death was of no concern to him."

"It is very possible that is just what your brother was; of no concern – like a stranger," he suggested. "After all, he had an odd way of doing business with his own family…" He hesitated while choosing a pair of slacks from the wardrobe. "…and then arriving unannounced at our home in Genoa. Well, that would always present a problem, no?"

"Why he had to involve himself in the money transfers," she said. "It made no sense."

"He didn't involve himself," Gio corrected. "That interfering fool from the local bank in Banjul; the Gambian capital, where he was negotiating with local tribal leaders – he did the damage!"

"I thought you said that Jock had probed the transfers for himself."

"No, he hadn't; not at first. The local manager knew of Forex international money trading. He too was a trader who, unfortunately, had contacts in the City of London."

Pulling on a pair of grey slacks, he began working a fine, leather belt through the waistband.

"And?"

"Simple," he replied, sitting down. The athletic figure crossed his legs, unfolded and then carefully pulled on a new pair of grey silk socks. "The trader's contacts saw that the values of some of the currencies were higher on specific dates than those my father was feeding to Jock."

"But Jock had written valuations, hadn't he?" she asked. "And they came direct from the company?"

"No, not really," he said. "They came on company paper but from *our* bank's printer. The currency values had been altered by a few fractions and the transfer fees, shall we say, *adjusted*, while being traded."

"So how did the Gambian make Jock wise to the corrections?"

Gio shook his head and laughed ironically.

"He had shown the banker a printout of AidenallafricA's transactions," Gio explained. "Knowing the man would feed the information of the charity's wealth to greedy local chiefs."

"Why the hell did he do that?"

"Jock's experience was," Genovese said easily, "that the sight of wealth would entice the chiefs further upriver into a bit of 'honest' corruption, while still supporting the charity's work. That way they would not want to attack the workers, or steal the supplies and resources."

Amelia gave a wistful smile. With a grudging admiration, she suddenly realised just how resourceful Jock had been.

"So rather than having them openly robbing us, we'd feed them a cut to make sure we were allowed onto their territory?"

"It was that simple." Gio smiled, and then went on, "Uncomplicated, until it appears he told Jock that he thought the figures on his balance sheets were fictitious. The banker then offered to prove they were fakes!"

"So what did Jock do?"

"Well, he decided to challenge my father..." Gio shook his head indignantly. "Flew over to our home to confront him!"

"Just like that?"

"After he had checked that the banker's figures were correct," Gio explained, "he worked out that a large sum – he thought around two million Dollars US – was being creamed from the charity by my fathers' bank, or by Forex traders. He was unsure as to where it had gone."

"What's that in sterling?"

"About £1.4 million."

Amelia raised her eyebrows.

"A pretty penny, indeed," she remarked. "And was he?"

"You think my father a dishonest man?" Gio said defensively, narrowing his gaze. "You have met him. He is a man of great honour and integrity, is he not?"

"I would not argue with the impression he gives, Gio, but sometimes with money - well, there are many great temptations," she said carefully.

"And you are correct; indeed, you are correct..." Sensing the need to protect family honour, his tone was now becoming more resentful. "But perhaps you should ask your own father about the money movements, no?"

Offended by the implication that his father had anything to do with the fabrication of financial information for a trusted client, his response had been deeply indignant. Although convinced his father was above suspicion, he knew that the bank had been linked to many unsavoury characters over the years. Yes, they altered the exchange rates slightly in their favour, but not to levels that had produced a $2million profit. He believed in his father's interpretation of these matters: a client's behaviour was a matter entirely for his own conscience and his God. Their bank judged not one person – nor the sources of their wealth. They simply did as a client asked providing it broke no rules for which they could be publicly criticised.

"If Jock confronted your father, why didn't he tell him the truth, rather than risk the bank's reputation?"

she asked. "It would have been easier."

"Confidentiality," he replied curtly. "Our reputation survives on it!"

"What should we do?" she asked.

"Nothing." The Italian smiled easily and put his arms around her. "Absolutely nothing."

"Are you sure?"

"We have done no wrong and," he said gently, "providing the situation remains unchanged, neither has your father. We should leave it that way. It is a family matter. When your brother has been buried, I will speak quietly with him and explain my concerns."

Pushing him away, she said, "And you think father killed Jock?"

"Who knows? As I've said, it is a family matter: a matter of honour. I do not expect him to tell me, do I?"

"No, I suppose not..."

"When the time comes I will tell him what I know and believe. I hope he can understand my position and continue working with our bank." Gio's accent thickened as his temper darkened. "My position on AidenallafricA's Board gives me the right to challenge him, but what he has done is probably not so wrong."

"'Not so wrong' is an interesting turn of phrase," she said, shaking her head. "My father may have murdered his own son *and* pilfered money from the charity, Gio."

"None of this is fact," he corrected. "And, unless it is proved to the contrary, then his honour is seen to have been protected."

"Bloody honour," she said, "is that all you Italian men think about?"

"Honour is sometimes all that lies between a good society and a bad one," he said stoically. "Everything else is corruptible."

Throwing him a hard stare, she stormed out of the room.

*

Lamont said into the mobile, "Got us nowhere."

Having arrived at the shore as the search was concluding, he felt deeply disappointed. However, no despondency weighed on his features.

"There's no trace of anything on the loch's shore to help us – at least nothing the dogs, or a metal detector can find. They're retracing their last scan down near the water's edge, then they're off…"

Pressing the receiver to his ear, he had to listen carefully for a moment, as the uniforms' loud background chatter interrupted the conversation.

"Aye, sir," he confirmed, "got that. I'm going back up to the house to talk to the family…. yes, and tell her of our suspicions… no, there's no mobile phone on the horizon either. Text that number through and I'll try it while I'm there. It might not be Jock's, but you never know; may just ring somewhere audible nearby… Yes, I'll thank Phil Mason for the work on the laptop. Yes… I'll ask, thanks…" Lamont's eyes narrowed as he listened. "At least that's something… I'll tell the others… Aye, they're with me at the moment…Yes, bye."

Closing the call and slipping the mobile into his pocket, he walked over to the dog van, where O'Leary and Tortolano were chatting with the search team's sergeant. One of the team's alert Alsatians, tail wagging, wandered past him with its handler. Patting its head absently, Lamont stopped and looked out over the Loch.

"Great view of the hanging mist from here," said Tortolano, interrupting his thoughts. "Makes a damp, driech morning more palatable."

He was about to respond when a metal detector's intense, high-pitched squeal, cut through the damp air. Down by the shore, the officer had taken off his headphones and squatted low. They watched as he began moving a few of the larger stones with his hands.

"Here, sergeant!"

Slapping at a midge as it feasted on his neck, the detective observed intently as the uniform trotted unsteadily over the thirty yards of heavy shingle up to where the sergeant stood. He was carrying something small in his rubber-glove clad hand.

After a brief discussion with the officer, the tall sergeant picked his way quickly but deliberately over to where they waited. He held out a small, brass bullet case on the end of a biro.

"Weatherby 0.30 calibre," he stated knowledgably.

Donning a protective glove, the detective carefully took hold of the casing.

Studying it for a moment, he said: "Might be a chance of a print if we're lucky."

O'Leary leant toward him to get a better look.

He asked: "Could it have been one of the shells used on Jock MacCaig?"

"Possible," the sergeant replied, breathing heavily after his exertions. Alistair McCusker was six foot three, and nearly as broad, but his enthusiasm for the job more than overcame any physical effort.

"That one and the Winchester .308 are commonly used in deer hunting," he explained. Reflecting for a moment on the shooting of Jock MacCaig, he clarified the remark. "The Remington JHP is more commonly used for accuracy, but the 'ammo' wouldn't have mattered too much with a big target like the MacCaig lad. Especially if he wasn't too far from the shore."

"Shooting your thing then?" Tortolano asked, impressed by the officer's knowledge.

"Aye," he grinned. "Up in these parts with the gun – a fine Sako rifle, Weaver Scoped, whenever the missus'll set me free."

Shaking his head at the broad knowledge of guns the man seemed to have, Lamont asked: "Are you saying that anyone with knowledge of a rifle could have pulled off those two shots?"

"Not quite," the sergeant said, and thought for a moment. "One through the heart and one through the head? Unless there was a great deal of luck involved, I'd guess whoever fired those two shots knew shooting – and the gun they were using – very well. Would need to have set the scope up with a couple of practise shots too."

"So it's likely the firearm was owned by the shooter?"

"Not necessarily," McCusker said. "But, in my opinion, it's more than likely."

Lamont studied at the shell case again before dropping it carefully into a small plastic evidence bag. He handed it to Tortolano.

"I've got to go up to the house," he said. "Can you whisk it down to forensics and get them to dust it for prints and lab it for DNA? Then check for suppliers of the shells and see who bought some in the last year or two?"

"Pleasure."

"Take the Mondeo," he said, glancing at O'Leary. "We should be in Pitlochry by the time you get back."

"Yes, if you must, but remember it's my only means of transport in this bloody wilderness!" O'Leary said. Then his face softened and he shrugged. "Ah, why not. I want to go up to the house anyhow."

"If you've got an objection," Lamont said, "spit it out."

"No," O'Leary muttered dryly. "What would I object about?"

The Scot was about to comment when the message tone on his mobile sounded. He glanced at Tortolano. "What time do you make it?"

"Eleven thirty. Forgot your watch?"

"In the jewellers..."

"Use the phone," she said, shaking her head. "It comes up on the screen?"

He shrugged and transferred the number from the text into his mobile directory.

"We'll see you later in Pitlochry, OK?" O'Leary threw his car keys over. "And no rallying!"

"Let's get up to Druin and try for some answers," the Scot said. "Maybe we'll get a response to this phone number. You never know."

He shouted across to the sergeant: "Big thanks to you and the team. Great help. Good work."

The officer waved acknowledgment and continued packing.

As he put on the seat belt, O'Leary asked: "What are we after?"

"Well," Lamont began, as he fired up the diesel, "we need to figure out whether the daughter could have flown back to Scotland, as the ghillie seems to think. We also need to talk to the Lord and Lady of the house again about their relationship with Jock. There are some email files that our tech guy, Mason's uncovered. They're from the deceased to her Ladyship – and with replies. Not tasty, but according to Moon, not without their romantic implications either. Hardly mother and son stuff, let's put it that way."

"Do you think we're likely to get anywhere?"

Lamont's face held a steely determination as he replied: "No, but it's time to get the gloves off. We now know enough to say definitively that the family isn't squeaky-clean, whatever public image they project. Giving them a little nudge might help."

O'Leary took a bag of cheese and onion crisps from his pocket and tore it open. "Are you sure about doing that?"

"We know they're not a tightly knit bunch," he replied. "I think that allows us some flexibility. It's already opened a few doors."

"So you think…" O'Leary spluttered, sounding unconvinced as he crunched greedily through a large mouthful, "that whatever's going on could be uncovered by putting a little pressure on them?"

He offered the bag toward Lamont, who raised his left hand in refusal.

"Yes, I think some pressure might help."

"Have we any concrete evidence at all?"

Exiting a sharp, tree-lined bend in the narrow road the Scot was forced to brake violently. A Royal Mail van, its indicators flashing, had parked with its rear end jutting out. He muttered an obscenity in the direction of the postman, straightened the car and drove on.

Exhaling loudly, he said: "There was the e-mail from Jock to young Genovese's father."

"Is it of any real value?"

"Yeah," he confirmed. "The note said that following their telephone conversation, he'd be leaving Africa that morning for Genoa. He was hoping to meet with Genovese senior at his home in the village of Saint Eusebio later that day."

O'Leary thought for a moment and watched as more dark, heavy clouds drifted over the rugged landscape. A strong breeze was getting up as it neared midday and the native alder and oak trees were already shedding their leaves. He finished the crisps, screwed the empty pack into a ball and tucked it into his jacket pocket.

Turning his attention back to Lamont, he asked: "Did the note say what the purpose of their meeting was?"

"Only that he wanted to see the AidenallafricA bank transactions in print."

"When was this?"

"One week before he was removed from the charity's Executive Board of Trustees at an extraordinary meeting."

"And you think that's a strong enough link to push things with MacCaig?"

"Well, it's shortly before he returned here and collected three bullets."

"So he flew from Africa up to Genoa, then returned here directly after meeting old man Genovese?"

"Seems that way," Lamont said thoughtfully. "And then went for a prolonged cruise on the Loch..."

"Package holidays ain't what they used to be."

Involuntarily, the Scot found himself chuckling.

"Can of petrol and a match was all he needed for the ultimate Viking experience."

Castle Druin pulled into view and the two officers braced themselves. Aspects of the investigation were crystallising and both knew it. It was about getting a result: though for Lamont the right result and a conviction.

The vibration of his phone interrupted the

detective's thoughts as he parked by the castle. Reading the text, he nodded.

"That sample taken from the loch side yesterday was most probably canine," he confirmed. "There were one or two more like it nearby, which suggests that the pack had stopped there, probably after a morning run from the kennels got their systems in gear."

"So?" O'Leary said, sounding unconvinced.

"Well, our supposition that Jock was being hunted," he explained, "seems ever more plausible."

Getting out of the car, Lamont cast a pensive eye over the estate toward the native trees bordering several acres of tidy parkland.

"Someone who knew both the dogs and this landscape used them to track him."

"But was the dog stuff fresh?" said O'Leary, swiping crisp fragments from his suit jacket as he spoke.

"Yes," the Scot confirmed, focussing on the castle portico. "And that means there are probably fewer murder suspects than we had five minutes ago."

"Unless we're wandering along the wrong path entirely," O'Leary proposed.

"Aye, well," he murmured grudgingly. As they approached the imposing entrance, something was nagging him again, but he dismissed it, knowing that not working alone was probably clouding his judgement. "That's not out of the question, either."

*

Busy hospital outpatient departments can be places of great introspection as people weigh their often complex health and future options. But for Elspeth, this was very familiar territory. She inhabited a world filled with stories of heart-warming bravery, courage and success, juxtaposed against grim failures, as the care process occasionally failed in its battle against disease and ill health.

Not unlike the vast majority of hospital waiting areas, the white-walled, open plan space was full of anxious faces and mothers with noisy, bored kids. Phones flashed, receptionists smiled tolerantly and printers whined, as the never-ending stream of humanity sought treatment. Walking ever more anxiously until she reached the consulting room door, the logical woman now fought to avoid running from the scene.

'Professor Allen', the sign read. Taking a moment to compose herself, Elspeth opened the door and pushed away another barrier between herself and the truth.

Lifting her eyes from the computer screen, the middle-aged secretary smiled.

"Prof Allen's expecting you, Doctor. You've to go straight through."

Hugh Allen rose from behind his desk and greeted her warmly.

"Elspeth lass," he beamed. "How are you?"

"Well, you know…"

"Grab a seat, grab a seat," he blustered, before she could elaborate. "Can I take your coat?"

"No, no, Hugh, I'm fine."

The anxiety in her voice was clear to anyone who knew her, and Hugh Allen knew her well.

"How was France?"

"Just what we needed," she said. "And the recommendation was great, thanks. What a find: sun, idyllic setting, good food – in fact everything you said. I brought you back a bottle of the local vintage – forgot to bring it with me today though."

"That's no surprise, but thanks anyway. Something to look forward to," he said, as she made herself comfortable. "Great that you enjoyed it. Eileen and I have been over several times. Love it!"

Resting one leg over the corner of the desk, the doctor unconsciously opened his top white coat button and collected his thoughts.

"Sorry Elspeth, this will be a little difficult," he said. "I rarely have to consult with members of our fraternity; far less ones whom I've known as friends for twenty years."

Elspeth had been to university with Hugh Allen. Even though he had been in the year above, they had become friends through their common research interests. Both were part of a larger circle from the medical faculty that still met socially. Having held a crush on him during those years, she was now extremely thankful the opportunity had never arisen for them to become lovers.

"Tell it like it is," she said stoically. "Please, I need to know."

"Like it is, is like it feels, Elspeth," he said quietly.

"The MRI scan shows some spread, though it's probably not been too rapid."

"What do *you* think?" she asked anxiously.

Now working hard to control the fear and the panic, she could feel her stomach churn.

"If the growth only began around the time you spotted it three weeks ago," he said carefully, "then there's a good chance we can excise the worst of it."

The word excise, she knew, meant 'cut out', and probably as a total mastectomy. Her own knowledge had allowed her to absorb that much without having to be told.

"And," she asked carefully. "You said, 'the worst of it'?"

He looked at her and shook his head.

"Don't honestly know, Elspeth. If I get you into hospital on Sunday, we can have you in theatre Monday morning at the latest. The biopsy and scan have defined the lesion, but now we have to control it."

"Take me through it," she said, her voice now weak. "I've sort of lost where things are up to in my panic."

"Well," he said, picking her notes off the desk and leafing through the reports. "Typically, you have a triple negative cancer."

Uncomfortable with his own candidness, he watched her for a moment.

"Go on Hugh, I'm a big girl!" she urged, forcing a smile.

"Yes, well," he said, gathering himself. "Okay, in your case our cell studies show that it has occurred because of the BRCA 1 failure. In other words, the BRCA 1 gene that normally inhibits cancer cell formation, as you know, is dysfunctional..."

"And the cell studies of the tumour?"

"The oncotype DX studies we're conducting of the cancer's cells will let us know what type of chemotherapy has the best chance of controlling it."

The word *controlling* sent a shiver down her spine, for she wanted to hear the words *kill*, or *eliminate*.

"Control, Hugh," she said breathlessly. "Just control...."

"Elspeth," he responded gently. "I haven't lied to a patient in all my years of medicine. I'm not starting now with one of the dearest people I know."

"Prognosis, Hugh," she asked gloomily, her eyes welling with tears. "I know it's guesswork, but please, what do you think?"

"If we can do better than control the growth, then I'll be the happiest man in the world – next to that husband of yours," he offered. "If not... well, with this particular cell structure there shouldn't be an 'if not'. We've got to it early enough and I'm the best."

Knowing he was being honest, Elspeth quickly wiped her tear-stained face.

"When do you want me in?"

"Sunday morning," he said firmly. "And go over to Rosythe Hall."

"Why there?"

"Haven't got a window here, Elspeth; NHS list as long as your arm," he said, shaking his head. "And besides, the after-care's better..."

Hugh Allen let his words hang, for she appeared shattered by the news. Putting a gentle hand on her shoulder, he rose from the edge of the desk.

"Have you discussed anything with Crieff yet?"

"No," she said eventually. "I'll need to do it soon though."

Hugh Allen's pager buzzed as she spoke. Glancing down he flipped the off switch before placing it carefully on the desk. Turning his attention back to his patient, he crouched slightly, looking directly into her eyes.

"Before Sunday, Elspeth! You'll need to talk to him before you go in," he said pointedly.

The advice was gentle, though much firmer now.

"He'll have to come to terms with things *with* you, not on his own. Important for you both, I think."

Hugh Allen paused to allow her to absorb the words.

"I can't begin to understand how difficult this will be, but you'll need him with you all the way from now on."

"I know," she said. "But the time hasn't been right."

Nodding his understanding, he asked: "How is he, anyway?"

Deliberately diverting focus away from the cancer, Hugh Allen knew he still had strong feelings for this dear friend. However, today he sought only recognition of his gentle patient management style. That was enough for him.

"Just the usual," she smiled. "Kind, distracted, pre-occupied, direct, busy – a little bit like you taking care of me."

"Well," he said, with a broad grin. "I've been outed. Still, get the man on your side quickly. He'll have his own anxieties to deal with. It'll take time – you of all people must know that, Elspeth."

Pushing herself up from the chair, she sighed.

"Thanks, Hugh." Her warmth was genuine, affectionate. "If there's anything I can do."

"Not just now, Elspeth," he said. "There'll be plenty of time for that later. That bottle of fine wine you brought back sounds good though."

"*Fine?*"

"You'd bring nothing less for a friend," he said, and putting his arm around her shoulder, guided her out into the corridor and waved goodbye. Returning to the office he spoke to his secretary.

"Tell Rosythe that we need a table and recovery suite for early Monday," he began. "Oh, and ask for the most senior sisters – tell them MacConnaghy's a must for theatre. And if anyone asks questions, tell him or her to bill me for the overtime required. I'll phone Matron myself later to confirm everything. Remind me."

With those words Hugh Allan was already heading toward the files on his desk to prepare for the next case.

Chapter 14

"Not be better to take Lord MacCaig in for questioning?" O'Leary suggested. "My guess is he thinks he can mess us around a bit. This is his land: the ancestral home. Perhaps he feels too secure?"

As they stood in front of the portico, Lamont looked at him.

"On the other hand," he offered. "Perhaps that's what we need."

"Why?"

The Manchester detective was trying hard not to sound exasperated.

"Well, if we take him in now the man knows exactly where he is with us: prime suspect land. Whereas, leave him here and he's probably less guarded and, hopefully, more informative."

"More likely thinks his allies in Dundee and Edinburgh – Chief Constable Brian Macalister, for example – are protecting him and his family in there from the wicked filth," he grunted, gesturing at the castle.

"Possible."

"And with that scenario, he's probably playing us along until we get bored and go away."

Raising his eyebrows, the Scot thought hard for a moment.

"Aye, there's something in what you're saying, right enough. I wondered that myself on the way up here this morning..."

O'Leary mimicked his habit of scuffing at the compacted gravel with his foot, but said nothing.

"But despite what we know about the family's financial dealings and relationships," the Scot added, "I'm yet to be convinced that the killer's in this house."

Taking his hands from his trouser pockets, O'Leary said: "What are we here for, then? I mean, are we here for his Lordship, or not?"

"His Lordship, as you call him, might appear bent, but we can't really prove that. At least not just yet," he said. "And no, before you ask, I don't think the old banker in Genoa hired a hitman to take a pop at Jock."

"What then?"

"See that Loch over there," Lamont said, pointing down the slope toward the west. "If I want to fish that there are two types of lure I can use."

O'Leary watched his partner with amusement written large on his features.

"If I want a quick catch, I throw a nice silver spinner in and let the fish rush after it. Easy." Lamont pursed his lips. "However, if I want to chase the fish and learn about it, I'll cast a fly over its resting place then observe, learn and try to get it to bite. If it takes the bait, I have the fish, knowledge of it and the real satisfaction from knowing I've outsmarted it."

"Sounds like we've been fishing in the wrong pool after all," O'Leary quipped.

"I'm saying this fish needs playing," he stated firmly. "We know too little about what lies behind these doors and I don't like *ones-that-got-away* stories. We want to get to the bottom of MacCaig's business, as well as catching whoever murdered his son. To me, it all feels wrong here."

"Anything you say," O'Leary agreed tamely, managing not to sound too sceptical. "Let's just hope you're not opening doors you don't know how to close!"

The Scot threw him a dirty look.

"Why do I get the feeling you're fishing me as well as the MacCaigs?"

O'Leary shrugged.

"You never recognise a good catch when you land one, I'd guess."

The Scot's detective wasn't thrown by his partner's one-liner and ignored the attempt to distract his thinking.

"Think I may have asked the wrong questions…"

"What should *we* have asked?" O'Leary tried, emphasizing the 'we'. "There are three of us on this case, not just you."

Lamont threw his fellow officer a glance and said: "Who else was here last Sunday?"

"What?"

"The staff all had the weekend off, so who *was* here?"

O'Leary seemed confused, and as Lamont looked at the man the penny began to drop as to what had been troubling him.

Agendas, he thought, *Good teamwork has a set of agendas...but O'Leary has one of his very own.*

"We know where Lady Helen and Lord MacCaig were," he said, more easily. "The daughter and the boyfriend were in France."

"Jock was here, and presumably the gamekeeper too," O'Leary added.

"Till Sunday, yes," the Scot agreed. "But did anyone else come here on the Sunday?"

"Not that we know of..."

O'Leary chewed on his bottom lip.

"Did the ghillie see anyone else?"

Lamont scratched his chin, then absently tucked his shirt further into his trousers and straightened the waistcoat. He gestured toward the rugged terrain north of the estate.

"Well, we know Tosland lives a mile or more that direction," he said. "He'd have no idea if anyone else was around. So while we're busy trying not to offend anyone, we're not asking the right questions."

During his first visit to Castle Druin, O'Leary should have enquired more thoroughly, but was reticent about upsetting anyone after being warned off by Inspector MacDougall.

"Okay, so we may have bollock'sed," he said. "But there's no point in wearing hair shirts. I mean; it could all be speculative."

"You believe that?"

The Scot knew that statistically, nearly ninety percent of those questioned in police investigations refused to answer any questions. So far they had been lucky; the MacCaigs hadn't closed the door on them and by remaining tactful, they might still get any additional information needed.

Pressing the ornately decorated call system, O'Leary could hear it ring several times before the door finally opened and Amelia MacCaig appeared, looking a little dishevelled and tired. She invited them into the grand hall.

"Sorry it took so long, but Dad's with the ghillie. They're out in the rear courtyard somewhere and the housekeeper's busy preparing lunch," she explained apologetically. Then, in a conspiratorial whisper, added: "Mrs Robb's as deaf as a post anyway!"

"No need to whisper then, I'd have thought." Lamont added tersely: "Is Mr Genovese still with you?"

Although stung for a moment by the pointed response, she recovered quickly.

"He's in the study, working. Why?"

"Could you ask him to join us please?"

Leaving them in the hall, she disappeared up the heavily carpeted stairs. While they waited, Lamont rang the mobile number that they thought may have belonged to Jock.

After a while, he said, "Sod all."

He put his own phone back into his pocket

"No surprises there, eh?"

"No," the Scot said, and shrugged. "Unless someone else had it, the battery would probably be flat days ago."

They were looking up at large oil painting of Colonel Stirling, the SAS founder, in his Scots Guards regalia, when MacCaig's daughter reappeared with her boyfriend.

"Father idolised him," she said, gesturing up at the piece.

"Hero of mine too," O'Leary concurred. "Tough man, right enough."

Unhappy at being kept waiting, Lamont interrupted the polite dialogue.

"Was anyone else here the weekend Jock died?"

"No," she said. "Not as far as I know, but you'll have to ask my father."

"And you, Mr Genovese? Do you know if anyone else was here?"

The slim Italian shrugged.

"We were in France," he replied, surprised by the question. "You were with us there on the Friday evening!"

"But Jock had been murdered on the Monday," said Lamont, coldly.

"So?"

"And neither of you left France during your holiday? I mean you could have returned by private jet, then left again."

Gio shook his head slowly, and still appeared confused by the questions.

"You own a private hire airline firm after all," the detective added.

"That is a preposterous!" the Italian fired back. "You are implying that one of us could have flown here, killed poor Jock, and then flown back to France?"

"Not implying anything," said O'Leary. "We're trying to establish who was in the castle grounds at the time of the murder."

"Have you finished?" Amelia demanded.

"Yes," he replied, almost smiling. "I'm sorry to ask these difficult questions, but we're not here to be sociable – as you must know."

"You may not be being sociable, but you're also not being very, I think, *sensible*, detective," the lithe Italian posed, turning away.

"Thank you both for your time," said O'Leary, but the couple were already heading back up the stairs without acknowledging the courtesy.

He muttered: "I think you've nicked his 'biscotti'."

Lamont said nothing as he headed off to the kitchen. Putting his head round the door, he asked the housekeeper if she could contact Lord MacCaig.

Mrs Robb took umbrage at the request, pointing out that she believed her employer was in the rear courtyard somewhere, but that she had better things to do than go hunting around for him.

The detectives glanced toward each other, but just

as they turned to leave, the elegant, stocking-footed Helen MacCaig came in through the rear hallway. Pale-coloured tights covered her lengthy legs, and the red woollen cardigan still hung loosely under the well-worn wax jacket. A skin-hugging, blue Lycra vest§ held pert breasts close to her bodyline.

Greeting them cheerfully, she washed her hands at the sink. Having been interrupted, Mrs Robb cleared her throat and tutted loudly.

"Sorry," she said. "My hands never seem to be clean when we meet, thanks to having to take off those muddy wellingtons, so I've given them a wash just for you."

As she drew close, Lamont couldn't help but notice the lazy smile shaping her full lips. He now understood how MacCaig had been swept under this woman's spell. Her manner and bearing, allied to a fabulous figure, could certainly draw an admirer closer than they might wish.

"It's good to see you both again, detectives," she said in familiar husky tones.

"Can we go through?" he asked, gesturing toward the dining room. "We'd like to ask a few questions."

"Can you bring us coffee, Mrs Robb?"

"Aye Lady Helen," the older woman said gruffly, throwing a forced smile. "Nothing else to do today, right enough. I'll bring it straight away. It'll have to be an 'instant', if you don't mind."

Glancing at each other, the detectives followed Helen MacCaig to the dining room.

"Too much work, or too short of patience?"

O'Leary asked.

"Both today," she said, as they reached the table and made themselves comfortable. "She's indispensable though. It's almost impossible to find someone with her qualities prepared to travel in and out locally."

"She's from the village?"

"No, Pitlochry."

"No chance of her indulging in gossip about the household, then?" asked Lamont.

"No," she replied. "Works six days although lives in five nights a week. Keeps her own house in the town. Alex says that in all the twenty or so years he's employed her, he's never had cause to question her confidentiality."

"Being a bit deaf must help, eh?"

"She's possibly not that deaf, detective. She can hear most things fairly well – when she wants."

"Was she fond of Jock?" O'Leary asked.

"Loved him," she replied. "He was quite young when she first came into service. Took him under her wing, so to speak. Apparently Alex's second wife didn't like that too much either."

"How has she been since his death?"

"She was devastated when Jock's body was discovered."

Wanting to move things along, Lamont glanced at his colleague.

"Were there any other house guests here after Mrs

Robb left for Pitlochry on Saturday evening?" he asked. "Or on Sunday for that matter."

"There are always comings and goings here," she said easily. "Ewan wanders in unannounced, and then there's Cameron; we use him for global accountancy matters. It's easier for him to visit weekends."

"And he doesn't mind? I mean, working at weekends..."

"Not if you like shooting as much as Alistair Cameron does!"

"Was he here the weekend before last?"

"Probably, yes – I think," she said uncertainly. "Though I don't always see him when he comes up for the shooting."

"Just for the shooting?"

"Yes," she said. "He and Alex have been acquaintances for years. Sometimes he doesn't need to chat about money, he just visits."

"What's his particular financial specialty?"

"Accounting mostly," she began. "Although he handles our family investment portfolio as well."

"And did you see him the weekend Jock went missing?"

"Funny you should say that," she said. "Now that I think about it, I saw his car in the rear yard on the Sunday."

Feeling a tingle of excitement rise in the pit of his stomach, Lamont still kept his features deadpan. He knew this lady was capable of deliberately misleading them. Her apparent sexual congress with Jock was testament to that.

"Does he have a wife, or friend who visits with him?"

"His wife pops up occasionally," she said wistfully, "but she's still a close friend of Alex's ex-wife and doesn't really take to me, I'm afraid. I see her when we have more formal events – Burns Suppers and the like – but we rarely speak more than a few words."

"I see," said Lamont.

He was about to ask again about her relationship with Jock when Alex MacCaig came in from the main hallway.

"Morning gentlemen," he said brightly, "At least I think it's still morning."

Throwing his jacket over a chair, he checked the time.

"Ten after twelve, never mind," he said. "Close enough."

"So my stomach says," O'Leary added.

Neither officer got up to greet their host.

"Has Helen been entertaining you then?"

"She was telling us about your friend, Alistair Cameron."

"Ah, yes," MacCaig began. "Alistair and I have been good friends for many years."

"How did you meet?"

The wealthy businessman thought for a moment.

"Well, in past years my father felt the estate was running into difficulties. He established that we needed more than just accountancy. We needed to move forward before the old house fell apart," he explained. "So he asked me to find someone with some investment acumen. He wanted to develop the limited money we were taking from the family's businesses at that time."

"And how did you find out about Mr Cameron?"

"Well, when I asked around, there were only three or four wealth managers in Scotland worth their salt," MacCaig said with conviction. "From those I researched, Cameron Corporate were the ones with the best portfolio results. Yes, there were a few well-established companies and banks with excellent reputations, but none particularly impressed me when I spoke with them. Alistair was the new kid on the block and seemed to have developed a formidable reputation. The others worked under a blanket of management layers. You couldn't see the wood for the trees."

"Money world a bit cloak and dagger back then?" O'Leary interrupted.

"There was 27% inflation, major industrial upheaval, worker revolt and the changes brought about by Mrs Thatcher," MacCaig elaborated. "Anyone who could make money in that climate had to be good. Cameron Corporate, through Alistair, were more than able to demonstrate an ability to invest a portfolio wisely – both for short-term gain and long-term security. As I said, the others had to contend with layers of management and internal scrutiny. Alistair saw an opportunity and bought into it there and then, while the others were twiddling their thumbs, or doing risk assessments!"

"And what role do Cameron Corporate play in AidenallafricA's money transfers?" O'Leary enquired.

Having revealed to MacCaig that their interests had widened, Lamont glanced at Lady Helen for a reaction. Although her face gave little away, MacCaig himself looked thoughtful, as though thrown by the question.

"Cameron Corporate take the Aid All Africa's monies," he said carefully, "and invest them in the money transfer market through their partner company in London. They use AidenallafricA as the trading vehicle for the Forex market, as you obviously know."

"And how closely do you keep in touch with the money's investment growth, or otherwise, while it's in this market?" Lamont probed.

"I'd be less than honest if I said I understood the complexities of financial trading on the international money markets," the man responded, sounding slightly embarrassed. "My lovely wife here helps keep a personal eye on things during her regular London visits."

"Does that satisfy you and the other Trustees?" O'Leary asked.

"We operate strictly within the Trustee Act of 2000," Helen MacCaig said defensively. "If there is any wrong doing in relation to our investments, then you'll find no guilt within these walls, officer. We do very little different to other charities…" Hesitating, she stared petulantly at O'Leary for a moment. "Lord MacCaig has run the charity for many years and brought great benefit to needy children across the African continent."

"And you have no concerns about gambling on Forex with donations given to meet the needs of the impoverished over there?"

"It's too easy to talk in terms of gambling charity assets," the man responded firmly. "We only do what the banks do – though more effectively, I may add."

"Effectively?" The Scots detective challenged the word, tilting his head slightly. "Forgive me saying, but if banks trade and lose money, then you still get your pound back. As far as I can see, if Forex trading fails for AidenallafricA, then you've thrown away other people's money. Money given in good faith..."

"Do I need my solicitor here, Detective Lamont?" he asked, coldly. "I mean; you appear to be inferring wrong-doing on our part."

"No, Lord MacCaig, you won't need your solicitor. The last thing we intended to do was cause upset." he replied, a wistful smile dancing on his features. "I think we'll leave it at that for the day though."

"Yes," Lady Helen said supportively. "I should hope you do. I've never heard Lord MacCaig's integrity so insulted."

"Really," O'Leary muttered.

Glaring at him, Helen MacCaig sighed and rose from the table.

"I think, if you prefer, Lord and Lady MacCaig," Lamont said, politely. "We could further our discussions down at the Pitlochry Office in the company of your solicitor – if we need to speak to you again, of course."

After waiting a moment in silence for the Peer to

respond, Lamont nodded and turned to leave.

"It's up to you," O'Leary added, following him. "We'll let you know if we wish to further the matter. You can decide then." Stopping, he turned toward the couple. "Is that alright with you?"

"Perfectly," said Helen MacCaig curtly.

"Oh, by the way, Lord MacCaig," said O'Leary, as he reached the entrance. "Are there any other sources of money being handled by Cameron Corporate for you personally – or the estate for that matter?"

"We've said all we need to today," Helen MacCaig interrupted.

"As you please." He shrugged and strode out into the shelter of the portico.

Alex MacCaig said nothing as the detective pulled the door closed. He stood impassively, hands in pockets, looking thoroughly depressed. The Scots detective thought his present dejected image would be hard to mimic. It was certainly no act, and seemed in stark contrast to his cheerful introduction only ten minutes earlier.

As they strode over the concourse, O'Leary took a deep breath of mild, clean, highland air.

"You know," he said chirpily, and exhaling loudly. "I could get the hang of living up here."

"It'll never get the hang of you," the Scot said airily. "You've no need to worry about that!"

"Yes, you're probably right there," he replied. "We'd better get the address of Cameron Corporate, eh?"

It had started throwing heavy spits of rain on a strengthening breeze and they hurried across to the car.

"Yes," agreed Lamont, thoughtfully. "We need a long chat with Cameron before he has time to gather his thoughts."

"Sure enough."

Now believing O'Leary had another, wider agenda with the MacCaigs, he asked: "What were the *other sources of money* you were fishing for?"

"Nothing," the detective replied. "Just curious."

Even though feeling certain there was more to this detective's line of enquiry than mere curiosity, the Scot decided to let it go. O'Leary would undoubtedly give him nothing, whatever line of enquiry he was covertly pursuing.

On reflection, Lamont knew there could be a thin line between the way the Charities Commission treated the two terms: investment and trading when it came to trustees' use of funds. He understood the distinction between those two, in relation to taxes payable by the charity, could be very broadly interpreted. Any financial wrongdoing would be difficult to prove. Perhaps, he thought, this was what his English colleague was chasing.

"By using a separate trading company," Lamont posed. "It could be that the financial side of this messy business is as much about tax avoidance as pilfering for personal benefit."

"Lost me," O'Leary said, quickly pulling the passenger door wide as the heavens opened. "You were right though, when you said we needed to solve the murder first."

Sliding quickly into the Audi out of the downpour, Lamont said: "Ah, were life that simple."

"What's on your mind?"

"None of this is simple," he added. "It's likely they'd claim that AidenallafricA – although a trading company for Forex – was in their opinion, an ethical line of investment."

"How do they get away with that?" O'Leary asked.

"My guess is they'd contend that the trading company isn't set up to make a profit, only to prevent others, i.e. the banks, from making use of charity money to further their own profits. And the banks are hardly popular at the moment, are they?"

"And tax?"

"That's for HM Revenue and Customs to sort out," the Scot winked. "As you said; let's just find the murderer."

Chapter 15

The two detectives met Tortolano back at the Pitlochry office and briefed her about the MacCaig interview. She listened intently as they recounted the key components of their dialogue at the castle. They then offered their respective opinions on the financial dealings of the charity.

"And neither of you think the MacCaigs were directly involved in their son's death?"

"That about sums it up," said Lamont, gesturing absently. He was staring through the office window at the comings and goings. There had been a surfaced thoroughfare on the A9 route since Wade's military road was built in the eighteenth century. A busy dual carriageway, hidden behind heavy woodland, now carried goods traffic and tourists to Inverness and beyond.

As the season drew to a close, fewer backpackers and roof-box adorned cars could be seen passing on the old Athol Road. For those not dependent on passing trade for a living, it was time to breathe a sigh of relief. Much of the clutter would disappear from the walkways, and shops would become free from most of the imported tartan tat. Sadly, he thought, the visitors didn't take the grim weather with them when they left. Hands in pockets, he watched as heavy rain droplets spattered off the roof of his car.

"What do you think?" asked Tortolano.

"Sorry," he said. "I was just thinking. Something's bothering me, but I've no idea what."

"What?" Tortolano looked amused. "About the MacCaigs, perhaps?"

"I agree with you, O'Leary," he said. "Something's not right..."

"Helen, Alex, the ghillie, Alistair Cameron?" she tried.

The Scot shook his head.

"Could it be difficult to believe that Lord MacCaig has little idea about the money movement?" O'Leary added. "I mean, I got the impression he's trying hard not to sound too aux fait with financial management."

"Aye, that's a tough one," he replied, pensively. "The money world appears to leave him cold, yet they're involved in complex and risky trading. Like all charities, it's a business centred on the use of money. Do good work, get more publicity, and funds are raised more easily."

Taking a tissue from the box on the desk, he wiped his nose and turned back to the window. He felt sure a cold was coming on.

"It seems certain Alistair Cameron understands the Forex movements implicitly," he went on, tossing the tissue into a metal bin by the desk. Taking a mint from his pocket, he stuck one between his teeth without offering them around. "And it could be that Jock has spoken to him before, or after, challenging his father."

"Or that MacCaig himself told Cameron of Jock's discovery," O'Leary chipped in.

"Does Cameron use a gun?" Tortolano enquired.

"Regularly," Lamont said, deliberately poking the glasses further up the bridge of his nose.

"According to MacCaig's wife, he's up here most week-ends," O'Leary added.

"You going to interview him?"

"Made an appointment with him for six this evening," he said. "His office is on Bothwell Street, in Glasgow's city centre."

"Want me along?" O'Leary asked.

"Or me?" she said, raising her lined eyebrows.

"It'll take two, right enough…"

He turned to O'Leary.

"Mind if I give her a sniff at the money man? It's a long way there and back for you."

"As long as you don't give her that 'sniff' you're carrying around with you," he nodded, "or the way things are going you'll both be in bed with a hot water bottle…"

Tortolano cleared her throat noisily and blushed.

"I think he means our own beds," her partner said, shaking his head and throwing a hard look at the Englishman. "Those Irish roots will get you in trouble one of these days."

"Don't worry, I'm in enough bother as it is," he replied, drily. "I'm even afraid of saying anyone has a jaundiced opinion for fear of a colour prejudice accusation being launched against me."

The young detective sniggered.

"Talking of prejudice," said her partner. "Do you mind putting together a report of today's interviews for Moon? I'll sort my own notes tonight. Spent too long covering my back on paper yesterday and not enough time asking questions. Anything we get out of Cameron this evening might confuse things."

"No problem," O'Leary said. "Be a pleasure. Can you give me a ring after you've finished in Glasgow?"

Nodding confirmation, Lamont then raised his eyebrows in the direction of the young detective. "Right, Stirling; then down to the big City at rush hour, eh?"

"Lead the way," she said, smiling.

As they left the office Lamont's phone toned confirmation of a text message. He was reading it as he got to the bottom of the stairs.

'Can we chat tonight? Missing you. Need you.

Elspeth

X

Lamont felt a moment of contentment as he accompanied the attractive plain-clothes detective out of the building. He opened the car with the remote as she ran across the courtyard through heavy rain, and then hurried to join her. While they waited at the Athol Road junction for a space in the traffic, the Inverness to Glasgow train trundled past on the main line opposite.

"Was that work?"

"My wife," he responded, smiling. "Post-holiday blues, I think."

"Lucky you've got someone."

"Luckier than you'd know..."

He swung the car out of the junction and accelerated southward toward the main A9.

"You got anyone on the horizon at the moment?"

"No," she said. "Footloose and all that."

"Easiest way in this job," he offered.

The rain eased and the wipers slowed to intermittent as they sped on through the Perthshire farmland. The road was heavily pooled with rain, but the four-wheel drive made light of it.

Forty minutes later he was briefing Moon on their progress and elaborating his suspicions about the use of charity funds. He then explained his concerns regarding the seconded detective's role in their investigations. Moon made a mental note, but didn't comment.

"Anything else?" the old man enquired, as his phone rang. After looking at the caller number, he nodded toward the door.

Taking the hint, Lamont was still considering Moon's lack of reaction over his concerns as he left the office. The detective wondered if the old man shared his thoughts about O'Leary. For all he knew, his boss had already been briefed about the detective, but didn't want to say anything.

He shrugged and let the matter lie. Tortolano's office was empty, but he came across her, cup in hand, returning from the coffee machine.

"I'm popping home to get changed. You'll need to dig around in the Perth Registry Office records again."

Even as his partner nodded her understanding, he was already on his way toward the stairwell. After driving home and changing out of his creased, damp clothes, he dropped Elspeth a text. He hadn't called in case she was busy, however his mobile rang a short time later and they exchanged a few pleasant words.

Explaining that he was on his way to Glasgow, he told her they would probably pass on the road. Confirming he'd be home by eight, he ended the call. As he set the house alarm, the thought occurred that she had sounded hesitant and tense, but he put the moment to the back of his mind. After all, her job was stressful and she couldn't always speak freely.

The detectives arrived in Glasgow shortly after five-thirty and dropped into one of the bars near Central Station. Tortolano chatted animatedly about the key principles surrounding interviews and he wasn't surprised to discover her knowledge was extensive. Although saying nothing to her earlier, he'd been impressed by her work at Castle Druin. It was just possible she could make a good partner. With the detective's intelligence and abilities, it would take no more than time and experience to hone those talents into a formidable skill-set.

Before finishing their soft drinks, Lamont outlined the areas of particular interest the coming interview might offer. She'd listened intently, easily grasping the direction he was taking. Excusing himself for a moment, he left her making notes.

While taking the short walk up to the Bothwell Street address in blustery evening air, he became aware of her excitement at the thrill of the chase.

Once upon a time, he thought.

"Does it always feel like this as cases develop?"

"Like what?"

"Well, sort of exciting."

"Only when you smell the kill."

"Hasn't this case given that feeling yet?"

"No," he said, striding out. "We're a long way from champagne and back slaps."

Cameron Corporate was in a neatly restored sandstone building and a close neighbour of the Scottish Cremation Society. From the names on the wall plaque, it appeared that a plethora of solicitors also kept offices in the building. She nudged Lamont as they passed the cremation office door and smiled.

"Some of the charity money hasn't gone missing…" Nodding toward the brass sign on the door, she joked: "It's gone up in smoke."

"Third on the left," he directed, ignoring the quip. "Switch on the serious button, this character could be dangerous in more ways than one."

"Why?"

"He's wealthy, connected, intelligent *and* a good shot," he muttered.

They stopped at the door to the accountant's offices. A security camera covered the entrance. The door was emblazoned with a large, round table motif. Each of twelve 'seats' was a gold 'pounds' sign, styled like an attentive person. Gesturing toward the impressive motif, the detective pushed it open.

The outer office was tastefully decorated and deeply carpeted. It smelled of wealth. Expensive looking solid wood desks, dressed with hand-stitched leather swivel chairs, occupied three of the spacious room's corners. The remaining one held secure filing cabinets and closed floor to ceiling oak shelving. A number of high quality flat screen monitors were positioned strategically around the walls displaying the latest financial data from the global markets. Another screen had the Bloomberg channel. A rotund female reporter was explaining the possible outcomes for bond purchases made by the Italian Government, elaborating on the likelihood of high interest rates on debt strangling their economy in the longer term.

His partner glanced over and Lamont pursed his lips.

"Home from home for you," he said, nodding up at the screen. "Italy."

She was about to respond when one of the doors opened and a tall, well-built man in his late forties came toward them. Smiling a practised, orthodontic smile, he warmly stretched out a hand and introduced himself as Alistair Cameron. Nodding politely toward Tortolano, the man led them through to a lavishly appointed anteroom.

Decorated in an opulent Art Deco style, the

detective presumed it was meant to ensure customers and colleagues alike felt comfortable. It oozed the wealth that was Cameron Corporate.

"Take a seat, take a seat. Coffee?"

The man gestured toward an Italian Espresso machine.

"No, thanks."

As they sat, Cameron politely waited until Tortolano was settled before speaking again.

"What can I do for you?"

"Thank you for seeing us," he began. "I know it's late, so we won't keep you long."

"What seems to be the problem, detective?"

Cameron eased himself into a comfortable position in the soft, upholstered chair.

"It's about Lord MacCaig."

The man shook his head dramatically.

"Terrible business with Jock, terrible…"

Distrust had already formed in Lamont's mind, so he decided to throw the curve ball early and try unsettling this smooth character.

"We're interested in the affairs of Aid All Africa – AidenallafricA to be precise, Mr Cameron," he elaborated. "As well as the unfortunate demise of Lord MacCaig's son."

"Oh, I see."

"Yes," said the detective, quietly. "Both are areas of interest to us."

The opening line had obviously worked, for after a moment's thought, Cameron said uneasily: "Perhaps I'll need to have my solicitor present in that case."

"Any reason, sir?"

"Well, these are complex and highly confidential financial matters, detective. There's a possibility – albeit a slim one – that I could be divulging information against the interests of my client."

"Then we'd be more than happy to have your solicitor present, Mr Cameron."

After a brief pause, Tortolano offered: "Keeps things nice and formal from our perspective, sir."

The man had clearly been thrown, and hesitated before getting up.

"I'll just see if George is free," he said, rising from the deeply padded leather.

As he left the room, the detective shrugged. He didn't particularly want the solicitor present, but it would make little difference to the interview. Glancing toward Tortolano, he smiled. For a fleeting moment, the detective felt like he was actually working with a partner – and the usually insular figure quite liked it.

"I think we might need to arrange a formal get-together in Stirling for this chap," she said, quietly.

"As long as he doesn't bring that," said Lamont, nodding up at the security camera, its red *active* light, blinking above the shelving.

"Oh," she said. "I see."

He stood up and took a closer look at some of the

art works adoring the room's walls. He was about to point out one of the original hangings when Cameron returned, accompanied by a ruddy-faced, grey-haired man carrying an A4 notepad. The man wore a pink formal shirt and grey herringbone bow tie. It gave him the surreal image, Lamont thought, of a character from one of Hergé's classic cartoon tales.

"Detectives, this is George Watson, my solicitor," Cameron confirmed.

"Speedy service indeed, Mr Watson," said Lamont.

The man offered a podgy hand and directed an awkward smile toward Tortolano.

"Our team live next door," he confirmed, resting the pad on the broad, marble coffee table. "Do a lot of work for Cameron Corporate when required."

"To be honest," said Lamont, disarmingly, "we hope our intervention doesn't bring Mr Cameron further need of your services."

"Can I get straight to the point then," Watson said. "I understand you have issues with Cameron Corporate regarding AidenallafricA, yes?"

"That's correct."

"But you are investigating the death of Lord Alex MacCaig's son, Jock, at this moment, are you not?"

"Indeed."

"From our perspective then, detective, if you keep the questions in this interview related purely to the demise of the unfortunate Mr Jock MacCaig, then an informal chat can go ahead."

The detective nodded.

"But off the record, so to speak," Watson added. "Agreed?"

Lamont directed a thoughtful gaze toward Alistair Cameron. The man was beginning to look somewhat less than self-assured. The detective thought the accountant had perhaps begun to develop an understanding of the very deep water in which he now swam.

"Providing your client knows we'll need to see him formally – and in the very near future – regarding the financial management of Aid All Africa's investment company, then we'd be happy to focus our chat today on Jock MacCaig's death."

The two men looked at each other and Cameron nodded.

"Though you need to understand," the detective added softly, "that at the moment, there appears to be a connection between Jock's recent knowledge of the management of charity monies and his death."

Having explained the link between Jock's murder and financial matters surrounding the charity, he had deliberately avoided giving away just how much the team knew. He suspected however, that Cameron, Watson and Lord MacCaig would already have discussed the matter in detail on the phone. Despite the close relationship Cameron had with MacCaig, he thought this man might be acting without his friend's full knowledge. The detective was developing the opinion that although Lord MacCaig was an astute businessman and networker, he might be overly trusting of those closest to him.

"Could you excuse us for a moment?" Watson

said. "I think Alistair and I need to clarify one or two matters."

Although the pair had left the room, the detectives could overhear a muted, occasionally heated discussion through the closed door. Then Cameron's raised tones came quite close to being audible. Smiling inwardly, he waited impassively while his partner studied her short, carefully polished nails.

Alistair Cameron returned to the room without the portly solicitor.

'Let's get on with it," he said, sitting down. Pulling his trouser knees up a little as he settled, the accountant added: "But first, please be clear; the charity, Aid All Africa, has at all times acted within the Charity Commission's rules of governance. I want that on record."

'We're grateful to hear that, Mr Cameron," Lamont said. "It's extremely important to us that the charity's work is undamaged in any way by these matters."

"That's exactly how Jock put it," Cameron said. "Though his language was not quite so eloquent."

"So when did you and Jock discuss this?"

"The Wednesday before his death."

"At the castle?"

"No," Cameron said, pointing a thumb over his shoulder toward a door. "Through there – in my office. Don't have time to trail up to Rannoch on weekdays."

"You were at Castle Druin on the Sunday before Jock died though?"

"I'm often there on Sundays."

"But a week past Sunday?" Lamont asked again.

"Yes, I was up seeing Alex about some shooting arrangements. It's the middle of the grouse season at the moment."

"Who else did you see there?"

"Just Lady Helen."

"And Jock?"

"He and I weren't on speaking terms. Not after the arguments he had with his father," he said indignantly. "Accusing all and sundry of robbing the charity. First, he'd tried to hassle young Genovese's father over in Genoa, then his own father – and then me."

Trying hard to keep within Cameron's wishes, Lamont stopped himself asking further about the charity's financial affairs. He was here to gain information that would lead to the conviction of a killer. Proving embezzlement from AidenallafricA, the charity's investment arm, could prove much more difficult. One step at a time, he thought.

"Tell us what you know about the argument Jock had with his father."

"As I've said, he was accusing everyone of conspiracy to defraud the charity and deprive African children of what had been raised to help them." Cameron added bitterly: "His father caught the brunt of it!"

"I see," he said, momentarily studying the darkening sky. Framed in the expanse of the room's smoked glass windows, the brooding scene looked particularly threatening though he couldn't think why. Surprised by being so easily distracted, the detective worked to keep his thoughts on track. "And did Lord MacCaig tell you this?"

"He was nearly in tears!" The man paused for effect, while shaking his head disdainfully. "I'll never understand how anyone's son could be so cruel!"

As Lamont listened, a heavy shower of rain swept in from the Atlantic and pattered noisily off the double-glazing. Across the street he could see the comings and goings of a few uniformed contract cleaning staff. Through the now watery distortions on the glass, they were readying the neighbouring offices for another day of commerce in the city.

"What do you know about Jock's relationship with Lady Helen?" Tortolano asked, sensing her partner had finished. "Were they on friendly terms?"

Studying her for a moment, he then glanced toward Lamont, trying to gauge what they already knew.

"Seemed friendly enough, though maybe too close," he replied, smiling wryly. "She was his stepmother after all, so you might expect that."

"Would you care to expand?"

Now appearing uncomfortable, the man sighed.

"Well, I think Alex thought they'd become too..."

"Yes?"

After moment's reflection, the accountant decided to be open with regard to Lady Helen's infidelity.

"I think familiar is the only word I can use," he said awkwardly.

"Go on…"

"Whatever I say sounds bad," he complained. Cameron ran a hand over his immaculately groomed but receding hairline. "Do you really need to ask these questions?"

"You said familiar," Tortolano probed, ignoring his protest. She eyed Lamont, but he appeared distracted, as though not really paying attention. 'How familiar did Lord MacCaig think they were?"

"He wasn't certain. Alex thought there might have been a degree of what he called, overfamiliarity."

From nowhere, Lamont threw in casually, "Sex, then."

"He isn't, I mean, wasn't, certain."

"And had Lord MacCaig challenged his wife about her relationship with his stepson?" he queried.

"Not that he told me."

"Would you describe yourself as Lord MacCaig's best friend, Mr Cameron?" asked Tortolano.

"I'd like to think so, though Alex has friends all over the world. He's very gregarious."

"Like his wife," Lamont stated bluntly. "And trusting too, apparently."

"Look, we're not here to talk about family relations – and you're never going to be able to prove any wrong doing on my part."

"But then," the detective offered, smiling, "if our line of enquiry becomes public, Cameron Corporate won't be a very attractive investment proposition, will it?"

"But that might damage the charity," Cameron pointed out, smugly. "And you can't afford that, any more than we can."

"How do you work that out?"

"Our political contacts believe that you are potentially surplus to requirements," he said. "Especially with the transformation process Scotland's police forces are about to go through."

Lamont studied him thoughtfully for a moment and didn't respond to the challenge.

Grinning stupidly, the accountant added: "And political fallout from any enquiry – especially if it harmed either Lord MacCaig's reputation, or Aid All Africa for that matter – could ensure your demise. As I understand it, and from Edinburgh, no less, you'll be told to keep your noses out if you pose a threat to the charity's reputation, even *with* due cause."

"And you think we don't have due cause?"

"No."

"We know someone appears to have made a profit: nearly one and half million, from trading AidenallafricA's money on the Forex market," Lamont pointed out, finally revealing his hand. "And we also know that Jock believed the accounts had been altered."

"And that it may have got him killed," Tortolano added, flicking a hair from her eye-line. "By the same person who altered the accounts."

"I wouldn't murder anyone!" Cameron protested loudly.

"But you did alter the accounts," Lamont

challenged. He leant toward the man. "Didn't you?"

"So-bloody-what if I did?"

"We can take that as an admission?"

"You can take a jump!" Cameron replied, rising from the seat abruptly. "I told you what would happen if you went too far."

"No, Mr Cameron," Lamont said quietly. "It's you who've gone too far."

"We'll see about that!"

"We don't believe you meant to murder Jock," he proposed, using the lie for effect. The detective had fabricated the statement, for he already knew Cameron wasn't a murderer.

"I murdered no-one! Are you stupid? I left Castle Druin just after ten on the Sunday evening and drove back to my home in Dunblane. I was in the house by midnight. Now try proving otherwise..."

"Did anyone see you?"

"Not in the house, no," he replied, thinking quickly. Then he got out his wallet and thrust a piece of paper toward Lamont. "Here, the receipt..."

"Wife charging you bed and breakfast?" Tortolano said provocatively, taking the paper from him.

"Went into the all night petrol station for milk before going up to the house. They'll remember me, too – full tank in the car and a carton of semi-skimmed..."

"Still had time to get back to Druin in the early morning though," she interrupted. "Receipt could be a convenient, but well thought out alibi."

"Wife came in just after six from Edinburgh Airport," he replied. "Wakened me up with a coffee."

"You won't mind if we confirm that of course," Lamont said.

"Be my guest!" He handed over a heavily embossed business card. "She's home now; ring her from here if you like…"

Getting the nod from Lamont, his partner went through to the secretary's office to make the call on her mobile. Now carefully measuring Cameron's reddened features, his thoughts focussed on the matter in hand.

"Did you see anyone else while you were up at the castle, or notice any strange cars as you were leaving?"

"That winding B road to Pitlochry has many strange cars on it toward the end of August," he said, still sounding angry. "It's the holiday season, after all. But in the dead of night on a narrow, winding back road, you see little other than your own bonnet, the centre line and trees!"

Relieved the man was calming down, the detective nodded and said, "Point taken…"

Tortolano returned before he had time to explore any other vague and irrelevant avenues of conversation.

"His wife confirms her return via Edinburgh," she said, sounding slightly disappointed. Looking at the accountant, she added: "Says she made you coffee as the six o'clock alarm went off by the bed."

Nodding his acceptance of the facts, Lamont rose from his chair and gave a quick stretch of his neck muscles.

"All right, Mr Cameron, we'll be in touch tomorrow. I'll need to have the charity's and AidenallafricA's books, as well as details of your own accounts. That includes those Manx ones that stay out of the taxman's reach."

"So, you're still going to try your luck?" he asked, sounding irritated.

"Not try, Mr Cameron…" The detective drew him a broad smile. "I'll have professional analysts pull those accounts apart, going back say, three years…"

Cameron looked at him with barely disguised hatred.

"Or you can try coming clean?" Tortolano said brightly.

"Why on earth would I admit guilt when I've done nothing wrong?"

"Forget Edinburgh if you think there's any assistance for you, Mr Cameron..." Studying him for a reaction, Lamont added: "We've our own friends there. Tomorrow: nine in the morning; the books. Detective Tortolano here will call in to collect them – along with your personal bank details. We'll arrange court papers, so don't bother trying to block things."

As he turned to leave, Lamont stopped and touched his pocket.

"I knew I had forgotten something."

Cameron's pose suggested a readiness to pounce on the detective, but instead he breathed in deeply and tried to gather himself.

"Yes?"

"You didn't say who else was in the house."

"Helen, Alex, Jock and…" Cameron paused thoughtfully.

"Yes?"

"Ewan might have been there," he said. "He's there most weekends, though you rarely see him."

"Does he shoot?"

Cameron smiled and shook his head disdainfully.

"You mean, 'did he shoot his brother'?"

"Simple question, Mr Cameron."

With a look of intense annoyance, the man said: "Yes, he shoots regularly, though rarely with the group."

It seemed to Lamont as though the accountant had consciously decided being difficult with their enquiries was futile.

"According to Alex, he's marksman stuff, but lazy. Don't know the lad very well myself. If I do see him, he's usually shuffling along, doing nothing useful. Alex adores him though. Was really hurt when custody went to the mother as part of the divorce settlement."

"And now he's with his father most weekends?"

"Apparently," the accountant replied. "Like I say, you rarely see him."

"And the last weekend Jock was seen alive?"

"Saw nothing of him. Too busy trying to keep the peace between Jock and Alex over the Forex account."

"And would Ewan have been aware of the arguments and the reasons for them?"

"Whole damned glen would have been aware of them," he added expressively. "They were bawling at each other – nearly came to blows!"

The detectives were forming a clearer picture of events leading up to Jock's death. Lamont suspected Ewan's name had been kept out of the picture, by family and friends alike, to protect him: but from what and why? He was also certain that the source of the heated argument – the money lost to the charity – was possibly down to Cameron or his associates trading badly on the Forex Market.

They left Cameron with another reminder to have the accounts prepared for collection the following morning. Stepping out into Bothwell Street, Lamont put a mint chew in his mouth.

"He nearly had a coronary. I like it when accountants look stressed and do that."

"Funnily enough, I did too," she said, smiling.

"Better prepare that request for the Sheriff Court when we get back," he said. "Just in case Cameron, MacCaig, or the other Charity Trustees decide to block access to the financial records."

"Will do."

Chapter 16

It was after eight o'clock by the time they pulled up at Randolphfield. Despite the late hour, Tortolano went off to make notes for the police legal team. They would have to work quickly. Preparing papers for the Stirling Courts in the morning would take time and seemed unnecessary, but it was just possible Cameron could try to block efforts to review his monetary activities.

Returning to his office, Lamont sat down and began dictating several paragraphs about the day's events for typing. He then sent a copy of the voice file to O'Leary by email. A few minutes later the phone in his pocket buzzed.

He listened carefully as his boss, ringing from home, advised him of the now intense Scottish Office interest in the case. It seemed MacCaig was asking questions via a friend in the Justice Department. In essence, Moon had been told bluntly that if they didn't tread carefully, or damaged the charity and Scotland's reputation, both could expect to enjoy new careers more focussed on their respective horticultural interests.

After elaborating at length on his current tactics, Lamont had the impression the old man was less than reassured. His explanation of the care taken not to upset anyone didn't seem to cut the mustard either. However, Moon seemed more placated after having it outlined where the detective thought their enquiries were leading. He went on to explain that money had probably been the cause of several disputes within the family preceding the murder.

Reflecting honestly, he confirmed that the identity of the killer, and reason for the murder, remained obscured by complex family relationships and hidden financial agendas. Even though he could hear Moon huffing and puffing as he spoke, he went on to clarify, that in his view, there had probably been nothing erroneous – other than misguided trading – on the part of the charity's financial managers. In his estimation, Cameron had been foolish, but no more than that.

This conciliatory line seemed to have settled the old man's anxieties about the prudence of his actions. After carefully describing the brief intervention from Watson, the accountant's lawyer, he indicated that if Moon agreed, they would apply for court permission to scour the charity's books. He explained that as a precaution, they had also asked for Cameron's personal bank account details.

Although agreeing with this line of action, the old man urged he take extreme care to avoid any media involvement for Scotland's reputation must not be damaged. And besides, he explained, the Charity Commission's rules on investments could be interpreted differently, depending on which way you chose to read them. Cameron's only crime, he suggested, was most probably the stupidity of allowing trading in riskier currencies. His efforts, he added, appeared no worse than most of the major banking players during the '08 meltdown.

Lamont wasn't quite so sure that such a simplistic justification could be applied to the accountant's behaviour. In his view, it hadn't as yet been established that the errors were indeed Cameron's own. Whatever direction they moved, he knew the team was now on very dangerous ground. The public flogging of Cameron and the other Charity Trustees would be certain to ensue following their exposure for any wrongdoing in the media. This could also be fatally damaging to their SPSA team.

He shook his head and thought for a moment before breathing a tired sigh of relief. While pondering the way forward, he felt dismay grow as another headache set in and cursed quietly at its onset so soon after the last episode. The inability to focus properly on the facts during their interview with Cameron had deeply disturbed him; and now this. The first wave of pain swept through, forcing him to cradle his head in his hands and swear loudly. Was he losing it? For a fleeting moment, he could feel himself falling, forever falling. The detective shook himself.

As he fought to concentrate, his first concern was that he would need to drive up to Rannoch tomorrow to interview the MacCaig's again. It was a lengthy trip; however, he was suspicious of the couple's failure to mention the probable presence of the other son, Ewan. The detective wondered if the motivation behind the family's behaviour had been purely emotional, triggered by the need to protect him from the fallout surrounding the death of his stepbrother.

Flipping the light switch on the way out, he closed and locked the office door. Pleased to see that

Tortolano's office was also empty, he walked out into the damp night air. After a quick glance at the car, he thought for a moment, then decided to walk home. Fresh air wouldn't ease the discomfort, but it would help clear his head and allow more time to reflect on the day's work. Striding out toward Stirling's, leafy Kings Park, and the comfortable Victorian house, he tried again to picture the scene at Castle Druin and the events that had led to a murder.

*

Elspeth was watching TV, magazine in hand, as he wandered through to the lounge and put his jacket over the settee.

"Multi-tasking again, angel," he said, and bent over to kiss her.

"Just reading the health columns, as usual," she replied, warmly, hugging him tightly for a moment. "Without these it's doubtful some of my patients would have anything to ask."

"Hey, that kiss was tasty," he said, planting himself on the arm of the seat. "You've been practising?"

"Need no practise. I'm already the best. Tell you what, I'll multi-task us a cuppa while I'm at it." As she got to her feet, Elspeth stopped and studied his face. "You've got a headache," she said knowingly. "Despite that pleasant attempt at a *hello* you look as though someone's given you a slapping!"

"Good idea with the tea, and thanks for the slapping compliment," he said, watching the tall figure admiringly as she headed through to the kitchen. "What kind of day did you have?"

"Wait a minute," she called, "I'm filling the kettle."

"Why don't you run the tap?"

Elspeth's face reappeared around the door.

"You're so *very* funny," she said, shaking her head. "Some things never change."

"I hope not."

As he wrapped his arms around her, Elspeth knew just how damaging his injury had been. The old Lamont would have tried to sweep her off her feet. Instead, he was too busy coping with pain. With her right hand, she pushed the hair from his forehead and gazed deep into his dark eyes. Tonight it was fortunate he hadn't been spontaneous, she thought, for the impact of revealing her secret would be painful for them both. Pretending all was well would be impossible. Elspeth knew she would have to tell him now. There would never be a better time.

Smiling broadly, he squeezed her buttocks gently with his hands, winked, and raised his eyebrows.

"Am I reading you right?" she asked, confused for a moment. "I thought you had a headache?"

"Elspeth" he said, with mock lust, "the headache will wait."

"It may wait," she said gently, touching his cheek with her hand, "but I'm afraid what we need to talk about won't."

"It only takes a yes from two consenting adults," he said suggestively.

Pushing him back to arm's length, she held his hands and said, "This is serious."

It was then he noticed tears forming.

"Is it that bad?" he asked. "Or have I done something wrong?"

"Neither," she replied, now sounding quite frightened.

"What's the matter?" he said, becoming more concerned as he finally grasped her anxiety. "Please… I know it's been too long… too painful!"

"Listen," she blurted out. "This isn't about you — or us!"

Stepping back, he felt as though something was seriously awry, but what? Could there be someone else?

Elspeth flopped onto the settee.

"Sit down," she said tearfully. "Please…"

Feeling certain that there was indeed someone else, he readied himself for bad news.

"I've got breast cancer," she sobbed, before he had time to settle.

All thoughts of infidelity, sex and police casework were swept away by that one, simple statement. He felt the colour drain as a wave of fear ran through him. Putting his arms around her, he held Elspeth gently, but close; closer than ever before.

"This is our battle, lass," he said quietly, but firmly, "Our battle — and I'm here, right here beside you."

As the shock struck home, he began to wonder how long she had known. Could it be she hadn't been able to tell him? A wave of choking guilt left him feeling physically sick.

After a few minutes gently cradling her, he managed to pull his thoughts together. Making them a drink, he sat beside her while Elspeth outlined what she knew. Elaborating about her state of mind and anxieties after discovering the lump, she then explained what had happened since that awful moment. Although reeling at the thought of what lay ahead, she managed to clarify the way forward through the coming days and months.

He didn't pretend to understand all the details, but resolved to read as much as possible about breast tumours. He would talk with her doctor, if the man could make time. At least then he'd feel able to give her knowledgeable support, rather than merely the kind words of an understanding husband.

He knew Hugh Allen socially. They had met many times at hospital and university alumni social functions. Although they weren't close friends, he'd been impressed by the surgeon's balanced opinions and strength of character. He seemed a good man, thankfully, for he was now a man in whose hands her life rested. Shivering as a cloud of fear hovered over his own pain, Lamont wondered how he could ever give the support this gentle woman needed.

The willowy figure grasped the very foundations of her fears, for Elspeth knew breast cancer physiology well. As a professional, she had dealt with many sufferers and understood implicitly the potential outcomes. If the worst were to happen, she knew her days could well be numbered, but had already determined to live them to the full. More importantly, being a pragmatist at heart, she hoped that if this were to be her time, she could bow out with courage and pride.

They lay awake throughout the night, but said little. Both knew there wasn't much that needed to, or could, be done to alter their circumstances. She had cried quietly on a couple of occasions: tears of relief; and tears for her man. People often forget a carer's struggle, but he hadn't in his time, and she wouldn't now. Having finally been able to share her fears and concerns about the future, she would try to support him. First, she would ensure all the old conversations about what to do, *if*, were reaffirmed and agreed.

When morning finally came, she shooed him out to work. Both her secretary and appointments clerk had been spoken to before leaving the hospital yesterday. They knew that all meetings and clinical work would finish for an indefinite period. This morning she would speak with the Departmental Director and run through her patient list, ensuring any priorities were identified.

By ten o'clock she hoped to be able to see her remaining inpatients. At lunchtime she intended to return home. Having promised herself that if ever the time felt right she would write a novel; it looked like now was that time. It would be a novel of life and love and pain; a synthesis of the endeavours of the many courageous souls for whom she had cared over the years...

*

Drumming his fingers on the wooden desktop, Moon looked across at the detective again and wondered what you could say to anyone at a time like this.

Shaking his head wearily, he offered: "There's

nothing else you can do, lad. She knows you're there."

He studied Lamont's tired features for a moment.

"You do need to be with her now."

"No, that's not the answer."

"No, I suppose she wouldn't like that," Moon reflected. "Too claustrophobic for a woman like Elspeth, eh? Bit too like you."

The detective nodded and said: "Look, if I need to take some time, especially after her operation, I'll just tie up the loose ends and go, eh?"

"Sounds good to me," the old man agreed, but he would hold his breath and pray it never came to Lamont needing time off-duty.

The room went quiet for a moment and the dull sound of commuter traffic on St Ninian's Road, the main route into the city, filled the void. Moon closed the first-floor window firmly with a loud tut. He sounded as though his concentration had been offended, rather than merely disturbed. The morning rush hour was well underway and he watched as the nose-to-tail queue of single-occupied cars and delivery wagons ground slowly forward.

Sitting down, he decided to get things back on track. Gloomily reflecting on Elspeth's problems would do little to help the man opposite, and even less to catch a killer.

"Where are we up to with the investigation then?"

After Lamont briefed him more fully on the previous evening's meeting with Cameron, Moon felt satisfied with the detective's analysis of the interview. He thought it would definitely be worth involving

Inland Revenue. That, he said, could be done discreetly after Tortolano brought the accountant's books back to Randolphfield. However, any threat to the charity's credibility following scrutiny of the accounts would have to be discussed with ministers at the Scottish Office before any action could be taken.

Accepting this with a frown, the dark-haired detective told him his thoughts on potential murder suspects within the MacCaig family. What he omitted to tell the DCC was that his suspicions had expanded beyond family members. But he would not brief the man based on a hunch, which was all he had at that moment.

"We'll have a summary meeting tomorrow," he explained. "I need to make sure we're pulling in the right direction."

"Good. That was always your style."

Understanding that he may have heard approval of his style for a moment, he gave the DCC a measured look of disbelief.

"What about MacCaig's other son, Ewan?"

"He's interesting, right enough. Seems to spend nearly every weekend at the castle. Never got a mention when I first spoke to the family, though. Stays in his own private world when he's at Druin. He's got a suite of rooms, a gun, shoots well and can work the dogs."

"He's a suspect?"

"Yes," the detective confirmed, without much confidence. "Could be the father's protecting him."

Pausing, Lamont looked thoughtful for a moment.

"And?"

"Like I said, MacCaig didn't mention the boy's name when we first interviewed him," he repeated, but a pensive shadow dressed the smooth features. "It was almost as though the lad was being deliberately kept from our line of fire…"

Tortolano put her head round the door.

"Morning gentlemen," she chirped. "I'm off to Glasgow to pick up Cameron's accounts. Anything else you want me for this morning?"

Lamont asked casually: "Did you get anything from Perth records office?

"Yes, the mother was an Ann Beattie. DOB…"

"That's okay." The detective cut her short, which didn't go unnoticed by the DCC. "Text it to me, will you?"

For a moment she seemed surprised, then nodded.

"Anything else?"

"No, not really. But don't upset him any more than we did last night. If you've any trouble getting the papers, give me a ring and we'll use the court documents the legal team are setting up."

"Doubt if he'll see me at all after yesterday. I somehow think the books will be left with the secretary."

She gave a little 'open and closed fingers' wave to Moon as she spoke. He grinned broadly.

"I'll ring Cameron Corporate before I leave to make sure we don't have our time wasted!"

After she'd gone, Moon, with a glint in his eye, asked how she was settling in.

"Needs more time," Lamont responded. "And to be a bit less emotive. Great potential though, and sharp as a tack."

"Can you work with her day-to-day?"

"Don't know," he replied. "That's the honest answer. But I'll do all I can to make it work. She's the right stuff, for sure. There's only the emotional side of things to get straight and…" He thought for a moment and scratched his nose as Moon waited. "Look, I like her – and she's good at her job. But whether she'll take to me is another matter."

The old man liked what he had heard.

"Team work is not just about liking your colleagues," he offered.

"I agree," Lamont said, shrugging. "But we're a small unit and any destabilising personality could make life very difficult. We – sorry, *I* – don't need moods and tantrums."

"That's fair enough."

Moon recognised the risks involved in bringing the girl into the team without letting her partner know more about her her. This may not have been his wisest decision, but the young officer had been earmarked for a bright future. He didn't believe recruiting her had been a mistake. Intelligence, drive and in-depth personality testing had shown she was the type who could provide a balanced support for Lamont. The DCC was certain of this, especially since the police psychologist had put the two profiles together for comparison.

"They were a very good match," she'd said. "Tortolano is probably as good a match as you could get for his personality type. She could compliment someone who's almost off the scale on intuition. This profile will also balance well against his high rating on introversion."

"Might have to go down and visit MacCaig's ex and the son, Ewan," said the detective.

Ruminations interrupted, the old man nodded.

"Could clear up some loose ends."

He waited for a response but got nothing other than the old man's interested gaze.

"You asked if I thought Lord MacCaig was protecting Ewan and the answer is possibly, but I have no idea from what," he added.

"He could have murdered his stepbrother, though?"

"As I said, it's possible, though there's not a shred of evidence to support that hypothesis," he offered. "But I don't think we can rule out anyone at the moment, even though I'm becoming more convinced that none of the family are involved."

Although having no desire to explore other lines of thought at this stage, he briefly explained his reasoning. Then the old man's phone rang, which Lamont took as the cue to leave.

Once back in his office, he made some notes then phoned Lord MacCaig. After confirming their meeting at Castle Druin later in the day, he asked about the son, Ewan. The man confirmed his expected arrival at the castle as usual on that afternoon.

According to his father, he was between jobs and liked to spend weekends at the estate whenever he could. Asked whether the young man would arrive alone, MacCaig confirmed this, conceding that he rarely brought friends with him. This concurred with what Alistair Cameron had said about the lad keeping to himself. Maybe he wasn't exactly a social isolate, but certainly seemed to find it difficult to have normal relationships. The detective understood enough psychology to know the lad's behaviour patterns were often precursors to deeper emotional problems.

Thanking the man, he hung up and then rang O'Leary to confirm he'd be up in Pitlochry in about an hour. With tourist numbers diminishing, and the rush hour traffic subsiding, the sixty miles into the Highlands could be covered quite rapidly.

Chapter 17

Sitting at the little desk, O'Leary was using his voice recording to prepare the typed report on yesterday's events. Unable to get the correct wording, he sat back and looked at the laptop screen. A week had passed since he'd found himself sitting alone contemplating the best way forward. For the time being at least, he had a meaningful role and the company of two other detectives. But he also had the irritation of a command chain, with its attendant, interfering support structure.

He had never fully appreciated how irritating a support structure could be, until now. However, he was more than grateful that a door had been opened. The fortress that was Castle Druin had been proving near impenetrable until Lamont appeared. There were other risks with having the Scots detective's lurking presence in the investigation, but he would face those hurdles if they arose.

O'Leary had always considered himself something of an atoll: pearlescent coral in the unforgiving ocean of promotion seekers and kow-towers. Both he and the Scotsman were kindred spirits in that respect and needed little support to function at their best. Although not liking the guy, after three turbid days together, he'd become aware the feeling was mutual.

However, he recognised and admired Lamont for seeking neither promotion nor favour. Guessing the Scot disliked the large majority of those above him in the police hierarchy, he assumed the man probably believed, like him, that their bosses misused both their position and power for personal gain.

*

On reflection, his sentiments would change nothing, but he had no regrets. In his opinion, he could stand proud, unlike many of his colleagues over the years. Despite the hardships and insults to his career, he had survived.

In the years before the Irish potato famine, O'Leary's long dead ancestors had also endured intolerable hardship, he mused. They had probably existed on root vegetables and water. With barely a roof over their heads and an unsympathetic, absentee landlord, a provider had no choice but to leave home when the crops finally failed. Abandoning a wife – and six hungry children at his already overcrowded mother's home – Eugene had packed up and joined the tidal wave of humanity leaving to seek work in foreign lands. Setting off for Scotland, he promised to send for the family as soon as he found a wage.

Brendan's grandfather, Pat, told him that his ancestor had arrived in the Central Belt in the eighteen fifties. Hearing of the newly developing coalfields, the man had been desperate, but full of hope. Sadly, he failed to recognise that his prospective homeland was as riven by religious bigotry and zealots as his native Ireland.

Despite trying feverishly to find work in the

developing Lanarkshire mines, he discovered that most of the pits in the area weren't hiring. Many fellow Irishmen were, in their desperation, openly begging for food. After a month of futile searching, the man was nearing starvation. According to family lore, despite having neither food nor water – far less money to send home – Eugene's luck had changed.

While searching for work as the morning shift arrived outside gates of the new Shotts Colliery in Lanarkshire, he had overheard a conversation between two of the pit deputies, or overseers. They were talking about a new mine, in Tyldesley, near Manchester. He'd listened as they mooted that the owners were desperate for workers of any denomination; caring little as long as a man was healthy and physically strong.

And that was all he had needed to hear. Despite the bitter winter weather, the two hundred miles south across the rugged, frozen Scottish Uplands and Lakeland hills, were covered on foot in less than four days. His first weekly wage packet of one pound sterling had arrived seven days later.

Within three months the family were happily crammed into their tiny, one-roomed accommodation. The mine owners had built rows of small terraced houses for their workers, who rented them for three shillings each week, but if you lost your job for any reason, homelessness ensued. In the days before nationalisation, this ploy alone kept most of the workforce subservient to their bosses.

Wondering if he would find the necessary answers in Scotland, Brendan put the memory of his grandfather's tales aside. The detective knew he would have to be very patient. Unlocking what his team believed was a tightly woven web of deceit surrounding the wealthy landowner would take all his patience – and luck.

Deciding the stale, heavy office smell could be alleviated by some fresh air, he tried, and not for the first time since his arrival, to open the old window. To his relief, after a deal of thumping, banging and scraping, he finally managed to prise free the sash frame. O'Leary drew a deep breath of cool autumn air as it wafted in on the breeze. The bent screwdriver, used to break through the many layers of paint, now lay on the narrow ledge as testament to his efforts.

Sitting down, he swung round and put his heels on the small sill. Satisfied, he clasped his hands behind his head, and breathed in the fresh scent of highland countryside. He watched as the two local policemen returned with their morning breakfast. Once a week, they had told him, they ate here. Thursday was their team social day. Despite nearly choking as they elucidated, he said nothing. Today, as usual, each carried a paper bag with filled rolls from the local café. The thermos flasks would soon be opening, and the smell of bacon would waft freely up to the first floor.

Needing answers, he thought it time to engage the two in conversation again. During the only discussion he'd had with them, Sergeant Weir was asked to confirm that Tosland had been at his brother's home in Kingussie before the murder. He had also told him to call into the Service Station on the main A9. Verification of whether Amelia MacCaig, or her Italian boyfriend, had been there for fuel late, he'd said, would certainly be helpful.

Normally, he would have made the enquiries himself, but this situation offered an opportunity to bridge the gulf with the local lads. It was just possible he may be in Pitlochry for some months, and would no doubt need their help at some point. After all, he thought, they must have some local knowledge concerning the MacCaigs and Castle Druin. Small communities talked; policemen listened.

He agreed, however, that Lamont had a point: in a tight-knit village like Kinloch Rannoch, where the sergeant lived, the man's family might even be linked to the estate in some obscure way. O'Leary understood this. Yes, it could compromise the credibility of the officer's police role, but the man must know the estate and most of its staff. Undoubtedly he would have spoken with many of them either socially, or in passing. It was also highly likely he had overheard crumbs of local gossip about MacCaig. His wife and kids would also feed precious snippets of fact, or fiction, pernicious or otherwise, concerning the estate and its inhabitants, into the occasional conversation. Information like that could yet prove helpful.

Rightly believing that success stories always attracted gossip in small communities, he knew MacCaig's fortune, allied to the man's political status, would give him near reverential standing. In Kinloch Rannoch, his kudos was further elevated by the local population's dependency on the estate's success. It was in all of their interests to protect Druin, and everything it stood for.

O'Leary put on his jacket and went down to the

kitchen at the rear of the building. He knew the two men would already be at the old Formica-topped table, tucking in heartily.

"Morning gents," he said. "Bacon smells good."

Hugh Weir looked up and wiped his mouth free of brown sauce with a monogrammed café tissue.

"One pound fifty," he said, holding up the half-eaten roll. "Worth every penny, too!"

As O'Leary sat down, Pete Wilkinson, the Constable, cleared the debris and made some space on the oblong surface.

"Would you like a cuppa?"

"Kind of you," he said. "As it comes."

The young officer poured him a cup from his own flask.

"Thanks," he said, sipping the brew and nodding approval.

"Spare roll here," said Weir. "I'm eating too much."

"Ta, but no," he responded, patting his abdomen. "Had a bite already."

"Up in Ma Brearley's?" the sergeant scoffed: "From what we've heard, you're brave."

"I'm getting used to it," he said, scratching his head. "If I just eat a slice of that warm bread masquerading as toast, close my eyes and dream…"

The two officers laughed.

"Anyhow, I'm shifting over to new digs tonight," he said. "Mrs Conroy?"

"Is she the tasty looking English woman; little

black Scotty dog?" asked Wilkinson.

"You know her?"

"Seen her out in the glen with the dog." He winked and grinned. "You should get on with her!"

"Because she likes dogs?"

"No," said Wilkinson. "Ah meant, she's new here too!"

"Yes," he said. "I'd figured that."

Taking another sip, he watched while the uniforms chewed heartily on their repast.

"Tea's really good," he nodded. "Thanks."

"Wife's own," Wilkinson said, through a half-chewed mouthful.

Keeping his eyes on the table, Weir said nothing.

"Yes?" O'Leary nodded his approval. "Worth keeping, that one."

"She's a great lass, right enough."

Changing tack, the detective said: "Mrs Conroy told me she's only been here since March. I'll be her first guest."

"Just what you need to settle in," Weir chuckled. "A virgin landlady!"

As the laughter subsided, he enquired: "Did you get round to asking if Tosland had been up at his brother's a week past Sunday?"

"I did," said Wilkinson.

Weir threw a glance toward the younger officer.

"Tosland and I go back a long way," he explained,

managing to sound almost apologetic. "Grew up here together; went to the same school. Thought I'd better let Wilkinson here sort it. You know the score..."

"No problem."

It was not the response O'Leary wanted to give the uniformed officer. In his view, local policemen needed to be part of the community, and yet head and shoulders above it at the same time. Everyone should know where an officer stood and what his values were. The sergeant seemed happy to have broken that unwritten rule.

"What did his brother say?"

Wilkinson took his notebook out of a jacket pocket.

"He said Mackenzie had been there, right enough," he confirmed, taking a telling glance over at Weir.

"And?"

Wilkinson stared at him blankly.

Displaying a level of patience he didn't feel, O'Leary tried again, gesticulating with open hands.

"And what time did he leave?"

While trying not to show his frustration, he knew this enquiry should have been conducted without involving these two. After all, Wilkinson had found the body and Weir's world was encapsulated by the local community. Perhaps Lamont had been correct: the neighbourhood was too closely related. It would be difficult to take anyone's word, including the local bobbies, when it came to one of their own kind.

"Early hours for him, apparently," said Wilkinson.

"Roughly?"

"Said he'd been sleeping." O'Leary tilted his head inquisitively. "Morning?"

"Yes," the uniform confirmed. "They'd been drinking. Well, he had after they'd watched the shinty on the telly. Said his brother left to return to Castle Druin sometime around five-ish."

"Shinty?" asked the detective.

"Scots game," said Weir, smiling. "Like Irish hurling."

"Ah," he said. "Bash a ball with a big stick then chase it toward a goal?"

"More or less..."

Turning his attention back to Wilkinson, he asked: "And Tosland had been at his brother's all night?"

"So the brother says."

"And what about the service station?"

"I went up there," said Weir, interrupting. "Hadn't been too busy, apparently. Lucky enough to get the lad serving on the night shift the preceding Sunday."

"Any help?"

"Yes," he confirmed, enjoying the detective role for a moment. "I got him to check the till receipts with his bosses, but there was no sale recorded to either a Genovese, or a MacCaig. Took a picture with me I had in the house."

O'Leary looked puzzled, but impressed.

"One I had of the school fair," he explained, proudly. "The MacCaig girl presenting prizes to the juniors. Close-up of our lad and his pal getting an award from her for the three-legged race a couple of years back. She's not changed much and it's as clear as day. Anyhow, the pump attendant didn't recall ever having seen her, and certainly not on that evening. There were only seventeen customers recorded for the whole night."

"I don't suppose Mackenzie Tosland stopped for fuel on the way back to the castle?" he asked speculatively.

Weir nodded toward the young constable. Smiling proudly, he took a deep breath.

"Strangely enough, yes," he confirmed, cheeks flushed. "His was the second last name on the list."

"That a problem for you?"

"As I've said, I know him." Weir then ratified his relationship with the ghillie. "His wife and I were once…"

"Friends?" O'Leary gestured his understanding with a shrug and a nod. "No problem with that."

He looked from one to the other.

"You're only doing your job – both of you – and you've done it well, thanks. I'm really grateful."

Finishing the drink, he got up from the table and pushed the seat into place.

"Keep what you've told me to yourselves for now, please."

Both the officers muttered agreement and nodded as he left, but when he was out of sight, Weir pulled a face.

The detective had nearly got to the foot of the stairs, but then turned back to the kitchen.

"Sorry," he said, popping his head round the corner. "The fuel; what time did Tosland get it?"

Opening the notebook again, Weir leafed to the appropriate page.

"Five-fifteen it says here; twenty quid's worth."

"Ta," he said. "Enjoy your breakfast lads."

Chapter 18

The two uniformed officers were hurrying out of the station as Lamont arrived. Chatting earnestly, they hardly noticed as he drove past them and parked. The police Land Rover had swung out onto the main road before his seat belt was unclipped. Getting out into the morning sun, he watched as they disappeared from view. Shrugging, he coded the door lock and went in.

Hearing his colleague's footsteps on the stairs, O'Leary shifted his heels off the sill and closed the file.

Knocking sharply, the Scot swung the door open and nodded.

"Good trip?" O'Leary asked.

"Indeed."

"Wait till you hear this…"

"I'm all ears," Lamont said, and wandered over to the window.

"Well," he began. "I was just…"

Gesturing toward the car park, he said: "No, let me guess: you've had the two smiling uniforms that left hurriedly in the four-by-four sacked for impersonating local constabulary?"

The Englishman laughed and said: "Sergeant Weir's pissed off, right enough."

"Gone home to change?"

"No," he replied, trying to regain some composure. "He's explained to me that his friend lied."

"And Sergeant Reid's friend is?"

"Tosland."

The smile left him and his eyes narrowed.

"Let me see…"

Expecting nothing of value, O'Leary leant back in the chair, satisfaction etched on his face.

"They went to school together?" Then the Scot added: "And Tosland's long dead wife, Norah, was Weir's first love?"

Clearly surprised, the detective constable sat up.

"Where the hell did you get that from?"

"He lied to me, so I checked."

"When did he lie to you?"

"When he drove me down to the jetty."

"Why didn't you tell me?"

"Wasn't sure," he said. "At least not till I checked the school records with education authorities yesterday."

"How did you get onto that?"

"Simple really," he explained. "When I was at the Loch with him, he claimed not really knowing the local bobbies. Well, it's obvious that he would have known them like brothers. He's ghillie on the bloody estate, after all! And if you'll recall, Helen MacCaig told us she didn't think we'd gone to question her about the poachers."

"Simple really; there have been regular incidents of poaching, which led to Weir taking statements from Lord MacCaig. According to the files in Perth, Weir also spoke to Tosland about it on several occasions."

"Doesn't mean he knew him that well though, does it?"

"Well, that and the fact that he'd been on the estate for many years and, more importantly, lives in the local community. Even though he's out at the castle estate, he visits the village pub – and the shop – regularly."

"So he uses the shop," said O'Leary. "You'd expect him to. But I mean, it still doesn't suggest he meets our man Weir there."

"No, but it got me thinking."

"About what?"

"Boiled sweets," Lamont said, taking out a mint chew and examined at it as he spoke. "He likes loose, boiled sweets. Sell them in the Rannoch shop – phoned the proprietor yesterday. He confirmed that Tosland goes in two or three times a week for supplies, of one sort or another. The local police also use the shop. Wilkinson buys the family's breakfast rolls most mornings. Also goes in occasionally to check up that all's well. Weir's used the place since he was a lad. Proprietor went to school with him. And Mackenzie Tosland..."

"That's what Weir just told me – well, more or

less..." O'Leary thought for a moment. "So, d'you think there's a connection to the murder?"

"Well, he and our friend, Weir, went to school at the same time. Not the same year, though."

"Yes, he said that when we first met," confirmed O'Leary, thoughtfully. "Implied today that he and Tosland's dead wife had once been close friends."

"The Education Authority records office in Perth confirmed that they were both there at the same time; but one year apart. Tells us little about the murder, only that some people in this little community seem to be avoiding the truth."

"I could have told you that," said O'Leary. "Found out this morning from Weir that the ghillie lied to us about coming back here late Monday afternoon too. According to the Service Station records he got fuel at 5.15 on Monday morning!"

"Do we know if he returned here though?" asked Lamont, putting the sweet he'd been holding into his mouth.

"Well, no. But it proves he didn't tell us the truth."

Chewing on the mint, he both looked and felt puzzled. One of his milder headaches was beginning and he'd found the expression of puzzlement a good disguise when the pain struck.

Great day ahead, he thought, as his hand involuntarily reached for the small titanium plate on his skull and rubbed it tenderly. Concern was growing in him about his own mental state, in particular the increased frequency of the pain and his inability to concentrate. Now weary, he didn't bother telling his fellow detective of having already checked the filling station records for the Sunday and Monday.

With genuine concern in his tone, O'Leary asked: "Are you all right?"

"Yes, no problem," he answered easily. "Did you get Weir to do the filling station check?"

"Yeah, seemed like a good way to build relationships. I might have to spend a lot of time around those two – in the near future at least."

"That's a realistic perspective. Just out of curiosity…"

"Before you ask, *no*, I've heard nothing from Manchester so far, or the Police Federation either, for that matter."

Nodding his understanding, Lamont said: "Guess it'll take time, eh?"

Sounding sympathetic to a fellow officer's dilemma was in his nature, though he struggled to recognise his own empathy in this instance. Perhaps, he thought, the Englishman noticing his discomfort had struck a chord. O'Leary had done nothing to suggest he held bigoted, or racist views, but there was something not quite right about the man's behaviour. A detective's job often meant having to live a lie, but in Lamont's mind, this went beyond professional parameters.

"Why do you ask?"

"Just curious," replied Lamont.

The man may not be without fault, Lamont thought, but he did seem to be an enthusiast for the job in hand. And at this moment in time, the job was all that mattered.

Putting aside the nagging concerns about O'Leary, he suddenly felt tired. Elspeth's health had momentarily slipped to the back of his mind. How could it? He would have more to worry about than mere work matters when he got home tonight. But despite her problems, he knew phoning Elspeth to show concern would not be welcomed. From that perspective they were very much alike.

After trying to weigh up whether this man had an inkling of his true role, O'Leary dismissed the concerns. Shrugging his shoulders, he took a deep breath as he got up.

"You've confirmed with his Lordship when the next interviews with them will be?" he asked, leaning back against the wall.

"Yes, we're over there this afternoon, around two," the Scot replied. "The other son, Ewan, is due on the scene about then. I didn't tell MacCaig that talking to his son was the purpose of the visit, though he'd guess that for himself."

"And he's happy enough to see us there?"

"Don't think *happy* is a word I'd use, but he'll tolerate another quizzing without legal help, or being dragged over here."

"Do you really think the son has anything to do with the murder?"

"Something about the Ewan lad's playing on my mind, but I haven't quite figured it yet…" A surge of pain made him struggled to concentrate for a moment. "Might have a better idea once we've spoken to him."

"We know he and Jock weren't big buddies," said O'Leary. "And the young man likes spending, but doesn't like working."

Shaking his head, the Scot worked to clear his thoughts.

"We'll get a more informed picture when we look at Cameron's books," he said. "Might give us a clue, but I'm not optimistic AidenallafricA's accounts will do us any good. Cameron isn't bent either, but he doesn't *dislike* manipulating figures. Whether he gambles badly on the financial trading markets is another matter entirely."

"Can we can pin a prosecution on him for that?"

"Depends what our political masters want. He may be off-limits if he has enough influence, or Lord MacCaig decides that he'll protect a friend in need."

"Is a friend indeed..."

"Sums up our role in this bloody investigation to a 't'," Lamont complained coarsely. "Fighting friends of friends of family…"

"Not like you – the frustration thing, I mean. Or is it?"

"You don't know me," Lamont replied briskly.

The abruptness of the response had displayed more than a hint of irritation.

Taken aback, O'Leary felt surprised, but said nothing.

After a few uncomfortable moments, the Scot said apologetically: "Too many woes at the moment."

"Need to talk?"

"No," he said. "Need time to think."

"Problems?"

"No, at least not here."

"Home's always difficult when it gets in the way."

Lamont almost reacted by braking one of his personal rules: keep work and home as far apart as possible. He had almost been drawn to talk about Elspeth. Explaining his personal circumstances to Moon was a necessary intrusion. This would have been something else. Besides, the man was a stranger, and one he didn't entirely trust.

Taking out his mobile and noting the time, he phoned Tortolano. While looking out at the Perthshire hills through the mist of pain shrouding his vision, he wondered how beautiful that scenery would appear if he didn't have a wife to share such experiences with.

The headache had come on strongly now. His neurologist once told him that, considering the nature of the injury, he had been lucky. He may occasionally get some warning of the imminent onset of pain in the form of an aura; a kind of precursor, or alarm bell. Explaining that auras came in different forms for different people, he'd said it might present as an itch, a smell, or a blurring of vision – anything. But no such luck: for him, the discomfort arrived unannounced. If he was lucky, and near home, the solution was a darkened room and two of the prescription painkillers to knock him out. Here, at work, it was grin-and-bear-it.

"Hi lass…" Grimacing while listening as she elaborated, he asked: "And how did he take it... Okay.

Made life easier… yes, get them to the guys in audit. They can comb through them… yes, you too… bye."

"She got Cameron's records without difficulty, then?"

"Left them on the desk apparently, as she said he would. Smart lady." Nodding toward his fellow detective, he smiled awkwardly. "Good reader of the script is young Tortolano."

Giving him a wry grin, O'Leary asked: "What about the fallout?"

"Moon's been warned that whatever we find in the accounts – either those belonging to the charity, or Cameron's own – may not be of use. National embarrassment, reduced confidence in Scottish charities, probable fall-off in donations, etc. etc.!"

"Pain in the ass."

"Quite," he added. "Still, the job's principally to find a murderer."

"What about the media?"

"There's almost no interest from them at all. Initial reporting of the death, summary of his family and role in the charity, and then nothing."

"You think Lord MacCaig's contacts have suppressed the media interest?"

"Very possibly…"

Lamont suddenly felt a little unsteady. Resting his hands on the window frame for a moment helped him balance and he hoped his colleague hadn't noticed. It was rare for dizziness to accompany the pain, but today seemed to be an exception. There was no medication he could take. Once the pain had begun drugs would do little to help, other than knock him out. And this was not the time for sleep.

"Out here in rural Scotland," he continued, "it'd cost the press a fortune. I guess the expense would be too much – both in time and effort – for the hacks and their bosses. They'd get little of interest up here to stimulate national sales. People would hardly be drawn to tales of rural intrigue – at least not from outside the three or so thousand souls in Pitlochry itself."

"Right enough," O'Leary agreed. "Don't blame the locals though. They won't talk to the press for fear of exposing themselves to MacCaig's wrath. The man runs this bloody community!"

"Talking of blood..." One of Scotrail's three-carriage First liveried trains caught his attention, as it trundled toward the small town's mainline station. Head aching, he turned to his colleague. "The full Coroner's report came in this morning." He shrugged. "Adds nothing helpful to the interim report we had at the beginning of the week; small quantity of alcohol in the blood and nothing else."

"No help, eh?" O'Leary said, pulling the crotch of his trousers free.

"No," the Scot confirmed, watching with distaste as the other continued to adjust his manhood. "Anyhow, we need to talk to the ghillie again. We can catch him before we see the MacCaig lad."

"You don't believe in hanging about, do you?"

"True."

As O'Leary began pulling on his jacket, the Scot

was already disappearing down the stairwell.

While they drove in silence toward Kinloch Rannoch, the breeze strengthened under a darkening sky. Within a few minutes, spatters of rain appeared on the windscreen. The occasional piece of dying foliage, stripped from native woodland by the wind, plastered itself to the glass. Squirting screen-wash at the offending debris when his view became obscured, Lamont cursed under his breath, although in truth, he was cursing life in general.

His world seemed to be in a fugue state. Elspeth was ill, the case was going nowhere quickly, he was losing concentration and feeling dizzy and O'Leary was but a ghost in the machine. To complicate matters, Tortolano, sensing his weaknesses, was already thinking for herself. As the tortuous B road skirted the shores of Loch Tummel, he wondered just what else could happen to alter his normally so predictable existence.

"Full wash-wipe bottle is a good idea up here in autumn," he said quietly, as spray blurred his view of the road ahead.

"Good idea anytime," O'Leary offered. "If it's not falling leaves, it's oil from trucks and delivery vans."

As they pulled through the crested estate gates, Lamont took the branch road to the left and drove up toward Tosland's cottage. When they arrived, the ghillie was in the cobbled yard; a broad, untidy space between the heavily fenced dog run and the cottage, chatting animatedly to a middle-aged woman.

"All right Mac," she was saying, as they got out of the car into a downpour. "Keep her inside and warm for a few days. I'll come over again on Monday. Phone if you need me before then, alright?"

Closing the driver's door for her, he said warmly: "Aye, thanks. Ye've been a great help."

Pulling on his coat, Lamont fastened the buttons as they approached the couple.

"Hello again," said Tosland. Rain dripped off the soaked beanie as he spoke, and ran down his nose. He wiped it away with the back of his hand. "This is our vet, Mrs Thompson."

"Hello," she said, in an off-hand tone. The woman gave them no eye contact. "Right Mac, remember: phone if you need me!"

Closing the window, she started the Mitsubishi's engine. They watched as it drove round the tree screen into the narrow track and disappeared through the surrounding woodland.

"Shall we get out of the rain?" said Lamont, glancing knowingly at his colleague. They followed the gamekeeper into the small stone cottage.

"That's a fine fire you've got there," said O'Leary.

Rubbing his hands together vigorously, he stopped in front of the wood-burner.

Tosland nodded. "It's no' usually oan in the autumn, but it heats the water an' saves oan the electric bill."

"Every little helps, eh?"

Nodding in agreement, he asked: "Wid yeh like a cup o' tea?"

"No," Lamont said. "Nice of you to offer."

"How can I help ye then?"

"Can you confirm what time you returned here from your brother's house in Kingussie, the Monday Jock died?" he asked, taking in his surroundings.

The pale green walls hadn't been painted for several years, but were decorated with a variety of modern prints and photographs of wildlife, as well as loch and mountain scenes. The little room was untidy, but not by any means dirty. A photographic tripod lay against the wall beside a bulky, old-fashioned television.

O'Leary had wiped the rainwater from his face with a tissue and was now looking around for somewhere to deposit it. Tosland reached out and took the soggy paper from him, dropping it onto the pile of logs beside the fire.

"Afternoon before a' goat back here," he replied.

"And what time did you leave Kingussie?" O'Leary asked. Picking up an Olympus camera he'd been eyeing from the mantle, he studied it enviously.

"Early oors, ah think," Tosland said, "must've been aroond five or so."

The ghillie put out his hand to retrieve the old OM10 camera from the other detective.

"If you dinnae mind…"

O'Leary handed it over. "Sorry."

"My first," he said, putting the camera back on its preferred spot. "Thirty years auld. Dinnae want it damaged."

"Like photography?"

"Best way tae shoot, if ye ask me."

Lamont thought the statement an odd one, coming as it had from a ghillie. Rarely had he heard of more contradictory hobbies; after all, the man bred game birds, and his wages were earned by leading men to positions from which they could kill both them and the red deer.

"Have you spoken to your brother in the last twenty-four hours?"

"Speak tae him most days," he said. "He telt me that ye've been checkin' tae see that a wis there, right enough."

"But you gave my colleague here," he said, raising a hand toward O'Leary, "the impression that you'd not arrived back till late afternoon."

"And that's as true as I said it wis."

"So where did you go after you left the Frodyke Filling Station at five-fifteen in the morning?"

"Why do ye ask?"

"Because we need to know, Mac," the detective stated firmly.

The ghillie shrugged casually and put another log on the fire.

"Listen," he said, "a young man was gunned down here last week. We really need to find the killer..."

O'Leary glanced at his partner before interrupting.

"Did you kill Jock?"

The question had been posed bluntly, but aside from a dismissive shake the head, the sturdy figure didn't react.

"Unless you tell us where you went after leaving your brother," Lamont said. "We'll have no choice but to arrest you."

"Whit fur?" the ghillie complained loudly. "I've done nothing wrong!"

"For obstructing our investigations for a start," said O'Leary. "And while we then carry out further enquiries into your whereabouts on…"

"Christ man!" he growled. "She's just bloody-well left! *That's* ma reason, man!"

"The vet?"

O'Leary had clearly been taken off guard, but Lamont didn't look at all surprised.

"Ah met her here at aroond ten o'clock," he explained. "Her man gets the 6.30 train tae Edinburgh. Even checked he went fur it. Then he flies doon tae London fur the week."

"Very convenient," muttered O'Leary. "Told me you weren't here until late afternoon."

"Can you tell us what time you got back here?" Lamont asked.

"Not long before she arrived."

"So, where were you between five-fifteen and then?" Lamont asked, unconsciously rubbing his head.

"Ah telt ye. Makin' sure her man goat the train. Then I drove here. Went intae the village shop first though, fur milk and some bacon."

"Bit convenient if you don't mind me saying,"

O'Leary said, looking at him disbelievingly. "Driving over to the village first – where the shop-keeper knows you – just to get milk and bacon. You could have picked that up on the way."

"Where?" he responded, frustrated by the questions. "There wis nane in the petrol station."

"Were the dogs in their kennels when you eventually got here?" Lamont asked. Putting a hand to his head, he tried not to allow his features to distort as another dark wave of discomfort struck.

"Aye," he replied. "Ask Beth, she'll tell ye."

"Beth?"

"Mrs Thompson," he confirmed angrily.

Clearly the ghillie hadn't wanted his relationship exposed by the investigation. Lamont began to wonder what else the man had hidden to protect himself, or the interests of his friends. Would he lie to defend an employer like Lord MacCaig?

Noticing his partner's apparent discomfort, O'Leary took the reins, asking: "How long have you and the good lady vet been associated?"

"What dis that mater?"

"It matters because we're asking!" Lamont demanded. "This is a murder enquiry, not a bloody polite conversation Mr Tosland! Now, an answer…"

The man's face set, and for a moment it appeared as though further cooperation was beyond him, but he sullenly said, "Three years."

"Does anyone else know? The MacCaig family, or their staff for example."

"No."

"But they would know when you were, '*indisposed*', and when the dogs needed to be back in their kennels," he argued.

"Ah always know if the dugs hiv been oot anyway," the man replied. "They're breathless, manky an' wet: canna be helped, livin' in a damp, boggy forest."

Although his vision blurred a little, Lamont maintained the thread of questioning.

"And you're sure they'd been out when you got back?"

"Aye. Lord MacCaig sometimes comes across an' lets them oot fur a run if ah'm late," he said. "So ah thought nothing o' it."

Having seen MacCaig return filthy from outside work, Lamont accepted this as being a reasonable assertion.

As the pain subsided a little, the misty veil began to lift from his eyes. Taking out his mobile, the Scots detective asked: "Have you a number for Beth Thompson?"

The ghillie hesitated for a moment before reading it to him.

Lamont keyed the digits into the Blackberry then pressed 'call'. There was no consistent signal.

"Great," he muttered.

Before he could ask, Tosland passed him the house phone. The number was already ringing.

He nodded in gratitude.

"Mrs Thompson… Detective Lamont," he began quickly. "Yes, that was us…. yes… Can we meet? Now, please… yes, your surgery in the village… no problem. Be with you in ten minutes? Good."

Gesturing to O'Leary, he popped another mint between his teeth and offered his thanks to the ghillie. Tosland ignored him. The man looked thoroughly fed up and offered no eye contact as they left.

Holding up his coat collar, Lamont hurried over to the car, his partner in tow.

"What do you think?" O'Leary asked, fastening the seatbelt.

Taking off the rain-spattered glasses, the Scot was using a tissue to dry them.

"Tosland might not have pulled the trigger, but I'm not convinced he doesn't know who did."

"You don't think…?"

"*We* don't think too clearly," he said, as another fleeting pulse of pain coursed through his head.

O'Leary didn't disagree and shrugged as his partner put a heavy foot on the accelerator. As the Audi threw wet grit and gravel noisily into the wheel arches and jolted forward, the Scots detective was angry for having missed the obvious by not thinking laterally.

"And when we do think," he complained, "it's usually about the wrong bloody things."

"What's wrong now?"

"Nothing that'll change the course of events. I just missed something obvious earlier in the week."

Chapter 19

The deluge had eased by the time they reached Kinloch Rannoch, although spits of rain were still blowing through the gusting wind. Half a mile east of the village, they turned off the road onto a short gravel track. The vet's practice lay no more than fifty yards behind a thicket of natural woodland.

'Rannoch Veterinary Surgeon', the tidy cream and green lettered, brass wall plate announced. Lamont thought the building looked relatively new. Built in the style of one of the local eighteenth century stone country houses, it sat beneath a natural slate roof. The property obviously served as both domestic and work quarters for Beth Thompson. Another large rectangular building with, 'Theatre Care Suite' on a sign by the entrance sat to the right of several tarmacked parking bays. The sound of the fast flowing River Tummel rushing through the glen below filled the air.

"Very neat," said O'Leary, taking it in. He stood for a moment absorbing the scene stretching from the river, nearly a hundred yards below, up toward the rugged Perthshire hills.

"Beautiful," he remarked. "Business must be good."

"Not short of a bob or two, the old veterinary types," the Scot agreed, getting out of the car. "These hills are full of lambs, beef cattle and working dogs; not to mention the local pets."

"Special, eh?"

There appeared to be genuine appreciation of the environment in the city dweller's eyes.

"You'll be wanting a job here next."

"I'll be wanting a job, full stop – any job," he replied easily, although too easily for Lamont's liking.

The Theatre Care Suite door opened and Beth Thompson made her way over to them in an outfit resembling sterile hospital greens.

"Thanks for seeing us, Mrs Thompson." Lamont extended a hand. He guessed the woman to be in her fifties, though she looked and sounded younger. Her long, neatly cut hair was kept back from her face in a ponytail. "Not interrupting, are we?"

"Yes, but I've ten minutes free," she said pleasantly. "Come into the house. My nurse is taking care of old Bert."

"Bert?"

"Sheepdog. The old boy's sired half the pups in this glen. He's a highly intelligent beast. Every local shepherd wants his offspring."

"I see," he said. "Good to be popular."

"Not a police dog then," O'Leary muttered as he followed them into the property.

Closing the front door, Beth Thompson asked if they wanted coffee.

Both men declined the offer as she led the way to her surgery office.

"Hope you don't mind coming through here," she said apologetically. "But I've theatre greens on and don't want them in the house."

"No problem."

Perching on a swivel stool at the desk, she said: "So how can I help you?"

"It's about Jock MacCaig's murder, Mrs Thompson." Lamont watched her face carefully and noted the slight flicker of her eyes.

"I thought it might be," she responded, suddenly sounding weary. "From what Mac told me on the phone anyway..."

"Tell me what you know about Jock MacCaig," he asked. The detective felt heavy with regret. He would rather not be here, asking questions, but had caught the inflection in her tone. Lamont knew his assumptions hadn't been wrong. Glancing toward O'Leary, he decided at that moment he had little choice but to be both blunt and brutal. Sensing there wasn't much time, he needed answers from her before confronting MacCaig.

"You see, we're confused as to why such a fine young man, who worked tirelessly for others – and much loved as he was..." Lamont let the words hang for a moment before continuing, "should end his days, body torn apart, floating on Loch Rannoch with his head blown open..."

"That's enough!" she cried angrily. "That's..."

Covering her face, the woman broke down and

began sobbing bitterly.

"He was your son, Mrs Thompson, wasn't he?" he said gently: "Your maiden name was Ann Bethany Beattie. Am I right?"

"Oh Jock," she sobbed. "Oh God, my boy… poor, poor, Jock…"

As he got up and went over to comfort the vet, Lamont looked across at his open-mouthed colleague, shook his head and shrugged.

"Tell us what happened, please," he said. "The father…"

A directive gesture sent O'Leary to find a glass of water. Returning after a moment, he passed it over.

When she eventually stopped sobbing, Beth said hesitantly: "Mac is – was – his Dad." Taking the water, she quietly thanked him for his kindness and took a sip. "We were young and wild. I never stopped loving Mac – even after Norah came along."

"Norah was his wife?"

"Yes," she said. "Couldn't bring him children, but he already had Jock…" She struggled for a moment before regaining her composure. "Even though he never knew."

"Do you mind taking us through the chronology of events, please," he asked. "It'll help immensely."

"Yes, sorry, of course."

Beth Thompson wiped her eyes repeatedly, as she explained how she had met Mackenzie Tosland. It had been during a winter ceilidh at the town hall shortly after she arrived in Pitlochry. The woman explained that the ceilidh was the biggest social event of the year in their community. Trying hard not to sob, she recounted how the tall, sandy-haired Scot had asked her to the floor for a waltz.

He'd said she looked like a lonely wallflower and his wife thought a dance would do her good. Afterwards, she had been invited to join them at their table.

Discovering she was a vet, newly arrived to work with the Pitlochry practise on secondment, he'd told her of the opportunity that had arisen in Rannoch. He explained that the elderly practitioner in the village had let the practice fall apart. A fine man in his day, he had been proving both increasingly difficult to get hold of and expensive. Apparently the man was using practise monies to subsidise excessive drinking and was desperate to sell up.

Grabbing the opportunity, she bought the practice using borrowed money from the local bank. Then, not long afterwards, she and Tosland had indulged in a wild one-night fling. She explained that Norah, his wife, had gone off to the city to visit her parents for a few days. She met Mac again purely by accident, but had not wanted any involvement with a married man, despite her attraction to him.

Rubbing his head distractedly, Lamont nodded his understanding.

O'Leary gestured over, glancing toward his wristwatch, but the Scot had already registered their time constraints. Keeping his attention focussed on the vet, he thought it possible she may yet reveal something of value.

Beth went on to explain that she had been celebrating her acquisition with friends in the local pub when Mac turned up. After inviting the ruggedly handsome local into the group as a courtesy, they'd got chatting again. Despite only wanting to thank him for his tip-off about the practise, one thing led to another and they ended up spending the night together.

The woman explained how, a few weeks later, she found herself single, deeply in debt to the bank, and pregnant. She hadn't told Mac: he was poor and already married. More importantly, her strongest instincts were to protect the man, for she had fallen in love with him.

At the time Tosland was working as a beater. When asked, he also acted as guide for wealthy hunters visiting the estates around the local Perthshire glens, or giving riding lessons in his spare time. Beth told them how, despite her emotions, they avoided further liaisons, even though she longed to be close to him. She had preferred their fling remain a secret to avoid hurting his wife. As a result, for years they'd done no more than pass a few warm words on the rare occasions they met.

Luck however, had not completely deserted her. One of the then Lady MacCaig's horses had required veterinary care. She therefore had little choice but to make repeated visits to the estate. The two women had become friends. Eventually, Beth told her of the pregnancy, but had never revealed who the father was.

Strangely, Catherine MacCaig had seemed thrilled, confiding that she and Alex were desperate to have children. The woman explained she had already lost three pregnancies through miscarriages. Tragically, eminent gynaecologists in London had confirmed that, for her, successful childbirth was highly unlikely.

And so a deal had been struck between the pretty young vet and the aristocratic couple. Beth however, promised herself never to reveal who the child's father was. If asked, she would choose to say it been the result of a passing acquaintance: an encounter with an attractive stranger during a trip home to England. The lie had worked. Both of the MacCaigs, excitedly planning for a baby's arrival, were too preoccupied to be concerned with fine detail.

The detectives looked on as Beth told them that it had all been too easy at first: she was pregnant; the MacCaigs wanted a child. It had been that simple. Lord MacCaig had even helped with the expenses involved in paying off her loan and mortgage debts to the bank. Further, the wealthy landowner then paid for hiring a locum vet. This ensured the practise was managed while she spent three months at her parents' home in Leeds. Free of prying eyes, the secret of the pregnancy had been kept safe.

The only complication had come when Alex MacCaig made it clear that, in keeping with family tradition, the baby had to be born on Scottish soil. Beth had then been forced to return to Perthshire for the birth. Staying in a discreet country hotel for more than a fortnight, she'd had frequent visits from the MacCaigs and the support of a private midwife, whom they'd paid to stay by her side.

O'Leary went over and comforted Beth as she became tearful again. Both detectives were deeply moved by her sincerity, whatever her role in their investigations.

After apologising profusely for the emotion, she went on to explain that during her long absence, MacCaig had hired Mac as ghillie. Shocked to see him at the estate, she realised that nothing could be said without revealing the baby was his. Apart from wrecking his marriage, she said, it would also have made it impossible for Mac to continue working at Castle Druin, and for her to remain the vet in this close-knit, rural community. So, despite the anxieties and internal conflict this brought, neither man was ever told who the child's father was.

Two years later she met and eventually married Harry Thompson, a London financier. At that time, he visited the glen fairly regularly on shooting trips. She explained – with the obvious discomfort of someone who feels they are being hugely disloyal – how they had tried unsuccessfully to have children for a couple of years before learning of his sterility.

"And how long have you been seeing Mac this time round?" asked Lamont, gently.

Beth looked at him and smiled weakly.

"It feels like we've never stopped seeing each other, really…" Her voice was full of regret and her eyes glazed over as she spoke. "But then three years ago, I went over to the kennels – one of my regular checks on the dog pack. Instead of him going on his way like he usually did, we just got talking. We're both lonely but…" She hesitated, and then sighed wearily. "I'd never stopped loving him."

"Did you tell your husband about Jock being your son?"

"No, there was no need," she said, quickly

gathering herself. "Promised myself never to tell anyone and I haven't. I told him I'd once had a child, but that it had been adopted long before I came to live near Kinloch Rannoch."

"And Harry works in London, you say?" His mind now working overtime, he asked, "Who for?"

"One of the big investment houses. Anderson Scotland, they're called.

"And do you think he suspects you of having an affair? I mean, we know he's away in London all week, but we all have a way of finding these things out, don't we?"

"It's possible I suppose," she replied. "Though I don't think Harry would let that go unmentioned."

"Would he be angry?" O'Leary asked.

"Angry?" Beth Thompson shook her head and laughed scornfully. "He'd be livid!"

"Can I clarify," said Lamont. "You do intend to tell him, don't you?"

"Yes," she replied regretfully. "Mac and I want to be together."

"By the way," he said. "Did no one ever comment on how much Jock resembled Mac?"

"I suppose they were rarely seen together outside the estate," she said, "and Jock was always so well presented in public – and well-spoken, too. And Mac is, well, like Mac."

"Can I ask one last thing?"

Beth nodded.

"Did you let the dogs out on the morning Jock died?"

"No," she replied. "Why?"

"A question, Mrs Thompson, no more," he said thoughtfully. "Thanks anyway."

As the officers rose to leave, she touched Lamont's arm.

"Find whoever killed my boy, will you?"

"I'll try my best," he said sincerely. "There's one photo I've seen of Jock with Mac. It's on the wall up in Jock's rooms at the Castle. You might ask Lord MacCaig for it."

"I will," she said, touched by his thoughtfulness. "That I will, thank you."

"By the way," he said. "What time does your husband normally get up to go into Pitlochry for his train?"

"Used to be around four thirty," she said. "But he sleeps in his own room these days, so I'm not sure."

They left Beth Thompson washing her face as she gathered herself for busy old Bert, the collie.

O'Leary nodded toward the theatre building as they stepped out into the fresh, moist air. "At least she's got that to keep her mind off things," he said, breathing in the strong smell of wet woodland.

"She'll need more than that after telling her man what she's up to," Lamont replied. Something was nagging at him again; something he'd forgotten, but he was damned if he could remember.

Bloody pain! he thought, wincing.

"Good one with the records offices in Perth," O'Leary said, as they got into the car. He noticed again that the Scot was rubbing his head. "Even better spot with the photo. Nicer if you could share these things."

"The records office search was young Tortolano," he responded, starting up the Audi and accelerating off in the direction of the castle. "Once she had the mother's name, I asked her to cross reference it against any marriages during the ten year period after the birth."

"Good on her, otherwise we might be chasing shadows in the Tuscan sun," he said wistfully. "Mind you, running around Italy with young Miss T to interpret doesn't sound too bad either!"

"Wouldn't for you, I suppose," Lamont grumbled.

"What's that supposed to mean?"

"Single, free," he said, "though a bit too long in the tooth."

"Missed out 'racist' in that jibe."

"Not proven," Lamont said, and winked. "Yet."

As they turned into the castle driveway, O'Leary felt a degree of frustration at gaining so little information about his own interests. He had learned a lot about Lamont during the past twenty-four hours, but that was it. It would now be difficult to make progress without revealing his true purpose.

The splendid oak door swung open and Lady Helen greeted them. Svelte and smooth in a tight fitting grey dress, the seductive figure coolly invited them in. Lamont noticed that her long hair was still tied back, exposing the exquisite shape of her high cheekbones and the smooth, warm complexion resting on them.

It was then the flash of guilt hit as he reflected on Elspeth. They had talked of it often: what would happen if either of them died? A deep remorse and discomfort cut him as he engaged Helen MacCaig's inviting eyes.

As she ushered them through into the dining room, he had the sudden urge to abandon the interview and head for home, knowing he was more needed there. Then the cold, logical, mental processes kicked in and his thoughts fell into place.

"Have a seat, Alex will be with you in a couple of minutes," she said. "He's out back. I think they're planning the beaters' route for the next shooting party arriving. Will you have coffee?"

"Yes, thanks, Lady Helen," O'Leary said. "That would be greatly appreciated."

"Could I ask before you leave," said Lamont. "Do you personally have any dealings with Anderson Scotland, an investment company in London?"

"Of course," she said easily. "They assist Cameron Corporate in the management of AidenallafricA's Forex investments."

"So you'll know Harry Thomson?"

"Not that well."

Watching her full lips enunciate the words, he heard the lie. It rang in his mind like an early morning alarm. He could almost feel them at times. Perhaps it was hand movement, or body language, or inflection in the tone, a momentary hesitation, or the eye movement – whatever, he knew.

"But you do know him?"

"Yes," she said. "He's senior partner in the investment firm we use down in Canary Wharf. Seems very competent. Deals mostly with Alistair Cameron."

"And he's a local too, apparently."

"Well, yes, lives nearby – he's the estate vet's husband, as it happens," she confirmed.

"Very handy," O'Leary said cheerfully, knowing there was no better way of gaining information than to distract an interviewee. "You'll be moving the Square Mile up here the way things are going. I can see it now: 'The Rannoch Eye' revolving over Pitlochry."

Lamont asked: "Shoots this estate?"

"Yes, but not very often. I don't think Alex likes him that much."

"And do you?"

"A business relationship, detective," she said. "Just business."

Helen MacCaig looked unsettled by the question, though she was a smooth liar. He gave her another verbal prod.

"Business?"

"Yes, detective – business," she said testily. "Is that all?"

"Yes, thanks again, Lady Helen," he said, running a hand slowly over the table, admiring its patina.

As she left, the detectives found themselves drawn to watch her lengthy legs stride casually out of site across the grand hall.

The Scot raised his eyebrows.

"And she knows it," he said scornfully. "Probably the most dangerous weapon in this house."

"That's for sure."

"You don't think we should call her back; ask her about Jock again?"

"Won't help us."

In the three hours since they'd left Pitlochry, the intense pain in Lamont's head had peaked. It was now subsiding and the accompanying wave of relief released a momentary glow of warmth through his body.

"No?" O'Leary appeared to be uncertain.

"Besides which, she'll only lie," said the Scot, quietly. "And we'll get ourselves flung out. Won't lead us anywhere either, trust me."

Looking at the complex character that was Detective Lamont for a moment, O'Leary decided the man knew where he was going, but didn't know how to take others with him. It seemed as though his perceptions and analysis of a crime stayed private: his very own personal property. Possibly this was a lack of trust; or even a fear of his thoughts and interpretations of events being ridiculed. He shrugged inwardly. When this enquiry had finished, part of him hoped he would never again hear of the moody Scotsman.

"Any thoughts on our new friend, Mr Thompson, the vet's hubby?" Lamont asked.

"Yet another complication in a tangled web of relationships and money," he murmured. Both men were being careful not to be overheard outside the room. "And that's about all. Another one that likes playing with other people's money. Gives me a headache!"

"Snap," the Scot agreed. "Still, check him out, will you?"

"If I must…"

Before O'Leary could ask what his colleague wanted to probe further with MacCaig, the peer strode into the room, closing the door firmly behind him. As he slung his heavy jacket over a chair and threw a silk scarf beside it, Lamont saw that the man's lemon coloured shirt and pale chinos were covered in heavy stains from working around the estate.

MacCaig noticed the look of appraisal.

"Wrong gear for the job, I'm afraid," he said, "but better than throwing them out when they've done their time, eh?"

"Would still be my best gear," said O'Leary. Having noted the expensive designer motif on the shirt's breast pocket, he added: "Even stained."

"Helen's ordered you coffee," he said, ignoring the remark. "Mrs Robb will be with us shortly."

"Great, thanks."

Lamont had been thumbing something into his Blackberry. Finishing the text, he pressed 'send'.

"Sorry," he offered, after a moment's silence. "Texting with these thumbs is never easy."

"Can't work those things myself," MacCaig said. "Gave up trying years ago."

"You don't mind if I ask a few questions again, Lord MacCaig?" he began. "I know we've made life a little difficult, but we're still trying to find your son's killer – as if you need reminding." Throwing an apologetic gesture, he said: "You know we're also happy if you feel you need legal representation?"

"I fully understand," he replied. "But for the moment, no."

The detective remained unconvinced by the man's composed persona.

"About your son, Jock," Lamont said, with a hint of compassion. "Did he know who his mother was?"

"No," MacCaig replied. It was clear from his expression that he wondered where the question was leading. "However, it never seemed to bother him."

"Did he ever ask who Ann Beattie – the woman whose maternal name is on his birth certificate – was?"

"He did once, as I remember," he answered, thoughtfully. "Would have been seventeen or eighteen at the time."

"And what happened?"

"I told him that she was a pretty young English girl who'd become pregnant by accident and, wanting to go on with her career, she'd offered him for adoption," he elaborated ruefully. "Not really a lie either."

"Do you know if he ever researched his roots further for himself as he got older?"

"I never asked."

"I see." Surprised, Lamont made a mental note. Changing the subject, he said: "You'll know we've been looking through the charity's investment accounts."

"Alistair's apparently under investigation now, yes?" MacCaig spoke briskly and let the question hang in the room's fragrant air.

"No, AidenallafricA's accounts are under investigation. I wouldn't want to personalise our enquiries, Lord MacCaig."

"Perhaps not," he said. "But my friend certainly feels threatened by your behaviour."

"If he's done nothing wrong, then there shouldn't be a problem."

"As long as you both know," he confirmed, narrowing his gaze, "he's a man in whom I have complete confidence. I don't want him besmirched."

This, Lamont felt, was the first clear threat that power and influence could be brought to bear to protect friends if necessary.

"And as you've said, he's a friend, Lord MacCaig," O'Leary added. "Who may have other matters that require the tax inspector's enquiries more than ours."

"So it would seem…" MacCaig put his hands in his trouser pockets and responded in a firm tone: "You'll appreciate I've also had to speak to my friends in Edinburgh?"

"Your political allies are of no concern to us," Lamont said dismissively. "Whatever we do here will be focussed entirely on finding your son's murderer;

not damaging the charitable cause he apparently loved and worked for so tirelessly."

He watched for MacCaig's reaction to the praise of his dead son.

"That's very considerate of you," the man said finally. "To recognise his devotion to Africa."

"Not at all," the detective said easily. "We believe that's how it was. But he was angry about the possible misuse of the charity's monies."

After a few moments thought, MacCaig shook his head and gave a heavy sigh.

"If that's a question, then yes, he was angry. I am too. But trust me, if anyone has been using, or abusing the monies raised by our charity for their own gain, I'll personally see to it that they never get close to money, or any other finance related matters, for as long as they breathe!"

The door opened, interrupting the powerful figure's flow.

"'Scuse me gents, your coffee," said Mrs Robb, coming over to the table carrying a small wooden tray with three tall, blue coffee mugs on it.

Distracted for a moment, MacCaig waited patiently until she'd put it down and left.

"Trust me gentlemen, I'll finish them, friend or not," he added threateningly. The anger in his voice was unmistakable "Your senior officer in Stirling has been advised of this too."

Expression oozing a mixture of confidence and belligerence, MacCaig looked like a man fighting to retain control of his world.

Believing he would be good to his word, Lamont accepted he was a dangerous opponent – but that wouldn't stop the detective seeking a positive result from their enquiries: not now.

Taking a glance over, he noticed O'Leary staring at the peer, eyes seemingly filled with contempt. Convinced his partner had another agenda in this investigation, the Scot thought it better to ease the growing tension. Whatever O'Leary's problem was; they were hunting a murderer.

"You said your son, Ewan, travels up from Cambridge today?" he asked.

"Yes, arrived earlier – just after lunch."

"You won't mind if we talk to him?"

His tone made their intentions clear, regardless of MacCaig's views. As he sipped the coffee thoughtfully, Lamont could see the bulk of Schiehallion through the long, gothic-styled windows, its conical peak lost in broken cloud. For a brief moment earlier in the day, he had wished himself up there in wild weather, rather than churning through MacCaig's complex personal life. It had been a bad day, he thought, when his concentration became diminished in any way. And today was bad. However, if it weren't for Elspeth's problems, things wouldn't be so unusual. Reassuring himself that she would be fine didn't help, but with each passing second he felt more like confronting the task in hand and less like escaping into a dull, deflated mood.

"If you need to," MacCaig said. "Though I can't begin to think what good chatting to Ewan will do."

"It may achieve little, right enough," O'Leary said.

"But he may throw a glimmer of light on something, eh?"

Glaring angrily in response to the supposition, MacCaig's growing dislike for the English detective was becoming ever more evident.

"Can I ask," Lamont said, "were Ewan and his brother friends?"

"Why?"

"We need to exclude Ewan from our enquiries, Lord MacCaig," he explained. "Were they friends?"

"No," he replied, after a moment. "They don't... sorry, they didn't get on. Sibling rivalry thing with brothers, I suppose."

"But they weren't natural brothers," O'Leary interjected. "Could that have affected how they got along?"

"I shouldn't have thought so," he replied, testily.

With the man now becoming increasingly irritable, Lamont thought it time to give him a jolt while his defences were otherwise engaged.

"We were chatting to Beth Thompson – as Ann Bethany Beattie now is – a little earlier," he said carefully.

MacCaig stared at him blankly, though seemed to realise that his private life had finally entered the public domain. A very personal dam had been breached and the floodwaters were inexorably rising.

"And what would you like me to say?"

"Well," he said. "She's the local vet, so you must have regular contact with her."

"Been here frequently over the years, yes."

"Get on well?"

"No reason not to." Looking deliberately from one to the other, MacCaig asked: "And just where are you heading with these stupid questions?" Raising his hand, the man gestured by waving an index finger. "You're very much mistaken if you think I'll tolerate them."

The Scots detective narrowed his eyes. It was a warning, right enough, but he wouldn't stop the line of questioning. Regardless of the man's defensive protests, someone in the community had committed a very well planned murder, and he wanted to know both who, and why.

"How well are you acquainted with Harry Thompson, her husband?"

"Not my type, though he does business for us through Cameron Corporate, for the Anderson Scotland group," he said, almost distastefully. "Shoots the estate by invite, as and when."

"As and when?"

"As and when I need to see him away from business," he said. "Keeps the two organisations' relationships sweet."

Despite having offered the veiled threat of no longer tolerating their questions, Lamont gauged that the man didn't seem particularly unhappy to continue fending them off. The passing thought struck him that this character may actually get his kicks out of verbal sparring.

"Detective, even when you don't like people, it's

still important they're offered your hospitality. Helps to make sure they provide the quality of work you want."

"And Thompson's work is of a high standard?"

"According to Alistair Cameron, it is," he responded defensively.

From his own, deliberate tone, the detective knew he appeared to be suggesting that impropriety coursed through this man – and his two financial experts – like blood through an artery.

"And he's a friend to you both?"

"No, Alistair's not too fond of him, although he introduced us," he said haughtily. "Mayors Burns Supper down in Glasgow a few years ago, as I recall."

"And how close was Jock to all this?"

"Jock played no part in any of it," he replied. MacCaig's voice still held a tone of intense irritation. "I'll not have my son's name derided or…"

Interrupting to make his point, Lamont said: "I didn't imply he *had* played a part, Lord MacCaig."

The detective had spoken very firmly. Now becoming more assertive, he suddenly sounded much less like a man concerned by whose toes he trampled on in pursuit of the truth.

Relaxing a little, O'Leary sat back as the show warmed up.

"And your point is?" MacCaig said.

"My point is, that we sense Jock's death may have had something to do with financial irregularities," said Lamont, pushing at the bridge of his glasses.

"You've tried that line already," he said, shaking his head dismissively. Despite knowing the risks involved in encouraging the questions, he smiled and ventured: "Go on then, how do you work that out?"

"Appears he'd found irregularities in the Forex dealings done on the charity's behalf. We know he'd gone to meet Gio's father at the Banco dei Lourgho Basso over in Italy before coming home."

"There was no impropriety there."

"Or so we believe," he agreed. The detective waited a moment to see if the man would be drawn further before continuing. "But the accounts may help us clarify matters?"

"Good luck with that one!" MacCaig exclaimed, but his face had paled considerably.

Changing tack, the detective asked: "As eldest male sibling, was Jock the principal beneficiary in your will?"

He knew before the man replied what the response would be, for Jock was not a MacCaig by birth.

"No, my estate passes to Ewan."

Belatedly, stung by his own utterance, he glanced over his shoulder to make sure Mrs Robb had closed the door properly.

"And does Lady Helen know this?"

"No, there's no need," he replied airily. "This is a family matter."

"So it may be," Lamont said, "but Lady Helen is family…"

He watched as the man squirmed visibly.

"Can I ask if Ewan is aware of the will and its contents?"

"Well, no…"

Only then did MacCaig understand where Lamont's questioning was heading.

"You don't think," he said loudly, "that one of my sons – or my wife for that matter – would do harm to each other for money? That's preposterous!"

"Is it?"

Rising slowly from his seat, MacCaig leant across the large table and looked at the detective as though he'd grown two heads.

"You *must* be completely lost in this investigation!"

"Are we?"

"You people have no idea what you're doing, or where you're heading," he challenged. Then, drawing a deep breath, he added: "And let me tell you, the chasm in front of you is very, very, deep!"

"Is that a threat?"

"Threat? For God's sakes!" he spat. "I mean, if these accusations are the best you can come up with, detective…"

Returning the man's hard eye contact, the Scot decided it was time to kick MacCaig in the balls.

"And what if I told you that Mackenzie Tosland was Jock's natural father?"

Eyes wide with surprise, Alex MacCaig stood frozen, like an alerted stag. Knuckles clenched against the table, he stared open-mouthed at Lamont. The detective could have driven one of the many antique Claymore swords that adorned the castle's walls clean through his stomach and had a lesser impact.

"Where did you find that out?" he asked.

His own words sounded weak as the revelation sunk in. It became clear, perhaps for the first time, the strange role that fate could play in determining your future. Pure chance, a gamble, or a thought: one fatal, decisive moment drew you forward to glory, or brought you to your knees.

"Guessed it at first," he responded. "Then his mother confirmed it this morning."

"I see..."

Looking on, O'Leary wondered if MacCaig might open up further if he briefly left the scene. He gestured discreetly to Lamont, then asked: "Would you like a glass of water, Lord MacCaig?"

'No," the man replied. The voice sounded empty and he rubbed his face, almost as though trying to erase the years of wear. "No, I'm fine."

The Scot knew this response was far from truthful. Over the years, MacCaig had been prepared to delude himself that all was well. The delusion was equally true, both in the financial world – where others were probably mismanaging the charity's resources – and in his emotional life. Helen MacCaig had been sleeping with his adopted son: a son whose natural father worked for the estate as ghillie and had done for more than thirty years. Chaos seemed to prevail in every corner of his life, but Lamont was still not convinced he was a mere victim of fate.

"We'd like to see Ewan, now please," Lamont said, assuming a commanding tone.

It had been his intention to ask MacCaig if he believed his wife and Jock had been a little too close, but decided against it. Eventually, the question would have to be asked, for he wasn't convinced Lord MacCaig hadn't played a part, by accident or otherwise, in his adopted son's death.

"Yes, I'll see that he comes straight down," he replied. The tone was dull and flat, from a man experiencing a rare taste of defeat. "You've no more need of me at the moment, I take it?'

Picking up the jacket and scarf, he had almost got through the door when Lamont's voice stopped him.

"Mac Tosland doesn't know Jock's his son, Lord MacCaig. Might be better if Beth tells him herself, don't you think?"

Without looking back, he grunted in agreement with the proposition.

"Oh, and your secret's safe with us. The local bobbies won't know either unless it comes out at some point in court, of course."

But MacCaig was through the door and gone without responding. Later, when the dust had settled, he would appreciate the detective's sensitive management of his personal secrets. At that moment however, he would have greeted their deaths with a sneer.

O'Leary swilled down the coffee dregs from his mug.

"Nice one," he said grudgingly. "Just don't offer

your services to the Samaritans."

Lamont threw his fellow detective a dark glance, but said nothing. As yet, no matter what they uncovered, their enquiries appeared no nearer to finding Jock's murderer and the case had become ever more confusing. This didn't usually trouble him during an investigation, but the security of his personal life had been undermined *and* he was trying to work with two new partners. Worse still, he was suffering lapses in concentration and a disturbing fear of revisiting that feeling of falling into a bottomless crevasse.

He wondered what someone like him, looking in from the outside, would make of his recent behaviour. Elspeth had a serious health problem, yet he was still at work, focussed and driven. Worse, his consciousness was occasionally being disturbed by other women's physical attractions.

Resolving to try sharing more *and* be a better partner, he would take a more thoughtful approach with Elspeth tonight. She needed tenderness and love. It was time to build those and a greater level of understanding onto the foundations laid in France.

The abrupt arrival of Ewan MacCaig, an almost dapper, youthful, but overweight replica of the middle-aged father, interrupted his thoughts. He watched as the man slouched noisily into the master's chair at the head of the table.

"Thanks for coming in to talk to us," said Lamont.

The man acknowledged his courtesy with an almost imperceptible nod of the head.

Noticing the resentment, Lamont wasted no more time being polite.

"We believe you and Jock could hardly be called friends?"

"Is that a question?"

"If you like…"

"True then."

Seemingly imperturbable, the well-groomed figure spoke without lifting his eyes and waited for the next question.

Glancing over at his partner, the Scot sat back while O'Leary led the questioning.

"Any reason?"

"No."

"Were you jealous of his relationship with Lord Alex, your father?"

"No."

Pausing, the detective thought for a moment. Deciding to attempt opening the dialogue up with a different line, he asked: "Didn't you admire his charitable work?"

"Why should I?" The young man lifted his head and looked at the detectives for the first time. Smiling for a moment, he shook his head. "Do you guys believe he was a saint?"

Lamont countered immediately. "Why would we believe otherwise?"

Smile now gone, the sullen figure shrugged, but didn't respond.

O'Leary glanced across at his partner, eyebrows raised.

"You knew he wasn't a MacCaig by birth, am I right?"

"Yes."

Putting his phone in front of him, the young man clasped his hands together on the table, stretching his fingers out against each other.

The Scot nodded toward the mobile, warning O'Leary that the conversation might be being recorded.

"Tell us what you thought of him," O'Leary tried. "In your own words."

"Lucky boy," he replied flatly.

"How do you mean?"

"Share in the estate, career, everything," Ewan said, with a cold smile.

Now that the dialogue had opened up a little, Lamont noticed that, like his sister, the man had an affected blend of hybrid Home Counties and Scots accents.

Lamont said, "Really?"

Looking up at them again, he responded with, "Yes, really." Then he smirked and said: "Won't get that now, though."

"From what your father told us," Lamont added brightly: "He wouldn't have got it anyhow. Nothing, zippidy-zilch, bugger-all, zero…"

Ewan's eyes moved quickly between the detectives, surprise and confusion sketched on his dull features.

Certain the words had sunk home, the detective added: "The will's principal beneficiary, as we understand it, is you."

"What do you expect me to say? Perhaps something like: damn, what a waste – and I murdered him for that money, too. How bloody inconsiderate of father not to tell me!"

Ewan MacCaig looked from one officer to the other again, his eyes filled with contempt.

"Get real," he said finally.

"You know," O'Leary chipped in. "We expected some humanity, but it seems you're missing that genetic link. Possibly any genetic link – to our species…"

The arrogant figure said with a sneer: "You'll get nothing from me about a MacCaig. Any MacCaig – even dead ones."

Glancing at each other, they knew the lad was right. He would give them nothing. But Lamont hadn't quite finished.

"Perhaps your father wanted you guys to earn your spurs," he said. "Though I think in your case, he'll have to find a donkey to saddle first."

Another discreet look passed between the two detectives.

"You don't want to work with the charity?" Lamont asked. Trying hard to live by the rules, he had quickly returned to a non-judgemental style.

"Why would I do that?"

The Scots detective raised his eyebrows.

"Fair point," he agreed.

"Are you interested in photography?"

"No."

O'Leary interrupted in a disbelieving tone. "You never take photographs?"

"My phone does the job," he responded, holding out the expensive piece of technology. "The camera was Jock's thing."

"Did you hear, or see, anything that might help our enquiries; say, on the Sunday before Jock was murdered?"

"No."

"And did you hear the dogs either then, or early on the Monday, when Jock died?"

"I left late Sunday evening."

"Okay" Lamont interrupted wearily. He had heard enough. "That appears to be all, though we may need to speak to you again."

As the man headed for the door, he asked: "Before you leave, can we ask how you got back home?"

"Car."

"Big one?

'Discovery, why?'"

Lamont shrugged, and said: "No reason, just curious. Thanks for your help."

As the heavily built figure went out, O'Leary followed him, closing the dining room door as the man disappeared up the broad stairwell.

"Think he killed the stepbrother?"

"Possible, yet it seems unlikely; despite his being kept out of our way."

O'Leary wandered round the room taking in their surroundings, then sat down again while Lamont scribbled some notes.

"Don't we need the search guys back again to see if we can locate the dead man's camera?"

The Scot felt puzzled as he put the notebook back in his jacket pocket, but made nothing of it.

"Might be worth a try."

"Hey, it might have a snap of the killer on it!"

"With biometric profile, no doubt."

"Or a befuddled Loch Ness monster," O'Leary joked.

Having shaken his head at the humour, Lamont realised the pain had now completely gone. A sudden sense of relief washed through him.

"Let's get out of here," he said. "I need some air."

Sometimes the pain destroyed his ability to think, but although it hadn't been bad today, the relief was only fleeting. It would be back. Now another headache consumed his attention. Despite the investigation being focussed it had answered too few questions for his liking.

And Moon would soon become concerned. A can of political worms lay open. To add to the stresses, the Scottish Force was about to undergo its biggest change for a generation. It would be radically slimmed, whatever the review threw up. However, if this investigation disturbed too many relationships, political or otherwise, they too could become victims of that radical slimming process. And Lamont didn't do diets.

Chapter 20

As evening drew near, Beth Thompson decided the time had come to tell Mac what he should always have known. For more than thirty years she had kept the secret, but everything had changed. Their boy was dead, yet even his natural father didn't know the truth.

She knew Mac had been very fond of Jock. They enjoyed a mutual interest: photographing wildlife and the countryside it inhabited. However, neither was averse to shooting and killing game when required. Although behaving like close friends, they rarely met away from the estate. It had almost seemed that Jock unwittingly treated Mac like an integral part of his family; dependable and always there in the background when needed.

But it would have been so different had she revealed the truth. If either man had known their genetic relationship, turmoil would have prevailed in their respective worlds. It would have unleashed destructive emotional forces beyond their control.

Beth now guessed correctly that the detectives investigating Jock's murder would have to disclose the truth to Alex MacCaig for their own reasons. She could do nothing to control that happening, but trusted their timing would allow her the opportunity to tell Mac before it became public knowledge.

However, delayed due to a heavy workload, in particular sheep she had to blood test for a local farmer, it had taken her more than six hours to get over to the ghillie's cottage.

She had thought of phoning, but a shock like this could only be delivered face-to-face. Besides, they'd now become both friends and lovers, drawing closer with each passing day. Revealing the truth to Mac in any other way was, for her, unthinkable. Beth had always been afraid of his anger should he discover the truth. Now she feared the damage his finding out from anyone else might cause.

Having chastised herself frequently, especially during the traumatic experiences of the past fortnight, she was angry at her inability to be honest with him before now. After all, it was a straightforward matter: his son – their son – was dead. She could only hope Mac would allow her the opportunity to explain. If he failed to accept her reasoning, then their love was finished. After all, both men had needed protecting, and if a mother didn't do that, who else would?

Beth's anxieties rose as she arrived at the cottage. Pulling on the handbrake, she could see Mac in the kennel block, feeding the dogs. Getting out and fastening the body-warmer against a cool breeze, she watched as he filled the food bowls. They never ate until after Mac had his evening meal.

'Pack leader', she thought.

Mac knew his place in the world, as did the dogs. From her point of view, she deeply envied the simplicity of his life. However, the complications about to be introduced in a humble, yet fulfilled existence were, to her, horrific. Their time together over the last couple of years had been wonderful, yet illicit. Despite giving herself freely when possible, she was still a married woman.

The practise also put serious restrictions on her freedom to be with him. Leaving the surgery for more than one or two nights a week, at most, was difficult and only possible if there were no call-outs, or sick animals in the hospital wing. If care was required, then Mac had to visit her. Neither liked this arrangement, as it meant increasing the risk of being caught. There was always the off-chance that someone would arrive with an animal seeking emergency veterinary care.

From Mac's viewpoint, there was a chance that he could be needed at any time by the MacCaig family. Living in a tithe cottage meant being onsite at all times. As ghillie, he was never supposed to be absent from the estate without permission.

Closing the compound's metal gate firmly, he walked past her toward the cottage, offering neither a greeting, nor even eye contact. Her heart sank in that moment. Had he already discovered the truth? There was a slim chance, she thought, that there might be some other problem of which she was unaware. But, as he threw open the door her hopes faded. Stomach churning, and with a rising swell of emotions, she bit her lip and followed him into the lounge.

"Talk to me," she said, pleading. "Please, Mac."

He slumped down on the chair by the fire without removing the work jacket.

"I'm sorry," she said. "I know what I've done. It

wasn't meant to be like this…"

"Alex MacCaig came to see me this afternoon," he began, almost as though he hadn't heard her speak. "Told me Jock was my boy. He was crying. It was like he'd been cheated: all angry and hurt and hating me."

"Oh, Mac…"

"Said it was my fault and asked why I hadn't told him. Wouldn't listen to me… didn't believe I hadn't known."

"I couldn't," she said weakly. "I tried so…"

Despite the offer an explanation, Mac continued as though she hadn't uttered a sound.

"Pleaded with him, I did," he said. "Promised the man I'd known nowt. But he said ah wis a bloody liar and good as killed the boy: Jock, my own flesh blood!"

Mac began crying, but as she approached, he pushed her away, angrily telling her to leave him alone. Standing in the middle of the little room, she felt quite helpless and lost.

"If I'd told you, then your marriage, your job, everything…" Imploring him to listen, she said: "They would all have gone. He was *our* son. I promised myself never to let anyone know you were his father: you, MacCaig, anyone…"

"But why?" he argued. "Ah'd hiv kept the secret."

"That wasn't possible. Remember your marriage, your life back then. You'd got the job here while I was away, pregnant and lonely…" Standing in front of the man, she was close to begging him to believe her. "It was impossible to say anything to anyone. Ask yourself, how could I? For God's sakes; it would have ruined his life; all our lives!"

"How can ye be sae sure?"

"Think about it," she said tearfully. "Think about his life here, on the estate; your life. And then there was MacCaig and his world. It was easy when he was away at school all those years. Didn't you ever notice how often I used to come over in the hope of seeing him: to be near him?"

"So it wisnae really about me?"

"No," she said. "Well, yes, in part. But I told you the truth: I'd never stopped loving you. I was always yours."

"And Harry Thompson," he said. "How does he fit in tae all this?"

"I fell in love – or infatuation. Perhaps lust or something – I don't bloody know! I've already explained to you: he swept me off my feet; then I wakened up."

Face wet with tears, Beth had her arms out, as though trying to embrace his pain.

"But it was too late," she said miserably. "The damage had been done and I couldn't go back. He was kind and gentle and thoughtful and asked for little in return. You were married and seemed happy."

"You said Thompson was jealous; possessive even," Mac challenged.

Although still angry, he now seemed calmer; listening to her.

"He's become that way in recent years," she said, trying to win him over. "But it wasn't always like that.

I told you all this when we got back together."

"Oh, I didnae bloody listen," he said. "Too busy lookin' at ye'."

Mac sat up on the chair. His expression had softened, though he still appeared lost.

"What do we do now?" she asked.

Looking up at her, she saw the sadness clouding his eyes.

"We bury our son," he said. "Then see whit life becomes after that. Jock comes first. Ah'll talk to MacCaig about him again. The man might just listen. If he doesn't?" Mac shook his head and shrugged. "Ach, we'll cross that bridge when we get tae it, lass."

Slowly getting to his feet, he took off the wax cotton jacket and dropped it onto the chair.

"Ah'll put the kettle oan," he said. "Ye'd better sit down before ye fall down.

Chapter 21

After dropping his colleague off in Pitlochry, Lamont had driven straight to his office. On the way down the A9 he phoned Elspeth. To his dismay she hadn't answered, so he left a short message hoping everything was okay and telling her he'd be home around seven. While focussing on the busy traffic, the detective then phoned Moon and updated him.

Arriving at Randolphfield and locking the car, he stopped for a moment and tried calling Elspeth. The home phone rang out for a minute, but there was no answer. He would have loved a few words, but mainly for his own reassurance. Guessing she would probably still be at work, busily tying up the loose ends in her caseload, he shook his head. From tomorrow the woman could focus on her own health.

Shrugging, he hurried toward the building's entrance. A sharp stab of anxiety kicked in as he thought about what Elspeth was going through. Dismissing it quickly, he climbed the concrete stairs, two at a time.

After several minutes checking mail and reminders left on the desk by Jean, he began preparing a summary of the investigation into the murder. Reading the note left by Moon gave him little, other than a degree of disquiet. They had already discussed most of his concerns on the phone, yet the old man still wasn't happy about the way he was running things.

He hadn't had the land between the Castle and the jetty searched for clues, mainly because of any media curiosity it would arouse. This worried the old man, despite the probability that both the camera and the phone lay in the loch's depths. However, he would share this with his new partner. Letting Tortolano have some insight into his personal decision-making processes would do no harm.

And a new factor had entered the investigation: the role of the ghillie and his lover. Lamont never failed to be intrigued by the sacrifices people would make to protect their interests. The dead man hadn't known his two acquaintances as parents, despite the fact both been close to him throughout much of his life. This made him wonder how Mac Tosland had reacted after being told he had been the dead man's father.

More intriguing however, was how MacCaig would react. After all, if Beth Thompson had been honest with him originally, a very stressful and difficult situation for all at Castle Druin could have been avoided. The man, Lamont thought, was not quite the calm, controlled persona he projected publicly. They had seen a dangerous edge to his personality during the interview today, but whether or not that anger had led him into crime was another matter entirely. He appeared, at least superficially, as clean as his public image.

Studying the wall chart, major decisions had to be made following a preliminary review of Alistair

Cameron's accounts. Primarily, it would be important to decide whether there had been any financial impropriety in relation to the charity's funds. The team understood however, that had there been any misappropriation a prosecution was unlikely – unless, of course, it could be seen to be in the public interest.

Legal action, Lamont knew from experience, was highly improbable. The old 'boys school' connections in Edinburgh would ensure that. Their principal motivation would be to look after one another and their respective public images. After all, damage one and you subtly erode the group's strength. Chip away at it often enough, and the entire house of cards could fall.

From the detective's cold perspective, anyone responsible for the abuse of funds should get their legal comeuppance. He would not readily give up chasing a conviction, even if it meant grief and turbulence for the team. It was his belief that the public would probably give *more* to charities, particularly if the evidence proved conclusively that the people in charge were *not* lining their own pockets.

Then there was the secondary matter of Cameron and MacCaig from a tax perspective. He wondered if the estate, or the interests of their associates, benefitted from the charitable status of Aid All Africa. There could even be direct involvement in tax avoidance.

He drew a deep breath and glanced at the wall clock. It was nearly seven and Elspeth should have been at home. Ringing the house again got no response. Knowing how she'd expect him to behave didn't make things any easier. After watching her stand by him throughout the biggest crisis of his life, he would now have the chance to reciprocate. Could he live up to her standards? After all, he wasn't a doctor with a sick wife, just a man who cared.

The detective grimaced as he opened the top file on his desk. Moon had placed yet another buff folder on his own 'important' stack. Having once asked the man why he put them there, Moon had explained that it meant he didn't have to verbally stress how important the contents were. And it always got his attention. Being slightly annoying was better, in the old man's opinion, than being unnecessarily direct.

After spending fifteen minutes reading and making notes, he threw it back onto the pile. The brutal murder of a drug dealer called Billy McFarlane in his former home village was the last thing he wanted to get into. He already had more than enough work with the MacCaig investigation, although this new case presented an interesting mix through the involvement of drugs and the use of extreme violence.

Perhaps Moon would agree to him running shotgun for his new partner. Tortolano could begin the enquiry and he would oversee her work; at least until he had a result in Perthshire. That way, he could ensure the hard-pressed Stirling detectives, in whose patch this problem lay, didn't make life too difficult for her. It wouldn't be for long either, since the MacCaig case, like all investigations, had a finite investigative lifespan in the active phase.

No, if Jock MacCaig's murderer could not be found in the next few days, he would leave O'Leary and the miserable MacDougall up in Perth to get on with it. There was always the possibility that the political voices in Edinburgh would draw a halt to his investigations anyway, regardless of progress. And they might do so a lot sooner than he would like, especially if his actions challenged the party line.

Throwing on his jacket and straightening the waistcoat, Lamont locked the office door and headed out through the floodlit, leaf-strewn car park for the walk home. Abercromby Place was quiet, almost deserted, under weak pools of fluorescent light. Manicured gardens dressed the large, Victorian houses as a cool breeze stirred gently waving foliage. Mature trees, their branches waving threatening shadows across lawns, further darkened his mood. Pulling up his jacket collar and quickening his stride, he leant into the chill evening air.

He had never stopped appreciating how lucky it was to live in such affluent surrounds. Yet very little of the good fortune had been due to his marriage, or career success. Unbeknown to the family, his father had traded equities in small volumes during the late sixties and seventies. Even his mother had been oblivious to this activity.

They had lived a modest lifestyle in the surrounds of a small, Stirlingshire mining village. However, when his father died, the portfolio had been bequeathed to him. Only learning of the investment folder at the reading of the will, he had been touched by his father's gesture, but assumed it would hold little other than sentimental value.

However, after examining the various papers, it transpired that any dividends earned over the years had been carefully reinvested. To his astonishment, closer scrutiny revealed that the portfolio held several nuggets. Shares had been purchased when some of the now large and well-known multi-national companies were in their infancy.

Elspeth had joked that his father had bestowed the gift as recompense; mainly for the equanimity he had shown in making him live with such an awkward Christian name. During his school years in particular, he had endured every proxy and informal moniker imaginable. The name, Crieff, had presented a goldmine for abusive remarks in the hands of schoolmates.

It hadn't been until he reached the age of twelve, after his father enlisted him at the local amateur boxing club, that the catcalls ceased. He had never become a good boxer, but he had learned how to overcome the fear of pain. At the age of sixteen, the athletic teenager discovered cross-country running as an alternative and less brutal way of releasing the daily fix of endorphins. Boxing had been left far behind, but four years of pugilism had seen the once introverted youth become a more rounded individual. Yes, he remained a quiet man, but had grown more thoughtful than introverted and confident with it.

Opening the wrought iron gate, he took the eight steps up to their front door in skipping strides.

"Home again!" he called, turning down his jacket collar. "You in?"

"Here..."

A wave of relief washed over him as her voice echoed back from the kitchen.

"Hi lass. How are you?"

Elspeth stood by the sink, peeling vegetables. He put a hand gently onto her shoulder, but she didn't offer eye contact.

"Tough day?" he asked, quietly.

"Not good, really. I tried to be all efficient and organised."

"Tying up loose ends?"

"Tying up *all* the ends," she said, fighting to contain the emotion. "And wondering if that was the end of everything I've ever worked for."

Wrapping his arms around her from behind, he kissed the side of her head affectionately.

"I remember lying in Intensive Care thinking the same thing," he said. Stepping back, Lamont gently squeezed her shoulders. "Then you told me the end of one strand of our existence doesn't mean the end of everything."

Studying his reflection in the kitchen window, she said: "Might well mean that for me."

Sounding weak and uncertain, Elspeth could barely contain her fears. Dying was something she'd never contemplated, till now. Even more frightening however, was the thought of leaving behind everything she loved and cared for.

"Might well have meant the same for me," he argued positively. "Certainly in the darker days, when I didn't feel I could fight any more."

Pulling her round and looking into the tearful eyes, he said: "If you hadn't been there to give me a reason for breathing, I'd have given up."

"I'm scared," she said.

"I know," he whispered, softly stroking her hair. "I know…"

"I'm glad you're here," she sighed.

"So am I," he said, taking her firmly by the shoulders. "Forgive the metaphor, but this is when, 'the tough get going'."

Kissing her on the forehead, he smiled.

"You're the toughest I know, so dig in. We're in this together."

Chapter 22

Awake early, Lamont showered and dressed then, after tidying the dishes into the washer, made a large pot of tea. Taking a cup to Elspeth, he left it on the bedside locker, although he didn't waken her. Instead, he settled quietly by the window and watched her for a few minutes. Their world had changed, and other than support this gentle woman, there seemed precious little he could do to alter anything. He'd never felt vulnerable, but the past few days had challenged his very being to the core.

Getting to his feet, he gently touched her shoulder. Feeling her warmth for a moment, he sighed as she murmured and stirred a little, but didn't waken. Quietly slipping on his jacket, the thought of writing a note crossed his mind, but he felt lost for words. After a few moments, he decided little more could be said. Words wouldn't change the process Elspeth had to go through, or add to what had passed between them. He was always there and would never leave.

The walk to Randolphfield passed quickly, almost too quickly, for he really wanted time to reflect on how best to offer support through the dark days ahead. Fear of losing her gripped him. All surgery came with potential complications and Elspeth's treatment would be no different. Knowing she was in good hands changed little.

Unlocking the office door, he sat down forlornly behind the desk and tried to concentrate on the MacCaig case. Checking the action plan thoroughly, the Scot gritted his teeth and began reviewing the facts again. Having not had to set out an investigation plan for some years, the board appeared messy and strewn with irrelevant detail. Surprisingly, he found this helpful. Much of it would normally have been buried away after being labelled as inconsequential. Having Tortolano on board had its advantages; not least of which was her ability to gain valuable information using logic and intuition. They would not have been able to identify the main suspects in this case quite so readily without her diligence.

Glancing out the window as he prepared for the conference call, he saw Moon's car arrive and drew a deep breath. It was only seven forty-five. The traffic on the main route into Stirling had gradually become heavier and the detective closed the window to restore some peace.

After making a couple of necessary calls, he found himself in the middle of speaking to the air travel company about their passenger log, when the gruff character's face appeared in the doorway.

"Yes... many thanks..." The detective nodded toward his boss as he spoke. "Get back to me when the computer comes back on-line then... great... speak to you in..." Lamont glanced at wall clock. "Thirty-five minutes? What's your name? Okay, got that," he said, making a note. "Big thanks, cheers."

"Early?"

"Too early." Gesturing toward the plan, he added, "Been here nearly an hour. Thought I'd better get my head back into this MacCaig thing."

"Good man," said Moon, closing the door and leaving him to his work.

He phoned Elspeth, despite knowing he really shouldn't. If her usual reaction to any fussing was to be expected, she'd argue and send him packing. But this was different. It rang for nearly a minute before she answered.

"Hi," he said, when she finally picked up the receiver. "How are you?"

The reaction was as he'd expected.

"Alright, alright," he said. After listening to her for a moment, he offered: "Yes, I am probably phoning more for my benefit than yours… No, I won't do that… No, and I know where the sun doesn't shine either, thanks."

Eventually, tired of being told off, he said: "Yes, I am being selfish and stressing you, and no, I won't phone again before six… yes… yes again, and only if I can't get home earlier than usual. And yes, I will stick my head up my own ass and smile."

Clever woman right enough, he thought.

Grinning as he slipped the mobile into his waistcoat, the detective settled back to ponder the evidence plan. Elspeth was indeed clever and knew exactly how to set him free to do what he did best.

Tortolano came into the office as the clock showed eight. She looked sharp: all polished olive skin elegantly moulded into a tight fitting, light grey suit and dark blue shoes.

"How are you?" she asked.

After a moment's thought, he decided not to tell her about Elspeth. It was personal. Besides, he didn't want the newcomer's reactions clouded by concerns that had nothing to do with her. Work was work, full stop. Home life had no place in a policeman's duties. Knowing things were never quite that simple, especially when matters became deeply personal, made little difference; Lamont had always kept emotions away from the job. He expected no less of every colleague, but was frequently disappointed.

"Very well, ta."

She could tell from his tired and strained expression that he was not being entirely honest, but didn't pursue the matter.

They chatted idly for a while: Tortolano about life and police work in general; he about career and promotions. Indulging himself for several minutes felt deeply therapeutic. Having judged himself as owing the young woman time to form a broader picture, he realised she had most probably already done so. As the conversation developed, the officer found his opinion of her abrasive character being subtly tempered to a more positive edge.

Hard-working and intelligent, yet wilful and opinionated, Tortolano fascinated him. Chatting with her now revealed another side of the young officer. They discussed her time at college, then her thoughts and feelings about the conduct of the investigation.

"It's very like the casework studies you read in college, although far more exciting," she confirmed enthusiastically.

"It's still people's lives, though," he said, running his left hand absently over the laptop keyboard. "Takes hard graft, intuition and a bit of luck to catch criminals; no matter how exciting or dull a case seems. However, it takes real skill *not* to offend the innocent."

Watching him push the glasses further up his nose, then pop a mint as he chatted, Tortolano tilted her head.

"I see you're perplexed by that," Lamont said.

"Not really," she said. "Just thinking about what you said and trying to put that into the context of the MacCaig investigation."

"Good."

Deciding she knew him well enough to confide her feelings, she said: "I'm a little bit anxious out there – in the real world, so to speak."

"Can I let you into a secret?" he said. "So am I."

"Really? You?"

"Yes, me," he confirmed. "Worry about everything."

"That why you don't like offending the innocent?"

"Part of it," he confided. He was being a little too open with Tortolano, but knew it may help their working relationship. "Perhaps I'm more afraid of failure."

"You're not known for that."

"Give me time," he said. "You'll learn how to crash ingloriously – and with little style!"

"Now, you are known for that!"

He appreciated the careful stroking of his ego and was in no mood to knock her back. Besides, events at home were proving more traumatic than he could have believed possible. The detective smiled wryly to himself: Moon had once said when you start sharing truths with a stranger you're seeking either sex or solace.

"Okay," he said, glancing at the wall clock. "Time to call O'Leary for the conference brief on the week's work."

As he keyed in the Pitlochry number, John Barton, from the audit department, poked his head round the door. The ruddy complexioned character looked puzzled.

"Hi," he said. "Got a minute?"

"No, but since it's you…"

The detective waved an arm toward a space at the table.

"It's those Cameron papers you dropped in yesterday afternoon," the auditor said, sitting down and acknowledging Tortolano with a nod.

"Problems?"

"Well, not with Cameron."

"How do you mean?" Tortolano interrupted.

"Well," he said, focussing his attention toward Lamont. "The problem, if you can call it that, rests in London."

"AidenallafricA?"

"Yes," the man confirmed. "The trading hasn't been too clever, to say the least."

"But not Cameron's doing?"

"No," Barton said. He screwed up his face as though bearing bad news. "In fact, from the story these accounts tell, Cameron's diligent work actually uncovered the mess."

"Anderson Scotland..." Lamont knew where the man was leading them. "Thompson?"

"Check!" Barton said. "And he's no longer a company partner."

Suddenly very attentive, he leant toward the accountant. "Since when?"

"Since yesterday morning, according to his stand-in."

Grinning broadly as he elaborated, Barton believed he finally had the jump on the erudite detective. "Spoke to him on the phone ten minutes ago. Money-making Londoners start early down at the Wharf."

"Well done," he said. "That's a pint I owe you."

Barton's smile evaporated and he shrugged. He knew Lamont rarely went near pubs, or drank anything stronger than Irn Bru.

"Thanks," he said grudgingly, rising from the table. "I'll get back to the invoices."

"Well, there we go," said Lamont, as his mobile began ringing. He already knew what Barton had just confirmed. Looking at the caller number, the detective smiled to himself. "At last!"

"Hello... yes... and on the twenty-second? Good... I

see... Could you repeat that please... last night? You're sure... Right, many thanks... yes, and can you email it to me?"

Watching him spelling out the email address, Tortolano began to catch the wave of excitement. Could it be a breakthrough had finally arrived? His face said it all. Watching him close the call, the young detective couldn't tell whether her emotions were of fear or anxiety, but could feel the pulse thumping in her forehead.

"Harry Thompson has a regular ticket for London Gatwick. It wasn't used on Monday 22nd of August, the day of Jock's death," he said coldly. "And further, a new ticket was issued in his name for another flight."

"When?"

"Late last night."

"He could be back in Scotland then?"

"He *is* back," he said. "And I think we may have a problem."

"We don't have a lot of time to get up to Rannoch, do we?"

"If the airline's bookings computer hadn't been down briefly for routine maintenance, we'd have known half an hour ago."

Scratching his chin for a moment and considering the options, he tapped the desk.

"Give O'Leary a ring and let him know what's happened to Thompson's job. Advise him of the man's change of schedule for the flight back to Edinburgh. Tell him I think the man's dangerous, probably armed. I'll talk to Moon. Can you phone Anderson Scotland in London? Ask them for Harry Thompson..."

"What if he's not there?" Tortolano interrupted.

"Of course he's not there!" Lamont snapped. "Just check! Tell them who you are and ask what his company status is." Pulling on his jacket, he said: "Ask if he still works for them. We need confirmation before we wade into Castle Druin again, or we'll get our arseholes stitched!"

Chapter 23

A thin band of morning mist hung low over the loch's quiet waters in the cold, autumnal air. Above it, shards of piercing sunlight dappled neighbouring mountains and higher stretches of the narrow glens. Rushing streams; like silent, glistening slashes from a distance; poured down the hillsides at irregular intervals. Grazing ewes were spread out across the slopes like dirty white spots, their numbers punctuated by the odd regal figure of a nervous stag, ever ready to bolt when it sensed pursuit.

Positioned by the old cobbled bridleway that meandered up toward Castle Druin, Harry Thompson glanced at the black Hublot watch. A thick cluster of midges swarmed around his head, but the hungry biting females rarely bothered him. This made his life in the hostile highland air more pleasant than for most.

Despite having found this beautiful Scots wilderness by chance, it had become his very own world. Even the trips to and from London were more exciting: like leaving behind a lover, knowing she would always be there, waiting. Unlike Beth, whose loyalties had gone.

On one of her frequent jaunts down to London, Helen MacCaig had gleefully revealed that she'd spotted Beth's car outside Mac Tosland's cottage. It was late at night and she'd called by on the off chance of having a chat about a difficult young gelding they owned. She told him the car had subsequently been there in the early hours on more than one occasion, for she'd checked; even observing their affectionate kissing as Beth left the love nest. She'd been a distance away, and had only seen them through thick woodland but, she'd laughed, it was 'mouth to mouth' and definitely not for CPR.

He'd been shocked; not only by the news that Beth was being unfaithful, but from the pleasure Helen had seemed to gain through telling him. As she lay in his arms, the woman goaded him, implying his wife's infidelity meant he was a failure. Helen told him that she couldn't understand why he should be troubled: after all, here he was, with her. And what was wrong with Beth having a bit of fun anyway?

Then she'd delivered the sucker punch. Laughing jubilantly, the woman reminded him that he shared her body with her husband – and Jock! *'Young Jock,'* she'd taunted, watching his shocked reaction to this disclosure. They had slept together, she laughed, long before she'd met and married his father. Thompson had protested vehemently at her behaviour, but she laughed at his anger.

'And besides, I enjoy him; why should I stop?' she'd argued.

Positioned beside the heavily overgrown track, he leant anxiously against a pine tree, eyes and ears focussing on any signs of movement. Even as he waited for her return and the tension built, he still wondered how anyone could be so sexually liberal and boast about it.

Bitch! he thought bitterly.

Jaw firmly set, he considered the fate awaiting all of those responsible for destroying his dream. Those foolish dreams of early retirement to a quiet life in the glens may now be over, but he would have the last laugh. The box marked *'Jock'* had been ticked: three more to go.

Excitement coursed through him. It wouldn't, couldn't, be long now. Her routine rarely changed. Even away from home, she was always up at six. But, it was now well after eight, and he'd waited in the damp morning air for over an hour. If she kept to her normal behaviour pattern, Helen MacCaig's ride back to Castle Druin was about to be rudely interrupted. Thompson felt the clothes sticking to him as the tension increased. Pulling at the moist armpits of his jacket, he worked to loosen them. Beginning to fear his plans may be thwarted, he wondered where else could she have gone? Thompson checked the ceramic watch again.

"Shit!" he said.

Gathering his gear, he was about to head back to the car when the distant sound of hooves on the stone bridleway broke the silence. Although the noises came from some way off, he smiled. The faint, metallic, clip-clopping of horseshoes on cobbles, meant the time waiting for sweet revenge hadn't been wasted.

Dropping the holdall and hastily unzipping it, Thompson brushed the insects from his face. Gathering his thoughts, he put the Beretta pistol back into his coat pocket along with the sheath knife.

Taking out the Ruger SR-22 rifle, he leant it against a tree. It probably wouldn't be needed, he knew, as the hooves were approaching slowly enough to ensure an easy target. However, active service in the Balkans had taught the man never to take chances.

A smile now dancing on his lips as the horse approached, Harry Thompson walked casually out on to the bridleway. Checking to make sure of the rider, he then threw a casual wave. Helen MacCaig looked surprised as she neared, but returned the gesture. Bridling the seventeen-hand chestnut mare, she reined in alongside him.

"Harry, darling, what a surprise! I thought you were still in London?"

"Popped back early," he said, taking hold of the bridle and stroking the mare's nose. "Can't keep away from Rannoch, or you for that matter."

"But what are you doing here this early in the morning?"

"Waiting for you," he said. "I thought you'd never get here."

"Sorry, I was late setting out this morning. Men and their needs," she said slyly.

"I've brought something you'll like, too," he said, feeling in his pocket for the knife handle.

"You're a randy bastard, Mr Thomson! You know I've already had to deal with Alex, don't you?"

"I only get hot when I think of you, though," he said. Thompson threw a suggestive glance down at the grass beside the track and gestured with his head.

"Can't you wait till next week when I'm down in

London?"

"But I've come all this way, Helen," he said, in mock plea.

Shaking her head in defeat, she said: "You do know the grass is damp, don't you!"

"I hope you are too," he grinned.

"We haven't much time then," she said, licking her lips sensuously. Unstrapping the dark blue cap and shaking free her flowing hair, she tossed the helmet onto the grass at his feet and swung out of the saddle, adding: "But for you, there's always a few moments, I suppose."

"For me?"

"Yes, this one will be just for you."

Barely had her riding boot touched the track, than the first sharp thrust of the six-inch blade cut through her clothing.

"And this one's for you, bitch!" he growled, driving the knife hard, up under the back of her ribcage a second time and twisting it viciously.

Almost simultaneously a gurgled scream was choked off by Thompson's hand closing over her mouth. Sliding the blade free, he again thrust the cold steel deep into her body. Helen MacCaig fell back, one foot caught in the stirrup, but as he reached the blade across her throat the mare bolted, pulling her free of his grasp.

Hitting the track violently as the horse galloped away, her head battered repeatedly against the leaf strewn stone surface. The body bounced along wildly like a rag doll for more than fifty yards, Thompson in hot pursuit. Then, thankfully for him, her boot broke free of its metal restraint. A wave of relief swept through him as Helen MacCaig's body thumped to the ground, then rolled to an abrupt halt. Breathing heavily, he stood over her, ready to deliver the *coup de grâce*. On closer inspection however, he could see from the bloodied, torn features that she was already near death.

Studying her battered face for a moment, the killer checked her wrist. She moaned softly, but the pulse was rapid and very weak. He had seen death faked during his years of military service, but this was no deception. Wiping the knife on the grass, he sheathed it. Then, catching hold of her collar, he dragged the dying figure the few yards into thick woodland. Carefully covering the now barely breathing woman's torso with loose foliage, he looked at her one last time. Finally deciding she could die slowly where she lay, he put an armful of bracken and branches over her face. Revenge was sweet.

Setting off after the mare, he found it a short distance away, grazing on the sweet grass by a low banking. Leading her into the trees, he left the horse loosely tethered to a branch. Before leaving, he stroked its flank and spoke soothingly to the animal. Thompson loved horses more than people.

Hurriedly checking the time, he collected the bag and rifle then headed off to find his car. Hidden from view on a little used forestry track down by the loch, it was more than a mile away. He now had little time. This was just another mission, and not unlike the ones he'd had to complete in the army. Except this was personal.

*

"What did Brendan say when you told him?" Lamont asked brusquely as they hurried to the car.

Glancing at him, *grumpy bastard* fleetingly ran through Tortolano's thoughts.

"Said he'd wait for us getting there!"

"You certain?" He clipped the seatbelt in place.

Staring over at him, she shrugged. "Like, I'm a liar?"

"I didn't mean that!"

Accelerating hard, the detective had to swerve crazily to avoid a motorist approaching from his left on the exit from the office block complex.

"All I know is that you're panicking!"

"Run through what Anderson Scotland told you again – please," he demanded, ignoring her.

"He's booked a ferry to Larne, car to Dublin, flight to Dubai, then on to Thailand," she reaffirmed. "Off for a new life, I'd guess."

"And the flights, ferry and hire cars were all booked in the Investment Company's account name?"

The signs for the motorway and Perth flashed past.

"Yes, so it seems," she asked. "Why?"

"At a guess, he'd figured it would be another three weeks before the month's end paper trail gave up the route taken," he explained. "Give him time to settle more scores, then disappear. A change of image, new passport and he'd be long gone. Possibly Asia, though more probably South America: and before we'd even begun looking for him. That's a fake departure scenario he'd already set up. Strange that Anderson Scotland uncovered the trail so early, isn't it? Could be his own doing, but I wonder…"

"Why do you think he's headed for South America?"

"Extradition treaties. Some of the South American countries don't have them with the UK. Apart from that, it's further away. And with fewer British influences, it's easier to get 'lost'."

"What countries?"

"Columbia, Costa Rica, Venezuela: God knows!"

Accelerating out onto the motorway, he cut across a line of fast-moving traffic to the outer lane. Horns honked loudly and offended drivers flashed their headlights.

"There are a few of them, right enough. Argie's haven't forgiven the Falklands. Doubt if they'd help either."

As the car sped toward Perth, they sat quietly for a few minutes. Tortolano felt the tension settle after his outburst.

"You haven't told me what you think he'll be doing up in Rannoch?"

The clock was showing more than 100 miles an hour as they flashed past Blackford and the signs for Gleneagles Hotel. Lamont swore as an overtaking Mercedes temporarily blocked their progress, forcing him to brake sharply. The detective flicked on the car's police lights. The bonnet grill began flashing blue and he accelerated away as the driver took the hint and swung in.

"He has scores to settle: think he plans to expedite them before he takes his leave."

"What scores?"

"Not certain, but I think there are one or two who'll be in his sights, literally," he said. "For example; both his wife and girlfriend have been, ahem, *unfaithful*. Apart from that, he could be interested in making a name for himself by taking out Lord MacCaig."

"What makes you think he hasn't headed for a ferry and the Dublin flight?"

"Not his style," he explained. "Could have been out of the country after the first murder. Must surely have known the money pilfering would eventually be exposed. I mean, the dead man, MacCaig's son, was hardly subtle in his approach after finding the financial discrepancies, was he?"

"You mean he's cold enough to think he has time to exact revenge and still get out of the country?"

"Possibly, although it's more likely he's either mad, or so egocentric that he thinks himself invulnerable."

Tortolano was now beginning to understand her partner's anxiety. "Will we be in time to stop him?"

Glancing across, he said: "If we are, it's a bloody miracle, right enough."

Police warning lights still flashing, Lamont took the two roundabouts leaving the motorway in the outskirts of Perth at a reckless speed. The Audi's tyres complained loudly. Switching on the police alarm to clear the road, he floored the accelerator again. With any luck, he thought, they were no more than thirty minutes from the castle.

"Give O'Leary a call and let him know where we are," he said. "Tell him we'll meet in the layby beside the A9 at the Rannoch junction."

"Like I said, what if Thompson's really headed down to Ardrossan for the ferry?" she asked. "Or found his way over to Dublin already?"

"Moon's sorting that side of things," he replied. "There's a general, 'all points', so the airports and exits from the country are covered. He's talked to the Gardai in Dublin too. You never know though, as you said, Harry boy could be playing a game of 'hide and seek' with us."

"Shouldn't we have let the MacCaig family know what's going on?"

"Discussed that with the old man," he replied uneasily. "He's giving them a gentle warning on the phone. After all, we don't want to start any alarm bells ringing too loudly, just in case. However, Lord MacCaig has been told we believe the man's armed. He's been asked to let his staff know the situation."

"What about the local officers?"

"Weir's been told to keep an eye open for him," Lamont said. "And to be aware that he's the main murder suspect, and quite probably armed and dangerous."

As they reached the road junction leaving the A9, he scanned the surrounds for signs of their colleague. However, as they turned toward Kinloch Rannoch, O'Leary's car was nowhere in sight.

"Ring him again," he demanded, as they sped on.

"And find out where the hell he is!"

"Aren't you going to wait for him?"

"We're already too late as far as I'm concerned," he muttered absently.

She found the number, pressed call then listened as the number rang, then cut to the service's voicemail. Trying a second time had the same result.

"Must be out of range," she said, looking worried.

"Yes, and we know where..."

Chapter 24

Driving through the estate grounds toward the ghillie's cottage, Thompson knew he had been fortunate. Had either the horse, or Helen MacCaig, made it back to the castle, his time as a free man could have been curtailed. Worse, in his view, those who had so cruelly ruined his life would not be punished. Catching his reflection in the rear view mirror, he saw that beads of sweat glistened on his forehead. Wiping them with the jacket sleeve, he smiled, took a deep breath and exhaled slowly. It was just like active service; dangerous, exciting and you were free to kill when needed. Killing, he thought, would be needed at least twice more today: Beth, and then, if there was time, that interfering accountant, Cameron, down in Glasgow. Both had betrayed him.

Nearly two hundred yards from where he knew the ghillie's cottage came into view, Harry Thompson pulled off the track into a rough passing place and stopped. It was familiar territory, but he was late. There was little he could do now, other than hope that Beth and her lover were still there. Getting out, he looked around carefully, face twisted into a grimace. This was how it would have to be. Strangely, he felt a degree of anxiety and, glancing down at his right hand, observed the slight tremor. It was always there going into action.

Taking another deep breath, he regained some composure, then, tucking the pistol into his waistband, patted it reassuringly. For a moment he thought of using the knife, but if Beth *was* with Tosland, there would be little chance of surprise. Besides, the ghillie was fit, strong and might get lucky. That thought persuaded him to slide two more clips of shells into his pocket.

Closing the jacket, he edged stealthily up the track. The ghillie was a hunter by instinct. Having followed the man on the many occasions they stalked together, Thompson knew he had excellent vision and acute hearing. The man's life was tuned to the countryside and any unusual noises near his home patch might easily be overheard.

Making his way forward as quickly as possible, he soon guessed himself on a level with the cottage. Taking great care to keep noise to a minimum, he picked his way through the thin strip of woodland. Crouching low, he felt certain of having heard an approaching car on the breeze, but the forest fell silent again. He sat still for a while, senses tuned, listening, but nothing stirred.

Letting out a deep breath of relief, he moved forward again. A few yards further on, Beth's pick-up came into view, parked in front of her lover's old four-by-four on the other side of the broad courtyard. A wave of relief brought the satisfied grimace back to his features.

Then, without warning, the hound pack began barking wildly, startling him. He swore viciously. Had his scent carried over to the kennels? Something had disturbed the pack, but what? Drawing the pistol from his belt, he took off the safety catch and checked the clip. Thinking quickly, he decided to rush the house before Tosland had time to react to the disturbance, but at that moment, the ghillie, wearing only a dressing gown, poked his head out through the partly open door.

Thompson froze. This was not how he had planned it, but perhaps Beth would come out too if the barking continued. He might yet be lucky...

"Quiet, dogs!" Tosland shouted.

As he watched, the ghillie stepped further out into the yard. The man looked around hesitantly, seemingly listening carefully for a moment. However, judging by his calm demeanour, Thompson guessed he'd sensed nothing and felt relieved. The ghillie waited till the pack settled a little, then went back into the house and closed the door.

The killer cursed quietly, for an opportunity had been lost. He could have finished Tosland where he stood, then gone in for Beth.

Beth, he thought, *Beth the unfaithful liar.*

"Beth," Mac whispered, as loudly as he dared. Having glanced out through the net curtains, he was now certain of not having been mistaken. "Beth!"

"What is it?" she asked, wandering into the little sitting room, towel-drying her hair.

"Get dressed, quickly!"

"What?"

"Do as I say!" he demanded. "Harry's out there

watching."

"Are you sure?"

"Beth, for Christ sake just *do* as I say – and quickly!"

He had spotted a shadow at first. Then a second glance had sighted what he thought to be a figure, crouching in the dense undergrowth by the treeline, no more than thirty yards away. Mac Tosland was both surprised and shocked, but had fought to keep his composure. Too composed, he thought, but it had seemed to work and he'd gotten back into the safety of the cottage unscathed. A glance through the net curtain however, revealed the shadowy figure of Harry Thompson. As the man stood up, Mac could see him clearly – and the pistol he was holding! Now they must get dressed quickly. And he needed a gun.

"Hurry, throw me my jeans and jumper!"

"Beth…" Pulling on the clothes she'd passed him, Mac was now beginning to panic. The fact that a moment ago, Harry Thompson's pistol was pointed toward him had begun to sink in. A sickening fear rose in his stomach. "Where are the keys?"

She shook her head and said fearfully: "I think you left them in the pick-up!"

"Shit," he muttered. "The gun store keys are on that bunch!"

"What?" she said, pulling on her jeans and fastening the tight zipper. "What are we going to do?"

Gesturing toward the kitchen, he said: "Out the back, quickly."

As she tried to pull open the rear door, Beth

discovered it was locked, top and bottom.

"Here," he said, pushing her aside. "I'll get it..." But, as he struggled with the loose iron handle, it gave way. Mac Tosland froze. Then he could hear voices in the yard and the dogs began barking again.

"Hear that?" she asked.

She made her way toward the front of the cottage.

"Wait!" he shouted. "Don't go near the door for God's sake, he's armed!"

Holding her back, he peered through the net. Harry Thompson was in plain view, but the gun was pointed across the yard. Someone had challenged him. The ghillie felt both frightened and puzzled. Who else was out there? Despite listening carefully, he could hear little other than the pack, now yelping wildly again in the cool morning air.

*

Spotting the empty car as he sped toward the ghillie's cottage, O'Leary drew alongside to check it was unoccupied. Killing the engine, he jumped out. The other car's bonnet was still warm, meaning there was just a chance he wasn't too late. Thinking quickly, he decided to make his way round to the back of the yard beside the kennels in the hope of surprising the killer, for he carried no weapons.

"Just my bloody luck," he muttered.

From the corner of the buildings, he'd felt a wave of relief as the cottage door opened. Watching, as Tosland came out to establish what had disturbed the pack, he knew no damage had been done – yet. But his heart jumped as he spotted Thompson, hiding just yards away in the undergrowth. He waited for the worst, but after shouting at the dogs, Tosland went back into the cottage unharmed.

Then the man stood up, pistol in hand. Suddenly the detective felt very naked and very much alone. Tortolano had warned him, but knowing there might not be enough time, he'd hurried over to warn the vet and her lover of the threat. Now, other than trying to surprise and distract the armed man, he could do little.

After a few moments, Thompson stepped warily out of the brush, checked around carefully, and then began to make his way toward the cottage door. The detective felt his heart miss a beat. Although his mind raced through the possibilities, few scenarios did not involve two innocent people being murdered. He had no choice: it really was now, or never.

Moving away from the cover of the building, he began walking toward the man.

"Harry Thompson!" he called.

Surprised, the killer turned, staring wildly at him for a moment, a twisted smile etched on his face. Then he raised the gun, aiming deliberately at the policeman.

"Jesus, Harry – it is Harry, isn't it?" said O'Leary, stopping. "There's no need for guns, man."

"Don't try the bloody familiarity routine with me!"

"Harry," he tried again, "you'd best put the weapon down. Don't want to get yourself in more trouble, eh?"

Brendan O'Leary's voice was soft, yet commanding. Although he had taken the killer by surprise, the gun still gave the man control. For a moment, he battled a cold, deep fear. It brought him close to turning and running from the possibility of death, but soon waned. Despite knowing his life was in real danger, he moved forward again, although more slowly.

Then, using his fingertips, reached into his front breast pocket and slowly took out the police warrant. He held it up on an outstretched hand.

"We're police," he said. "My friends are closing in from the estate perimeter. It'd be better if you put the gun down and talk to me before this gets messy."

"Liar," he argued loudly, clearly refusing to take the bait. "There's fuck-all to talk about."

As he walked slowly forward, the gun remained pointed at O'Leary's torso.

"You know, I wondered what had the dogs barking!" he said, looking around anxiously.

O'Leary could see a strange, leering grin etched on the killer's face. Like someone deranged, he thought, and knew then things would not end well.

"A lonely policeman, eh," said Thomson, suddenly feeling a thrust of panic.

In the distance, his fears were confirmed: a police siren, barely audible, but there, none the less, wailed on the breeze. Gritting his teeth, he grasped that it would not all finish as he'd planned. It was now everything *and* nothing.

O'Leary had gradually slowed, almost to a halt, but – throwing caution to the wind – began moving forward again. Then the cottage door opened wide and Mac Tosland came into view. For a moment, the detective felt a glimmer of hope, but as Thomson swung the gun round he could see that the ghillie was unarmed.

"Stand still!" Training the weapon on the detective again, he screamed: "Move a leg and I'll kill you!"

Then, raising his eyebrows inquisitively, he glanced toward the ghillie. "Where is she?"

"I'm here," Beth said fearfully, stepping out from behind the door. "What do you want, Harry?"

"We've a score to settle," he said, shouting wickedly over the pack's manic barking. "Just you and me."

"What score?" Tosland demanded.

Thompson didn't respond, but stared hard at his wife, trying to decide if he should finish the job and kill her now, or wait.

The ghillie said bitterly: "Beth's done nothing that you haven't been doing for years!"

Watching from the side, Brendan O'Leary saw his chance. He began taking careful, but quicker steps toward Thompson, getting ready to spring forward. Now, no more than fifteen feet away, he lunged directly at the man, but the killer swung the gun round...

*

A deep sense of frustration and foreboding gripped Lamont. At the castle, MacCaig confirmed that Moon had phoned to warn of their concerns for his safety, though he couldn't understand why. Still, they'd locked down the building, waiting to be told all was well.

Asked if his wife was home, he'd explained that she was out riding. Although now a little late returning, he said this was nothing unusual. Apparently, she often varied her route, or stayed on at the stables to groom the mare. He guessed she was still over at the stable block, though not carrying a mobile phone, so he couldn't check. The man hadn't heard from O'Leary either.

Curious, Lamont asked: "And did you inform your wife of Deputy Chief Constable Moon's concerns?"

"No need," MacCaig replied airily, "she's a big girl." Apparently enjoying the surprised expressions on the officer's faces for a moment, he added: "Helen can look after herself, trust me. Besides, she knows Thompson rather better than I. They're on *very* good terms…"

MacCaig deliberately let the sentence hang.

"I hope you're right about her well-being!" Tortolano said tersely.

Ignoring her concerns, he said: "May I ask: why are you so concerned about Harry Thompson?"

Studying at him for a moment, Lamont thought throwing a right hook seemed like a good idea; it may just dispel the complacency.

"Without leading you off at an unnecessary tangent, Lord MacCaig," he said, determined to bring the man to terms with what was happening, "we think he may have been involved in your adopted son's murder."

"I see…"

MacCaig didn't seem troubled. This apparent lack

of concern for his wife's safety left the detective mystified. However, given the peer probably already knew her time in London was spent pursuing a clandestine relationship with the currency trader, perhaps this wasn't too surprising. Little ever confounded or shocked the detective, at least not where people were concerned, but he firmly believed her life to be in grave danger.

Although becoming ever more anxious to discover O'Leary's whereabouts, Lamont knew public safety came first. Protecting both Helen MacCaig and Beth Thompson was of paramount concern. Local police had just confirmed to his partner that the veterinary surgeon couldn't be contacted. Equally troubling, the MacCaig woman was, he believed, alone and potentially exposed to the killer somewhere in this vast landscape.

So, despite concerns for their missing colleague, he and Tortolano drove first to the stables. With no sign of Helen MacCaig, they drove carefully down the rough bridleway, hoping to warn her of the potential danger.

The four-by-four covered the bumpy, cobbled ground quickly. Failing to spot her by the time they arrived at the junction with the road to Rannoch village, he had little option but to change priorities and search for O'Leary. Assuming the detective would be looking for Beth Thompson, he guessed they could be together at Tosland's cottage. There was just a chance, albeit a small one, but things were becoming desperate.

Trying the Manchester detective's mobile again, Tortolano still got no response, but left another message. Deeply concerned, they sped round toward the ghillie's cottage. Gripping the seat belt across her chest as the trees flew past in close proximity on either side, Tortolano was more worried about her partner's driving than their colleague's safety. Then, suddenly, he braked violently. Tyres complaining loudly, Lamont struggled to retain control as they slewed to a halt. Stopping no more than a few feet from O'Leary's car, he let out a sigh of relief. Blocking the route ahead, it had been abandoned haphazardly, the driver's door wide open. As he pulled on the handbrake, loud voices somewhere ahead cut across the noise of barking dogs. Lamont, heart in mouth after the near miss in the car, sensed the urgency in him rise.

*

"I said *stand still!*" screamed Thompson and pulled the trigger. A loud 'crack' burst from the pistol and the dog pack fell silent.

O'Leary's mouth opened in astonishment as the slug lodged in his upper abdomen. He crouched, and then dropped to his knees, groaning. Staring toward his assailant, a surprised look on his face, the detective then turned his gaze toward Mac Tosland. What could have passed for an apology crossed the pained features, before he fell forward onto the cobbles, grasping his stomach.

"In the house!" The gunman demanded, striding forward. "Now!"

"You can't just leave him there!" Beth protested.

"In!" he instructed. "Or you'll join him sooner than you need to."

O'Leary heard the cottage door slam closed through an intense, nauseating wave of pain. Trying desperately to lift himself onto his knees, he managed to get both hands on the floor and push hard. However, overcome by shock and pain, he slid forward again and his face ground against the cobbles. Warm blood oozed from the wound onto his hands. He knew, in that frightening moment, there was little time left.

Sirens?

Certain he could hear sirens again, coming and going on the cool morning breeze, the detective tried to smile through the pain. A glimmer of hope flashed briefly in his mind, then O'Leary fell unconscious.

*

Waving the revolver at the couple, Thompson directed them toward the worn two-seater.

"Down!"

"Why this?" she asked. Then, for a moment, a terrible thought snatched at her consciousness. *"YOU!"*

"Woman, you never stop accusing me, do you?" he mocked. "Killing you will make me very happy."

"It *was* you..."

Beth made to get to her feet, but he moved forward, swinging the gun back as though to strike out. She cowered, arms shielding her head for a moment.

"You killed Jock, didn't you," she said tearfully. "*Our* son..."

"Whose son?" he demanded. The mocking expression had left him. Thompson now looked confused. He screamed: "*Whose son?*"

"That was my boy!" she said bitterly. "You killed my boy!"

"Jock MacCaig?" he said, shaking his head. "I don't get it. *He was our boy*? But I..."

Sobbing loudly, she said: "No, Harry... he was *my* boy!"

Watching intently for an opportunity to intervene, the ghillie's eyes never left the weapon in the man's right hand. Despite being no more than seven or eight feet from it, he knew the distance might as well be a million miles. Shifting position slightly, he noticed Thompson's eyes catch the movement. A moment of despair grabbed him, for no matter how quickly he tried to launch an attack, the old seat's cushioning would absorb precious momentum. The man would shoot him more easily than he had the policeman. Yet the ghillie knew there would only be a few more moments to act. The revelation of having murdered their son would not pre-occupy the killer for long.

Confused, Thompson stared at his wife.

"So who was the father?"

"That's of no matter to you," she said with contempt.

In the background the sound of the police sirens had now become clearly audible. Looking coldly at her husband, Beth began to accept that she would probably die here. With that understanding, the panic subsided almost instantly, replaced by a strange feeling of inner peace.

"You'll kill me, but you'll always wonder who Jock's father was. You can rot your years away in prison wondering."

"So you think!" he spat, though still appeared puzzled.

"I felt guilt for hurting you; horror that you might get more hurt from finding out by chance, but not now, you murdering..."

*

"Wait there!" Lamont shouted.

The young detective watched as her partner sprinted off up the track before she had time to react. As he disappeared from view, she got out and ran after him.

Despite running hard, the Scot tried to remain vigilant in case the killer bushwhacked him. Thompson, he thought, was clever, seemingly having planned for all eventualities. Rounding the treeline into the courtyard, his heart sank. In the middle of the yard lay O'Leary, a pool of blood around his body.

Glancing around for the perpetrator, he hurried over. The English detective, bleeding heavily, was still alive. Kneeling, he took off his jacket, rolled it up, and then shoved the bundle under his head.

"Can you hear me, Brendan?"

O'Leary's eyes opened, gradually focussing. "You never use my name..."

O'Leary wretched and coughed, blood spewing from his mouth.

"At least, not one that you haven't heard few times already, I'd bet."

"True..."

The wounded man spluttered, grimacing with pain.

"Take it easy, help's on its way."

"It's bloody painful," he groaned.

Quickly unbuttoning the waistcoat, Lamont folded it and pressed it against the wound.

Wincing, the man swore loudly.

"Sorry," said Lamont. "We need to stem the bleeding. Can you hold that there?"

"Never liked that colour..."

Breathing short shallow breaths, he coughed again, projecting spatters of blood over his colleague's face.

"Think the bastard's nicked your lung," the Scot said, quickly wiping his cheeks, "but that'll sort."

"Hope so."

"Got to go now," he said, putting a reassuring hand on the wounded man's shoulder. "Before Thompson does any more damage. Take it he's in there?"

"Yep." he spluttered: "He's got Tosland... and... and..."

"It's alright," he said. "I'll sort it. You need your strength."

Arriving breathless from her exertions, Tortolano knelt by his side.

"Wait there till I get back," he said. "If the killer appears, run for it, okay?"

Looking at her partner with alarm, she nodded, but would wait with O'Leary no matter what transpired.

"Not planning... on moving... till then…" Coughing blood again, he made a horrible gurgling noise. "Sorry..."

"So am I, Brendan," said Lamont. "So am I. But we'll sort that when you get yourself back on your feet, eh?"

The wounded man forced a smile and, as consciousness left him again, the Scot patted his shoulder.

Getting to his feet, he wiped away the fresh blood spots from his face as anger rose like a cold, misty shadow. He hadn't known a feeling this strong since being bullied at school.

"Think the cavalry are close by," he said. "Better get him help."

Fists clenched, he hurried toward the cottage door.

"Careful!" she called after him.

But he heard nothing as he tucked the glasses into his trouser pocket. Knowing a tactical team was already on the way made little difference. Lamont was beyond stopping. A colleague's injuries made things personal. The dogs had begun barking again. Through the noise, he could hear the emergency sirens and voices shouting nearby.

"Hang on," Tortolano muttered, watching her colleague stride toward the cottage. The unconscious detective's breathing was wet and shallow. This wasn't good and she knew it. "They'll be here in a minute."

*

Thompson's eyes were filled with hatred. A misshapen smile returned to his lips as he levelled the pistol at his wife. Then Tosland, realising this would be his last chance, threw himself forward, but just as he did so, the cottage door burst open and, head down, the detective launched himself into the room.

Shocked, Thompson hesitated for a moment, uncertain in which direction to shoot. But, as Lamont tried to gain his bearings, the gun swung toward him. Luckily, Tosland managed to catch hold of the man's arm and push him off-balance. They grappled for a moment and then crashed against the wall together, before falling over the television, knocking both it and a brass table lamp to the floor.

They wrestled violently for control, but with one hand free Thompson had the advantage and pulled the lithe ghillie over to his side. Seeing this, Lamont kicked out viciously, knocking him back, just as a shot rang out. The detective felt the heat sear pass his face through a deafening roar, but the bullet only tore into the plaster above the sofa. Beth Thompson screamed as it showered her with dust and dirt.

Reacting swiftly, Lamont grabbed the man's other wrist and threw a solid punch to the solar plexus, then launched another powerful uppercut to his chin. The man's jaw cracked and the pistol fell free. Seeing this, Tosland seized the opportunity. Grabbing the brass table lamp, he swung it forcibly, tearing the power plug from the wall as it smashed, weighty base forward, into Thompson's head. The killer groaned and fell limp.

Getting to his feet shakily, the detective kicked the gun away. He had begun helping Mac Tosland to his feet when two armed response officers burst in, rough handling them to the floor at gunpoint.

"Clear!" someone shouted.

A moment later Tortolano arrived with the team commander.

"Good to see you," Lamont said, getting up and dusting himself off as one of the officers hastily led Tosland and Beth out to the safety of the yard.

"And you," she said. The young detective began pulling Thompson's arms free to clip on a pair of handcuffs.

"I'd put them away," he said, taking the glasses from his pocket. "Check for a pulse first, though."

Shaking her head, she said, "Think he's dead..."

"Could have been me and the others, bar for a bit of luck."

Lamont went outside, where two medics were feverishly working to resuscitate his colleague. Hurrying over, he crouched beside them.

"How is he?"

One of the paramedics glanced at him.

"Poor," he said, as he introduced a venous line into the unconscious figure's arm. "Lost a great deal of blood."

"Bring the trolley over!" he shouted. Without looking up, he said: "We'll stabilise him, then he'll need surgery, pronto."

A short time later they found themselves watching helplessly as the ambulance doors closed.

"Where will they take him?" Tortolano asked.

"Perth, apparently."

There was nothing else Lamont wanted to say. He had been there himself, wounded and fighting for life, and not so very long ago either.

As the emergency vehicle pulled away, he went over to the senior firearms officer.

"Take it easy with Tosland," he said. "Saved three lives in there."

The officer replied, "And took one."

Shrugging, he left the uniform to his well-planned post incident routines.

The lethal blow that killed Thompson had probably saved their lives, so his interview was likely to be a mere formality anyway. A Coroner's Court would sort it out, eventually. Yes, he would need to be properly interviewed, but not until he had fully recovered from the shock. The Perth team would take care of that. Lamont too, would need to explain both the gun discharge and the lethal blow that finished the killer.

He went over to where the forlorn figure of Beth Thompson stood.

"You alright?"

Eyes glassed over, she seemed in a state of shock.

"My son..." she began emptily. Looking back into the busy cottage where the police team were surveying a murder scene, she added: "And now this...and Mac."

Putting a comforting hand on her shoulder, he

said: "Mac saved us both."

"He shouldn't have had to. It was my fault for not seeing what was happening."

"You're asking a lot of yourself. I know Harry was your husband, but the man was clever and devious," the detective said. "There was nothing anyone could have done."

He wasn't being entirely honest, but then, what did that matter to her now?

She began sobbing. He motioned over one of the female constables to take care of her.

"I'll be back to see you in a few days," he said gently. "We can have a chat then."

Despite the need to complete the investigation, he decided that the paperwork could wait. Collecting his jacket and the bloodied, filthy waistcoat from one of the officers, he watched for a moment as they marked out the spot where O'Leary had lain. He had begun walking back towards the car when Sergeant Weir arrived.

"Bit of a mess," he said. "By the way, your car's been moved out of the way to get the ambulance and the police team through. Here's the keys, took them from the ignition." As he handed back the fob, Lamont gave him a puzzled look.

"How did you know we'd be here?"

"Post mistress in the village shop," he said, sagely. "Seems the whole bloody village knew of the vet's goings-on. The wife too – everybody but me!"

"Aye, villages can be like that," Lamont said.

"How does it look for O'Leary?"

"Not good," he replied, shaking the feeling off. "Though we won't know until they get him to Perth. Should have been airlifted, but the chopper's tied up helping injured climbers."

"I hope he's fine," said Weir. "We were getting to like him."

"So were we, sergeant," he replied, thoughtfully. "So were we."

"There's been a report from Lord MacCaig that his wife went out riding earlier, but hasn't come back yet."

"Big of him," said Lamont.

"Constable Wilkinson and a few of the Perth lads have gone off in the Land Rover to search the bridleway. They'll drive out from the castle and follow the track to the Loch, then round to the village. Some of it'll need to be on foot, though."

"Tortolano and I did a quick scan of the bridleway ourselves, but there was no sign of her."

Taking out the mobile, he quickly checked the time. Helen MacCaig had been out of contact for close to three hours.

"Let the lads know we only went as far along the bridleway as the main road, then turned back here."

"Right," Weir said. "I'll tell them now."

"Given what's gone on in there, anything could have happened. If I were you, I'd split the team. Get some out to the village to track back toward the castle. No point in taking chances. Lord MacCaig says she was well acquainted with Thompson, but I've the feeling she may have offended him somehow."

As Weir left to broaden the search, Tortolano had been listening carefully.

"Do you think he's killed her?"

"I think she could have been a target," he said. "And from what we've heard from Anderson Scotland down in London, our friend Cameron would have been his next port of call. Seems the man decided to settle all scores before taking his leave."

"I'm glad we stopped him when we did," she said. "Though seeing him dead was..."

"It was perhaps unnecessary, but in the heat of the moment..."

He wondered for a moment how his partner would cope with such dramatic events when they had eventually sunk in.

"Is that your first body?"

"In the field, yes."

"Do you good," he said roughly. "You okay to go on?"

"Why would I not be?"

"Oh, just thinking. O'Leary and this mess: bit of a tough introduction."

The discussion was interrupted by Weir, jogging back toward them.

"They've found a horse!"

After hurrying back to the car and extricating it from between the trees, they followed Weir's police

Land Rover to the bridleway. By the time they reached the spot where the mare was tethered, officers had already noticed bloodstains on the track and followed them to where Helen MacCaig's body lay. Wilkinson called them over, and then was violently sick.

"There!" he said throatily, pointing toward a thicket of undergrowth. "Sorry, can't help it – you'll see…"

"You seem to have a nasty habit of finding Thompson's victims," said Weir.

While the constable finished retching his abdominal contents, Lamont went over to the bloodied pile in the undergrowth.

As Tortolano looked on, he helped Weir uncover the battered body from the loose bracken. It was a grim task. Head twisted awkwardly to the side, they could see the face had been pummelled and torn. Even from a glance, it was clear the almost unrecognisable woman in the undergrowth was beyond help. A large, bloody stain had spread down her back onto the breeches. Two or three small slashes in her riding jacket told them she'd probably been stabbed.

"Seal it off, sergeant," he said. "Keep everyone else away until the scene-of-crime guys have time to get over here."

Tortolano looked disgusted. "We drove past her!"

"We weren't searching the bushes, lass!" he said: "Give yourself a break."

"But the blood on the track…"

"Look at the state of it. You would need to walk deliberately along a path as rough as this to have a chance of seeing anything!"

"I suppose," she agreed slowly, pushing the hair from her face. "Do you think he made her suffer?"

"I'd guess she was left to die here, right enough. Mind you, from the mess she's in, I doubt she'd have known too much about it. Forensics will give us some answers, though."

"Judging by the scuff marks, it looks as though someone's surprised her, right here," he said, crouching by the track. "Then the horse has broken free. Clever bastard's been careful enough to catch it and tether it out of sight. Didn't want the alarm raised too early. Our man needed time – had other work over at the cottage. He'd have known where Beth and Tosland would be."

Before leaving the uniforms to seal off the area, he borrowed one of their badged, fleece jackets from the Land Rover to keep out the cold. As they made their way over to the castle, he wasn't looking forward to meeting MacCaig. Despite the man's apparent indifference to his wife's delayed return when they'd spoken earlier, he would no doubt blame the police for not protecting her.

Taking out the phone, he checked for a signal then phoned Moon. It only took a few minutes to brief him on the damage perpetrated by the killer.

Chapter 25

Driving up toward the castle, it looked grey and bleak under an overcast sky. It was as though Druin had taken on a defensive, threatening posture in response to recent deeds. As he pulled on the handbrake and got out, Lamont felt as dull as the turreted building. It was cold for early September and he felt both tired and weary. The detective zipped the fleece and headed toward the portico.

"Shock," the young officer remarked. She pressed the doorbell. "You should be wrapped up by the fireside."

Drawing her a look, he was still pondering a sarcastic reply when MacCaig opened the stout portal. As he ushered them into the hall, the man seemed crestfallen, almost as though he already knew what they were going to tell him.

After briefing him and offering their condolences, the detective felt ever more certain the wealthy landlord had been aware of his wife's philandering. However, her untimely and brutal death still hit him hard.

"And was it Harry Thompson?"

"We think so," he said. "Although it'll need forensic confirmation."

Lamont knew that it might yet be MacCaig who murdered her, or planned her death using Thompson, but that now seemed highly unlikely. Something told him, that with MacCaig's wealth, he'd always use a third party for anything illegal.

"I see," he said, taking a deep breath and exhaling slowly. "Is Mac alright?"

"Yes," he confirmed. "Bit of a hero, really."

"You mean Jock's father was a hero," MacCaig said, a regretful smile passing his lips. "No need for any sensitivities here, officer."

"No."

The wealthy landowner still looked forlorn, but his voice held some satisfaction; as though a loose end had been tied up. The detective noted the reaction.

"No one to blame," the man offered wistfully. "It was just timing really; it's all about timing, don't you think? Another time, another place, and who knows..."

Showing them to the door, he thanked them generously for their courtesy.

"If you would both accept an invitation to Jock's funeral, I would be honoured to see you there," he said. "You found his killer, and probably helped save the charity's reputation. Jock would have been grateful for that."

Knowing it may not be within MacCaig's power to arrange the funeral, he said nothing. But, the man seemed to be trying to build bridges – or curry favour.

"We'll try," said Lamont, politely.

As they turned to leave, MacCaig stopped them.

"Wait," he said, "I nearly forgot. If it's at all possible, give my regards to your colleague, Detective O'Leary."

"He's in hospital in Perth," he said. "Took a bullet doing his duty."

"I do hope he recovers. Give him my thoughts."

They could feel him watch while they crossed to the car. When the door closed, Tortolano exhaled loudly.

"Strange man."

"Respect to him for what he's coping with, but he's too smooth a character for me, despite his attempts at warmth," he said. "I'm only surprised he isn't blaming us for the murder of his wife."

Tortolano shook her head and laughed: "He may do yet!"

On the return journey, Lamont dropped by Perth Infirmary. He had stopped for flowers at a service station and carried them with him into the reception. They were directed to the Intensive Care Department, where a uniformed officer from the Perth force was already on stand-by outside the entrance.

"Detective Lamont." Flashing the warrant card, he added: "This is Detective Tortolano. How's O'Leary getting on?"

"He's been taken for emergency surgery," the policeman said. "Think they expect him to be in there for a good wee while."

"I'll leave these flowers with you. Make sure he

gets them, eh?"

As they sat down in the waiting area, the uniform went off to deposit the flowers. A passing nurse pointed to the hand lotion holder on the wall.

"Have you?"

"No, but we will," he said. "Can we see a doctor about our colleague, Detective O'Leary?"

"I'll find out who's dealing with his case," she said, elbowing through the swing doors.

The detectives got up and were rubbing some of the antiseptic fluid from the dispenser into their hands when a young female medic in theatre greens came out.

"Dr Strickland," she said. "I'm responsible for Mr O'Leary."

"How is he?"

"Well, he was very weak when he arrived. We've tried to replace some of the lost blood, stabilise him, and then get him down to theatre as quickly as possible."

"Will he make it?" Tortolano asked.

"If the internal damage can be repaired and the bullet removed..." She paused reflectively for a moment. "He'll be very fortunate to survive. He's fighting for his life."

As his partner drew in a sharp breath, Lamont uncharacteristically put a comforting hand on his young colleague's shoulder.

"Thanks doctor." Handing her a contact card, he said: "If you hear anything, could you let me know on this number please?"

"Can do."

"He has no family," the detective added. "So it's important."

"I understand," said the medic. "I'll call you as soon as we know how he is."

"Has he any belongings here – a mobile phone perhaps? He only joined us recently on temporary placement from Manchester. I could be doing with it to phone his friends and colleagues and let them know what's happened."

"That would be nice," she agreed. "I'll ask Sister to get it for you. Wait there a minute."

Curiosity writ large on her features, Tortolano looked at him. He winked, but said nothing to avoid being overheard by the constable, who had returned to the door.

The Sister appeared a few minutes later.

"This isn't normal, you know," she complained.

"Getting shot in the line of duty isn't either, Sister," he said. Lamont held out his I.D. for effect. "Especially not when you're two hundred miles from home and friends!"

"Well, I suppose…"

She passed him the mobile.

"Thanks. Make a note of where it's gone, just in case, will you?"

"It's in the records already."

They drove in silence toward Stirling, each taking

stock of the horror that had so quickly unfolded. After barely twenty minutes on the road, his phone's ring-tone sounded. The young detective watched attentively as he set the car's hazards and pulled over onto the dual carriageway's hard shoulder.

Listening for a moment, he looked over and slowly moved his head from side to side.

"Thanks, doctor. I appreciate you taking the trouble," he said. "Yes, I will, thanks... bye."

Checking his mirrors, he turned off the hazards and indicated. They bumped off the grass verge back onto the inside lane.

"They did everything they could."

"You didn't like him anyway," she said bitterly.

"No," he corrected, taking the car up to the speed limit. "I didn't trust him. A bit different, I think. Don't you?"

"If you say so."

"Why do you think I made the pretence of asking for his phone?"

"Pray tell, master," she replied, sarcasm oozing from the words.

"Because I want to know who he's been dealing with and why!"

"Sure that's not a bit paranoid?"

"Look, he's a drug squad officer from Manchester, allegedly suspended for racism," he began. "Yet he's probably the least bigoted character I've ever met. More than that, he doesn't – sorry, *didn't* – behave like someone on suspension. He was composed, pleasant and controlled. Not a hint of, 'why should I bother, I'll get hung anyway'."

Through the anger and shock, Tortolano was becoming curious. "What do you mean?"

"Well, a large percentage of the officers suspended for any reason lose their livelihood, pension, everything," he explained. "O'Leary looked like the least troubled man in the force!"

Glancing over as he steered the car past a motorhome, he asked: "Did you even once hear him say he was worried about how things were going?"

The young officer thought for a few moments. "So you think there was another reason for him being here?"

"I don't know, but my curiosity will make sure we bloody well find out!"

Tortolano brightened up a little.

"That would be a nice memory for him. Better than nothing."

"Yes," he said. "Better than nothing."

If only he had waited a few minutes, Lamont thought angrily.

Watching the Perthshire countryside fly past as he drove, the man was locked in his own private battle. The officer's death had awakened another, deeper anxiety: What if Elspeth didn't make it?

The craggy, imposing landmark that is Stirling Castle seemed to take forever to appear. Ugly scaffolding, visible for miles around, adorning the Great Hall throughout its long renovation, had recently been removed. The fortified structure's bright sandstone façade now stood out like a beacon on the town's skyline. The castle remained *the* focal point in Scotland's history, crystallised into one iconic, picturesque cameo.

As they drew into the office car park, the sun began throwing bright shafts of light between thick, windswept clouds, helping blow away his self-inflicted gloom. For Lamont, the MacCaig case hadn't closed. Yes, the murderer and his motives had been identified, but the investigation had thrown open other doors.

Chapter 26

"I know this isn't the time," said Moon, carefully. The man leant against the door jamb trying not to appear demanding. "But how did one of our men end up dead?"

For the past fifteen minutes, as he'd sat behind his desk, the detective had been trying to answer that very question. Drafting out the report had seemed near impossible; a task riven with emotion and self-blame. The young detective had joined him and stood, arm draped over the filing cabinet by the window, but could offer little support. He stopped typing and looked up.

"He wasn't supposed to be there on his own," he explained, shaking his head. "Before leaving here we called him and told him we were on our way. Asked him to wait for us at the Rannoch junction."

Tortolano nodded as the old man gave her eye contact.

"Better finish getting it written up then," he said, glancing down at the laptop. "We've press running all over us. They're trying to establish how an unarmed detective from Manchester ended up confronting a dangerous gunman at Castle Druin in Perthshire. They're taking the line that he was acting under orders; chasing down a drugs operation that was being run on Scottish territory by an English team!"

"How did they get hold of that?"

"Someone from the *Dundee Courier* found out where he came from, then made a few phone calls to the press down in Manchester. Discovered he had been investigating major drugs and child trafficking gangs in the area over the past two years."

"What?"

"We've a three-way dialogue going on now between ourselves, Edinburgh and the Manchester Force. To complicate things even more – as if we needed it – MacCaig's decided to stick his thruppence in!"

"What if he *was* investigating drugs and child trafficking here?" Tortolano quizzed. "Shouldn't we have been told?"

"He was supposedly suspended in Manchester," said Moon. "Awaiting a disciplinary hearing."

"Allegedly," said Lamont. "What if that's a pack of lies? I mean, how did he end up in Pitlochry, for heaven's sake? It's a bit far-fetched if you think on it."

The DCC shrugged.

Weighing his growing suspicions aloud, Lamont said: "If strong Manchester relationships were established during the riots down there, then isn't it just possible that someone in Holyrood agreed to help them track down a drugs source? After all, it would help us too, if you think of it: nipping a supply chain in the bud."

"We know a lot of stuff comes in through the

Highland ports, right enough," the old man said. "But I'd have been told if someone was sent in to investigate. After all, it may be child trafficking, as well as drugs."

"But would you?" he asked, sounding more sceptical. The detective got up and stood by the window, his mind racing.

"You don't get on with the Tayside Chief, do you," he stated. "So why would he tell you what was going on? Perhaps they thought the fewer people that were aware of the enquiry, the less chance of it being blown open. What if O'Leary wasn't in Scotland purely by chance when young MacCaig got shot?"

Tortolano chipped in: "It's a fair point."

"The situation at the moment is that we're involved in the murder of an officer from England," Moon said impatiently. "He was killed by a madman who'd been pilfering charity funds from an overseas investment company in London. They were moving sterling abroad for a charity run by Lord MacCaig and his family. Now, write this lot up for God's sakes, so I can explain our actions to Edinburgh!"

Shoulders hunched, hands dug deep into his trouser pockets, the old man turned away abruptly and bustled out of the office.

"I thought it sounded good," said Lamont and shrugged. "Whatever, the old man's pissed. He knows we've been shafted and his pride's taken a dent. He'll be back."

Tortolano didn't respond at first. The detective was angry with herself, believing she should have been firmer by telling O'Leary to stay put until they arrived.

"It sounded good to me as well," she said, after a while. "Almost too good."

"Wasn't your fault, you know," he remarked, sensing her discomfort. "Nothing else you could have done."

"Perhaps…"

Leaving her dwelling on matters, Lamont got on with the draft report while she gazed out of the office window. Occasionally, he would look up and seek her agreement about a paragraph, or a phrase, but both were deeply immersed in thought.

The DCC reappeared fifteen minutes later.

"There's a search warrant on its way," he barked. "It'll be on Jean's desk in thirty minutes. You two get back up to Pitlochry and check out O'Leary's office and his digs. Pick up any belongings before anyone gets a chance to bury them in a cupboard somewhere! We need his files, mobile and laptop!"

"Got his mobile already," Lamont said, holding it up.

"Have it checked out thoroughly then."

"I thought you wanted this case tied up?"

"I do," Moon said gruffly, managing to sound like a dog fighting for a bone. "But I told a former colleague from the Police Federation down in Manchester that O'Leary'd been killed in the line of duty. Apart from being shocked by his death, he said he'd been a bit puzzled by O'Leary's disciplinary. Seemed to think it was a strange case. Apparently they'd been asked not to move too quickly in gathering evidence; the complainant may eventually let things go!"

"And you think the complaint may have been fabricated?"

"Well, I thought about our conversation a few minutes ago and then reflected back to my old chum's words," the DCC explained. "He said the criminal allegedly offended by O'Leary during the arrest, hasn't been seen or heard of since the complaint was lodged."

"Interesting," said the detective, thoughtfully. "A bit too convenient, eh?"

"It gets better," said Moon, scratching his chin. "He thought it all a bit strange that accusations had been brought at all. Apparently the black officer supporting the racism allegations was a friend of O'Leary's. They were drinking buddies."

"Knew something was wrong when I first met him," said Lamont. "Relaxed about the disciplinary, easy-going, stress free. He was even supposed to be a womaniser but, as far as I could see, he never gave out any real vibes. He liked our friend here, but that was curiosity…"

Tortolano grunted disapprovingly and was about to argue, but he cut her off.

"My only concern at the moment is why he confronted Thompson without being armed."

"We went unarmed," Tortolano interrupted.

"Not the point! Covert drug squad and knew there was something suspicious going on with Thompson? He would surely have been armed. The only detractor could be that his cover would have been blown if we'd found out."

"How I see it, too," Moon agreed.

"There's something else," she said, seeing sense in their argument. "Don't you remember saying that the paper trail from Anderson Scotland seemed to have revealed Thompson's planned trip abroad a little too early? In my view it shouldn't have appeared before the end of the month."

"Ah, yes…" Gesturing toward her, he thought for a moment or two. "Perhaps he *was* fed to us by O'Leary. It's possible he'd already spoken to them seeking information about the man."

"We'll find out," Moon nodded. "I'll give them a ring. You two get up to Perthshire and dig around."

The two detectives looked at each other. Lamont felt close to searching for excuses and almost found himself citing Elspeth's condition. They had already covered a lot of miles and were tired. However, after reflecting on the case, he knew he desperately wanted answers, and they wouldn't come if the evidence disappeared. After collecting the search warrant and grabbing a sandwich and tea to go, they made their way back to Perth.

*

At the Tayside Headquarters, Lamont expected to find the dead officer's belongings had already been removed for forensic examination, but was relieved to discover they were still in store. After a protracted discussion with the quartermaster, he signed the release forms and the clothing package was passed across the counter. Placing it on one of the nearby chairs, he donned a pair of rubber gloves. Carefully taking out the blood-soaked items, he searched through the pockets.

Finding nothing other than a set of keys, he then emptied the contents of the man's wallet. Apart from the usual bank, credit cards and currency, it held little. There were several receipts for minor purchases of little interest. Putting them back into the wallet, he decided the contents could be studied more closely at a later date.

Folding the clothing back into the plastic bag, he placed it on the counter. The officer, who had been trying not to watch them rifle through the belongings, was now very curious.

"Were you looking for anything in particular?"

"No," he lied. "But we'll take the wallet and keys with us. We need a closer look at things."

"I'm not sure you can do that," the uniform said, hesitantly.

Glancing at his partner, Lamont didn't want to show the search warrant, for he was uncertain as to whether the wording would cover this situation.

"We've a warrant," he said firmly. The detective flashed the paper in front of the desk officer. Reaching across toward the desk phone, Lamont said: "I'll just ask Inspector MacDougall why you're obstructing our progress."

"No, no," he said quickly. "There'll be no need for that. What, with your warrant and..."

"Thanks," he said, glancing over at his partner. "Right, we'd better get back down to Stirling."

Tortolano was about to ask *'where?'*, then realised

what he was up to.

As soon as they settled in the car, she asked: "Aren't you being a little too guarded?"

"Possibly," he said, putting his foot to the floor as they cleared the city limits.

"What did you expect back there?"

"McDougall, acting under instructions from his Chief – blocking any attempt to remove O'Leary's belongings."

"What about his laptop?"

"That's why I've got the foot to the floor," he said, grinning. "If things are as we've imagined, then Sergeant Weir, or someone else, will be asked to get that piece of technology down to Perth, ASAP."

"You any good with android phones?" he asked, tossing O'Leary's mobile into her lap.

"Ha!" she exclaimed. "Same make as mine."

"See what you can get out of it, then."

"Do you really think this mess is drugs, or child trafficking?" she said. "Only, I'm beginning to wonder now that we're in Perthshire. I mean; it hardly seems possible that anything like that could happen out here."

"That's probably the best reason there is for running anything illicit in the Highlands," he said. "Who would believe it possible?"

"So you reckon the laptop's important?"

"The email accounts and hard drive are worth examining," he said. "Or possibly even any memory sticks he may have left behind. We'll have a sniff around, but I don't think we can be certain of anything."

Glancing across at her as they entered another brief stretch of the A9's picturesque dual carriageway, he nodded and smiled.

"I know," she said. "Keep an open mind till we find out what's really going on."

*

Twenty minutes later, as they drove into Pitlochry Police Station, the detective found himself drawn to reflect that only a few hours ago O'Leary had been going about his business with a purpose. Now he was no more than a memory.

How quickly life changes, he thought, while wondering how Elspeth would be feeling. A surge of guilt reminded him that he really should have called her before setting out. Instead of briefly calling home to check her well-being and change clothes, he had taken the spare trousers, shirt and tie from his locker and given himself a thorough wash in the changing rooms.

Pulling on the handbrake, he looked across at his partner.

"Still okay to get on with this?"

Steeling herself, the attractive officer returned the look and nodded.

Coding the digital lock, he opened the door and they headed up to O'Leary's office.

It was unlocked. The room appeared as though it had been vacated in a hurry. The detective shook his head sadly. The laptop lay open on the desk, 'asleep', and his office chair had fallen back against the radiator. Lamont straightened it and sat down.

"Have a look who the last calls were made to and received from?" he said.

Tortolano put the mobile on the desk and pulled out her notebook.

"'*To*' was an 02052362812 – the Forex company number at 5.15 last evening. The '*from*' was us, this morning.

"Very clever," he said, pulling a face. "You could have told me."

"You were talking," she said. "I was working on this and listening while you drove. Multi-tasking: it's a woman's thing; you wouldn't understand."

"Check the recordings will you?" he asked. "Or have you done that already?"

"You'd have heard if I had," she said. "Besides, might have interrupted that flow of venerable wisdom."

They heard a noise downstairs.

"Is that front door self-locking?"

"Yes," he confirmed. "It'll be Weir, or the lad. Shut that door, will you? Best keep the chat to ourselves."

As they began playing through the saved voice recordings, he got up and checked the open cupboards and drawers for anything that might help. Finding little of interest, he used O'Leary's keys to open the stationery drawer in his desk. It held one 16GB memory stick and a few blank sheets of paper, but nothing else.

After ten or so uneventful minutes listening to O'Leary's occasionally personal recordings, he gave up.

"We'll take this back to Stirling. The tech boys can go through the laptop and stick. They'll need to check if there are any locked files. Buggered if I understand these things," he said. "Let's go find his digs. At least we know he called Anderson Scotland."

As they headed past the reception desk, he noticed Weir in the station office. The sergeant was on the phone, but finished the call abruptly as he walked in.

"Sorry again about O'Leary," he said, looking a little flustered. "We were just beginning to get to know him. Seemed okay."

"Good officer," he replied.

"Yes," Weir said. "Not the sort you'd have thought would end up here, on some kind of placement for whatever."

Guessing the uniform was on a verbal fishing expedition, perhaps hoping to find out what he could for the gossip, Lamont ignored the bait.

"Hopefully, there will be a representative of Perth Police down at his funeral," the detective said, optimistically. "No doubt someone will let you know the arrangements, eh?"

"Manchester?" said the sergeant. "Bit far, considering we hardly knew him."

"Suppose so," he concurred. "Anyway, hopefully you'll not see us again for a while. All the best."

"Aye," he said. "And you too."

The detective registered a hint of relief in the man's tone and headed out to collect his partner.

As they got into the car, he could see Weir through the front window, already on the phone.

"Trust him with your life?" she asked.

Lamont looked at her and pulled a face. "Wouldn't trust him with yours."

Chapter 27

The detective's lodgings, he thought, were not at all as had been described. Fastening his coat, he noticed the neat, older styled bungalow wasn't as scruffy as the man had portrayed it. Checking in his notebook that they had arrived at the correct address, he stuck it back in his pocket and glanced around. Most of the cars were no more than a few years old. Those not parked in their own driveways probably belonged to tourists trying to avoid the town's parking fees, he thought.

Mrs Conroy had the door open before they were through the garden gate. Standing on the front step, arms folded, she watched their approach. Lamont felt a little uncomfortable for a fleeting moment, but let it pass. Judging by her pert figure and pretty but stern features, he decided O'Leary might not have been a bad assessor of landladies after all. A neatly trimmed, black Scotch terrier sat by the woman's legs. It showed them a healthy set of teeth, growling loudly as they neared.

"Quiet Angus!" she said firmly. "They're Police."

Contradicting the picture O'Leary had painted, she was small, almost petite, and the closer he got the more attractive she looked. With long, dark brown hair tied behind her head in a ponytail, she was, he guessed, in her early forties.

Introducing herself, she smiled and shook hands. Ushering them through to the neat, tidy lounge, the landlady offered them a cup of tea. Thanking her, they said yes, but explained the nature of their visit. Lamont showed her the search warrant.

"You were welcome without that," she said, gesturing toward the papers. "He was a fine man and anything that gets to the bottom of his death is alright with me."

"That's really kind of you," Tortolano said. The young detective wondered how she knew O'Leary was dead and threw her partner a glance. He too had registered the remark. "Can we look through his room while the tea's brewing?"

"Of course," she said. "This way."

Still growling, the little Scotty scraped past them to be at its master's heels.

The bungalow had four bedrooms, and the landlady had chosen to give her guest one of the two with en-suites. O'Leary had portrayed the accommodation, like its owner, as worn and tired; yet it was neat, tidy and clean: very clean.

"You only take the one lodger?"

"More than enough," she said. "Could manage two, but the mess would get the better of me."

"How long had Detective O'Leary been here?"

"Just arrived," she said.

Realising that O'Leary had shifted digs, he nodded and smiled to himself.

"Something wrong?"

"No, no," he said. "You keep a tidy house, right enough."

"Thank you. His room's here," she said, opening one of the bedroom doors.

Lamont thought she seemed remarkably agreeable to their questions and search warrant, despite having only briefly known the dead officer. He intended to establish why.

"Have a good look around. I'll go and get that tea for you."

After packing O'Leary's meagre belongings into the suitcase stored under the bed, the detectives looked around. Anything helping to shed light on the officer's role in Pitlochry could prove valuable. However, the room had been meticulously cleaned and polished. Even clothes in the chest of drawers were stacked with military precision.

"Do you still think there's more to O'Leary than we knew?"

"Anything's possible," he said, lifting the small bedside rug and looking underneath. "We'll know more when we scan through the computer files and that memory stick."

Tortolano shrugged.

Gesturing toward the door, he added: "She knows more than she's saying."

Not disagreeing, Tortolano had a quick look around the small en-suite, while he checked beneath each drawer and piece of bedroom furniture in turn.

"One almost new bar of soap, a wet razor, shaving foam, aftershave and spare blades in the medicine cabinet," she said. "Nothing else."

Putting the wash bag into the wheeled case and zipping it closed, he towed it into the lounge. As they sat down, the landlady returned with an overfull tray and set it on the glass coffee table. After pouring their drinks, she offered across the scones and biscuits.

"Thanks for your hospitality, we've only had a sandwich on the way here," he said, jaws working on a caramel wafer. Wiping away the crumbs, he asked: "Did anyone call to let you know we were on our way?"

"No," she said. "Should they have?"

Lamont shook his head and took a sip of the hot tea.

"How well did you get to know Detective O'Leary?" Tortolano enquired.

The landlady's eyebrows twitched and she looked more than a little uncomfortable as she replied: "Hardly had time to say hello."

"Did he give you any packages to keep safe for him?"

"No, sorry."

The young detective was becoming ever more curious.

"Did he mention anything about his work?"

"Not a great deal," the woman replied, picking up her mobile, which had begun flashing. As she read the text, she smiled. "Sorry, text from my boss."

"You mean landladies have managers now?"

"No, but Manchester's drug squad does," Conroy said quietly. She put the mobile back on the coffee table and stood up. Extending a hand, she introduced herself.

"D.C. Mary Conroy."

Nodding, Lamont said, "Good ruse."

"Undercover?" asked Tortolano, taking her hand.

"Yes," she confirmed. "That text was my boss in Manchester. He's just talked to DCC Moon, in Stirling. He'll be up on Monday to brief you more fully."

"About?"

"We can't afford eighteen months, or more, of painstaking work to be destroyed. Brendan thought you were discreetly chasing for answers, though."

"Who's your boss?" Lamont queried.

"DCI Martin Hulme, North West Regional Drugs Liaison Unit," she replied. "Good guy, but I'll let you judge for yourself when you meet him."

"How many in your team?"

"Only five on this case, though there are twenty-seven in total."

He shrugged.

"Well, well, you never know who you're talking to these days."

Mary Conroy smiled.

"From the lack of surprise on your face, I'd guess we were right that you suspected interference."

"Yeah," he said.

400

The detective felt relieved that his nagging doubts about O'Leary hadn't been misplaced.

"Good cover, wasn't it?" said Conroy.

"Very," Tortolano agreed. "We knew all wasn't well but..."

Interrupting, her partner said: "By the way, we're really sorry about Brendan. Were you two close?"

"No," she said sadly, "he was a bit of a one-off. Few got close.

"Can you brief us informally on the situation?" he asked. "Or do we have to wait till next week?"

"'Fraid so," she responded. "We've long since learned that communication's better if it's delivered with one voice. Keeps things sweet. Besides, this business is all too complicated for my little mind. I'm just a housekeeper."

"And the dog?"

Tortolano was stroking the Highland Terrier's head.

"He's mine right enough. Could probably tell you more than me!"

"I doubt that," he said.

"Professionally trained," she said, and winked, "although he tries to hide it. It's important that I'm a convincing widow. This cute little fellow helps start conversations with other dog owners. They can give quite a bit of local information at times. Also allows me to wander into places I wouldn't normally be able to go. At least, not without it looking unusual."

"Like Castle Druin grounds," he said.

"Possibly..." Connor seemed keen not to be drawn further. "Sorry, but we'll be able to talk properly after our bosses get together on Monday. Alright with you?"

"Frustrating, but fine," he said grudgingly.

"It'll have to be."

"We'll keep up the act as we leave, then," he said, finishing his drink. "By the way, you make a great cuppa."

"Thanks."

"We'll leave Detective O'Leary's case," he said, nodding at it.

"Good idea," she said, smiling warmly. "Our responsibility."

As they got to the door, Conroy put her hand on the Yale, and said: "By the way, what did you hope to find here?"

"A gun, perhaps?" For a moment Lamont seemed dismayed as he spoke. "Your colleague went after a killer unarmed, despite the fact we warned him."

"I asked him to wait," Tortolano said sadly. "Message never got..."

"Not your fault," said Conroy. "His choice. He wouldn't want to take a weapon in case it blew his cover – and the case."

"Where is it?" Lamont asked, bluntly.

"The pistols are stored under the floor beneath my bed," she said.

Conroy found herself looking the Scotsman over

properly. "O'Leary would have liked you."

"Wouldn't have known it," he said.

"Not his style," she added. "Letting anyone know where they stood. Least, not till he was sure."

*

It was nearly 5.30pm as they passed Auchterarder village and drove through the rich, arable farmland. Using the 'Bluetooth', he tried to call Elspeth, but got no answer.

Tortolano noticed his disappointment.

"Your wife?"

"Yes..."

"Problems?"

"Not really," he lied.

Exhausted and a little dumbstruck by the day's overwhelming events, he got back to his desk to find a string of messages on the answer machine, but only one sticky note on his laptop screen. It read: 'Ring Elspeth when you've time'.

Dropping it in the bin, he lifted the phone, but got no answer from the house. He tried Elspeth's mobile number. It only rang twice before she answered.

"I'm in Rosythe Hall," she said. "Hugh found a cancellation. They can have me in theatre in the morning."

Lamont swallowed hard, but couldn't respond.

"You hear me?"

"On my way," he said anxiously. "Need anything?"

"Only you..."

Lamont knew how important tying up his work on the MacCaig investigation was, but it would have to wait. He dropped O'Leary's laptop, memory stick and mobile phone off in the Technical on Phil Mason's desk and hurried out to the car.

The early evening traffic on the Glasgow road didn't slow his progress, and he pulled up outside the hospital after less than thirty minutes. Tired and weary, but worried for his wife, Lamont got out, straightened the creased trousers, and glanced around at the setting.

Rosythe Hall sat in manicured gardens on the northern edge of the city. A pleasantly restored Victorian building housed the reception and offices. The more recently constructed clinical facilities radiated out from the Grade 2 listed hub. He was impressed.

The receptionist directed him toward one of the four wards. Elspeth had her own room. Glancing through the window, he could see her sitting by the bed, listening to something on the iPod. The image brought an instant surge of relief.

"Hi! You look great!"

As she took off the earphones, he bent over and pecked her cheek.

"What did you expect, a corpse?"

"Don't joke, I've been worried."

Although his tone was light-hearted, she knew it was meant.

"Great they're getting things done quickly, isn't it?"

"That doctor *is* looking after you, right enough!"

"Phoned at three. Said he could operate tomorrow morning following a cancellation!"

A strong vein of both excitement and anxiety coloured her tone.

"Haven't brought anything," he stated apologetically.

"Oh," she said, pulling a face. "What would I need in here, Crieff? Don't worry yourself, the hospital has everything!"

Smiling at her stoic humour, he pulled over a chair.

"You worried?" he asked. "Or is that another of my more idiotic questions."

"Funny you should say that," she replied thoughtfully. "Guess I am worried, yes, but more relieved."

"Not surprised!"

"Yes, it's three weeks since I found this lump and life's been something of a blur," she explained. "I've been through every emotion in the book; from terror, to horror, to guilt – and back again."

"What is there to be guilty about?"

Elspeth looked at him apologetically.

"That I should have told you before we went on holiday, or at least while we were there. I intended to but..."

"But you weren't sure, were you?"

"No. I just kept thinking how well we were getting on. Unless you'd forgotten, we've had a rough time over the past few years. It was great to feel like your wife again, not just someone I shared a house with."

"Is that how it's felt?" he asked, now feeing awkward.

"Well, a lot of the time, I suppose..."

Lamont didn't know what to say for a moment and stared out of the window.

"There's no need for angst," she said. "We've lived with that long enough already."

Nodding in agreement, he said: "You're right, I suppose."

She studied him for a moment.

"Where's the jacket and waistcoat?"

"It was the detective up in Pitlochry; O'Leary," he said, momentarily reliving the horror. "He was badly wounded and they got messed up helping."

Elspeth knew little of his work, for he wisely shared few of the day-to-day goings-on.

"My God Crieff, that's dreadful!" she said. "Are you alright?"

"Yes, but he died later in Perth Infirmary. They couldn't stop the bleeding..."

"Oh my," she said. "I didn't know. There was something on the news, but I wasn't paying attention."

"You've other things to deal with," he said reassuringly. "And now I have too."

"Yes..."

"When you're through all this, we'll sort out the children thing," he said awkwardly. "It's important."

"Before I get *too* old," she said. "Or the chemo makes it impossible."

He smiled, but she looked at him anxiously.

"I fear dying without having…"

Leaning across, he held her tightly. There was nothing to say that would help. He thought it funny how the desire to procreate hit you when your life felt threatened. He could remember having had similar thoughts during his own long recovery.

"Go home," she said softly. "Get some rest. I'll be pre-med from about nine, so you could come back earlier if you like?"

"I will," he said. "Is there anything I can bring in for you?"

"Just yourself," she said, "minus the guilt and angst about things you think you're failing on." Squeezing his hand, she said: "You've no failings in my eyes."

Lamont kissed her forehead.

"Likewise." He her a gentle hug.

*

After a long hot shower, he threw on a dressing gown and poured some fresh orange juice. Gulping it down, he collected the day's soiled clothes, put them into a plastic bag then dumped it in the bin at the rear of the house.

After a night of disturbed, violent dreams, he rose at five. Slipping on the training gear, a hard jog took him round his usual route of the city's Kings Park. Eventually, he turned back into the old town and up

Broad Street to the castle esplanade. Checking his time on the sports watch, he made a mental note to collect the other one from the jewellers'.

It had been a good run. Leaning breathlessly against the parapet, he absorbed the expansive view of the meandering river Forth, flowing through the flood plain. The town's other tourist draw, Rochead's 19th century gothic revival monument to William Wallace, stood tall on the far side of the valley, its 220ft sandstone walls dressed by cold light.

The morning was fresh and brisk, though a red sky glowed off to the east, out toward the estuary. Fleetingly, he thought of the brave souls who had absorbed the same historic view over the centuries. He wasn't at all superstitious, but looking over at Bruce's figure gave him an idea. Walking over, he touched the plinth and glanced upward.

"That was for luck."

Jogging the mile or so down to the house, he showered again then dressed quickly before driving back to Rosythe Hall.

It had barely gone eight o'clock when he opened Elspeth's room door. The bed had gone. He sat down, shocked. Perhaps luck hadn't been on their side? Then, with a sigh of relief, he realised the missing bed meant she had probably already left for theatre. Lamont hurried back to the ward Nurse's Station to find one of the staff. A tall, bearded male in uniform caught his attention.

"I'm Mr Lamont," he said. "Do you know if my wife is in theatre?"

"Yes," the nurse confirmed. "Prof Allan was in

here at seven. He said your wife's case was important and didn't want to keep her waiting. Even called the theatre sister in early for this morning's list."

"Thanks," he said, with considerable relief. "Where's the hospital café?"

"Through that door and to the left. You'll find newspapers there, too. If we need you I'll come through."

After two anxious hours and three coffees in the restaurant, he finally decided to go back to the room. A few anxious minutes later, the ward Sister popped in to tell him that Elspeth was in the recovery area and seemed fine. She informed him, however, that it would be unlikely he could see her for a few hours.

Relief flooded through him and he thanked her for letting him know. Trying hard to relax, he took a few deep breaths and slowly released them. He always feared the worst where health matters were concerned. Putting his coat on, Lamont wandered out to the car. Feeling quite lost, he sat quietly behind the wheel for a few minutes.

One personal problem appeared solved, but another battle was brewing on the horizon. Work never left his thinking for long.

If MacCaig had been the undercover team's target, then he was indeed a cool customer. And an extremely well-connected one, at that. However, after Monday, he would most probably become a name on a closed case file. Not liking it that way didn't matter; it was the nature of the job. You didn't always get what you wanted. Castle Druin was now likely to be someone else's problem. Jock MacCaig's murderer was dead, as was his own part in any further investigations into the family's activities. After the North West Regional Drug Unit assumed command, they would undoubtedly go their own way. He would be shut out. Unless he could find a back door...